I0824640

IN THE COUNTRY I LOVE

IN THE COUNTRY I LOVE

ALAA AL-BARKAWI

PEACHTREE Teen

Peachtree Teen
An imprint of Peachtree Publishing Company Inc.

Text copyright © 2026 by Alaa Al-Barkawi
Jacket and all interior illustrations copyright © 2026 by Nabi H. Ali
All rights reserved. No part of this book may be reproduced, transmitted, or stored in an information retrieval system in any form or by any means, graphic, electronic, or mechanical, including photocopying, taping, and recording, without prior written permission from the publisher. Additionally, no part of this book may be used or reproduced in any manner for the purpose of training artificial intelligence technologies or systems, nor for text and data mining.
Printed and bound in January 2026 at RRD, Dongguan, China.
Edited by Zoie Konneker
Book design by Lily Steele
PeachtreeBooks.com

Content Advisory: This narrative contains mention of Islamophobia, xenophobia, racism, war, genocide, violence, sexual assault, death, grief, PTSD, alcoholism, bullying, and mental illness.

First Edition
1 3 5 7 9 10 8 6 4 2
ISBN: 978-1-68263-810-1 (hardcover)

Library of Congress Cataloging-in-Publication Data

Names: Al-Barkawi, Alaa author
Title: In the country I love / Alaa Al-Barkawi.
Description: First edition. | Atlanta : Peachtree Teen, [2026] | Audience: Ages 14 and up | Audience: Grades 10-12 | Summary: Told in multiple voices, two Iraqi American best friends, a struggling teen father and the community's golden boy, see their forbidden friendship ignite a chain of events that exposes family secrets and forces them to confront questions of identity, faith, racism, and justice.
Identifiers: LCCN 2025046833 | ISBN 9781682638101 hardcover | ISBN 9781682639054 ebook
Subjects: CYAC: Best friends—Fiction | Friendship—Fiction | Self-actualization—Fiction | Family secrets—Fiction | Muslims—Fiction | Iraqi Americans—Fiction | LCGFT: Fiction | Novels
Classification: LCC PZ7.1.A392967 In 2026
LC record available at https://lccn.loc.gov/2025046833

EU Authorized Representative: HackettFlynn Ltd, 36 Cloch Choirneal, Balrothery, Co. Dublin, K32 C942, Ireland. EU@walkerpublishinggroup.com

To my family and to my country.

And to all the refugees searching for home—
wherever it may be

Bismillah al-Rahman al-Rahim

In the name of Allah,
the Most Gracious
and the Most Merciful

DEAR READER,

I have always been fascinated by the relationship between home and violence.

I was born in a refugee prison camp on the outskirts of Saudi Arabia after my family was forcibly displaced from Iraq, alongside thousands of other Iraqi Shia Muslims, in the early nineties as a result of Saddam Hussein's brutal dictatorship and failed US foreign policy.

My young parents had to raise four small children in this camp, which was riddled with human rights abuses: torture, starvation, sexual violence, unlivable desert conditions, and much more. Thankfully, soon after I was born, the United Nations High Commissioner for Refugees chose to help my family escape the camp and resettle as refugees in the United States. This was a process based mostly on sheer luck.

Unfortunately, a few years later, two major events happened: 9/11, followed by the US invasion and occupation of Iraq. Some of my earliest memories are watching images of Iraq being bombed through our Arabic satellite TV. Bloodied bodies pulled from the rubble. Parents grieving their dead children. Buildings turned to ash.

Yet, in the US media, our people were not portrayed as victims, but instead as villains. Iraqis, and by extension other Arabs and Muslims, were viewed as a monolith for terrorism. Our language, our clothing, and our homeland were deemed as barbaric and extreme.

By the age of five, I learned not to tell people where I was from. We were already hated for being Muslim, but being Iraqi meant the target on our backs grew even bigger. I swallowed parts of my identity, afraid, even though we were the ones being perceived as dangerous.

Once again, a place that was supposed to be my family's refuge had become unsafe for us. But here we were, living in a country that was actively destroying our own.

I didn't know how to define home. How could it be America when we were told we didn't belong? How could it be Iraq when we weren't even allowed to go back? Iraq, the place where most of my family still lived, was also the place my classmates' family members were being deployed, whether intentionally or not, to hurt people who looked just like me.

Home felt complicated and unknown. Most days, it still does.

The US invasion of Iraq left over one million Iraqis dead and millions more displaced. As a modern society, we have still not reconciled what it truly means to violate a people and their country with little to no accountability. Nor do we offer much visibility from the perspective of the victims. While there is a plethora of media about the invasion, it is almost always through the eyes of the military and veterans. For decades, Iraqis have been invaded, occupied, and killed, but there are rarely stories told for us and by us.

This is why, even after twenty years since the invasion and continued occupation, *In the Country I Love* has become one of the first young adult novels to feature Iraqi characters by an Iraqi author.

This book was written to bring awareness to the realities of Iraqis and Iraqi Americans in a post-9/11 world. It is also a story that centers Shia Muslims, a minority sect in Islam, whose practices are steeped in social justice but often misunderstood and demonized. Under Saddam Hussein's regime, Shias were targeted, imprisoned, and brutally murdered en masse. Because Shias have been historically ostracized by governments and attacked by extremist groups across the world (like ISIS), I wanted to share some of the practices and traditions that have been misinterpreted and underrepresented—Muharram, Laylat Ashura, and Arbaeen—hoping not only to shed light on the diversity of Muslim stories, but to show that Shia Muslims are just as Muslim as anyone else.

Although Iraqi and Shia representation in mainstream media is long overdue, this book does not encompass all the rich and diverse perspectives of those identities. It is simply a reflection of *my* perspective growing up with those identities in a post-9/11 world. The novel also explores traditional cultural Iraqi family dynamics from the perspective of a community that did not have access to education and safety, and certainly won't represent every Iraqi family.

Since 9/11, there has been pressure on Arab and Muslim voices to be more palatable to Western audiences by letting go of tradition or religious practices—or for us to play the part of the perfect victim. Having to prove over and over that Arabs and Muslims are just as complex and flawed to those outside our communities is one of the most dehumanizing acts we can inflict upon ourselves. In writing and sharing this book, it is my goal to not succumb to this pressure; our stories deserve to be told with all the messy nuances that make us human. Due to the real-life events that inspired *In the Country I Love*, you can expect to read about heavy and oftentimes uncomfortable topics. Please take care of yourself and read the trigger warnings before you begin.

As you embark on Yassir's, Khaled's, and Kawther's journeys, you'll witness firsthand how imperfect each character is, and how the inevitable reality of violence and the idea of home can blur into one. While violence can obscure the idea of home, it is up to each character to find a way to extricate one idea from the other—or not—if they choose to. Some characters aren't brave enough to embrace their identities, just like I wasn't when I was younger, but some will fight their hardest for their truths to be heard—the way I am trying every day, starting with this book.

In the Country I Love offers the story of one small community's experience, but can be a reminder to all readers that with home, there is heartache, but there is also love, too. In our current political climate, we are collectively experiencing the frightening reality of violence defining our understanding of home, and what it means to fight against hate. It is not easy to be brave, but it is worth it to try.

With love,

ALAA AL-BARKAWI

SKY

Delicate whispers in the dark.

That's how I find the most interesting things.

The ones that are not supposed to be found. The creatures left behind. Their breaths rattling in the zephyr of my wind, praying that this moment will not be their last.

I heard the whimper first.

Before the crowd gathered at Twenty-First and Main, twilight and crimson lights illuminating their shocked faces. I heard it before the ambulance screamed down the street and swallowed the body—a boy—in one large bite.

Now, I am not all-seeing, nor am I all-knowing.

I can only see what the humans choose to expose to me. Bombs sweeping buildings clean, children hunting each other on playgrounds, men breaking promises down on one knee as they sputter meaningless words like *Will you marry me*.

I don't answer prayers, either. That is not my job.

Nor can I discuss secrets of the universe, although I do know many.

But I can tell you this: When that boy, face smeared with blood and dirt, whimpered, I found a shadow leaning over him. Then the shadow walked away. When the shadow returned, he brought with him the police and their sirens, and the onlookers whose hands covered their mouths in horror.

When the shadow leaned into the light as the cops began their questioning, I recognized his face. He was skinnier. A green military uniform no longer engulfed his body, but the grimace that bit the inside of his cheeks was the same. Years ago, when a dead little boy lay face down in the mud after a rainstorm in Baghdad, the shadow looked up at me and stared and stared and stared. By the time I stared back, he was already being dragged away by his superior officer to give a report.

I try not to pay attention to soldiers. There are too many of them. While many humans linger in my memory, the soldiers and their work haunt me most. If I tried to keep track of them all, I'd never rest.

However, they leave behind the delicate whispers I like to find.

The ones I like to follow.

The ones I like to soothe in their last moments, my warmth cupping their chins as they release their final breaths.

As I said, I am not all-seeing, nor am I all-knowing. But one day, when the earth has folded over and become obsolete, I will testify what the humans did to one another before they enter the hereafter.

I found the ambulance resting on the shoulder of a hospital curb in silence. But the body was gone. Yet I could hear the whimper still.

So I followed it.

1

YASSIR

FORTY-EIGHT DAYS BEFORE

On the eve of Imam Hussein's murder, Yassir Al-Azzawi watched the masjid fill wall to wall, and wondered where his mouthy best friend was among the chaos. Of course, he wouldn't be allowed to talk to Khaled even if he found him. So he observed the crowd in boredom, knees sinking into the stained salmon rug where Baba ordered him to sit.

At the masjid, even the walls grieved. Black satin was draped over every inch of the room, with glittering Arabic calligraphy looping brilliantly over the cloth. Splotches of fake blood dripped at the diacritics of the painted words to symbolize the sacrifice of Imam Hussein and the seventy-two companions who had accompanied him in battle over thirteen hundred years ago.

Umm al-Banin. Ya Abbas.

Most Arabic words had withered in Yassir's head. When he tried to resuscitate the language to speak it aloud, he never made the right sounds, but to his surprise, the names of Ahlul Bayt were still perfectly intact in his head.

"Here."

Baba returned with two half-broken turbahs in his palms, the consequences of coming late on one of the most sacred nights of the year. Yassir grabbed the smaller rock and stared at Allah's name engraved in the clay. His thumb lingered over the faded Arabic, but he stopped himself from tracing over it.

"You will stay here and pray. You will not speak to anyone. You will not move from this spot unless I tell you to. *Understood?*" Baba's lips were an inch away from his ear, the scent of secondhand smoke heavy on the collar of his black dishdasha.

Yassir couldn't keep his eyes from rolling. "Yes, Baba."

Baba side-eyed Yassir's rotting lemon-yellow hoodie, something he had done several times on the car ride from school. Yassir had foolishly thought he'd be driven straight home, where Mama's cooking awaited to silence the miseries of the day while Yasmin made a mess like she always did, spitting up milk and stew onto his jeans.

But now he understood why Baba had been adamant this morning that Yassir wear his black sweatshirt. The one that now sat damp in his gym locker after Alex and Khaled had spilled beer all over it during lunch.

When Yassir had come home with a one-month-old who shared his DNA and the dimple in his left cheek earlier this year, well, he was lucky he had not yet been shipped away. But if Baba caught Yassir drinking again, a one-way ticket to Iraq would be in his hands the next morning, as promised. So Yassir had borrowed Alex's smelly yellow hoodie and dealt with Baba's disappointing stares. Stares he'd gotten used to long ago.

"Get up," Baba commanded as the chaos of the room came to a standstill and men and children took their places for prayer. Yassir stood up and placed his hands over his ears before settling them down at his sides as salat al-maghrib commenced.

It had been 1,147 days since Yassir had made salat.

One thousand, one hundred and forty-seven days since reciting a meaningful "Allah *is* the greatest, most compassionate, most merciful" kind of prayer. He had been sandwiched between Baba and his older brother then, the scent of Ali's strong sandalwood cologne seeping into the air as he lifted his hands to his ears, Baba's voice commanding the next movement.

That day, Yassir had thought of Ayah's face after each rak'ah, recalling the moment they'd been reunited on the first day of freshman year after years of separation, when hope and excitement had foolishly mixed in his stomach.

Allahu akbar.

The motions of worship were engraved in his muscle memory. The words he'd assumed were long forgotten slipped out beneath his breath. He lingered with his forehead on the turbah when he was supposed to. Stacked his feet after sujud.

Allahu akbar.

Yassir whispered it as each man lifted his forehead from the Persian rug. He whispered it when they put their hands together in dua and lifted them toward Mecca. He whispered it, the scent of rose water and boiled rice clinging to the air.

Allahu akbar. Allahu akbar. Allahu akbar.

Yassir opened his eyes as a harmony of prayers filled his ears. Everyone, including children as young as six, closed their eyes and asked Allah to make their dreams come true. To watch over their families. To get the bombs and corrupt government out of Iraq. Maybe even to lower their car payments, or something.

Tonight he wouldn't even bother.

Despite what his parents believed, praying would not solve any of his problems. It hadn't fixed a single thing in their lives before now, anyway.

The prayer ended, with several men extending their hands to Baba. When Baba smiled at the uncles, Yassir could see the worry deeply lining his cheeks, where the dimple he and Ali had inherited met with a grimace. Sleep deprivation was tucked under the puffy dark parts of his father's eyes. Yasmin's teething cries kept him up at night, too. Sometimes during salat al-fajr, Baba would lay her fussy body at the center of his sajadah and whisper prayers in her ears to make her pain go away.

Guilt settled between Yassir's ribs.

He looked away. Even when others extended their hands, he knotted his fingers together, acknowledging no one but himself.

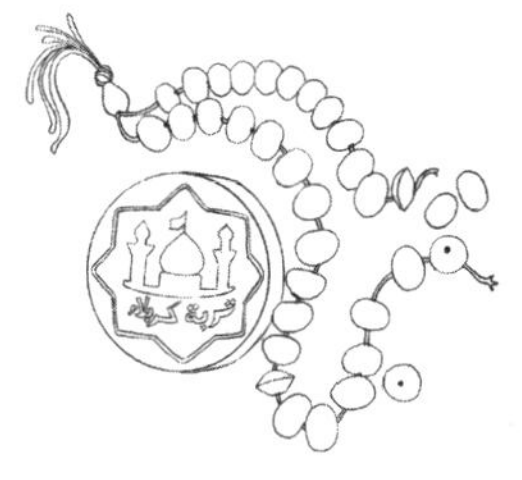

2

KHALED

On the eve of Imam Hussein's murder, Khaled Al-Hakim drove back to the masjid with a smile on his face.

Tonight was the eve of Ashura. The most sacred day of the year. The day that reminded him that sacrifice for justice was more important than anything else in the world. His body buzzed with the nostalgia and purpose that Ashura brought each year . . . oh, and the beer he'd drunk over lunch.

He shouldn't have done that. But he had been so stressed about sending the letter to his superintendent, and before he knew it, he found himself drinking what Alex called liquid gold (although in Khaled's mind, murky Coors Light was far from that). It had been a while since he had done that—drinking in the day between rants in the car with his friends—mindlessly forgetting just how many sips he'd had until the last drop hit his tongue. Even Yassir, who had much bigger things to worry about, had stared at him in concern from Alex's back seat.

On Tuesday, during the sixth night of Muharram, Khaled had proudly made the call to prayer in the masjid. Now, with the alcohol still in his bloodstream, his prayers wouldn't even be valid. The last time he drank, he'd carried the guilt for months. Now he felt it all over again, and it was too heavy to pretend.

To avoid lining up with the crowd for jumu'ah prayer, he had volunteered to buy every single carton of water from the nearby deteriorating grocery store for the special meal being served.

At least tonight was a special night. Tonight he wouldn't repent alone on his prayer rug at home. No, he'd quietly repent to Allah among the dozens of Iraqi Shias who spilled into their masjid, the air laced with sweat and worship. A night filled with sweet milk and stories about the past and stirring wishes into giant steel pots of qeema until the sun rose again.

He couldn't wait to hold his hands up to the ceiling and beat his chest so hard that after everyone shouted *Ya Hussein* in unison, a dozen tiny red dots would adorn his skin the next morning like a memorial.

Khaled wished life were always filled with excited Muslims gathering for a singular purpose. In his white, conservative city, this was rare. The only Muslim left at his school was Yassir Al-Azzawi, although Yassir didn't consider himself much of a Muslim these days.

For now, in the comfort of his Buick, Khaled lightly beat his chest with one hand, clasping the steering wheel with the other. The voice of Bassim Al-Karbalaei, his favorite Shia eulogy reader, pumped loudly from the car's raspy sound system. He didn't even care when strangers gave him bizarre looks as he drove down State Street, windows down, listening to Arabic poetry, because for the first time since he'd gotten kicked out of his American government class, he felt at peace.

Khaled swiftly parked a few lots away from the masjid—as the five spots allotted to the masjid were beyond overfilled. Only moments ago, the sky had been painted a half-bitten plum, orange and purple hues stroking the golden horizon. Now only lit cigarettes glowed under the dim streetlight where Iraqi men gathered like moths.

"Khaled, habibi!" they shouted, spotting him. "Salaam!"

"Khaled, how's your heart, habibi?" another shouted. "You doing okay?"

Khaled felt a tremor snake up his arm, but he shook it away, along with the question. He shouted his salaams back, pushing the water cartons over his skinny knees as he waddled to the masjid's entrance.

His eyes took in how many new bodies had entered the building since he'd left for the store. His bones settled at the sight. This masjid was Iraqi and Shia. Most masjids around town were the same, nearly exclusive to the small pocket of communities that lived here. The Sunni Bosnians had their own masjid—the Somalis, too.

He loved these people. He loved how loud and funny they were. How sweet and gentle they could be, too. Most Iraqis here had been forced out of Iraq during the 1991 revolution—the same time his parents had. Some had come here after. During the famine in the nineties, the US military invasion of 2003, or the invasion of ISIS a few years after. Many were refugees who had clung to one another, the way his and Yassir's family had when they'd first arrived in America.

Nearly every family dreamt and endured the same things. With his own family dwindling, he found comfort in the presence of these people—even if they were traditional in every sense of the word; marriage always came before college, and college rarely came at all. Khaled's dreams were bigger than the dreams of those who had come before him, and they admired him for it.

Outside the hellhole of Chapman High, there was a place where he was respected. Where he belonged.

"Just put them over there," Baba said, clasping Khaled's shoulder. "How many more did you bring?"

Khaled sighed. "I cleaned out the store. I promise. I won't drink water tonight, if that helps."

Baba ruffled his hair, the tobacco stains on his teeth exposed. "We need you strong during the latmiyat today. Drink water or you'll pass out. Remember when you were six and you passed out because you refused to drink anything? Muharram isn't Ramadan, habibi."

Khaled laughed at the memory. "I know that now, Baba."

"When you're done, start taking food over to Khala Amirah for the women's section, okay? The place is packed."

Khaled nodded and stared at the makeshift kitchen, his jaw dropping at the sight. He blinked several times, making sure what he saw before him wasn't a mirage. Sure enough, Yassir Al-Azzawi (who Khaled jokingly called Yassir Al-Harami) stood in the same ugly yellow hoodie he'd had on since lunch, ladling lamb tashreeb from a steel pot larger than half of his body.

If Baba hadn't been lingering around, he'd have taken a picture to commemorate the moment.

Yassir's father, Sayed Rahman, must be trying to get Yassir to accumulate good deeds in his latest attempt to save Yassir from sin. Perhaps if Yassir behaved like the pious boy his father wanted, the Sayed would stop threatening to send him to Iraq.

Khaled began to take the sayenas filled with mountains of rice, fluffy khubz, and Yassir's tashreeb back and forth to the partition that separated the women and men, where Khala Amirah, one of his mother's friends, and a few other aunties gratefully took the trays, admonishing him for getting taller just as they had done every night since Muharram, when the mourning observance started eight days ago. By the fourth trip back to the kitchen, Yassir had a hand to his nose. He had never liked lamb. Sayed Rahman had become cruel.

Look up, harami, Khaled texted him. Yassir continued his ladling.

"Khaled." Baba's arm was warm on his shoulder. "The trash is piling on the corner outside. Go toss it. But take someone. Stop doing everything on your own."

Grabbing two bags of trash in each hand, Khaled scanned the kitchen again. He knew the perfect companion—but the ugly yellow hoodie had disappeared.

3

YASSIR

Before Khaled's father could spot him, Yassir dropped the ladle Baba had shoved into his hand and ran. Within a minute, he was on the other side of the parking lot, crossing close to State Street.

Yassir walked until he could no longer hear the faint noise of worship and dinner and laughing and crying. He walked until the streetlights had dimmed so much in the distance that he could barely spot his own hands in the glow of moonlight. It was not the first time he had done this, and it would not be the last. He would have kept going if it hadn't been for a set of footsteps behind him.

He always ignored strangers on his walks, as it was the safest, most practical thing to do in the middle of the night. There was also the fact that he was perpetually shy, which Ayah always teased him about. Despite the quiet stares and rare words he used when interacting with other students at Chapman High, he was somehow still more popular than her.

To be handsome and quiet, she'd laugh. *What a privilege.*

A shadow of spiky hair scrawled over the sidewalk, silencing his thoughts of Khaled's second-oldest sister.

"Come inside before your dad beats you up."

He's not the father I'm afraid of right now, Yassir wanted to say.

At Yassir's silence, Khaled continued. "Yalla, Sayed Yassir! He's looking for you."

"Stop—" Yassir caught the annoyance in his own voice. "Don't call me that."

Being a Sayed meant people in his community expected him to be an example of piety because his bloodline was tied to the Prophet Muhammad. The same bloodline that included Imam Hussein, who was the Prophet's grandson. As the more devout of the two of them, Khaled was jealous of the title, which was why he rubbed it in Yassir's face any chance he got.

Yassir stuffed his hands into the pocket of his hoodie and continued to trudge in the opposite direction, toward the streetlights, toward Yasmin, toward home. Even though it would probably take an hour to get there, he couldn't go back to the masjid.

"Are you upset or something?" Khaled asked, marching after him. "Or are you just seriously that allergic to religion?"

"I just don't see the point," Yassir said, going with the second option. It wasn't like he could tell Khaled the truth. "And I know you don't care, either, Khaled."

"Me? I'm the one who reminded *you* that today was Laylat Ashura. When you wore black this morning, I was actually proud!"

Yassir spun, finding his best friend only inches away, with hulking, reeking bags of garbage hanging at his sides. "I think you're just good at faking it. Remember how you spilled beer all over me today, *Sheikh Khaled*? How are you not still drunk?"

Khaled wasn't just perfect at being religious. He was perfect at sinning, too.

"You . . . you drank, too," Khaled retorted.

"Not *four cans*." Yassir shook his head, staring down the street. "Listen, I can't stay. If you want to help me out, you can give me a ride home. If you don't, you can find my murdered body in the morning." He pointed to the end of the dark alley. "That's where I'll be."

He twisted around and continued walking, hoping to scare his best friend away. The last thing Yassir needed in his life was for Khaled to get hurt. To get in trouble.

Watching him drink earlier had made Yassir feel sick. Although Alex had been the one to offer the first sip (Alex was *always* the one to offer the first sip), Yassir had encouraged them by joining in. He didn't know how to make Khaled stop doing the things he'd regret. It was only a matter of time before he'd regret being friends with Yassir, too.

The garbage bags scuffed against the concrete. Despite his words, his friend only clung closer. Typical Khaled.

"Don't you have, like . . . uncles' asses to kiss and marriage proposals to accept?" Yassir huffed. "This is why I don't call you on my walks anymore, Khaled. You're annoying as hell."

"How many times do I have to remind you that walking in the middle of the night is reckless behavior!" Khaled hissed, before dropping the bags dramatically. "When Yasmin grows up an orphan, then you'll be sorry."

Yassir pushed a middle finger up and Khaled laughed.

"Aw, Yassuri . . . you mad, habibi?"

Yassuri.

Ayah used to call him that. Ayah, whose hands lingered in his under their desks in biology class. Ayah, whose tear-streaked face was the last he saw of her as Khaled's father tore her away from him.

Hajji Abu Abdalla didn't let go of the past easily. After all, he had proudly worn the name of his son who had died in the Rafha refugee camps for as long as Yassir had known him. When he'd spotted Yassir for a brief moment at the masjid last year, rage had filled his eyes. Yassir didn't want to know what they'd look like now, despite the time that had passed.

"Just go away," Yassir grumbled in defeat. "I want to be alone."

It was Yassir's fault that the tension between their families had become worse. His fault that his best friend had started drinking.

And genius Khaled was none the wiser.

The jingle of keys rang in the air. Yassir turned.

"Listen, I do have asses to kiss and proposals to turn down, but I'm not going to just let you walk in the dark like some creep."

"Are you going to take me home?"

To Yassir's surprise, Khaled nodded. "If you're going to be a stubborn asshole, then yes. Because believe it or not, I don't want to see anything bad happen to Yasmin's dad. Even if he's an idiot ninety-nine point nine percent of the time."

Yassir narrowed his eyes. "Say wallah."

"Why do you want me to swear to God if you don't even believe in God anymore?"

"Just say wallah."

Khaled never went against his word when God was involved. "I'll tell some little kid to tell some little kid that you got a ride home from an uncle, they'll play telephone and tell your dad. Got it?"

Yassir stared at his best friend, unconvinced.

"Wallah," Khaled finally huffed, his keys reflecting under the dim streetlight.

Yassir smiled, crossed over and grabbed two garbage bags from him, and began walking back toward the masjid.

"Are you going to throw the trash in my car?" Khaled asked, pointing to the dumpster at the gas station across the street, where a blue dinosaur sign glowed in the moonlight. "I'm parked in the church lot next door. Besides, we need to make a quick pit stop first. I need like eight shots of espresso to keep me alive tonight."

"Right. You need to play golden boy for the rest of the night," Yassir scoffed as they launched the bags into the dumpster. "Just look at the collar of your dishdasha, Amu Khaled—might as well start wearing tucked-in golf shirts and a Bluetooth earpiece at all times."

A deep laugh escaped Khaled. A sound Yassir hadn't heard in so long, it nearly jarred his core. Maybe he *was* still a little buzzed from lunch today. "Literally slap me if I ever get to the Bluetooth era."

"I'll keep that promise," Yassir said as they began to walk toward the gas station. "Wallah."

When they were kids, they'd beg their fathers for a few bucks to buy as many candy bars as they could afford at this exact store. Back then, Laylat Ashura was one big sleepover. Blankets lined the floor of the masjid, sandwiches and chai passed out at intervals, the projector displaying the journey of pilgrims in Iraq making their way to the city of Karbala. The boys would sneak Ayah peanut butter cups and sour Skittles through the barrier that separated the men and women. Kawther and Fatima would scold them for wandering off so late at night, even if it was just a street away.

They would stay awake until sunlight peeked through the windows, the scent of qeema and hareesa filling the tight building. While Yassir had stopped attending years ago, Khaled still stayed up through the night every year. Whether it was out of obligation or choice, Yassir didn't know.

Khaled stepped inside the gas station first. The owners had changed over the years, so Yassir no longer recognized the interior. It seemed like the staff didn't recognize them, either, because as soon as they stepped onto the bright linoleum, two pairs of eyes were pinned to Khaled and his long black dishdasha, a distasteful look in each pair. Yassir took a sidestep away from his best friend.

"Damn, I forgot to wear my suicide bomb vest," Khaled muttered, rolling his eyes as he walked toward the coffee machine at the back of the store. The cashier, a young white man, made direct eye contact with the woman cleaning a hot dog machine.

"Shut up, Khaled," Yassir seethed, a few feet behind his best friend. "It's not funny when you say things like that."

"Why not?" Khaled asked as he reached for the largest cup on the counter. "It's what they're thinking. Haven't you noticed everyone is on edge with us lately? Even outside of school. You know that dude from the grocery store off Carter Street who wears those big-ass American flag shirts? Less than an hour ago, I asked him where he kept the cases of water bottles and he looked at me like I walked in with an AR-15 shouting *Allahu akbar!*"

The hot dog woman stared at them. Yassir attempted to smile at her, but she didn't smile back. Anxiety prickled his skin.

"I mean, if one of us is wearing something offensive, it's you." Khaled continued his spiel, pointing at Yassir as he grabbed two large foam cups. "Don't you know that yellow is probably the most disrespectful color you can wear today, Mr. Al-Harami?"

"Shut up." Yassir didn't like being called religiously forbidden, even if his actions these past few years often amounted to that. "Besides, it's royal *gold*."

"It's pukey lemon and you know it. Everyone at Chapman agrees with me—that was my most popular op-ed of all time."

"The only thing they've ever agreed with you about," Yassir said. "Aren't you banned from the school newspaper this quarter?"

Khaled pouted for a moment, giving his silent answer, and Yassir laughed.

"It's not funny," Khaled said. "It's basically a gag order."

"I wish it was," Yassir muttered, and Khaled flipped him off. There was a buzz in Yassir's pocket, silencing his laughter. *Baba.* He rejected the call immediately. "Khaled, you done? My dad's calling and if we're caught together your dad is going to freak out and . . ."

And I'll be fucked, he thought.

Khaled shook his head. "If your dad catches you with me, he's going to think I'm putting you back on the right path. Besides, my dad isn't going to be looking for me, he trusts me—"

The words dissolved on his tongue as his gaze caught Yassir's. He didn't need to say them aloud for Yassir to know what he was going to say.

Unlike your dad.

Khaled turned and hit the side of the sputtering machine until it spewed boiling-hot coffee, splashing from his cup and burning his fingers. "Ya Allah," he sighed loudly. "Save me from this misery."

A dry cough echoed through the gas station. Yassir looked up. Hot Dog Woman was near the cash register now, cell phone in hand. Yassir's stomach churned.

Khaled wasn't paying attention and continued his prayer. "Ya Allah, grant me the patience to get Yassir's whiny ass home and allow my body to be properly caffeinated."

He actually cupped his hands together momentarily in dua before letting out a chuckle. Hot Dog Woman and the cashier exchanged another silent look.

"Stop talking," Yassir whispered, tightening two lids on Khaled's various cups. "You're making them nervous, dude. This is why you got kicked out of government class."

Khaled's voice echoed loudly now. "Hmm, pretty sure that was due to racism, *Michael.*"

Yassir gaped at Khaled, his words barely pushing between his teeth. "*Are* you drunk?"

Khaled simply clicked his tongue as he strolled to the cashier, who grimaced at him.

The man scanned the barcodes on the cups. "That's five-seventy-five."

Khaled patted his dishdasha. "Shit. I forgot my wallet in my car."

Yassir searched his pockets and pulled out a five-dollar bill. "Return something, Khaled," he said.

The cashier shook his head. "You already filled those drinks up. You need to pay."

"We only have five," Yassir said nervously, fishing his empty pockets. "One of us will come back and pay the rest. Our car is just down the street."

"You think I trust ISIS wannabes to come back and pay? Your people are always coming in, causing a ruckus," the cashier growled.

Yassir blinked.

Khaled's face turned stony. "How about you kiss my ISIS ass?"

"Khaled."

"Forget the purchase. I think you two need to leave now." Hot Dog Woman spoke up.

The cashier took Khaled's coffee and dumped it in the trash can behind him. "Get out. You can't just saunter in and terrorize my store."

"Terrorize?" Khaled echoed. Then he laughed. Hard. The same condescending laugh he used during his outbursts at school. The kind that had gotten him kicked out of government class and banned from the newspaper.

Yassir didn't want to hear what would come out of Khaled's mouth next. He clamped a hand over Khaled's shoulder and yanked him back. "Khaled, let's go. Sorry for the inconvenience, sir."

Khaled shook his head, his dark brown eyes filling with rage as he shoved Yassir away. "Why are you apologizing to them?"

"Because you're being offensive!" Yassir said.

"They just called us terrorists and you think *I'm* being offensive?" Khaled scoffed. "Ya Muhammad. Ya Ali. They took one look at us and decided they knew everything they needed to know. It's like they *want* me to promise to blow this place up just to justify their assumptions!"

"Out." Hot Dog Woman pointed to the door. "Now!"

Once she put her cell phone to her ear, Khaled finally seemed to come out of his trance. Before he stepped outside, he held up two middle fingers to the man and woman in the store. Yassir dragged Khaled by his sleeve, only letting go once they hit the end of the street.

"You need to stop being an asshole," they both shouted at the same time. "No, *you*!"

Khaled pushed a frustrated hand through his spiky hair. "You need to stop pleasing every damn white person who comes your way. Did you miss the part where they called us ISIS wannabes? Wake up, Yassir! They don't care about you."

"Me?" Yassir echoed. "This is coming from the hypocrite whose best school friend is Alex, the whitest kid I've ever met."

Khaled laughed. "Oh, no, you forgot to count yourself there. *You're* the whitest kid I know. Even your daughter is half white. You forget who you are half the time. You're embarrassed to be around me. You're embarrassed to be around other Iraqis or, God forbid, anyone who looks Muslim. Your family is Muslim, whether you like it or not. I'd rather be a hypocrite than pathetic."

Yassir didn't reply. It had been a mistake going home with Khaled. Everything he ever did with Khaled turned out to be a mistake.

They trudged back to the parking lot in silence, finding Khaled's Buick parked just a few feet away from Yassir's father's taxicab.

"How am I supposed to make it through the night if I'm about to fall asleep at the wheel? Can you drive? Oh, wait . . . you lost your license."

Yassir sighed. "Thanks for shoving that in my face."

"I'm bringing it up because I just remembered." Khaled shook his head. "Honestly, if I hadn't sworn on behalf of God to take you home, I'd drag your ass right back to your dad right now. Also don't give me that look, I'm good to drive. I'm not drunk."

The Buick beeped open. Yassir hesitated before he slipped into the passenger seat. He caught a glimpse of little kids shoving each other across the road in the cramped masjid parking lot. He and Khaled used to do that when they were little, and Hajji Abu Abdalla would grab them by the collars of their shirts and swing them until they were dizzy and giggling into the crook of his arms, as he commanded them to go back inside and listen to the sheikh's lecture. Always with kindness. Patience. Yassir couldn't remember what it was like to be treated with those virtues anymore.

"Listen, Yassir, what I said before . . ." Khaled's voice softened now. An unspoken apology in his tone. "I take back what I said about Yasmin. I don't care what she is, she's still my goddaughter."

Yassir rolled his eyes. "For the *billionth* time, she doesn't have a godfather."

"I'm still her uncle, then, even if our siblings never married." A pang of sadness entered Yassir's chest for what could've been. "I'll always be Amu Khaled."

Khaled yawned. Yassir could see his own childhood reflected in Khaled's face. Every izzema dinner and s'more at the campfire. Every superhero movie and water gun fight. Everything good, everything whole, before Kawther tore their families apart. Before Ayah got married and left, too.

Khaled sighed deeply. "I miss her."

Me too, Yassir thought.

He hadn't seen his daughter since he'd kissed her sleeping cheeks goodbye that morning. The thought of her cries made his stomach clench. Sometimes it was hard to see all his mistakes in her eyes and rock her to sleep.

Yassir tapped the screen of his phone, finding notifications of three missed calls from Baba covering Yasmin's giggling face in the background.

He texted his father, despite knowing that Baba struggled to read text messages. I'm tired so I got a ride home. Sorry, Baba.

He hoped the word *sorry* would work in his favor for once.

Bassim Al-Karbalaei's voice trickled out of the speakers in the Buick. Khaled was right, Yassir was a coward.

But just before their escape, red and blue police lights illuminated their faces.

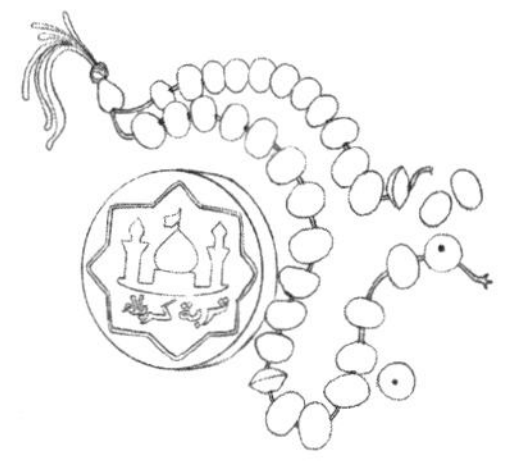

4

KHALED

The last time Khaled Al-Hakim had spoken to a cop was when he was beaten at the school playground ten years ago. Kawther had called the police and Khaled had stared at the officer then, just as he did now, his mouth frozen open.

The officer tapped on the window.

"Please step out of the car, sir."

This was wrong. Khaled Al-Hakim was not the type of kid to get pulled over.

"Out of the car, sir."

"Khaled," Yassir urged, pushing his arm. "Do as she says. *Hurry*."

"You with the curly hair," the officer said, pointing at his best friend. "You too, okay?"

Yassir slammed the passenger door and Khaled's spine jolted. His body followed Yassir's on autopilot. Of course Yassir knew what to do.

Khaled watched as his best friend dropped his arms, no longer hiding his fists in his hoodie. Yassir didn't look the officer directly in the eye, but he didn't look at his feet, either.

"You drunk, kid?" the officer asked Khaled.

"N-no," Khaled stuttered. "I'm not."

"You look paranoid."

"Should I be?" Khaled asked.

"*Ihmar,*" Yassir muttered beneath his breath in Arabic. "Iskit."

Shut up, dumbass.

Right. He should do that.

The officer's gray ponytail shone under the dim streetlight. "Got a smart-ass here? You know what's easier than asking questions? A Breathalyzer test."

Shit, he could hear an audience of uncles and little kids approaching them.

"Don't talk," Yassir whispered to him as the officer grabbed the test from her car, her eyes flitting between them and the inside of the car every few seconds. "You know they can use what you say in court."

"I'm legit going to piss my pants," Khaled said. "I swear to God. I'm going to pee right here."

"Shut. Up."

The officer came back. "I got a disturbance call from that gas station back at Twentieth and Main. I was told two boys who seemed a little intoxicated came by and started threatening the workers. They said they drove a Buick. One in a black dress. The other in a bright yellow hoodie. That sound familiar?"

"It's not a dre—"

Yassir nudged him.

For once, he should listen to Yassir Al-Azzawi, the kid who had a kid and a DUI and a revoked license.

Yeah. Yassir the Wise. The great mistake.

"I'm sorry, Officer." Khaled started over and Yassir's eyes widened. Khaled's years as a debate champion and spending local Arbaeen walks passing out flyers about Imam Hussein to random bystanders had prepared him for this moment. "There's a big misunderstanding. We're not intoxicated, okay? We're Muslim. We're not even religiously allowed to drink. And the building behind us? That's our mosque. It's a holy night. We stay up and make prayers on behalf of Imam Hussein and his family. Do you know who he is? He sacrificed his life—"

"Put your hands down where I can see them!"

The officer did not care to learn about Imam Hussein or the fact that Khaled talked with his hands a lot.

Yassir chewed his lips nervously.

Khaled Al-Hakim wouldn't go down without a fight. He held still. "The gas station workers were being racist. I swear. The clerk called us ISIS wannabes."

"They said you threatened to blow up the station."

"That was an exaggeration, ma'am."

A faint scent of cigarettes lingered in the air. The uncles were approaching with a million Arabic questions.

Khaled, habibi, what's going on?

Why is there a cop?

Are you in trouble?

Khaled attempted to turn and assuage them, but the cop barked at him. "Turn around so I can see you!"

Khaled gulped and turned. Yassir's mouth trembled.

The cop stepped closer to Khaled as more uncles approached. Little kids, too. Fear suddenly gripped Khaled. Videos of cops body-slamming and gunning down innocent people on the street flashed in his mind.

"Khaled, what's happening?" Hajji Majid asked as he approached. "Why is there a police officer here?"

Hajji Abbas inserted himself between Khaled and the officer. "Why are you questioning these boys?"

"I need you all to step back!" the officer shouted, a hand to her holster. Sweat trickled down Khaled's spine. The Hajjis simply stared at her until she gave another warning, and they took a step back.

The woman grimaced. "Listen, boys. I can believe people say nasty things. But from the looks of how you're acting, I'm going to administer a Breathalyzer test. Tell your friends to take at least ten steps back. You can even tell them in your language, okay? Let's be reasonable."

Khaled silently stared at the uncles, who watched in awe. Khaled had never been in trouble. At least, not like this.

The officer stuck the Breathalyzer tube in his mouth. "Blow."

Khaled stared at her, eyes pleading. She had no idea just how this simple thing was going to completely ruin him.

"Fuck," Yassir muttered.

"You're next, Curly," she said. Her gloves pulled away and she announced the results. "Blood alcohol level is zero point oh three eight. You might want to stop lying, kid."

Khaled closed his eyes.

"You a minor? Got your ID?"

"It's in the car."

"Tell me where it is, I'll grab it."

Khaled's voice quivered. "Cup holder."

"Stay where you are. Hands stay in the air. Understand? If you move, I *will* Tase you."

Yassir swore beneath his breath again. Khaled closed his eyes and put his hands up. *Bismillah al-Rahman al-Rahim. Ya Allah, please wake me from this shitty dream.* But when he opened his eyes again, the crowd had doubled in size.

He spotted Baba's confused face in the parking lot. Then his father was running over.

"Khaled? What's happening?"

"Sir, I need you to take ten steps back!" the officer instructed as she began to test Yassir's blood alcohol level.

"This is my son," Baba said, his voice cracking. Khaled's heart seized.

"Oh?" the woman said as she read Yassir's test. "Zero point zero one. How long has it been since you both consumed alcohol?"

"Alcohol?" Baba echoed, his eyes wide. "Khaled, what is she saying?"

The woman shook her head as she wrote on her notepad. "There was a disturbance at the gas station next door. These two were accused of harassing the workers; they both just failed a Breathalyzer test. Your son's blood alcohol content is zero point oh three eight. Not drunk. But he might have been at one point."

"Drunk?" Baba murmured in disbelief. His eyes bored into Khaled for only a moment before he turned to Yassir and asked, "What have you done?"

5

YASSIR

The minute the officer drove away, the yelling began.

"I asked you to take out the trash, not act like garbage yourself!" Hajji Abu Abdalla spat at Khaled, his eyes still glued to Yassir.

Khaled, who always had a million words in his mouth, stood in silence.

Khaled could argue with any teacher, any rich kid whose parents had power, he even backtalked the cop, but if there was one person Khaled couldn't stand up to, it was his father. He respected him too much.

Just after the officer finished writing the citations, Baba's eyes found Yassir through the crowd. Hajji Majid, Yassir's old boss, pestered the officer with endless questions until she finally got into her car and drove away. They would learn how much their fines would be in court.

Court.

In a few months, Yassir was supposed go to court to get his license back, and now he was facing another underage drinking fine. Worse, Baba's disappointed eyes were getting closer and closer. Running away from his father would be pathetic, right? Having the eyes of every Iraqi uncle watching his nightmare unfold, shedding light on his sins, on his friendship with Khaled, on this latest fuckup, felt pathetic enough. His heart was still racing. Each time the officer had touched her holster, all he could think about was Yasmin. How this morning, when he'd barely given her a glance and a peck on the cheek before school, could've been the last time he ever saw her.

Baba's cologne flooded his senses now. Yassir extended his arm in hopes his father would just grab him by the sleeve and drag him to the cab and take him home and scold him in private. Instead, Baba stopped a few inches away from him.

"Going around with kids who will impregnate the first white girl they meet?" The Hajji's voice had grown quiet as Baba approached, but his words cut through the air. "Is that the future you want, Khaled? This is the future you are asking for!"

When Yassir was a toddler, he used to call Hajji Abu Abdalla *Baba*, because he acted as his second father. The Hajji's eyes would illuminate each time Yassir called him that, and he would ruffle Yassir's hair with pride. He used to keep a photo of Yassir in his wallet. First grade, gap between his teeth, cheeks still chubby.

Now the man stared at him in pure disgust. It was what Yassir had been trying to avoid, even if he deserved it.

"B-Baba." Khaled stuttered his first word since the cop had left. His eyes momentarily caught Yassir's. "I was just taking Yassir home."

Yassir grimaced. Khaled never stayed silent when he should. Not in school. Not in the gas station. Not now.

Khaled saying his name only disgusted the Hajji more as he continued with his *The Al-Azzawis Are Not Your Friends Anymore* speech. It was a speech Yassir had heard multiple times since the age of ten. The kind that caused his parents to squirm in silence—as if their families had not once been intertwined as one. His parents always just stood and took the insults, just as Baba did now. Sometimes Yassir wondered if it was in their blood, to take the insults publicly, while the real battle happened quietly at home.

"You don't let your son near mine," Hajji Abu Abdalla said, turning to Baba, clutching a fistful of Khaled's dishdasha sleeve. He sounded desperate. "How many times do I have to beg your family to leave mine alone?"

Yassir's eyes caught with Khaled's for a moment—glossy, raging with sadness. Khaled looked away. *Please don't say more*, Yassir begged Hajji Abu Abdalla silently. *Don't say Ayah's name. Don't say what I did. Don't. Don't. Don't.*

But after a few silent moments, uncles surrounded Hajji Abu Abdalla, telling him to go back inside and to praise Allah to calm himself down. He eventually nodded, dragging Khaled away.

"Yassir."

A hopeless stare that often filled Baba's meek eyes locked with Yassir's. The disappointment overflowed, sobering in an instant whatever buzz Yassir might have had left in his system. When Yassir had brought Yasmin home for the very first time, Baba had looked at him with the same expression.

What have you done?

Hajji Abu Abdalla had asked him the same thing not so long ago.

Under the amber streetlights, Baba looked twice his age. He stepped closer and closer until he placed a hand on Yassir's shoulder. His breath was slow and jagged enough to pierce Yassir's anxiety.

"Where were you?" Baba's breath tingled on Yassir's cheeks as Baba tried to piece together the past twenty minutes. "I told you to stay."

The stiff collar of Baba's dishdasha scratched Yassir's neck.

He had never been this close to his father.

Baba smelled like spicy Iraqi cologne and the green mouthwash they kept in the bathroom. Their foreheads touched. The smell felt comforting, like home.

Home.

How had it only been three hours since school let out and he missed home?

Home was Yasmin.

Home was regret.

Home was Baba's rough hand connecting to his cheek for the very first time, providing the cleanest, sharpest slap Yassir had ever heard.

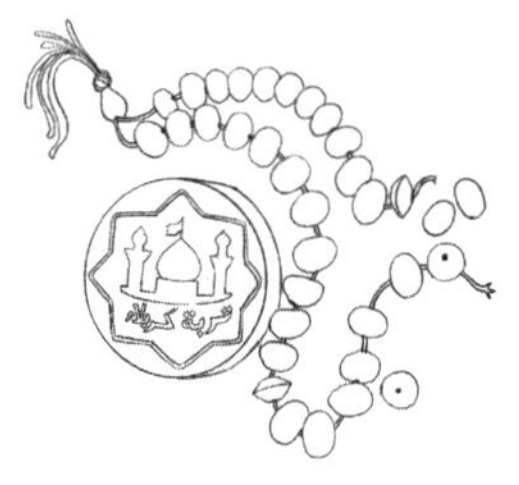

6

KHALED

FORTY-FIVE DAYS BEFORE

On Monday morning, Khaled stayed in sujud until his feet fell asleep. Until he was sure the words from the turbah rock engraved his forehead, and his prayers for forgiveness were automatic on his tongue.

"Khaled."

Every morning, every evening, and every moment in between after the events of Friday night, he had fallen to his knees and asked God to forgive his sins. While the blue and red police lights had sobered him up that night, it was Baba's eyes—glistening with anger, disappointment, and something wild and unknown in between—that would not stop haunting him.

How many times? Baba had asked later that night, after sending Khaled home.

I don't know, Khaled had admitted, foolishly. But the truth was that he'd lost count months ago.

Do you know your prayers might not be valid for forty days? Baba had reminded him. *Yet how many times have you come and prayed by my side as if you were clear of sin?*

While beliefs were split on forgiveness for drinking alcohol—whether it was forty days or immediate mercy from Allah—one thing was clear: Khaled had to stop.

He wanted to return to the way he used to feel before. Before everything in his life had become unrecognizable.

Allah does not burden a soul beyond what it can bear.

Yet there were days when Khaled could not bear it. He'd just never wanted to admit it to anyone besides himself. Now every Iraqi within a fifty-mile radius knew.

"Khaled."

A hand shook his arm, and he forced himself up before Kawther could touch him again. After nearly eight years of silence, his oldest sister stared down at him, hands nervously tucking into the pockets of her black pin-striped pantsuit, a small leather briefcase at her side, the strap thrown over her baby-blue hijab. Sometimes he'd wondered if she had lied about law school, using it as an excuse to run away from their family. For all he knew, she could have been a dropout, living in a van in the desert. But right now, she kind of looked like a lawyer. Now she said she was back for good, attempting to fit her life back into theirs as if they had not learned to live without her.

"Baba asked me to take you to school. He had to take the sheikh back to the airport before heading to the shop, and Mama . . ."

She didn't have to say it.

Mama was more interested in staring at the walls in her bedroom than driving Khaled to school. Since Kawther had returned, Mama rarely left her room anymore. After Friday night, Mama had avoided both of them.

Khaled nodded, silencing the dozens of questions that spawned each time Kawther looked at him. He tightly wound his prayer rug, grabbed his backpack, and followed her outside, sliding into the Honda Accord that shivered each time she started the engine.

After eight years, she still had it.

She'd given up everything—all of them—but not this stupid old car. The car she used to drive him and Ayah to dentist appointments and doctor visits. The car where they'd sip on milkshakes when the summers were harsh and the house was boring. Both jealous of and annoyed by the decaying leather seats, Khaled leaned his head against the window, his brain begging for sleep as she drove.

"I took my ACT here," Kawther said as they neared Chapman High. "Do they still have that fancy little fountain in the quad? I remember Baba was so fascinated when he saw the building. He must have really wanted you to come here."

Baba didn't care where he went to school. It was Khaled who had begged for him and Ayah to come to this insufferable institution. If not for his commitment to the debate team, he would have switched to a public school long ago, but a Chapman diploma carried a lot more weight than any regular high school diploma. Besides, he couldn't just abandon Yassir. If it weren't for Chapman, he might never get to see his best friend again. Although after Friday night, he wasn't sure if Yassir wanted to see him again.

Khaled stared out the window. He had approximately six minutes left of this car ride.

Kawther cleared her throat awkwardly at his silence. He'd only seen her once in the past eight years, and that was over a year ago. After that painful visit, she'd left them in the dust again. He wondered what it would take to scare her off now.

"Oh, before I forget, here's this back," she said, sifting through her briefcase at a stoplight. She retrieved the cell phone that Baba had confiscated from him on Friday. Khaled knew that his father had asked her to snoop for him, since he didn't understand all the English messages and apps on the phone. "Baba said you can have it back since he needs you to take care of the orders at the shop. I didn't pry, I swear. I just told him I saw everything so he would let me give it back. I'd rather you be honest with me than invade your privacy if you're into other trouble."

Khaled swallowed. He wondered if she'd seen his endless texts with Yassir. The voice notes that had gone unanswered. The complaints he'd made about her return. With all that she had done to their families, he decided he wouldn't feel embarrassed or bad if she did pry. She should know how much he hated her.

"Also, about the arraignment." Kawther's voice thickened. "I talked to Baba, and we thought it was best that I represent you instead of a public attorney. I'll pick you up from school on Wednesday and we'll go straight to the courthouse. I'll do the talking, okay?"

He continued to say nothing as she began to give him the rundown. From the uncertainty in her voice, it seemed like he would be her first real client in a courtroom.

Great.

Khaled stared at the car's digital clock. *Four more minutes.*

"I'm sure you feel scared," she said. "But you need to be honest with me, Khaled. Was that your first time drinking? Did Yassir give you the alcohol?"

If she hadn't run away, he wouldn't have had to hide his friendship with his oldest friend from his parents in the first place.

"If he did, you really need to rethink your relationship with him. His family . . ." Kawther stopped.

His family *what*?

Was also torn apart by her leaving. Ali had been so heartbroken, he'd left for Iraq, got married there, and moved on, only returning to America for short visits every few years.

His family also hates you.

At the next red light near the strip of small shops, Khaled could see the red brick towers of Chapman High peeking over the tall oak trees.

Two more minutes.

He unclicked his seat belt.

"Khaled—" she said, attempting to grab his arm, but he already had one foot out of the car and was slamming the door behind him before she could object, as the stoplight turned green. He trudged toward the school, the sky pelting rain as his sister's car squealed away. He watched as flocks of students scuttled over pristine stone steps into the building as a harsh gust of wind chilled his bones.

The minute he crossed the threshold into the warm building, he found Principal Delpy standing in the hallway, gesturing for him to step into her office.

7

YASSIR

A small gray bruise had appeared just below Yassir's cheekbone. It was firm and sore, and Yasmin loved to poke at it, just as she loved to pick at the three thick moles dotted across his neck.

While he attempted to brush his hair before leaving for school, she curled her hand around the frayed hem of his jeans. He gave up, throwing his hood over his head, and picked her up before pushing the soft chestnut ringlets out of her face and kissing her temple. She began to cry as he handed her to Mama, who sat half asleep on the couch. He followed Baba out the door, holding back tears of his own.

In the car, Baba slid on his thick black sunglasses, avoiding eye contact. Yassir didn't want an apology, and it wasn't like his father would offer him one, anyway. As on most rides with his father, they did not speak aside from Baba whispering astaghfirullah over and over until it blended with the verses of Quranic Arabic murmuring from the speakers.

His father could thank or praise God, as he did often at home, between sips of chai as the Arabic satellite news blasted from the television, but it seemed that whenever Yassir was in his vicinity lately, Baba always asked God for forgiveness.

Before Yasmin, before Yassir's first car and his first DUI, Baba had spent the ride to school telling funny stories about customers he'd met on his fares. He would ask Yassir about his classes or say how proud he was of Yassir's good grades in math. He even used to ask Yassir about his dreams, about what he wanted to be. Yassir never had an answer.

Baba wanted him to become a doctor or engineer, but he'd always end the conversation with *It's your choice, habibi. Do what makes you happy*.

Now Yassir didn't know what it felt like to be happy for longer than a few seconds after Yasmin's cute smiles or Khaled's ridiculous jokes. Everything that brought him any sense of joy these days inevitably reminded him of his failures. Yassir didn't know if he could achieve a happiness that would not disappoint Baba in the end.

Yassir closed his eyes, and when he opened them again, the Crown Victoria was pulling toward the same cold curb Yassir would be expected to return to at the end of the school day.

"Mikey!" Alex yelled from the parking lot, hands cupping his mouth. No one called him Mikey except for Alex. It was weird to have a nickname for his fake name. It only confused his father more. His father never asked why he went by Michael, and he commented little about it.

Yassir slammed the passenger door, waiting to hear the cab crunch over the gravel before acknowledging his friend.

"Oh my God, Mikey," Alex gasped as he approached. "Did Khaled finally beat you up?"

Khaled couldn't even beat a boxing bag properly. He'd had to switch gym courses junior year because he sprained his hand on the first day of class. As many times as Yassir and Khaled had verbally fought, they'd never beaten each other up. However, when the police officer had handed them fines like gift certificates last Friday, Yassir had wanted to clock his best friend in the face *at least* once. Maybe several times.

Yassir shook his head at Alex as they walked to first period, avoiding the hallway that connected to Principal Delpy's office. If she saw him, she'd pull him into another unsolicited lecture about his failing grades. As one of the five anonymous scholarship recipients in a school that promised Ivy League hopefuls, he wasn't just tarnishing his own reputation but also Delpy's attempt to make the school more inclusive of kids with lower socioeconomic status. A status that, unfortunately, belonged to Yassir as well.

After Chapman's low rating for its diversity practices in the latest edition of *Private School Quarterly*, Delpy was grasping at straws. It didn't help that Khaled had put the school on edge with his fight with their American government teacher last week. But Khaled always kept the school on edge, even when he put his feet up in class and quietly observed.

And Yassir was working on the failing grades. As much as a kid with fifty-eight missing assignments and a baby keeping him up at all hours could. But by the time he got up every morning, he had accumulated about twenty minutes of rest total, which, unfortunately, made the smooth, shiny desks of Chapman High incredibly enticing for napping.

Yassir slid next to the seat Khaled would be sitting in if he could learn to shut his mouth for once. Although Yassir was failing American government, too, there was something specifically about Wells's monotonous voice that made him unable to resist his exhaustion. It was also easier to fall asleep without Khaled arguing with Wells or Miles every few minutes. Maybe they would get through an entire lesson today. A solid fifty-five-minute nap.

"We're circling back to global extremism," Wells said as he queued up a slide deck with those exact words bolded in black above a map of the Middle East and Africa. Alex's hand shot up.

"Mr. McClusky, the bell literally rang less than five minutes ago." Wells raised his eyebrows, annoyed. "There will be no hall pass privileges without a valid excuse."

Tommy Smith, the class pothead who occasionally supplied Yassir with joints for free (Tommy had a charitable heart), was to blame for that one. He left class so often that teachers had lobbied to be given the choice when to restrict hall pass privileges. Sometimes at Chapman High, students were treated as future leaders. Other times, like they were still in the first grade.

Alex stuttered, "Um, no . . . I just thought, well . . . I just thought we weren't going to talk about terrorism in class anymore?" His eyes darted back to Yassir. "Because of like . . . that incident last week."

If Khaled getting kicked out of a class was considered an incident, well, Chapman High had gone approximately five days without an incident. For Khaled, that was a new record. But this time, Yassir wondered if both of them had gone too far. Khaled had angered nearly every teacher in this pompous private school, but Yassir had never seen a teacher have a full meltdown the way Wells had, face red and spit flying out of his mouth as he slammed his hands on his desk. If it hadn't been for the large desk acting as a barrier between them, Yassir wondered if Wells would've assaulted Khaled with his fists instead of his words.

Now Mr. Wells clicked his tongue at Alex. "The student who was triggered by last week's assignment has been excused from today's class. It's a sensitive topic for them."

"We all know it's Khaled, Mr. Wells," Brooks Stewart said, and Miles laughed.

Everyone knew what had happened because Khaled had told Alex and Alex had told everyone he knew. Despite choosing Yassir and Khaled as his best friends, Alex was pretty well-liked.

Mr. Wells rolled his eyes, neither confirming nor denying the obvious truth, as he played a documentary about the rise of Al-Qaeda, narrated by a retired CIA agent with six Purple Hearts or something. Yassir felt the class's eyes creep over him.

Freshman year, after he and Khaled had reconnected at Chapman, Khaled had told everyone that they were cousins. Now anytime someone bad-mouthed Khaled, they also shot inquisitive stares at Yassir. Like he was Khaled's public relations representative. Or worse, Islam's public relations representative.

Wells scanned the classroom. "Take notes, everyone. There will be a quiz at the end of class. Michael, wake up. Hoodie off."

Yassir sat up and sighed. He clicked his pen and listened to the documentary.

". . . the Quran is often a tool used to incite violence . . ."

The video showed a group of men praying before the image transitioned to faceless men in dishdashas and agals shooting at a building.

Yassir's chest burned. He was sick of videos like this always playing at school. He thought about the man at the gas station calling them ISIS wannabes. Khaled's outburst. The cop touching him.

Alex poked Yassir with the end of his pencil, pulling him back into the moment. "Did you know Khaled was excused from class? What if they're getting him kicked out? Man, I knew he shouldn't have written that letter to the superintendent last week."

Yassir felt the bruise on his cheek sting; there were a lot of things Khaled should regret now. He couldn't decide if it was more foolish for his American government teacher to assign a presentation about a terrorist organization of the student's choice, or for Khaled to choose the US military as his subject.

Khaled had only gotten as far as relaying the details of the Blackwater massacre before Wells walked to the front of the classroom and yanked the flash drive out of the computer.

"Clearly you didn't follow instructions. Take a seat."

"But I didn't even get to the part about soldiers raping girls younger than your daughter, Mr. Wells," Khaled had said, putting on a pout. It was clearly the wrong choice of words, because Mr. Wells's face became stone. "I have like three more massacres I wanted to talk about. You think that poor little boy's brain sliding out of his head thanks to Blackwater contractors is the worst it gets?"

"Sit. Down," Wells repeated.

Khaled smirked all the way back to his desk. The next presentation, which was about the Charlie Hebdo massacre, appeared on the screen. Khaled blew out an audible breath and tried to exchange a look with Yassir, but Yassir put his head down on his desk.

When the class dispersed, stares and whispers aimed at Khaled continued as they shuffled out. Then Wells's meltdown began.

"You think it's funny to offend half the class?"

"Who?" Khaled had laughed, his tone dripping with sarcasm. "Name me someone who isn't terminally racist, and I'll believe they were actually offended."

As Wells had continued raging, he'd noticed Yassir still lingering at the door. Before Khaled could turn and see him, Yassir had walked away.

Now, light suddenly spilled from the corner of the classroom, interrupting Yassir's dozing. An office aide poked their head into the room as the documentary played. Sophomore year, Ayah was an office aide during first period. Sometimes she'd interrupt Yassir and Khaled's calculus class, and she'd smile at Yassir when Khaled wasn't looking before handing her note to the teacher, her gaze soft, her lips pink, the golden honey in her eyes filled with a secret just between her and Yassir.

"Now?" Wells sighed loudly at the aide, reading the piece of paper before his eyes caught Yassir's.

Yassir braced himself.

Delpy better *not* be summoning him. Whether it was for his failing grades or Khaled pulling him deeper into shit, he didn't want anything to do with it.

But Wells looked away and paused the documentary for a moment. "Okay, class, I have to step out—Vice Principal Beckett will step in soon. Turn the quiz in to him."

What if Khaled's complaint to get Wells fired for Islamophobia had actually worked?

Alex's hand shot up instantly and Mr. Wells looked like he was going to have an aneurysm.

"No questions—"

"I really need to pee," Alex whined, shaking his legs for drama. "I drank like an entire iced macchiato before class and it's hitting me now."

Giggles swept through the classroom. This was extremely typical of Alex.

Mr. Wells sighed, giving in. "C'mon, I'll make sure you actually head in the right direction."

Alex nodded vigorously and stood up, smirking at Yassir. He clearly wanted to snoop on his way to the bathroom.

The minute they both stepped out, soft chatter filled the room as the documentary continued to play.

"Look, it's Khaled's dad," Miles muttered, and Brooks laughed. The screen filled with an older dark-skinned man in the center, eyes fixed on the camera, loading an AK-47. He looked nothing like Hajji Abu Abdalla. He didn't even share the same language or ethnicity. But it didn't matter.

The kids at Chapman, the gas station clerk, and everyone else who was intimidated by the presence of anyone who even appeared to be Muslim didn't care to think of them as anything but dangerous.

Despite their parents not having spoken in eight years, Khaled would never let anyone say this about Yassir's father. But as in all situations that made him nervous, Yassir found that silence lived more comfortably in his mouth.

He said nothing. Just like the day he'd brought Yasmin home, dodging questions from his mother and older sister about the wailing one-month-old in his arms and the old white couple who'd come to waive their rights over her. Just like the day Hajji Abu Abdalla had confronted him, or the day Ayah had left for good.

Uneasiness prickled between his ribs.

Despite being the son of a revolutionary who fought against Saddam Hussein's brutal dictatorship, Yassir Al-Azzawi rarely pushed back. Sometimes it was easy to forget that Baba had once stood up against injustice. The only injustice Baba had ever stood up to since then was Yassir's bare cheek in the moonlight.

Words began to form on Yassir's tongue, but before he could find the strength to speak them, Vice Principal Beckett was there, silencing the giggles that echoed throughout the classroom.

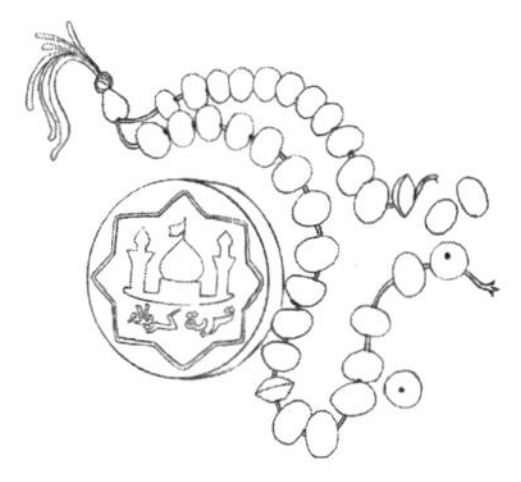

8

KHALED

"Sorry for being late, I had to escort Mr. McClusky to the bathroom," Mr. Wells said as he crossed over to shake hands with his bosses before he took a seat on the blue chair adjacent to Khaled's. "He's a wanderer."

Khaled tried not to turn his head to the glass wall facing the hallway. Alex's snoopy ass must be lurking around, waiting to share gossip about Khaled's mission to get Wells fired.

"Khaled," Mr. Wells greeted him, his ears redder than the paint splotches of fake blood Baba had made Khaled dribble on the masjid Muharram drapes. Khaled ignored the man whose last words to him last week had been *I'd rather eat dog shit than teach you* and *If you come back in here, you're getting an automatic failing grade.*

"Are we sure we don't want parents here?" Mr. Marks, the stuffy superintendent, said, glancing at his watch. Principal Delpy and Khaled both shook their heads immediately.

"We didn't have time to schedule the Arabic interpreter," Principal Delpy said, arms folded in the corner of the room. "Last time we had a bit of trouble understanding everything Mr. Al-Hakim said."

Two years ago, when Khaled complained about Ayah's hijab nearly getting pulled off in gym class, Baba came into the office in a fury, startling the principal as he relayed to her in extreme detail the poor conditions and torture he had endured in the Rafha refugee prison camp. How their family had nearly starved to death, that the Saudi soldiers used electric wires to damage his spine after he protested over the inadequate food rations for his pregnant wife. And that he hadn't lost his firstborn—Abdalla—whose name he still wore like a badge of honor, only for his kids to suffer at a private school that cost more than the down payment of their house. Delpy, who was made visibly uncomfortable by it all, simply tightened a smile, promising she'd take their complaints and safety seriously.

"I didn't mean to pull you out of first period, Ryan, but I felt that it was urgent that we get this taken care of now, as this letter has reached the board of trustees, too," Mr. Marks said with great annoyance. "I wanted to get some procedures straight, Mr. Al-Hakim. First, I can't just fire a teacher because someone asks for it. A thorough investigation must be conducted, and mediation is always the first approach. While Mr. Wells will express his own feelings, I think it's important to note that your teacher was purely reacting to an extremely insensitive presentation that distressed your fellow students. I take student safety very seriously. So"—his dark brown eyes met Khaled's—"welcome to mediation."

Mediation?

His teacher insulted him and threatened to fail him, and they were going to mediate?

"Mr. Al-Hakim, let's start with you." Mr. Marks shuffled the paperwork in his hands, where Khaled's rage letter sat at the top of the stack. "I've reviewed the rubric and I have to say, I'm inclined to believe Mr. Wells was within his rights to threaten to fail you for the assignment. It seems that you misinterpreted instructions."

"What exactly did I misinterpret?" Khaled asked, trying to use his level debate voice. Calm but pointed. "He asked me to present about terrorism based on the definition he taught us, so I did."

"Calling your classmates' family members who served in the army, some who were killed by terrorists themselves, terrorists, is extremely offensive, Khaled," Mr. Wells piped up. "I told you to present about an *officially recognized* terrorist organization, and the United States Army, despite your interpretation, doesn't count."

Mr. Marks and Delpy stared at Khaled to confirm that this was what he had actually done.

"No." Khaled shook his head. "It wasn't just the army; it was the entire US military."

Silence.

"Is this funny to you, Mr. Al-Hakim?" Mr. Marks asked.

Yassir always complained that Khaled's pompousness was visible in his eyes. "No."

"Mr. Wells?" Mr. Marks said. "What do you think?"

Khaled's government teacher blew out a breath. "I think we've had so many complaints over the semester, I've lost count, but on the day you made that presentation, I had at least nine parents call that evening, asking why I'm teaching their kids to hate this country. I think Khaled is a bright student, I do, but he doesn't care for education, only provocation of his classmates. I have never felt this stressed teaching a class in my ten years at Chapman High . . . Which is why I agree with Khaled's letter—I'd rather not return to the classroom if it means he will be there."

Dr. Delpy's jaw dropped. "Ryan—"

Khaled's head whipped around in shock.

Mr. Wells shook his head. "He's made classmates cry, he's angered parents, and these are things that happened before he even entered my classroom. Khaled, you clearly were accepted into this prestigious institution for a reason, but I am asking that we stay separated. Otherwise, I will hand in my badge and keys today. I'm sorry that it's come to this, but I am not in the business of allowing students to hijack my classroom."

Hijack.

Khaled's eyes turned to his teacher. The man who'd screamed at him just days ago now frowned as if he were the victim. He was painting Khaled as more than an occasional class disrupter—as a legitimate offender, a danger to his classmates. Between the gas station employees and Mr. Wells, Khaled wondered if there was anywhere he'd be allowed to tell the truth.

Marks raised a bushy gray eyebrow at Delpy. "How many complaints has Mr. Al-Hakim had?"

"Six," Delpy said, arms folded. "Just this year."

Khaled bit his lip. He was only aware of three, and two were from Miles, who he disregarded since Miles had choked him on the playground in second grade, blaming Khaled for his brother dying in Iraq. Miles hadn't really stopped taking it out on him since then.

"How many last year?" Marks asked.

"Four," Delpy answered. "Two in sophomore year. Zero in freshman."

Khaled swallowed. She had this memorized. Each year his tolerance for the offensive comments he received at school and for the way the school handled his complaints was further depleted. There were plenty of instances of discrimination he hadn't reported. But after Ayah had dropped out last year, he no longer cared to spare anyone's feelings. It wasn't like anyone had spared hers.

"A steady increase?" Marks noted. "It is very concerning to hear that you have so many complaints regarding your behavior."

"But this meeting isn't about those other complaints," Khaled insisted, frustration rising in his throat. "This is about my teacher screaming at me and cursing me out over a class assignment. Why am I the only person in trouble here?"

"This isn't about getting *you* in trouble." Marks frowned. "Your history of class disruption must be taken into account. Clearly, we can't put you both in the same classroom while we make our final decision regarding disciplinary action for both you *and* Mr. Wells. This decision will be made internally. Mr. Wells, your students rely heavily on you, especially as state exams are approaching. Mr. Al-Hakim—" Marks's eyes narrowed at Khaled. "It's too late in the year to switch your schedule. You will replace your first period in the classroom with independent study in the library with Mrs. Marsh."

So Khaled was the one being kicked out of class? Great.

Perhaps this was a trial from Allah. For all his stupid indiscretions.

Khaled straightened, hoping a tremor of anxiety was not visible on his folded hands. "And . . . how long will this decision take?"

Delpy spoke up, addressing both of them now. "I'll have to look into the other open complaints against you and speak to the students in Mr. Wells's class before making my decision. A thorough investigation will take up to a week or two. I'll review hallway footage, see if there were any eyewitnesses who can confirm either of your statements. Once the investigation concludes, you will each have one week to appeal the decision if you don't agree. Processing your appeal will take longer."

"In the meantime, Mr. Al-Hakim, you'll be on academic probation," Mr. Marks added, "meaning you won't be able to attend any extracurricular activities until the investigation is complete and you've accepted whatever penalty Principal Delpy deems appropriate."

Khaled couldn't keep his voice from cracking. "Even . . . debate?"

Delpy sighed. "Even debate."

In three weeks, he was supposed to be winning the debate championship for Chapman High and securing a full-ride scholarship to the political science program of his choice. If this investigation ran long, or if he appealed the decision, his probation period would prevent that, and everything he had worked toward for the past four years would be meaningless.

Don't you get tired of fighting it all? Ayah had whispered to him a few weeks before she dropped out.

Delpy's pink nails pushed against her blazer. "Again, we would hate to see this issue preventing Mr. Wells from doing his job, or Khaled from earning his education here at Chapman. I expect both of you to be on your best behavior these next few weeks and to remember the core values of our school. If either of you has any additional information for me to consider or if you change your mind about your desired outcomes for this situation, please let me know."

It's useless to try. Yassir knows it. I know it. When will you finally get it? What are you even fighting for?

Even though his sister no longer attended Chapman, he was fighting for her. Fighting against all the bullshit that had caused her to leave this school, and to leave him, too.

Mr. Wells's eyes briefly met Khaled's, and it was clear that he would not change his mind. He said his goodbyes and left.

"Go ahead and finish first period in the library," Delpy told Khaled. "I'll let Mrs. Marsh know to expect you for a full day on Wednesday during the next period rotation."

Except on Wednesday I'm being arraigned, he thought.

He nodded, shook his superintendent's hand, despite the urge to spit in the man's face, and trudged toward the library. He whispered the prayers in his head from this morning. Surat al-Fatiha. Falaq. Ikhlas. Despite his best efforts to remember God for comfort, as soon as he was welcomed by the smell of dust and peeling paint in the library, all he could think about was how badly he wanted a drink.

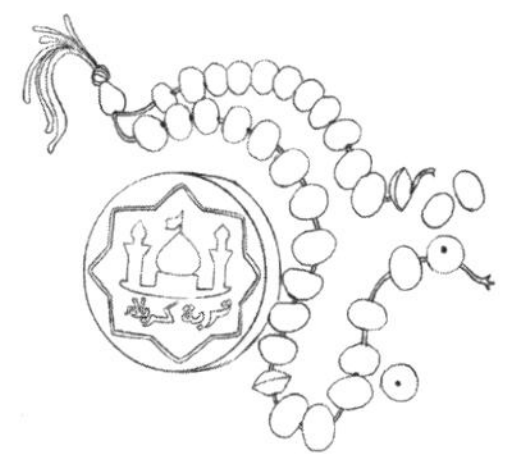

9

KHALED

At the end of the school day, Khaled found himself crossing toward Alex's bright blue Jeep, tucked at the edge of the student parking lot. Khaled reached the car door and found Alex telling a story while Yassir sat slumped, his head resting on the passenger-side window. Khaled tapped the glass.

"Khaled!" Alex shouted excitedly, pulling the window down and startling Yassir awake. Yassir's mouth fell into a line at the sight of Khaled. Yassir hadn't seen or spoken to Khaled since Khaled had silently watched Yassir hold his stinging cheek as he was shoved into his father's cab. Khaled had sent him a text after his interrogation in Delpy's office, but it had gone unanswered.

"Are you both just sitting . . . around?" Khaled wondered.

"By sitting around do you mean Mikey being my therapist?" Alex asked. "Because yes. He's a good listener, despite the fact that he keeps falling asleep. Want in?"

"I need a ride home," Khaled said. "So I guess."

The door was unlocked and Khaled slid across warm leather into the back seat, staring at the dark brown curls that shone gold under the dim sunlight.

"Why are you here? Don't you have a daughter to take care of?" Khaled asked.

To his surprise, Yassir responded. "My dad got a dispatch a few hours away. My mom doesn't like driving when she has Yasmin because Yasmin always has a crying fit, and I'd rather eat my own hand than listen to Delpy remind me of my failing grades again and why I've disappointed her. So Alex's cheese puff car it is."

"I told you I'd air things out if the smell bothered you." Alex sighed. The only thing Alex was addicted to more than iced macchiatos was twenty-ounce containers of cheese puffs.

"There's a thing called the public bus," Khaled said. "Runs until five for this route."

"You know my dad doesn't like me wandering off." Yassir raised his middle finger, pointing with precision though his eyes were closed. "Also, don't talk to me."

"I'm not talking to you. I'm talking *at* you." Khaled groaned, seeing the Coors Light bottle tucked under the passenger seat. "You drinking?"

Silence.

"No." Alex eventually spoke for Yassir. "He said he wants to reform."

"Subhanallah," Khaled joked, but he also meant it. If Yassir had quit drinking, then he knew shit was serious. Yassir did not believe in God much, but maybe he believed in being sensible. Something Khaled needed to believe in again, too. Silence dragged on as Alex fiddled with the Jeep's heater.

"Did *you* come to drink?" Alex asked after a moment. "Is that why you came over?"

Yes.

No.

"Of course not," Khaled said, reformed, too, pushing down the uncertainty lingering with his words. "I came for the ride. Besides, on Wednesday—" The thought of the arraignment pinned him down in that moment, though he didn't want to think about it. The car felt stuffy. He unbuttoned the top of his shirt. "Crack open a window, will ya? I'm getting stress palpitations."

"It's just toxic cheese puff inhalation," Yassir muttered, and Khaled bit down a smile.

"What's the verdict, anyway? You obviously didn't get Wells fired today." Alex rolled the window down, letting drops of rain sprinkle over his dirty-blond hair.

"I—well, I . . ."

"Spit it out," Yassir muttered. "You got fucked over, didn't you? I told you not to send the letter last week."

Yassir avoided conflict at all costs. Which was perhaps why he was avoiding Khaled now, too. Khaled shrugged. "Well, I can't let Mrs. Marsh spend first period alone."

"The librarian?" Alex asked as he turned around to face Yassir, mouth agape. "Duuuuude. *You* got excommunicated?! Permanently?"

"Not yet—there's an investigation happening. Delpy said she'd look into hallway camera footage and question whoever left the class last and might have seen the Wells meltdown. If this shit isn't figured out soon, I won't even be able to compete in the debate championship, since now I'm on academic probation." Anger rose again in his body. "Damn this school."

"Even the championship?" Alex inquired, tugging on Yassir's gray hoodie sleeve. "You sure you didn't see anything, Mikey? You're always last to leave, since you're always half asleep."

"I didn't," Yassir said.

Silence filled the car as Yassir shifted in his seat; shades of brown and purple painted the left side of his light brown cheek. Guilt festered in Khaled's gut, and he again eyed the beer bottle peeking from under the passenger seat.

I'm sorry, Khaled wanted to say out loud, in the silence of the Cheese Puff Jeep, but his words came out aggressive instead. Protective. "Ya Sayed, seriously? Cover that bruise on your face with a Band-Aid or something. People will think you're abused or getting into fights."

"This"—Yassir half turned, pointing at his cheek, suddenly seething—"is all your fault and you know it. I don't care about covering up your mistake. I asked for a ride home, not to get arrested with every Iraqi I know watching."

"Arrested?" Alex yelped. "Why am I just hearing this now? It's the end of the damn school day!"

"Technically we weren't arrested," Khaled corrected.

"Fuck you and your technicalities, Khaled," Yassir said.

"I didn't ask your dad to slap you," Khaled said.

Alex tapped a hand on Yassir's arm. "Your dad did this, Mikey? Is it . . . because of the baby?"

Yassir shrugged away at his touch. "It's nothing."

Alex frowned, shaking his head. "Wait, who got arrested? Why do you two always keep me out of the loop! I thought we were three musketeers? Amigos? The perfect triang—"

"Don't talk to me," Yassir said to Khaled, ignoring Alex. "I want nothing to do with you, not until I know I'm not going to prison or something."

"Prison?" Alex echoed.

"You won't go to prison!" Khaled exclaimed. "I swear. I've been praying all weekend that nothing will happen to us."

"Praying?" Yassir scoffed. "Why don't you do something that would actually make a difference, Khaled?"

Khaled frowned. "Like what?"

"Go apologize to the gas station clerk! Maybe they'll remove the disturbance charge."

Khaled stared at his friend incredulously. "Why would I apologize to those assholes?"

"Because for once in your life you need to learn to shut the fuck up!" Yassir fully faced him now. "Go and get Wells fired. Will it make you feel better? Will it make your intoxication charge go away? Or mine? No. Just go and do what you want, Khaled, you've never asked anyone's permission anyway."

Why did you tell Baba about what happened at school? Ayah's voice had seethed in his ear as they watched Baba storm from the house. *Don't you know each time you make a fuss it makes our lives worse? Everyone at school is making fun of him now, too.*

Khaled stared at his best friend. Was this making his life worse, too? "What does Wells even have to do with you?" he asked.

"What do you think? Everyone knows you're cousins," Alex said.

"We're not real cousins," Khaled and Yassir both said. Although Khaled had never minded if they were mixed up as real family—like they should have been before Kawther ruined everything—it bothered Yassir no end.

"I get secondhand bullying for being your best friend," Alex said. "And Michael is stared at like a monster. Kind of like how everyone looked at you during your presentation."

"Is that true?" Khaled asked, turning to Yassir. It wasn't that he was oblivious, but it wasn't like Yassir could just easily escape stereotypes because he called himself Michael, either. No matter how many times he and Ayah used to tell him this, Yassir wouldn't let go of the fake name.

Alex nudged Yassir, eyes on the rearview. "Time to break up your fight. Yellow cab is approaching."

"Shit," Yassir swore under his breath, throwing his gray hood over his unruly hair and shoving himself out of the Jeep. "Bye, Alex."

"See ya, Mikey! Thanks for the thera—"

The door slammed.

"—py." Alex's words faded to a soft whisper. "You know, he's a shitty listener, but I can never get mad at Michael? Sometimes when I look at him, I just want to burst into tears. Maybe because we knew him before . . ."

Before he became a dad.

Before, when Yassir would do all the driving, all the laughing. Ayah was so fond of him, too, always saving room for him at the lunch table, even though he didn't join half the time.

Khaled watched his friend run to the end of the parking lot under the sinking sun, the yellow cab glowing under the shades of approaching maghrib.

So much about Yassir had changed.

But not their friendship.

"Don't yell at him so much, either—I was going to fight you if you had really punched him. Don't you ever think it's our fault he's in such a bad place? We're the reason he got his first DUI and now you're going back to court? Of course he's terrified. He's going to get it so much worse than you." Alex sighed.

"He is?" Khaled asked. Last summer, Khaled and Alex had stupidly left bottles in Yassir's rusty Camry and he'd gotten pulled over after missing a stop sign. He barely even drank that day. But he was the one who got in trouble.

Khaled stared at the ceiling of the Jeep.

The guilt now seeped deep into his bones.

Alex was right.

"What do you think I could do?" Khaled asked, his voice thickening. "To help him, I mean. He obviously won't let me talk to him."

"Well, be nicer—he's a sensitive kid. And, I don't know, plead guilty? Make sure he doesn't get charged with anything. It will be your first time—so they'll go easy on you. Give you community service or something."

Khaled raised an eyebrow. "How do you know so much about the law?"

"My parents are divorce attorneys, duh. They used to make me go to Future Lawyers of America summer camp."

"That's a thing?" Khaled asked.

"Unfortunately, it's very much a thing. Imagine seventh graders in pantsuits and smacking each other with gavels. It was chaos!"

It was definitely something Kawther would've begged their parents to let her attend if she had known it existed. Of course, Khaled could verify this advice with her, too, if he was actually talking to her.

While Khaled would not apologize to the gas station clerks, taking the fall for last Friday's events was the least he could do. Just like his prayers, he would keep atoning for what he'd caused. He owed Yassir at least that.

Alex put the car into reverse. "Still need that ride home?"

"Yeah," Khaled said reluctantly, watching the yellow cab disappear into the distance. "Take me home."

10

YASSIR

FORTY-FOUR DAYS BEFORE

"Yassir." Mama's tired voice broke as she placed a freshly bathed Yasmin in his arms. "She has a fever again."

The minute Yasmin had seen him after school today, she'd opened her mouth wide and bit his face, rubbing her aching gums against his cheek. She looked as plump as the day she came into his life, but her eyes were much bigger, wider, and lighter brown, her curls damp against her face. Mama was right, her skin was too warm.

Yassir's chest panged with guilt. He took the syringe filled with pink liquid medicine from his mother's hand and attempted to put it in his daughter's mouth.

"Just like this, Yasmin," he said, his voice soft as he opened his mouth wide. He waited until she opened up her mouth wider, laughing; then he pressed the plunger. But instead of the pink syrup filling her mouth, it dripped all over her face and onto his lap. Yasmin stared at him in confusion before letting out a guttural scream—the kind that made his bones shake.

"Not like that," Mama sighed, her graying hair loosening from her ponytail.

She grabbed Yasmin from him, settling the baby over her black night dishdasha. Yassir stared at his mother, who easily got the medicine into Yasmin's mouth.

"Just go to sleep, habibi," she told him, her eyes filled with empathy. "I got it."

He hesitated, seeing the exhaustion in the grimace on Mama's lips. He knew she was sick of correcting him.

That's not how you change a diaper, she's leaking everywhere.

That's not how you feed her, she'll choke.

That's not how you put her to sleep, she'll suffocate.

Just as he was about to reach for his daughter, hoping for a second chance to prove himself, cold air pushed through the living room, along with Baba. He stepped inside, slipping off his brown loafers near the front door, a lime-green sibhah in his hand.

"What's wrong with her?" Baba asked in Arabic, hovering over the decaying leather sofa, automatically pushing a light hand over Yasmin's hair, just like Yassir had.

Nothing is wrong. Everything is wrong.

Mama shook her head, thin gray curls sticking to her forehead. "She's just fevering."

"Again?" Baba asked. Concern dripped in his tired voice, and Yassir's rib cage burned.

I'm sorry she's here. I'm sorry I ruined my life. I'm sorry it's ruining yours.

"I'll make an appointment," Yassir said automatically. "I'll make an appointment to make sure she's okay. Here, let me try to—"

Mama clicked her tongue, patting Yasmin as Baba sighed.

"Just go to sleep," Baba muttered. "Fatima will be here around seven tomorrow morning."

Yassir couldn't tell if scolds in Arabic from his parents or in English from his sister were worse. Fatima only came around to lecture him lately, escorted him to appointments Baba didn't know how to handle; and like at many moments in his life, he was both grateful for and regretful about it.

Yasmin whined into his mother's shoulder, and Yassir dropped his arms to his sides. She didn't want him. She never wanted him in the evening, so used to Mama comforting her to sleep. Before Baba could remind him, Yassir twisted away, trudging to his bedroom, trying to push the tears behind his eyes.

The door jammed and he sighed, kicking away Yasmin's ocean-themed walker—a hand-me-down from Fatima's younger son, Yousef. Stacks of homework taunted him at the corner of his desk, and the floor was covered with Yasmin's toys. He grabbed a teething toy in the shape of an octopus that sat over his pillow and stared at the ceiling. He could hear Baba pass through his and Mama's bedroom, and then moments later, he could hear the Quran blasting from the living room.

So much for sleep.

At least Yasmin had grown used to the noise, probably the same way Yassir had when he was young—the sacred words stamped over his brain, even if he didn't quite understand their meaning. But the noise was different now. Yassir grew up with Khaled and Ayah bickering in the corner of the living room, both of their older sisters giggling on the sofa, Ali shushing them all as soon as salat commenced.

The sounds of home.

At least, what it used to be.

Yassir blinked. At some point, the Quran recording faded away. The hallway light flicked off. Doors clicked shut. And a deep quiet took over the house. Yassir asked his eyes to close, asked his brain to turn off, but when the tears wouldn't stop pounding behind his eyes, he sat up and grabbed his sneakers from the corner. He crept through the house and stepped through the garage, away from Mama and Baba's bedroom, from Yasmin, and walked into the darkness.

Not even half a mile into the night, his phone buzzed.

He closed his eyes, hoping that when he looked down, his lock screen would be an image of the starry night sky, a thin crescent moon glowing deep in the center. Ayah had drawn the picture for him. Another secret between them.

If I call you tonight, will you answer?

He would get up in the middle of the night just to speak to her. Knowing very well that when the sun rose and Khaled sat between them in the lunchroom, they would pretend that they hadn't spoken for hours the night before.

It didn't really matter what she talked about, Yassir just liked to listen to everything about her. They talked about everything and nothing. Reminiscing about their favorite memories as kids, about her fear of failure, or her relationship with her mother. Kawther had practically raised Ayah and Khaled herself until she left for law school, and Ayah had become resentful of both her maternal figures. But lately she had gone shopping with her mother, learned how to make traditional Iraqi meals, and their bond seemed to be mending. She spoke about wanting to become a graphic designer, even though her parents did not find that to be a decent career. Like his own parents, they approved of three professions: medicine, engineering, and law. Stubborn, she continued to pursue it.

It's not like I've given up on all my dreams, Yassir. I have just given up on you.

His phone kept buzzing, and when he opened his eyes, Yasmin's smiling face with marag dripping on her chin stared back him. Disappointment filled his chest, and he hated himself for it. Notifications popped into his phone like fireworks. All from *Sheikh Khaled*.

There were many things Yassir regretted in his seventeen years, but sharing his location with Khaled Al-Hakim made it to the top five.

Yassir ignored the message and found Ayah in his contacts. All the way at the bottom, where he'd hidden her.

Night Sky.

He wanted to call her, just to hear her voice.

Even though she'd blocked him before she left to marry a stranger from Ohio.

He wished, at least, he had saved her old voice notes. That he could go back and hear her laugh again, whispering *I miss you*, though she'd seen him nearly every day. He'd never admitted that he missed her, too.

Only now it was too late.

He lifted the phone to his ear and gave in to Khaled's messages instead.

My Yassir dumbass senses were tingling. Khaled's voice was thick with sleep. Unless by some chance he was drunk. Yassir hoped not. *One day I'm going to tell Yasmin that her dad was a reckless creep strolling around the neighborhood—in fact, is she around? Have her call me. I'm sure she's just dying to vent to someone about you. I've become an expert in pissed-off baby babble.*

Yassir rolled his eyes and played the next voice note.

I'm going to keep leaving voice notes until the stupid blue dot on my map—that's you, by the way—is back to its home address. I still don't understand why you're on this wandering bullshit. Remember when I used to disappear as a kid? You know how my dad got me to stop? He told me how a jinn took over my great-uncle's right leg. Khaled knew jinn stories were off-limits. Asshole. While Yassir's belief in Islam—or any religion—had slowly slipped over the years, he couldn't help but still believe in jinn. *He went to the market in the middle of the night one day, then he began to kick the shit out of everyone, men, children, women, saying the devil was inside him. He ended up kicking some military officer, you know, one of Saddam's guys. Next morning, my grandmother asks for an imam to come over and secretly exorcise him, but it was too late. That evening, Saddam's men headed to the house, put a bag over my great-uncle's head, and shoved him into a car. My family never saw him again. And if you think that's bad, let me tell you about my dad's neighbor . . .*

Yassir turned the corner, the air crisp but not yet cold against his face, pausing the voice note about jinn before the fear could make his skin crawl, and found himself at the intersection near his old middle school. *Ass-here*, the kids would snicker, kicking him out of his chair. *No, my ass is here! Not yours.*

It was the first time Yassir was the only Muslim kid in school. The only kid from Iraq. The only kid who didn't know another kid, with the Al-Hakims on the other side of town, the richer side, without him.

Then, on the first day of eighth grade, his substitute science teacher had accidentally mistaken him for a kid named Michael, a dark-brown-haired boy who moved to the lower level of biology.

"Oh, sorry, that's not your name. How do I pronounce . . .Yasseer?" she had asked, her eyes widened with confusion.

"Oh, I actually go by that now," Yassir had said, nodding. "You can just call me Michael."

After a few weeks, *Ass-here* was retired from the school's vocabulary, and he never went back.

Yassir's phone buzzed, this time with a call from Khaled.

He stared at the caller ID photo of Khaled giving him the middle finger. He sighed, rejecting the call as he trudged up the block. After a few minutes of silence, he received another voice note.

If Yassir didn't turn back now, neither of them would sleep, and if he turned off his location, Khaled would probably call the police. Or worse, he'd show up himself. But Yassir didn't want to acknowledge Khaled, either. Friday night had been a wake-up call for their friendship. It should've ended when Yassir drove Ayah away, pushing their families farther apart than ever, but he was too ashamed to tell Khaled the truth.

After a few more steps, he pressed play on the next message. *Abu Yasmin . . . I saw you turn the corner. I know if you turn the next, you'll be able to take that shortcut back to your neighborhood . . . Abu Yasmin,*

Khaled's voice crooned softer and softer. *Go home, ya ihmar. Everything will be okay, I promise. Tomorrow I'm going to fix everything. Just show up on time, dress decent. It's all you have to do . . .* His voice sputtered into silence.

Fix everything? Was Khaled finally going to listen to Yassir and apologize to the gas station employees?

Yassir immediately called Khaled, but after several rings, it went to voicemail. He must finally have exhausted himself.

Idiot.

Yassir sighed, turning the next corner toward home, spotting the yellowed chimney on his parents' roof peeking out beneath the moonlight.

He let the coo of crickets fill his ears, the cold breeze dip deep into his lungs. He stared at the night sky again, watching the shimmering light of the stars and the clouds still visible in the glow of the streetlamp.

Then he dialed, this time for Ayah, hoping she'd miraculously answer.

SKY

Near the hospital, I spot a wide walnut-colored building painted in pale moonlight. It has aged over time. It stands tall, but parts of the windows have visibly decayed, rust eating the edges of its structures. Just like the hospital, it's the kind of building where humans change once they've entered it.

The last time I saw the whimper's family all together was in this exact spot. Two young women walked opposite each other, their eyes pasted to the wide concrete steps that stood before them, as a young man trailed close behind. Sadness sank deep into the lines of their cheeks. Tears streamed down only one face, yet anger was clear across each of their mouths.

It shocked me, to see them this way. I remember when they first arrived in this land, and when they lived in the land before it. I had seen the history of their pain, their loss, and the lives they had created with each other until this moment.

I wonder, would they still have entered that building if they had known that the last twenty years during which their lives had been intertwined would come to an end? Did they know that when they stepped into that building, it would be the last time their families would be considered one?

If I could have warned them that day to stop, I would have. But I cannot interfere in the lives of humans as much as they interfere in mine. Had I known what was to come, I would have shifted the clouds, changed the winds, ignited a storm. But as I said, I cannot see the future. I can only observe and remember. Yet I cannot help but wonder, if they had not entered, if the whimper had had his entire family behind him and not just the one he was born to, would he still have met his fate?

But I know better. It did not start there, on those concrete steps.

Before the whimper, there was the crying girl who had not been protected. And the boy who saw unspeakable things. And before that, the boy who chased after people who did not love him enough to look back.

The events that led to the whimper's tragedy—the failures of humans—stretch farther back in time, back to a country his parents were forced to flee long ago.

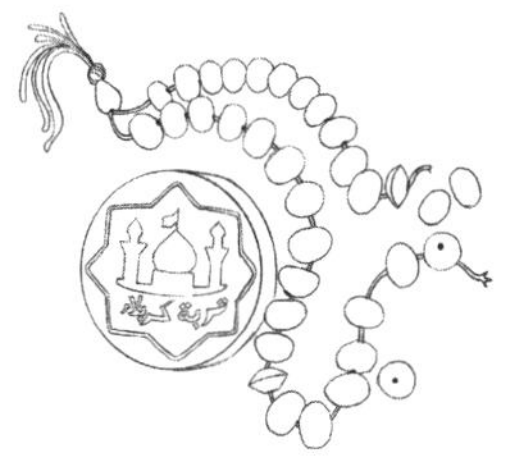

11

KHALED

FORTY-THREE DAYS BEFORE

Khaled and Kawther straightened up as they entered the courtroom with five minutes to spare. Fatima and Yassir walked in just as Judge Kasey, a stout Asian man, approached the court with a smile. Fatima was in a long black blazer and dress, a hijab that matched, and Yassir in the black button-down he'd worn to homecoming last year.

Please let me go first, Khaled made a silent dua. *Please let me go first.*

"Good afternoon, everyone," Judge Kasey said as he sat down, his nose dipping into the paperwork in front of him. "Angel Roberts? You're first."

Two gentlemen walked to the podium. Khaled fidgeted. If Alex and his internet sources were right, he needed to go first and admit guilt to remove blame from Yassir.

"Remember what I mentioned in the car," Kawther whispered. "If there are any questions, I'll do the talking. We can't argue against the blood alcohol level. Luckily, the disturbance charges were dropped this morning, but the call was still mentioned in the police report. All you have to do is say you're not guilty so we can move the case forward."

Khaled nodded, a small relief settling in his stomach. Things were already going his way. He hadn't called the gas station and apologized like Yassir had asked, but it seemed like the owner didn't want any fuss and had dropped the charges anyway.

He watched as a few more clients and their representatives were called to the podium, and when his name was finally called, he whispered a relieved thanks to God. Kawther stood up first, smoothing her gray blazer, and Khaled followed her to the podium.

"Is your full legal name Khaled Mustafa Al-Hakim?"

"Yes," Khaled confirmed, his voice breathy in the microphone.

"And you live at 2877 Sunstone Circle in Riverside City?"

"Yes," Khaled confirmed again, his voice beginning to shake like it did sometimes before debate tournaments. He cleared his throat.

"Mr. Al-Hakim, you are being charged with public intoxication after a disturbance call was made last week on the twenty-first of September. I would suggest that if you're threatening to blow up anyone's business establishment, it won't end well for you. If this is true, learn to hold your tongue." Judge Kasey sighed, his voice rasping from the speaker. "It seems the establishment has dropped the disturbance charges on their own, but you're not off the hook for the underaged alcohol charges. You have a class B misdemeanor with a maximum sentence of a one-year suspended driving license, one hundred hours of community service, a free mental health assessment with a licensed therapist, a state-run Be Alcohol-Free class, and a seven-hundred-and-fifty-dollar fine. Do you plead guilty or not guilty?"

The word was heavy on Khaled's tongue. He knew what he had to do. He was ready to face the consequences.

"Guilty," he blurted as his sister's eyes widened.

"Khaled," she whispered. *"No."*

"I plead guilty," Khaled affirmed. "I am fully responsible and sorry for that night. Please don't punish Yassir, who is in this courtroom today. He's my best friend and he didn't do anything. This is all my fault. I convinced him to drink. I convinced him to go to the gas station—"

"Khaled." Kawther grabbed his hand, squeezing it tight. He didn't flinch.

"Are you an attorney or family?" Judge Kasey asked.

"Both." Kawther cleared her throat as Khaled tossed her hand back to her. "Apologies. My client—"

"Pleaded guilty," Judge Kasey interjected. "Do you two need a moment to counsel?"

Khaled felt his sister's fiery stare, but he wouldn't look at her.

"I plead guilty, Your Honor," he said again firmly.

Judge Kasey looked at them pityingly. "I accept this plea, and while I find it admirable that you want to take responsibility for your friend's actions, he will get his turn. Because this is your first offense, I will keep your license suspended for six months with a mandatory Be Alcohol-Free education course and a five-hundred-dollar fine. Next offense won't be so easy. Understand, Mr. Al-Hakim?"

Khaled nodded, his heart hammering so hard he had to hold his chest. "Th-thank you, Your Honor."

Judge Kasey pounded his gavel. It was over.

Just like that.

Only six months without the Buick. An online course. A fine.

He was so damn lucky. It could've gone so much worse.

Alhamdulillah, he repeated to himself. *Alhamdulillah, Alhamdulillah, Alhamdulillah.*

Judge Kasey called the next name and Khaled held his breath. "Mr. Lokuru."

They sat back down in their seats.

"How could you be so careless?" Kawther seethed as she began to lecture him. "Are you purposely trying to rebel against me? I'm trying to help you—"

"Mr. Al-Azzawi." Judge Kasey's voice eventually silenced her, and Khaled's heart pounded again, hoping his efforts had worked. That Yassir would only get a slap on the wrist.

Yassir and Fatima stood up and walked to the podium. They did not have an attorney, not even a public defender. Why were the Al-Azzawis always stuck defending themselves?

"Yassir Al-Azzawi at Eighteen Thirty-Four Sunflower Road? Sorry, I'm not good at pronouncing names."

"Yes, that's correct," Yassir murmured into the microphone.

He fidgeted as the judge read the same maximum sentence charges as Khaled's.

"Do you understand these charges?"

"Yes."

"Do you plead guilty?"

"Yes."

Khaled nearly got up out of his seat. "What the hell," he whispered.

Judge Kasey frowned. "I see you're the continuation of Mr. Al-Hakim's story. But this isn't your first offense with alcohol." The judge tsked. "You got a DUI nearly eleven months ago. You weren't driving this time, but do you know what it means getting caught drinking twice before the age of twenty-one?"

Yassir didn't reply.

"It means you're going to get a seven-hundred-and-fifty-dollar fine, one hundred hours of community service, free bimonthly visits with a licensed mental health professional, and Be Alcohol-Free educational training like your acquaintance here. The last judge must have taken a glance into your puppy-dog eyes and felt bad, but I don't take minors' second offenses with alcohol lightly. If I see you in court again, you will serve time in juvenile detention. Or jail—looks like your eighteenth birthday is coming up." He shuffled the paperwork, glasses riding the middle of his nose. "Do you understand these charges?"

Yassir nodded.

"Do you plead guilty?"

"Y-yes," Yassir stammered, and Khaled felt his blood pressure skyrocket.

Judge Kasey banged his gavel and Fatima and Yassir returned to their seats. When the arraignment was finally finished, Khaled immediately ran into the hallway, trying to catch up to Yassir, who had just ruined everything.

"What the hell?" Khaled shouted, unable to control his anger. "Why did you plead guilty?"

Yassir turned around, staring at him. "Because I thought I was supposed to. You did, I thought—"

Khaled couldn't help but let the next words fall out of his mouth. "Are you an idiot? Didn't you see me taking responsibility?"

"Responsibility?" Yassir echoed. "Didn't I tell you to apologize to the gas station employees? You're lucky they dropped the charges on their own. I took responsibility the first time, Khaled, but this time it's your fault. Nothing you said to the judge would change his mind about me because of my priors. Because you left alcohol in my car a year ago and *I* was the one who got screwed over! It seems like anytime I'm around you lately, my life gets worse."

"You think I'm the only reason your life is so bad, Yassir?" Khaled scoffed. "Have you forgotten how you ended up here in the first place?"

Yassir's eyes faltered. "Have you?"

Kawther put her hand on Khaled's arm, catching her breath from running after him. "Both of you stop yelling in here. Unless you want the judge to give you an even harsher sentence for court disruption?" Kawther said. Her eyes momentarily caught Fatima's; Fatima stared back, her mouth agape. Perhaps it was not so easy to look at her oldest friend, knowing all the devastation they'd left in their wake. At least he wasn't the only one who had a hard time looking at his sister.

Fatima broke eye contact, grabbing her brother's sleeve, guiding him out. "Let's go, Yassir."

"Yassir—" Khaled began.

"That's *enough*, Khaled," Kawther said. "It's over. You didn't listen to me, either."

He shrugged his sister's touch away and stormed out of the building, Kawther pathetically calling after him again. When she finally caught up to him at the Honda, she unlocked the car and immediately blasted the heater as she trembled. Khaled stared at his hands.

"I'll explain everything to Mama and Baba so you don't have to. Baba says he wants you home now, so I'll get you an excuse for second period, too."

He shrugged.

"You should've let me handle it." She tried to meet his eyes. "I may be your sister, but as your lawyer . . . that was a mess."

Khaled turned and stared at her. Then he spoke to her directly for the first time since she'd arrived two months ago—no, since she'd abandoned him eight years ago.

"Sister? I don't have any."

☽

"What did they say?"

At home, Baba was waiting by the front door, Mama staring at a muted latmiyat procession on the television, her face pensive. At least she was out of her room, no longer lying on her side quietly in bed. Baba followed them into the living room, taking a seat by Mama as Khaled and Kawther stood before them. Khaled's anxiety kept him still. His parents had never looked at him like this before.

It was the way their faces had looked when Kawther left—when they'd whispered to each other, ignoring both him and Ayah when they asked where Kawther had gone. It was the way they'd stared when Ayah lay on the couch, saying she didn't want to go to Chapman anymore. That she wanted to live a different life.

"Outside of the car privileges being revoked, he just has a fine and an online class," Kawther answered for him. Despite how much he still hated her, he was grateful in that moment.

"How much is the fine?" Mama asked quietly, her eyes still on the television.

Kawther cleared her voice. "Five hundred dollars."

Mama clicked her tongue. It was lower than Yassir's, but it's not like he could gloat or take comfort in the fact.

"I'll pay it with my own money. I have some saved up," Khaled finally said.

Baba's eyes caught his, disappointment overflowing, just as they had on Friday night. It was the kind of look Khaled imagined Sayed Rahman gave Yassir each time he saw him. How could Yassir stand it?

A nauseous feeling snaked over Khaled's gut. He wondered what kind of scolding Sayed Rahman was giving Yassir now. Khaled had tried to protect his friend and all he'd done was get him into further trouble.

"Kawther, can you take him to work tomorrow after school?" Baba said as he headed toward the keys sitting on the entrance table. "He'll work until closing every day until he leaves."

Now Baba was speaking like Khaled wasn't even in the room. Like he wasn't even alive.

"Leaves? Where is he going?" Kawther asked.

Baba stared at Kawther, who stared at their father with the same twisted confusion Khaled must have had on his face.

"Is he going somewhere?" she repeated.

Baba nodded. "He's going to Iraq, and you're going with him."

12

YASSIR

After dodging Alex's questions about court and Khaled's absence from school all day, Yassir braced himself as he slid into the passenger seat of his father's car. To his surprise, Baba held a greasy mechanic's uniform.

Yassir couldn't get a job without affecting his family's government-funded insurance, but he'd worked at Hajji Majid's auto repair shop during the summers for cash under the table. Everything he'd earned working there had quickly dwindled from Yasmin's expenses, though, and he hadn't worked there since Ayah left.

"Fatima said you have a fine," Baba muttered. "Pay it off."

Yassir took the old shirt and nodded.

When they pulled into the parking lot, terror bit into his insides at the thought of seeing Hajji Abu Abdalla, whose own mechanic shop was next door.

"Don't even try to talk to Khaled if you see him," Baba muttered. "Stay inside at Amu Majid's shop, got it? He's doing us a big favor."

Yassir nodded. Avoiding Khaled would be the easy part, if Khaled allowed it. "Okay, Baba."

Baba got out of the car as Hajji Majid appeared from the small gray brick building, smiling with a cigarette between his teeth. "Yassir! Habibi!"

The man enveloped him in his arms, grazing Yassir's cheeks with kisses before he grabbed his chin and observed his bruise, clicking his tongue at Yassir's father as he spoke in Arabic. "This is no way to treat such a sweet child, ya Sayed. Yassir is the nicest kid I know."

Yassir couldn't help but weakly smile back at him.

"Just come right to the register, I'll have you count the till."

Yassir nodded in agreement. Before his father could slink away, Yassir decided to be brave. He tapped Baba's shoulder. He couldn't spend an entire shift not knowing.

"Baba—" Yassir's voice cracked.

Baba turned around, raising an eyebrow.

"What . . ." Yassir began in Arabic, but he didn't know how to convey *Are you sending me away?* in the right words without making a mess, so he landed back on English, as always. "Are you sending me to Iraq?"

Baba's eyebrows creased together in confusion as he answered in Arabic. "How exactly am I supposed to send you when you have fines and court orders?"

Yassir swallowed.

"Just go to work," Baba grumbled. "But if you don't do what I ask, Yassir . . . you won't get another chance."

Baba slid back into the Crown Victoria and drove away, and Yassir was filled with relief.

He had to do better, not just scraping by each day. He needed to pass his classes. He needed to graduate. He needed to do right by Yasmin. There would not be another chance.

In the corner of his eye, Yassir could see a strip of Hajji Abu Abdalla's shop across the shared lot. Laith, Ali's high school friend and Hajji Abu Abdalla's part-time employee, stood by the cash register. If he was here, that meant Khaled wasn't clocking in today.

Something wasn't right.

Khaled never skipped school, and he rarely missed a shift at work.

Yassir slipped inside Hajji Majid's shop. He smiled at Hajji Majid's jokes and drank the chai he served as he sifted through receipts and complaints the man had a hard time understanding with his limited English. Every so often, Yassir would turn his head, catching sight of Laith's curls and yawns, hoping he'd see Khaled instead.

By nightfall, after Yasmin had rejected him again for sleep, Yassir stepped outside the house. He didn't have to worry long; like clockwork, Khaled texted him immediately. This time, without a voice message. The words jarred Yassir instantly.

Don't stay out too late, ihmar. I know you're mad at me, but I'm calling an emergency meeting at that random café with the horses. Tomorrow after school. Bring the baby.

☽

FORTY-TWO DAYS BEFORE

Khaled had skipped school again.

"Maybe his dad beat him up for the court shit?" Alex had speculated at lunch. Alex must've seen Yassir's bruise and assumed all Iraqi or Muslim parents were the same. But whenever Yassir thought about either of their parents, it had always been softness that came to mind.

Soft words as callused hands ruffled his hair between soft, fitful laughs.

It was only in the last year that both of their fathers' softness had been replaced by jagged anger. Anger because of Yassir.

But would Hajji Abu Abdalla take it as far as pulling Khaled out of school to get him away from Yassir? Did he know about Khaled's incident with Wells? With a pang of guilt twisting his rib cage this morning, Yassir had attempted to cross toward Principal Delpy's office and tell her the truth about what he'd seen—she was going to find out anyway if she reviewed the hallway tapes—but the minute he'd spotted her office, he'd chickened out. He was barely hanging on by a thread as it was.

Luckily, Hajji Majid didn't need Yassir back at the shop until the weekend, so he was free this afternoon. Because he was around to watch Yasmin, he convinced his mother to go to the grocery store and stepped out with Yasmin in the stroller as soon as she left.

As they walked, the clouds parted, revealing a glassy blue sky, the color of Yasmin's mother's eyes. He had messaged Emily a few times with updates about Yasmin's milestones, but she'd simply reminded him that she did not want to be involved, before blocking him. So he left it at that. Yassir shook his head, avoiding the thought of her.

Walking with Yasmin was so different from walking alone, when he could disappear into his thoughts. Walking alone relieved stress, but now his spine straightened, his mind obsessing over the cold temperature, how much sunlight hit Yasmin's face, whether the uneven sidewalk tossed her around too much. But she smiled, staring up at the sky, and he smiled back, rushing into the coffee shop to escape the wind.

Inside, he found Khaled leaning against a chair, sipping a cup of coffee as he scrolled on his phone. Khaled had called for an emergency meeting a handful of times before.

First, nearly two years ago, when Ayah had decided she wanted to drop out to marry the son of a car salesman. Then the day after Khaled drank alcohol for the first time and looked Yassir in the eye and asked *Shit, man, am I going to go to hell?* Most recently was when he tricked Yassir on Father's Day so he could hand him a pack of diapers and a card that read *Happy Baba's Day, Shithead*, which had caused Yassir to actually cry in public and Khaled to panic, shoving thin brown napkins at him, begging him to stop.

But Khaled's face lit up now as he spotted Yasmin, a goofy look immediately softening his normal broodiness, and Yassir wondered if his panicked thoughts were all for naught. Renewed annoyance prickled at him. If this was all for dramatics—maybe an apology—he'd rather just punch Khaled in the arm. But once Yasmin smiled widely at Khaled, Yassir's irritation softened. Yasmin hadn't met many people, but she'd immediately liked Khaled, as if she remembered when he helped bring her home nearly six months ago.

Khaled was quiet as he switched to godfather mode: unstrapping the baby from the stroller, removing her hat and coat, and squealing at her small, fuzzy brown boots. "God, that's adorable," he laughed. He asked the barista for a high chair and ordered Yassir a large latte with a triple shot of espresso. Khaled already knew how tired Yassir was.

"So, you're alive," Khaled said as he easily opened the applesauce jar with a satisfied smirk. He plunged the small plastic spoon into the jar and held out the brown goo to Yasmin. She was unimpressed, her eyes fixed on the walls instead. "Would it kill you to actually answer a text message?"

"Just because I'm not talking to you doesn't mean I'm dead," Yassir scoffed, although he was relieved that Khaled was alive, too.

"Might as well be dead," Khaled muttered, and he began to make annoying babble sounds at Yasmin, who was only half amused.

"If you keep doing that, I'm leaving," Yassir said. "Why are we here?"

Khaled ignored his question, attempting to get another spoonful of applesauce into Yasmin's mouth. He failed. "Were you at the shop yesterday?"

"My dad is having me work shifts at Hajji Majid's to pay off the fine, thanks to you," Yassir said, unable to keep the irritation out of his voice. His anger from yesterday still felt fresh. "Are you following my whereabouts in the daytime, too? You know, I have better things to do right now, like our physics project—"

"Oh, you're actually doing homework?" Khaled raised an eyebrow. "Shocking."

"Get your portion done tonight," Yassir said. "I need to pass everything, or I truly will be fucked. Baba would've already shipped me away if I wasn't just slapped with court orders."

Khaled tightened his hands over his coffee, not speaking. Something stirred in Yassir again as Khaled pushed Yasmin's soft ringlets out of her face. He looked pale.

"Khaled, what's going on?" Yassir asked. "Are you getting kicked out of school?"

Khaled shook his head. "Not yet."

"Debate team?"

He shook his head again, biting his lip.

"Home?"

Khaled stilled.

"Khaled, spit it out already. Are you just being dramatic like always—"

"My dad is forcing me to visit Ayah," Khaled said with finality.

Yassir stilled, too. Yasmin continued to fidget in his friend's arms, drool dripping onto his jeans.

A year and a half ago, they'd sat in this exact spot and Khaled had asked him if he knew why Ayah suddenly wanted to drop out. *Did someone say something to her at school? She won't tell me anything.*

For a moment, Yassir no longer felt that his own father was cruel—the slap notwithstanding. If Yassir's father knew the truth about him and Ayah, this would be his punishment from hell. And Yassir knew that, in a different way, it was for Khaled, too.

"When?" he finally asked, trying to keep his voice steady.

"Two weeks. Baba thinks it's perfect timing, considering fall break and that I can be there in time for the Arbaeen pilgrimage to cleanse my soul. Right in the middle of the stupid school investigation and the debate championship, too. If I go now, I lose my chances at that scholarship, but he doesn't believe I can do it here on my own. Fix my iman. I need to convince him that I'm fine, it was a mistake and—" Khaled shook his head. "God, I didn't even tell you the worst part yet. He's making me go with Kawther. After eight years, she's listening to my dad's demands? She must have fucked up in LA, that's truly why she's back. She's packing her bag as we speak."

While Yassir was no fan of Kawther, either—considering she had been the one responsible for driving their families apart in the first place—he didn't hate her like Khaled did. He'd been hurt when she chose a new life over Ali, over all of them, but when she was in California, there was still the possibility that their families could move past what had happened. But then Yassir had destroyed any hope of their families reuniting.

"I won't go. I can't," Khaled said.

Yassir grimaced. "What are you going to do? Run away from home?"

Khaled shook his head. "Kawther doing that was enough stress for my parents. I think the only way out of is this is for you to . . ." He hesitated. "I . . . I need you to talk to my dad."

Yassir stared, dumbfounded. "Do you have amnesia? Because less than a week ago, your dad looked at me like I was the shaitan himself."

"That's my whole point," Khaled said. "My parents are pissed because they think I'm going to . . . end up like you. They probably think I'm gonna—" He didn't finish his sentence, his eyes descending on Yasmin.

"Become a teen dad like me?" Yassir asked, swallowing a lump in his throat.

Khaled shifted in his seat. "Listen, I know I got you into this court mess and you're rightfully pissed at me. I will take all your shit, all your insults, I'll even work more shifts and pay back your fine myself, but I can't go."

Khaled paused. "You can't let me see her yet," he pleaded.

Her.

Ayah. In Iraq.

A tremble of disgust cracked under Yassir's tight jaw. A few moments of silence fell between them, and Khaled shook his head, fierce desperation igniting in his eyes.

"C'mon, Yassir. I didn't mean to get you in trouble, you know that, but can you do this one thing for me?" Khaled asked. "I swear I will never ask you for anything in my entire life. This is why I asked to see Yasmin now. This is my last favor, I swear. I just need you to tell my dad who I really am, because he doesn't trust or believe me anymore. All you have to do is remind him that I'm not a liar—that I pray. That I repent. That I don't do anything else—have never done anything else that would even amount to a sin. I just need you to try." His hurried words came to a halt, Khaled looking defeated at Yassir's silence. "C'mon, what will you lose if you just speak to my dad?"

You.

If he talked to Khaled's father now, there was no way the truth would not come out.

Yassir's cheek ached, although the bruise had started to fade.

Yasmin's laughter pulled him back to the moment, and he watched as Khaled disengaged from the conversation to give his daughter a quick silly face. She loved Khaled. Even though she barely saw him, she loved him, and maybe Yassir didn't want to take that away from her. Not yet.

Or maybe he was still a selfish coward.

He could risk Khaled being angry with him now. He couldn't risk Khaled knowing the truth—not only would their friendship dissolve, but Khaled would never forgive Yassir. He would hate him. For being the reason Ayah left. For being a liar.

The past few days of fuming and ignoring Khaled would not compare to the unknown hate that Khaled owed him.

"Khaled, I have everything to lose," he finally said, because it was true. "You're holding my daughter, aren't you? She's all I have. The minute I speak to your dad it will blow up in my face. No doubt, he'll get Baba involved, and my dad already told me this is my last chance. I need my diploma from Chapman. I need my job. Both of which I could lose if Baba really means it. I'm trying to catch up on my schoolwork—" Khaled rolled his eyes, like he didn't believe it. "And maybe I don't feel like getting slapped in the face again, either."

Khaled huffed as Yassir began to gather Yasmin's stuff. He took his daughter back from Khaled. But first, Khaled gave her a goodbye peck on her rosy cheeks.

"I'm sorry," Yassir finally murmured, as if the pathetic words meant anything at this point. Khaled stood up.

"Where are you going?" Yassir asked, brushing down Yasmin's silky brown hair with his fingers before putting the beanie back on her tiny head.

"Home," Khaled said. "To try to convince my dad once again that I can't go. Yasmin, do me a favor and throw up on your dad's lap later, okay?"

"Khaled—" Yassir began, but Khaled simply flipped him off and walked away.

Yassir strapped his daughter back into the stroller, even though she gave him a fight. She resisted, whimpering when the damn seat belt wouldn't click back into place, until a nearby customer leaned down and helped.

"Just like this, sweetie." The older woman smiled at him.

He nodded gratefully, embarrassment warming his ears.

"This baby is yours? She's beautiful."

"My little sister."

The lie slipped out of his mouth so quickly, he barely had time to realize he had done it. He had never said that before, but he never liked going out in public with Yasmin, afraid of what people would think of him.

"Well, your mother must be grateful for you babysitting."

He smiled sheepishly at the woman and waved goodbye, then stepped outside, where it felt like the temperature had dropped twenty degrees.

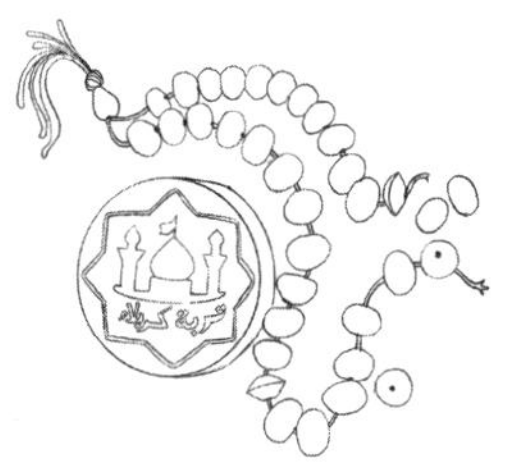

13

KHALED

Khaled knelt on the carpet and put his hands together.

Baba stared at him, confused. "Khaled, what are you—"

"Please, Baba, I can't go to Iraq. Please, I . . . I need more time. I'll go next summer. Even when it's so hot my flesh will melt—"

"Khaled." Baba shook his head, his eyes turning to watch the sheikh's Muharram lecture on the television screen. "Go pack. You leave in a few days."

"Baba, you can't take me out of school this month. It's really important that I'm at school right now. Principal Delpy is deciding—well, I mean, I have the debate championship. I worked very hard—"

"Worked hard?" Baba asked incredulously. "Is that why you drink? You can't handle the stress?"

Khaled blinked at the accusation. "I . . . I've stopped forever. Wallah. Why won't you believe me?"

Khaled hoped his words were true. He had not had a drop of alcohol since Laylat Ashura. Each time he felt the urge, he knelt in sujud or repeated the meditation surahs in his head. Even though he still felt the same—crumbling and confused on the inside—at least he had self-control again.

Baba's eyes softened for a moment. Sadness, not anger, stared back at Khaled. "I trusted you to handle yourself because you said you could. I gave you time, didn't I?"

Last year when Mama had visited Ayah, Khaled had not been brave enough to see her, so Baba had stayed with him. Then, when Baba made a quick trip over the summer, he'd asked if Khaled was ready, but Khaled asked Baba to delay, and Baba was still gentle in return.

"I'm not trusting your judgment anymore. Everything you've ignored for the last year, where did that get you? How many more DUIs do you need? Kawther said Yassir had two. Do you want to become like him?"

It all came back to Yassir. Yassir, who only had his DUIs because of Khaled. Who would never have gone to the party where he met Emily if Khaled hadn't invited him.

Khaled shook his head. "I'm not like Yassir, Baba. But it wasn't his fault I drank. It was mine. Every mistake I make is mine, not his. You can't blame him for everything. Outside of you and Mama, he's the only family I have now."

"He's not." Baba shook his head, his eyes now ignited. "You have an entire family an ocean away. But you think all you have is that reckless boy?"

"Yes! And you took him from me," Khaled said, now shouting. "Why do you still punish us all for what Kawther did?"

If Kawther could overhear his words from her bedroom, he didn't care.

Silence seeped between them, and Khaled wondered if he'd taken it too far. Baba stared at the TV with a blank expression.

After a few moments, Khaled stood up, defeated. He'd have to try again tomorrow. He could try convincing Mama . . . if Mama would even look at him.

"Ayah," Baba said quietly as Khaled began to step away. "There are many reasons why you can't be friends with Yassir, but the most important one is Ayah."

Khaled stared blankly at his father. "What does Ayah have to do with this?"

Baba shook his head, a deep anger returning to his eyes, just as it had on Laylat Ashura. "So you spend so much time with Yassir, but not once did you notice him trying to have a haram relationship with your sister? Do you think that's respectful? Why do you think she suddenly wanted to leave and get married?"

Khaled shook his head. He felt a tremor coming up his arm. "Baba, what are you talking about?"

14

YASSIR

FORTY-ONE DAYS BEFORE

"I'm concerned about you, Michael," Mr. Porter said, taking a seat in his swivel chair as the rest of his physics class filed out. "Do you have a reason why you presented on only two of the twenty-four slides you were assigned?"

Yassir's cheeks heated up. "I—I lost track of time."

"You seem . . . distraught. Everything okay at home?"

Yassir shrugged. All he could think about was his best friend's pissed-off expression at the coffeehouse yesterday. How he had disappointed and failed Khaled over and over again.

"I noticed the bruise on your face is healing. That happen at home?"

Yassir shook his head. "Nope. Got in a fight."

"With who?"

"I would tell you but then I think you'd get me in trouble."

Mr. Porter sighed. "It's good you're finally awake, but you have only a couple of weeks to get your grades up. You know when the quarter ends, right?"

"November eighth," Yassir said.

"Surprised you remembered."

It was the day of Yasmin's doctor's appointment, which he'd finally been able to schedule. He promised himself that by the time to take her in rolled around, he'd be free from the misery of first quarter.

"I know because it's close to my birthday," he said instead, which wasn't a lie.

"Well, let's hope you have a *happy* birthday. Get in contact with Khaled and redo the presentation. Remind him that he's received zero points for the assignment, too, got it?"

Khaled, who was not in class again today, hadn't bothered to complete his half of the project or answer Yassir's calls last night. Yassir nodded and Mr. Porter dismissed him for lunch.

To his surprise, when he stepped into the cafeteria, Khaled was standing at their usual table, speaking to Alex, who wore a confused expression.

The urge to yell at Khaled was strong. But as Yassir approached, he saw that Khaled's eyes looked empty, and he realized he had nothing to say. Frustrated, he turned and walked the other way.

Then Khaled began shouting his name, but not in the way he usually did. Not in the *Salaam, Mr. Al-Harami* or *Ya Abu Yasmin* or any of the other random and rude and affectionate ways he'd call Yassir. Instead, he just said his name, voice cold and emotionless.

"Yassir!"

Yassir froze. When Khaled caught up to him, his eyes burned with rage. He looked just like his father had when he'd found out the truth about Yassir and Ayah.

"Is it true?"

Yassir blinked. Khaled's mouth trembled, his fists clenching at his sides. Yassir hadn't seen him this way since Ayah left.

Ayah.

Don't touch me anymore, she told him in a haze of rushed words as he had tried to pull at her sleeve, tucking his fingers between hers, like he always did. *I can't do it anymore, Yassir. I can't wait for you to care about me.*

"Is it true?" Khaled repeated, voice breaking. "Are you keeping secrets from me?"

Is what true? Yassir thought, but his mouth was as slack as it always was in these moments. At the masjid before his father slapped him. At the gas station. At the classroom door when Wells was screaming at Khaled. With Ayah.

Yassir took a step back as Khaled took another step forward.

Then another.

"Is there . . . are you keeping secrets from me?" Khaled breathed heavily. His body shook. "Think, Yassir! Be honest, are you keeping secrets from me?"

Bile rose from the bottom of Yassir's stomach.

Don't tell Khaled, don't you think he'll get weird? That he won't understand?

Yassir couldn't tell Khaled, not like this, not in front of all these eyes. Ayah left and got married. She was gone from him forever now. The secret would stay between them. It was supposed to stay between them. He'd promised her.

Now his best friend was five, four, three inches away from him.

"Yassir. Say something."

Yassir blinked. His mouth was dry.

At the sound of his silence, his best friend pulled his arm back and punched Yassir in the face.

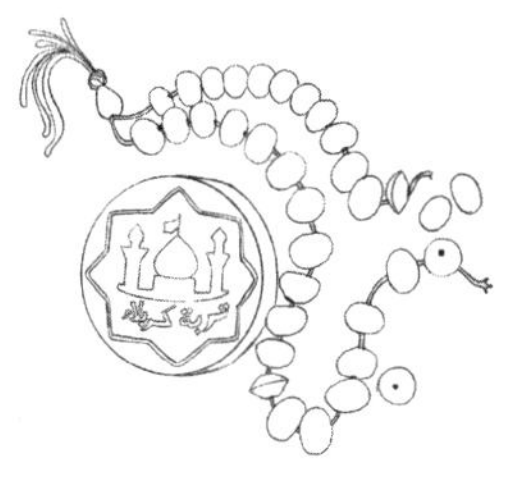

15

KHALED

"Don't worry," Khaled said to Vice Principal Beckett, who stood between him and Yassir. "I'm not going to hit him again."

Beckett merely shook his head. His dark brown hair was buzzed close to his scalp, and he had an army tank tattoo on his wrist, visible each time he shook someone's hand. Khaled didn't know when he'd deployed or which country he'd exploded—Iraq was a fifty-fifty—he just knew the man was friendly with Miles, thus making him an enemy by extension. Khaled always avoided him. Of course, Beckett was the one who'd pulled him off Yassir before he could get another punch in.

"You okay, Michael?" Beckett asked Yassir, who held a bag of ice to his face. The top of his cheek and part of his eye were already swelling.

When Yassir didn't answer, Beckett blew out a frustrated breath. "Physical fights are unacceptable at this institution. Remember *decorum*. Our first school value."

Khaled rolled his eyes.

"Just expel me already," he muttered. "I'm so done."

Beckett shook his head. "That's for Dr. Delpy to decide—" His phone buzzed. "Excuse me. Your father is finally calling me back." He stepped away with the phone to his ear.

Khaled would be afraid, but he thought Baba might be proud of him for punching Yassir. Even if he got expelled, what would be his punishment? The Buick was already gone. He had a criminal record. He was a pariah at school. And he was being sent to Iraq with one estranged sister in order to visit another.

Baba was right. He was losing himself—losing everything—but for *this*? A school that had consistently failed his family and a friend who had lied to his face for over a year?

The ice bag crackled in Yassir's hand.

"Are you even going to apologize?" Khaled whispered. "Or are you going to just stay quiet like always?"

If it hadn't been for the late-night texts and phone calls on Ayah's old phone, Khaled might not have believed his father's accusations. But Yassir had been leaving in the middle of the night long before Yasmin was born. When Baba showed Khaled the messages, it clicked.

Everything about Yassir Al-Azzawi clicked.

And the most aggravating part was that Khaled had missed all the obvious signs.

The first day of freshman year for him, sophomore year for Ayah, they both spotted Yassir at orientation. Ayah was the one to call him over. Ayah was the one who brought them all together again.

She was the one to always remind him to include Yassir, to save him a seat at lunch, to check on him, even after she dropped out and left for marriage.

We can't control her, Yassir had said at the coffee shop nearly two years ago, *just let her go, Khaled.*

"How is it so easy for you to let us go?" Khaled asked. Eyeing the swelling of Yassir's face, he felt a pang in his chest. It was stronger than the tremor in his hand. Something that gutted his marrow. A feeling he had only felt once in his life, yet still familiar.

Yassir bit his lip. Silent. Pathetic, like always.

"What am I talking about?" Khaled continued. "You never fucking cared about us, did you?"

Yassir's eyes glossed over. *Let him cry*, Khaled thought. *Let him feel guilty*.

"You're supposed to be my best friend. All I've done is worry about you, try to protect you—"

"Me?" Yassir finally interjected, anger gritting his teeth. "You only care about protecting yourself."

"At least I protected *her*!" Khaled shouted, unable to keep calm anymore. "How many times did you act like you didn't even know her? Funny enough, I thought you were keeping a respectful distance! You never stood up for her when people made fun of her hijab or the way she looked. And now I'm learning you liked her, just when no one could see. When I couldn't—" As another tremor of rage shook his body, Khaled stopped talking.

Yassir still had nothing to say. He only stared at his feet.

Khaled hoped each word was a knife twisting deeper and deeper into Yassir's guilt, if he even felt any.

"You're so pathetic, Yassir. If you don't stop being such a fucking coward, everyone in your life will leave you behind. Do you understand?" Khaled asked—he knew he was yelling now. "I always thought it was Kawther's fault that our family was destroyed, but it's *your* fault, isn't it? If you don't change, you're going to lose Yasmin one day, too, and I'm not going to be around to help you anymore. And you won't have anyone to blame but yourself."

"Khaled."

Khaled's eyes shot up at Principal Delpy, who stood in the doorway to her office. "Come inside. Michael, if you'd like, you can go to the nurse's office. We can chat later."

Yassir nodded but didn't stand up.

"Khaled," Delpy repeated, her eyes flickering fire. "Inside. *Now*."

Khaled hesitated. He knew that when he stepped inside that office, it would be the last time he'd ever be friends with Yassir Al-Azzawi.

Khaled took a moment to look at the boy he'd known since he was born. He stared at the pitiful brown eyes, searching for some sign of regret. He stared at the disheveled curls that peeked from the top of the gray hoodie, and Yassir's thin, slouching lips, the lips that had lied to him for nearly two years. He stared at the boy who was every swing set and Eid breakfast and bike race. The boy he'd thought he knew better than himself. The boy he'd thought was his best friend. The boy he had risked everything for.

Then Khaled pushed down the tremor that threatened to snake up his arm one last time and walked away. He took a seat in his usual spot, his hand throbbing. If his hand hurt that much, how much had Yassir's cheek taken?

"I've expected a lot of things from you since you set foot in this school, but I truly never expected this—"

"Am I expelled?" Khaled asked, cutting the principal off. He didn't have time to argue. He had a lot left to pack before leaving.

"No," she said, flustered. "I haven't had a physical fight in this school in years. But I'm following policy. You're getting suspended. Five days. And unfortunately, because of this infraction, Mrs. McCarthy has decided to remove you as captain of the debate team."

Khaled looked up from his pulsating hand. "It doesn't matter," he scoffed, tears welling in his eyes. "I won't be here for the championship anyway."

Delpy frowned, confused. "Did Michael tell you about the hallway footage between you and Mr. Wells? You do not need to use physical force to make a point, I was just about to deal with this myself and notify you that we had a witness . . ."

She continued to speak, but he was no longer listening.

Yassir had seen what had happened between him and Wells?

Khaled's right fist buzzed with anger again.

Whatever regret he might have felt at this moment no longer existed.

Baba was right. Yassir Al-Azzawi could never be his real friend.

Khaled shook his head, interrupting Delpy.

"After my suspension, I'll be missing thirteen and a half school days starting mid–next week because I'll be going to Iraq a few days before fall break begins. I'll send a signed note excusing the absences through the mail so I'm still following policy." He emphasized the last word.

Delpy blinked at him; she couldn't seem to keep up with her shock anymore. "*Iraq?* Is it even safe there?"

"Didn't know you were concerned about my safety, Dr. Delpy," Khaled said as he stood up. "We're done here, right?"

He caught a glimpse of his principal nodding before he walked away.

SKY

It's strange that humans will hurt each other with the same hands they cup in prayer. They look up at me with regret and resentment, pleading for forgiveness I cannot give.

What they don't know is that they're not the only ones capable of regret and resentment. I may not see all their transgressions, but I see many.

Being a witness is not so easy, either. The rocks and trees, the mountains and plains, they are lucky, as they are stationary. Stuck in one place; for them, the humans come and go. For me, they remain, for generations and on and on as long as they live. I can always find them, those delicate whispers.

But sometimes I am far too disturbed to carry out my duty.

How am I supposed to soothe a jaw?

A dark thumb left over from a blast?

A small arm still holding a piece of chocolate in its hand?

A brain that slides out of a child's head as his father wails, his eyes rolling back in agony?

How am I supposed to endure the sounds of bullets that don't stop raining from the machines under my belly and onto the families crossing the road? How am I to endure it again and again until I can longer recognize the whispers between mangled souls and limbs?

Sometimes I must look away. When I can no longer stomach the sight of those who died, I look for those who lived.

This is why I have followed the whimper's family for so long.

I remember the day the new families arrived in the land filled with broad mountains that peeked over the horizon, slick concrete roads, and snow that welcomed them at their knees.

The children were frightened, of course. They had never felt such sensations before. But I will admit, I do enjoy seeing horror press against human faces when it's over something trivial. The ice that slipped under their shoes, the anxious cries that soon turned into laughter, shoving snow over the coats that still had price tags attached to the sleeves.

A blond woman spoke to the parents as they moved boxes into and out of a white building that was shedding paint like a second skin. Although the children chased each other, a booming voice forced them to stop.

A human can always recognize when they're unwanted.

Since they had landed, other humans had stepped out of their own houses, watching the families, fear and curiosity in their eyes. They had never seen other humans look or dress the way the whimper's family did. A man walking a small dog nearby shouted something that caused the blond woman to pause her conversation and yell something back at him until he shrugged and walked away.

These humans were not like me. They did not know what the whimper's family had had to endure to step over the snow like they did. They were leftover people from a conflict their new neighbors would not know or care about. I watched as the parents startled, calling the children back before forcing them to disappear into the building. I watched the parents stare around at the other humans who watched them. Now they were afraid, too.

Refugees fascinate me, how they flee the violence I am forced to witness and start over again and again in lands where they are not welcome. How their search for home never ends. How their fear never quite disappears, it just changes.

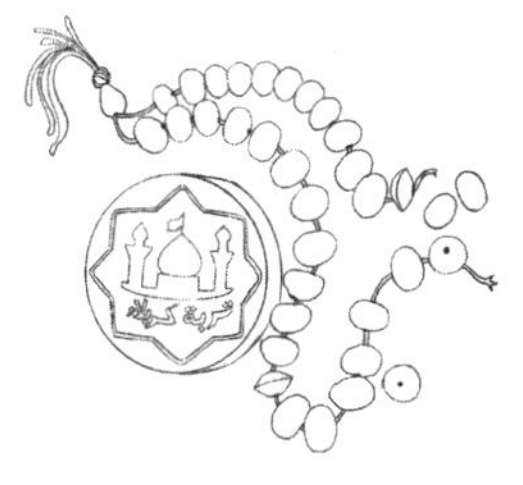

16

KHALED

THIRTY DAYS BEFORE

For the first time in his life, Khaled could not distinguish his family from the crowd.

"You think that's him?" Kawther asked, referring to a tall man in a navy blazer near the exit of the Najaf airport. She tugged on her long black dress, straightening her hijab, self-conscious without an abaya on—the standard dress code in Najaf for women.

Khaled pushed the luggage cart through the airport, not responding to her question. He hadn't exchanged a word with her since they'd left their parents' home nearly thirty-eight hours ago. If Yassir had known that Khaled had spoken less than ten words in the past two days, he'd have thrown a party. Khaled shook his head, pushing the thought of Yassir away, his knuckles still red and achy, even after two weeks had nearly passed since he'd punched Yassir.

"Definitely not him," Kawther muttered as the man turned away from them, smashing a cigarette under his loafer. Khaled's eyes still searched for the elderly man who'd descended from the plane before they had. The one who had pressed his lips to the earth, sobs escaping his body, until other passengers groaned for him to move. Khaled wondered what regret that man held, for him to kiss the earth like that. To kiss Iraq like that.

After ten minutes of walking in circles outside the airport terminal, searching for faces they wouldn't recognize, he felt a tap on his shoulder.

"Khaled?" a tall, baby-faced boy whispered, staring at Khaled's black Class of 2019 Chapman hoodie.

Khaled slowly nodded, taking the boy in.

He couldn't be older than ten. Thick straight brown hair dangled over his dark eyes, hiding the hint of green in them. The boy wore a blue-collared shirt with the word *Nike* misspelled in the center. Like almost everyone else, he sported black sliders, except that a large bandage covered a third of one of his feet.

"We were wondering where you two went!" the boy shouted, a smile spreading across his face. "We thought we missed your flight. My mom was so worried, she was trying to call your mom!" The boy spoke in Arabic so quickly, Khaled wondered how he registered a single word. All Khaled's years of learning Arabic through muffled conversations between his parents, and the eccentric vocabulary of community uncles, were no match for this rapid fire. The boy extended his hand. Khaled shook it before giving the boy a grazing kiss on each cheek.

"My name is Hassan," the boy said. "I'm your uncle's son."

"Of course," Kawther said happily as she introduced herself. Hassan led them toward a small group of people Khaled realized were no longer strangers, but family.

"We found you, we found you!" they exclaimed as he was passed through hugs, cigarette-laced smiles, and joyous laughs. Khaled's arms froze, feeling robotic. He hadn't been embraced by family like this since he had been beaten up by Miles in the second grade. But it hadn't been Mama and Baba who hugged him and kissed his cheeks like this. It had been Yassir's parents. Now the squeezes to his shoulder felt unfamiliar, almost painful. He didn't quite know how to wrap his arms around his relatives.

When he looked over, Kawther seemed familiar with the movements. Perhaps she had been hugged by friends in LA, the new family she'd created without him.

Resentment filled his stomach as they hugged Khalee Jafaar, their mother's brother, then his wife, Samira, who smiled widely, exposing her bright pink gums. They were passed to an old woman who he knew was his great-aunt, but everyone called her Bibi, as if she were his mother's mother.

"Salaam 'alaykum, Bibi," Khaled whispered, kissing both of her cheeks. She looked to be a thousand years old. Her skin rippled in thick wrinkles, like desert sand. Her hands were soft like the dough Mama used to knead with Yassir's mother as they baked traditional bread in the kiln, when she could convince her to get out of bed. Bibi grabbed his face, kissed each inch of his cheeks as tears ran down her face.

"Habibi," she sobbed. "Habibi, habibi, habibi."

Khaled froze.

It was astounding to see almost his entire lineage staring back at him. He didn't know these people. Yet their touches felt familiar, their faces warm, their tears legitimate—as if they had missed a boy they'd never met.

"You okay, habibi?" Khalee Jafaar asked, putting an arm around Khaled's shoulder, leading him off from the group as Bibi pulled away and kissed Kawther next. "Your mother told me you're having a hard time. She told me that"—his voice got low, so low that Khaled wondered if he imagined the words escaping his lips—"sharab."

Alcohol.

Khaled pretended not to hear him, embarrassment warming his cheeks. He knew Mama was close to Khalee Jafaar, but not close enough to reveal his darkest secret. His parents expected a changed boy in return for the sick one, the one who couldn't stop drinking the past year, even when he wanted to.

The boy who had become a liar, despite how much he valued the truth.

The boy who needed to see his sister, after a year of pretending she'd never existed.

Maybe his father had been right: He was becoming just like Yassir.

Reckless.

Before Khalee Jafaar could say anything more, Khaled walked a few steps ahead, grabbing the heavy luggage cart from Hassan, who was attempting to steer it, and followed his family home.

17

YASSIR

TWENTY-NINE DAYS BEFORE

"*Yalla*," Baba grumbled. "It's time for salat."

The adhan whispered close to Yassir's ear. He instinctively pushed it away, throwing the fuzzy gray blanket over his face, careful not to disturb Yasmin, who was miraculously still asleep in the crook of his arm. Despite the bassinet tucked between his bed and the wall, she rarely lasted the night on her own.

"*Yalla*," his father repeated, pushing the blanket off his face. "It's time for Allah, habibi."

While that word never left Mama's vocabulary, it had been so long since Yassir had been called habibi by his father. Guilt burned his rib cage. He groaned and shoved himself out of bed and into the bathroom.

He should've seen this coming. His father's latest attempt to save him from sin.

"Hurry," Baba muttered as Yassir stared at the sink, feeling thirteen again, when he used to bother fasting for Ramadan and would have to wake before dawn just like this. Would Allah care if he was one minute late to salat? You truly couldn't be late to salat, right? If Allah was so forgiving, could He forgive Yassir for staying up late, working on his English essay, and taking care of his eight-month-old daughter?

Yassir splashed water on his face while his father observed, his arms folded at the doorway. The bags under his eyes were so tender, they looked wet.

"Did you make niyyah?"

Yassir ignored him, wetting his right arm twice and left arm once, just as Hajji Abu Abdalla had taught them when they were little.

"Why is your face still like that?" Baba asked, pointing to his left eye, which was still partially swollen shut thanks to Khaled, who was probably on a plane right now. Or maybe he had arrived. Yassir didn't really know what the journey to Iraq was like.

He shook his head, wiping the top of his head and feet. "Yasmin dropped my phone on my face."

Baba shook his head at the obvious lie before he stepped back into the hallway. Why would he even care after already leaving a bruise on Yassir's face, anyway? Yassir followed him into the chilly living room, lit by a single bulb attached to a ceiling fan, on the brink of burning out. Yassir unfurled the auburn-orange sajadah, placed his wet hands over his ears, and loudly whispered the adhan and iqamah.

"Salat is in five more minutes."

Yassir paused. "Then why did you wake me up?"

"You should be awake for Allah before you pray your thanks."

Yassir stepped off the prayer rug and plonked down on the couch.

"Don't sleep."

Yassir closed his eyes. He thought about checking on Yasmin, but he was so damn tired he didn't think he could even get up after lying down.

When the five minutes were up, he heard his father recite the adhan.

Sluggishly, Yassir got up and followed along. His parents had always preached about salat curing everything. Headaches. Poverty. Greed. Depression. Yassir didn't buy it then, and he didn't buy it now. Yassir couldn't quite pinpoint when he'd stopped believing in God, but he'd never believed all the stories, never felt moved by the prayers the way Khaled did. The way everyone else did.

After the two rakkats were finished, Baba handed him a bright turquoise sibhah. It was time to recite thanks to God one hundred times. There wasn't supposed to be compulsion in Islam, yet Baba had no problem trying to shove it down his throat any chance he could in hopes Yassir would magically become the perfect Muslim.

"Astugfirallah."

Yassir's eyes jolted open—he had fallen asleep with his legs still folded, head bobbed to the side, fingers still nibbling the edge of the sibhah beads.

"Finish your istikharahs. Then go to bed," Baba commanded. "You have a long day ahead."

After school he would complete his first community service shift before closing at Hajji Majid's shop. His bones were tired enough that he could weep at the thought of it.

"*Subhanallah. Subhanallah. Subhanallah,*" Yassir whispered loudly enough to reassure his father the deed was done.

Subhanallah. Khaled would laugh if he could see him right now. *Mr. Al-Harami found God?*

Yassir's left eye stung as he thought of Khaled's broken voice screaming at him before he swung his fist. Yassir deserved it. He deserved more.

When he finished the istikharahs, he stepped back into the bedroom and crumpled near Yasmin, who was still sleeping soundly in her zip-up swaddle. He snuggled close to her, smelling the scent of her baby shampoo at the tips of her hair, but her skin felt warm again and a dread filled his stomach. He'd try to beg for an earlier doctor's appointment for her, just as soon as he woke up and the office opened.

If you don't change, you're going to lose Yasmin one day, too, Khaled's angry voice returned to him, *and I'm not going to be around to help you anymore.*

He'd get things right for once, without Khaled, as soon as he could get a little rest. But just as he closed his eyes, his alarm clock rudely went off, alerting him it was time to wake up for school.

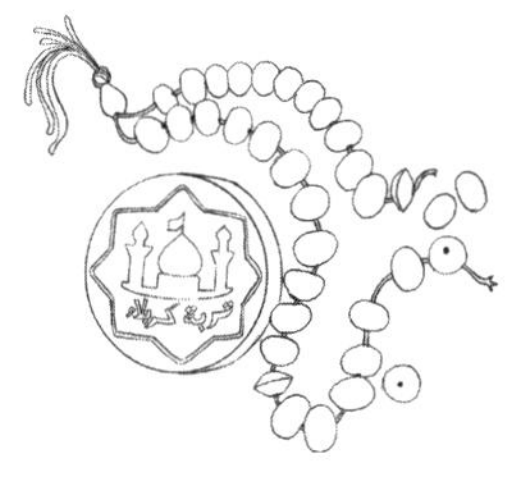

18

KHALED

TWENTY-THREE DAYS BEFORE

"Pray right here," Khalee Jafaar said, scooting a turbah to the center of the dark-green-and-gold sajadah as Khaled's uncles cupped their hands around their ears, commencing maghrib prayer.

Khaled stepped between his uncles, avoiding the snickering faces of his younger cousins behind him. Hassan and Ashraf had either become fond of him or enjoyed roasting him. Either way, Khaled offered them a smile.

He smiled through pinched cheeks and trays of bacha, although boiled lamb head—an Iraqi delicacy—was his least-favorite dish by a long shot. He smiled through questions about America and school because he didn't want to admit that he felt hated in the country that his relatives admired. He smiled because he did not want to disappoint a family that shared the small bump in his nose and the deep shadow of purple beneath his eyes.

After seeing their eager, hopeful faces, he understood why Baba had asked him to lie about Mama when they asked how she was doing. So far, Mama's side of the family was nothing like her at all. They were loud, they laughed between bites of meals and games of mahabis. They loved life.

And even those who were not alive were still included.

Khaled's eyes caught the photo above the mantel, the one that watched them all as they prayed. Faizal. Mama's youngest brother. He wore a fitted beige suit; a thin mustache peeked over his pale white skin; a bright cerulean sky was painted above his head. Khala Rahma told Khaled that his nose and cheekbones resembled his late uncle's.

He didn't know how Faizal had died, but the way most of the family hadn't said his name much, he knew better than to ask.

"Allahu akbar," Khalee Jafaar's voice quietly echoed, and Khaled prostrated, the regret in his stomach burning with each rakkat.

Right now, his debate team was probably packing their bags to head to Pennsylvania. Trying on the new team jackets that had arrived as soon as he left. Practicing their last rounds together. Earning scholarship money that should've been his.

"Allahu akbar."

He descended into sujud.

Despite being surrounded by his family, in a country he'd always dreamt of visiting, all he could feel was regret for what he was missing back at home. Perhaps Baba was right—by the time Arbaeen commenced and he visited Imam Hussein's shrine, he would be able to truly move forward.

When the prayer ended, his uncles shook his hands and ruffled his hair, and then they did what all Iraqi uncles did: pushed their dishdashas to midthigh so they could sit comfortably as they talked shit about the Iraqi government, sifting multicolored sibhah beads between their fingers.

Just a handful of years ago, none of them could dare to speak against the government, unless they wanted to be taken away, tortured, and never seen again. When he looked around the room, watching the smiles of his older relatives, he wondered how much they had endured all this time.

But his view was blocked as Hassan and Ashraf sat in front of him. His cousins sort of looked like Faizal, too. Khaled wondered if he resembled his father's side just as much as he resembled Mama's side. When he'd asked Khalee Jafaar if he would be able to see Baba's family a few days ago, Khalee Jafaar had simply given him a nervous smile. Even here, Khaled still had to endure the secrets hidden in his family's expressions.

"So, America," Ashraf said, tapping Khaled's knee. "Think you can get me there?"

"Your mom won't let you go." Hassan snickered without looking up from the phone. "She says you're too stupid for the schools there."

"Ihmar," Ashraf said, punching their younger cousin. "Have some respect for your elders."

Ashraf and Hassan quarreled every minute they were together—Ashraf was apparently the reason Hassan had an injured foot. But the two didn't seem to take each other's words harshly or hold grudges, just like Khaled and Yassir when they were younger.

"If you want to know your future, go ask Bibi Amal for a reading," Hassan scoffed, his eyes meeting Khaled's. "A year ago, he asked her if he'd go to America, and she also told him he was too stupid—"

Ashraf gave their cousin a light slap on the back of the head and stood up. "Let's go. Before she falls asleep."

Khaled followed his cousins to the next room over, where the women lounged around watching a Turkish soap opera between sips of amber chai. Kawther sniffled into a wad of tissues as she stared at her feet. She'd fallen ill as soon as they landed and didn't look any better than she had this morning. Khaled was grateful for the time to stall before traveling to see Ayah.

Back in America, with his veins still pulsing after punching Yassir, he'd packed with urgency to see her, not caring about anything he left behind. But now that he was closer than he had been the past year and a half, he no longer felt ready to face her, or to face the truth.

Ashraf sat down in front of Bibi Amal. She had dark sunspots painted around her face and cataracts in her left eye. Despite that, she found Ashraf's face and smacked it lightly.

"Respect yourself," she spat.

"Bibi." Ashraf kissed her hands. "Can you do a reading?"

"You're not going to America," the old woman said. "I told you to do better in your studies!"

Hassan cackled and Ashraf scoffed. "Fine. I'll just live with you forever. I can't have you getting in trouble alone, can I?" He smiled mischievously at her, and she gave him a playful slap on his left cheek, grinning. "What about a reading for our American cousins?"

"No, Ashraf," Khala Rahma said, pulling her son back. "Your bibi is tired."

Bibi Amal shook her head, her eyes now descending on Khaled. "Bring me my trinkets, Samira."

"But—" Khala Samira began, standing at the doorway, carrying a tray of fresh tea.

"Bring them," Bibi Amal sternly repeated as she ran her fingers through Ashraf's hair.

The boy lay back into his great-aunt's arms, and a pang of jealousy swept through Khaled's body. He had not gotten to know either of his grandmothers before they passed away. He had spent his entire life believing that his life was exponentially better than those here, but watching his family interact awakened an emptiness in his chest that he knew could never be filled. He wanted his great-aunt to hold him, too, and play with his hair.

Samira returned with a small black sack. Bibi Amal observed what was inside, clicking her tongue in satisfaction before she juddered the bag violently.

Khaled frowned uneasily. Baba always reminded him that there was Allah's will and free will, and no in-between. Coffee grounds and random objects could not determine fate. He'd heard his father lecture his mother each time she left to get her fortune told by someone from the community, including weeks before Ayah's engagement, which, according to his sister, was a deciding factor in her marrying Haydar.

The woman saw it so clearly—the move to Ohio and everything. Crazy, right? She even knew the first letter of his first name, though we hadn't told her. She says I'll be happy.

He'd been sick of seeing Ayah cry at school. Yet he did not want her to be happy. Not if it meant she would leave him. Not if it meant leaving them all for some guy she barely knew, too, even if Mama explained that it was perfectly normal to marry at that age. Mama was only seventeen herself when she married Baba, but it pained Khaled that she'd allowed Ayah to follow in her footsteps. Especially since Kawther had clearly proved it was the wrong choice. He knew Mama regretted letting Ayah go through with it—but it was far too late to change the past.

"You're first?" Bibi asked him, and Khaled stared blankly. He knew a few Iraqis back home who partook in the activity. Others rejected it and used only the Quran to help guide their decisions. He hadn't seen anyone try to tell their future with trinkets before. He wondered if it would be a betrayal of Baba if he did this. If it would be a betrayal of himself. Ashraf nudged him, and everyone else looked at him expectantly.

Khaled had come to Iraq to experience it as it was, in hopes it would change him, make him better. But more than anything, he wanted to understand Ayah better. So he nodded and the reading began.

"Allahumma salli 'ala Muhammad wa Aali Muhammad," his great-aunt whispered over and over until she spilled the trinkets from the black bag and onto the carpet. They looked like junk. Multicolored plastic gems. The illustrated face of Imam Ali on a broken key chain. A pink rubber heart. A toy spider. A dark blue stone shaped into the evil eye. Every trinket in the pouch was starkly different from the last. Part of him wanted to scoff, but the other part imagined his great-aunt picking out each item over the years, gently placing them in the bag like precious treasure.

"Do you see this?" Bibi Amal asked, pointing to a small heart-shaped indigo stone.

Khaled nodded. "Yes."

"This is you." She held up a large rusted key before setting it down where it had landed on the carpet. "And see this? This is your pathway. You are close to unlocking what you want in life. But there is something—someone—who always gets in your way."

Delpy. Wells. Superintendent Marks. Miles. Brooks. The list went on.

"I see a boy. Tall. Your age. He is young, but he holds a baby."

Khaled stilled.

"It seems you're holding each other back. Yet you worry about him, even if you try not to. Don't worry, he'll be okay. He will have a lot of pain in his life, but you will be there, by his side."

Khaled swallowed, hoping it wouldn't be true. Only once since coming here had he opened the location tracker, watching the little blue dot until it returned home. He promised himself he wouldn't do that anymore. He hoped that when he arrived back home, he'd have let it go—the desire to drink, the desire to be Yassir's friend, the desire to keep fighting for things and people that didn't even love him back.

Bibi continued to shuffle and picked up what looked to be a small evil eye. "You're a troublemaker, aren't you?"

Khaled swallowed, briefly making eye contact with Kawther as Khala Rahma laughed off the accusation.

"No, no, Bibi, he's a good boy. His mother always says he's reading Quran and even leading prayers at the masjid. Better than Ashraf." She clicked her tongue and Ashraf rolled his eyes.

Bibi tapped his head with her knuckles. "Well, if that's true, why have you upset your mother? I see her crying about you for days."

"How do you know it's my mother?" he asked quietly. It was rare that Mama acknowledged him anymore, especially since he'd been caught drinking. Her crying over him would feel like an honor.

"Because this is her trinket," Bibi Amal said, pointing to the plastic spider. "Because I know my niece. I've seen her in every family member's fortune."

"Why? Is she special?" Kawther spoke up, her voice thick.

"When someone ruins a family, they stain an entire generation. Allah yarham Faizal. I knew the same thing that happened to my sister would happen to your mother."

Faizal? His mother . . . a stain? Khaled's eyes caught Ashraf's, but he looked away, face flushed.

"Bibi," Khala Rahma warned, voice wavering. "Not now. The kids have been through enough."

Bibi shook her head, gathering the trinkets and stuffing them back into the bag. "You." She pointed to Kawther. "Come closer, habiba."

Kawther hesitated a moment before she obeyed. Bibi shook the bag before spilling the trinkets onto the carpet.

"Bismillah al-Rahman al-Rahim," she whispered. She pointed to the plastic pink bubble key chain. "This is you. And see this?" She pointed to an empty spot on the carpet where the trinkets were scattered. "This is your path. It's open to whatever you desire. Whatever it is you choose, you will find blessings in it."

Khaled could see relief fill his sister's face, as if she found hope in their great-aunt's words.

"But I also see death. Lots of it. You are surrounded by it and people will remember your name for it."

"Guess she's going to be a serial killer," Khaled muttered to himself. Kawther cleared her throat nervously, explaining that she wanted to go into human rights law, and Bibi beamed with pride that there was a lawyer in the family. Khaled wondered if their family knew what Kawther had sacrificed to get her degree.

Bibi Amal continued, "There is someone who still owns your heart, but it's time you take it back. Trust your instincts, as they are always right the first time. Trust God, as I know you are a woman of faith. You see this key?"

Bibi Amal pointed to a looped gold chain that was now attached to the heart-shaped indigo stone.

"People will try, but no one will unlock your heart. *You* are meant to unlock it. It is your choice to love and accept love. It will always be your choice. Don't forget that."

Kawther nodded, lifting the tissue away from her face. Something clouded her eyes. Khaled wondered who still owned his sister's heart. He wondered if it was the guy who had left Band-Aids on her face right before she ran off eight years ago. The man she wouldn't speak of.

Khaled had asked his parents if the scrapes on her chin were the reason she had left them, if someone had hurt her. Mama had simply told him not to bring it up again. He didn't. And then it became normal to stop bringing Kawther up, too.

Ayah always reminded him that Kawther was selfish. That if she really cared, she would be honest and not leave them. But whatever had happened to her, why could she still not tell him the truth?

Bibi clicked her tongue, sighing. "Have you visited your little sister yet?"

The room grew dead silent. Nausea rose in Khaled's throat.

"N-no," Kawther stammered, her eyes catching Khaled's. He tore his gaze away. "I haven't been well—"

"Go visit her. She's right by Imam Ali's shrine. You could walk there from Jafaar's house if you wanted. I saw her husband just last month. He's a kind man, don't you think?"

Khaled swallowed, thinking of the unanswered calls from his brother-in-law the past several months. He didn't like to think about Haydar. Kawther hung her head. She'd never met the man who took their sister away.

"Bibi, I think that's enough," Khala Rahma said. Bibi simply shrugged and finally packed her things. The room resumed its affairs from before the reading started, chai and laughter and a soap opera.

Ashraf tugged Khaled's sleeve. "Hey, follow me," he said, pointing to the stream of smoke moving from the hallway to the outside courtyard. The uncles were outside smoking now. Ashraf nodded to Kawther, too.

"Where are you taking your cousins?" Khala Rahma asked accusingly, pushing a steaming cup of chai toward Khaled, who stood and politely rejected it.

"I want them to teach me about how I can immigrate to America!" Ashraf smirked at his mother. "I don't want you to give my plans evil eye, Mama. Hassan, don't follow us, this is talk for those fifteen and up."

With the roll of Hassan's eyes, they followed Ashraf back into the empty prayer room, each settling on a cushion.

"I'm sorry," Ashraf said. "I didn't mean for Bibi to say those things about your mother." He shook his head. "I didn't imagine she'd say those words in front of you both."

"Can you tell us what she meant?" Kawther stared at her hands quietly, a tissue between her fists. "I want to know."

Ashraf's eyes moved to a photo on the wall. Khaled recognized Faizal's face. "Do you know how he died? He became a shahid in 1991."

Shahid. A martyr.

"How did he become a shahid?" Khaled asked, thinking of the photos that lined the streets of Najaf, martyred boys and men who were killed trying to protect the country from being taken over by ISIS. It wasn't uncommon for an Iraqi household to have at least one shahid in their direct family line.

"The uprising," Ashraf said quietly, eyes darting toward the door. Almost every Iraqi uncle he knew growing up, including Sayed Rahman, had been part of the revolution against Saddam Hussein. President George H. W. Bush's government had dropped leaflets from the sky, claiming they would support the revolutionaries like his father, like Faizal, if they fought back against Saddam. They'd lied.

Ashraf continued. "Your father and Faizal were best friends." This surprised Khaled. In all of Baba's eccentric stories of the past, he had never once mentioned Faizal's name. "Like most young men at the time, they knew how to shoot a gun after being forced to fight in the Gulf War. People in the neighborhood say your father shot a few of Saddam's men near Imam Ali's shrine. I don't know if it's true, but after the Americans went back on their word, Saddam regained control with their help. Saddam's government killed anyone who stood in their way. Women. Children. They did not want prisoners, they wanted corpses. And the military put a bounty on your father. When your father heard, he got scared. He took your mother and ran to the border. My father went to find them and help them hide, but they had disappeared. Faizal had gone searching, too, but he was kidnapped."

A heavy silence filled the room as Ashraf paused, eyes still glued to the door.

"Your parents escaped in a cargo van to Saudi Arabia with the other refugees fleeing that day. Meanwhile, Faizal was beaten by the military before the police shot him seven times in the back."

Khaled's entire body went cold. It was the same chill he'd gotten when hearing about his family's homeland over the years. Heinous crimes committed by the Iraqi government and by the US military. The mass disappearances and graves. The unlivable conditions in the Rafha camp. The shooting of Iraqi civilians by US Blackwater contractors. The Haditha massacre, when it happened again, this time in people's homes. The bombing of four hundred Iraqi civilians in the Amiriya shelter in 1991.

Ashraf's voice was merely a whisper now. "No one will say it, but Bibi, Allah yarhamha, our mothers' mother, blamed your parents for Faizal's death. Our uncle was just a kid, only sixteen. Your parents didn't know he had died until months after they left. Your mother was pregnant with your older brother, Abdalla. They had limited contact with your mother, but they didn't want to upset her while she was pregnant. I guess it wouldn't have mattered."

Abdalla, Khaled's elder brother, was alive for less than twenty-four hours before his heart stopped. All of Khaled's life, he had wondered why something lay irreparably broken in his mother's eyes. He looked for answers in the archived reports. He looked for answers in Baba's stories. But the answer had always been here, in his uncle's house.

"It wasn't their fault," Kawther finally whispered. "They didn't know."

Khaled stared at his sister, wondering if her words were true. If Mama and Baba had never fled, perhaps none of them would even be alive, but maybe Faizal would be.

"I'm not saying it is their fault, I'm just saying, they have not been forgiven," Ashraf said. "Your mother is still part of the family, of course, but your father has never visited since he left. Perhaps he feels too . . ."

Khaled's eyes returned to Faizal's photo. Smiling. Flowers near his eyes. He couldn't imagine a boy who looked so alive in the photo being filled with seven bullets.

"Guilty," Ashraf finally said. A familiar tremor seized Khaled's arm. All this time, Baba wanted Khaled to face his mistakes, and yet Baba couldn't do it himself?

Shame and running away seemed to be inherited traits in his bloodline. Even here, his family was broken, and it was always one of their own breaking them apart.

"Hey," Kawther said, tapping at Khaled's arm. "You're shaking."

He shrugged her off and realized that Ashraf was no longer in the room. Outside the hallway, all the lights had dimmed. Time had passed without him knowing, and he thought for a moment that he might be like Mama, too.

"We've been here a long time. I'm not sure if you heard, but Ashraf apologized for telling us. He's really sorry," Kawther whispered. After a few moments of silence passed, she spoke again. "Bibi is right. We should visit Ayah soon. Whenever you're ready. I'm sorry we haven't gone yet. I'm starting to feel better—"

"We're about to start the walk for Arbaeen," he said, regretting his words when he realized he'd accidentally spoken them aloud.

"It's okay if you're not ready to face her . . . it's okay if you're scared, Khaled. I am, too."

He shook his head, standing up and leaving the room. She followed him into his aunt and uncle's bedroom, which had been cleared out to make room for them. He dropped onto the floor mattress several inches away from Kawther's.

That night, for the first time since he was nine years old, Khaled dreamt of being hunted.

19

YASSIR

TWENTY-ONE DAYS BEFORE

"You're ten minutes late, Michael," Greg, the community coordinator, who couldn't be older than his brother, Ali, scolded with hands on hips. "Again."

My baby was having a crying fit before I left.

"There was traffic," Yassir said instead.

"You must be fancy, Mike, getting a cab to drive you around," Arnold, his fellow community serviceman, said. Last week, he'd taken a sip of Mrs. Gratton's whiskey when she wasn't looking. "You rich or something?"

"We don't like to keep clients waiting," Greg continued, pointing to his pickup truck full of household products, the kind they had to use to get the four-year-old coffee stains off an old woman's kitchen counters last week. Dead cockroaches had been fossilized into the sticky granite countertops. "Remember, I sign off on your hours."

Arnold rolled his eyes. "Well, can you add five minutes to my hours? I was here early."

"I would if you had helped me load the boxes," Greg scoffed as Yassir and Arnold slid into the passenger seat. Arnold's T-shirt was soaked with the scent of cigarettes, but Greg didn't say anything about it.

"Where are we going this time?" Arnold asked.

"Another apartment. Guess a renter needs help moving out. Resettlement agency called this morning. Their caseworkers are booked to the brim."

"If there are maggots in the kitchen pantry again, I'm out," Arnold said.

Yassir shivered at the memory. Arnold had opened a cabinet and immediately gagged, which made Yassir gag, and Greg had to hold a mask to his face as he tried to reassure the woman that her infestation wasn't that bad and that they were just being dramatic teenagers.

Out of all the organizations Yassir could have chosen to do his community service hours with, he was starting to realize VolunteerCorps was the wrong choice. Based on the website, he'd thought he'd be reading books to little kids, not having to clean up hoarders' houses or help strangers move. After today, eleven hours of community service would be complete. Only eighty-nine left to go.

Greg parked in front of the apartment complex's entrance and Yassir blinked, twice for good measure. Although he had been young when they moved out, he'd have recognized the peachy paint anywhere. The white stone fences. The graffiti scrawled on stop signs between the speed bumps. He could spot the purple-and-silver playground nearby.

He and the Al-Hakim kids used to play cops and robbers, house (Khaled always played the dog), and tag on the monkey bars until their mothers dragged them inside for dinner. Yassir could still remember the last time they all played together, before the Al-Hakims moved to a nice big house. He, Ayah, and Khaled clutched at the playground sand and stuffed handfuls into their pockets. A memento.

Hajji Abu Abdalla had scooped Yassir up because he was skin and bones and he could easily do that back then, even with his bad back.

Sorry, Sayed, Yassir is our new son! He's living with us!

Yay! Ayah had shouted. *Finally, Yassir gets to live with us!*

In the distance, he could hear kids still kicking and screaming as they slid down the worn-down silver slide, the kind that had always burned their asses in the summer heat.

"Move it, Mike," Arnold said, rousing Yassir from his daze. "Don't you listen?"

"S-sorry," Yassir replied. "I used to live here."

"Wow, really?" Arnold looked up at the building. "This place is for low-income people. I thought you were rich?"

Yassir ignored the comment, grabbing the boxes from the bed of Greg's truck.

"So, who are these people?" Arnold asked. "Another old lady?"

Greg shook his head. "I think it's a bigger family. They just got to the US a few months ago. That's all I know. Rent is rising . . . Guess they couldn't keep up."

That was one way to say they got evicted.

"Really puts things into perspective, huh, boys?" Greg asked, sighing.

Arnold nodded. "I'm poor, too. Are you a trust fund baby, Greg?"

"Do I look like one?"

"Kinda," Yassir muttered. Greg did like sweater vests.

Arnold laughed, slapping Yassir's back, which made Yassir instantly regret saying anything.

"Let's go." Greg scowled. "I would like for us to finish before the sun goes down, got it?"

Yassir moved forward, but each step brought a flood of old memories. Scrawling chalk on the pavement and skipping over sidewalk cracks. Ali pushing him on the swings so high, Yassir thought he would disappear into the sky. He and Ayah making mud houses in the sandbox while Kawther and Fatima gossiped on a nearby bench.

In front of the apartment, four little kids were singing a broken nursery rhyme.

"Your parents inside?" Greg asked.

The kids stared at them blankly before one of the youngest ones slowly nodded. The door cracked open, revealing a pregnant woman and a man in a wheelchair, presumably their parents. The mother had a dark purple hijab wrapped around her face, a box full of dishes in her arms. The father held a garbage bag filled with clothes.

"Hi, we're with VolunteerCorps," Greg said, flashing his badge. "We're here to help you move out. Okay?"

The mother stared at them. The father looked at them curiously, then pointed at Yassir. He spoke in a language Yassir didn't understand.

"You speak Arab, Mike?" Arnold asked, eyes wide.

"No. And that wasn't Arab*ic*," Yassir said, correcting him.

"How can you tell if you don't speak Arab?" Arnold asked.

"I just know," Yassir said, giving a sympathetic shrug to the father.

Greg began speaking to them slowly, trying to translate words from his cell phone. "Oh, they're from Afghanistan." Which meant they were probably speaking Dari or Pashto.

"Oh, shit," Arnold said. "That's rough."

"There's kids here," Yassir muttered. "Watch your language."

Yassir had become more aware of the words he'd used around Yasmin. He had always told Khaled to be careful with his words, but Khaled never listened. Yassir just didn't want his daughter's first words to be *ya ihmar*.

Greg listened to his phone translating again. "They said their caseworker is coming in an hour to pick them up and take them to their new place. Earlier, I was told they need their deposit back, so make sure you wipe everything down, boys."

"Everything looks pristine to me," Arnold said, shrugging as he gave one little boy a high five. "Good work, team!"

"We still have to double-wipe and help them move the heavy stuff," Greg said.

They got to work, starting with the kitchen, pulling out dishes from the higher shelves and placing them in boxes. Everything looked used.

Mismatched. Donated. When they first moved to America, Yassir's parents had to live this way, too. A few of those old dishes still lingered in Mama's kitchen cabinets.

The pregnant mother came to his side, trying to pick up the dishes and set them in boxes, but Yassir politely shooed her away.

"It's okay, we got this."

She smiled at him and said, "Alhamdulillah," which made his cheeks warm. Her gratitude reminded him of his own mother.

They wiped down the clean kitchen counters and fridge. It wasn't so bad, but it felt demeaning. The mother and father had already worked so hard on it.

"So, Mike," Arnold said. "Was your apartment shaped this way when you lived here?"

Yassir looked around. Greg was outside, directing things, or whatever Greg did. He shook his head. "No, it had the opposite setup. Kitchen and living room were switched around."

"How long did you live here? I mean, maybe it's a good thing these people are getting forced out. This place is tiny as hell."

It had been cramped for them, too. Ali and Fatima had shared a room, and he would sleep between Mama and Baba, clinging to Baba's sleeve at night when he was cold.

Still, it was blissful.

Maybe that was why the family looked so defeated. They had just gotten to America, and they were already being moved elsewhere. Maybe the kids liked the monkey bars just as much as he had. Maybe they felt at peace when the crickets chirped at night and the faint glow of the city peeked from the greasy window.

Yassir shrugged at Arnold. He worried the universe was trying to fill Khaled's absence with an even chattier kid. Arnold kept talking.

"Can't believe these guys are from Afghanistan, like all the way from across the world? Don't you think it's crazy our generation watched a war break out on TV? Wild, huh?"

Not as wild as living through war.

It wasn't like he had lived through war himself. But Mama and Baba had. They'd survived several in Iraq and then watched another one on the TV in their living room. Yassir would catch glimpses of the rubbled buildings and the bloody bodies being pulled out of them, clips of mothers screaming on live television, smacking their heads in grief. Whenever Yassir thought about Iraq, grief was the only thing that came to mind. Grief from the wars, grief through commemorating Imam Hussein. It was so rare that he saw any happiness on the screen. When the Iraqi national soccer team had won the Asian Cup a few years ago, the celebrations lasted for months. It was so different from what he'd experienced before, he felt completely disconnected from it. When was the last time anyone was that happy?

He wondered if Khaled remembered that time. What Khaled was doing there now.

He wondered if Khaled had visited Ayah yet.

Yassir's stomach twisted at the thought.

"I mean, they have so many kids, though, kind of irresponsible, right?" Arnold said as he began mopping. "Like how do you make kids while living through war?"

Yassir tried not to roll his eyes.

When Mama and Baba arrived in the United States, they came with the Al-Hakims. Two young couples. Three small children between them. People must have looked at them and thought they were irresponsible, too.

No language. No money. Only each other.

That was what Khaled's dad used to say proudly, especially when Khaled and Yassir fought over something stupid. *Why do you two always fight? You only have each other.*

"Where are you from, Mike?" Arnold asked. "Those people seem to think you're not from here and you look a little more brown than Italian, you know what I mean?"

Yassir did not know what he meant.

"Are you also from Afghanistan? Is that why you look so uncomfortable? Man, my cousin got blown up there. He survived, though. But I'd never sign up for that military shit."

Yassir shook his head. "I'm not from there."

It was close enough that it didn't matter, though. If people knew someone who served in the military or had been killed there, they'd stare at him in blame. Iraq and Afghanistan were the same that way. Miles had beat up Khaled years ago for that very reason.

"Oh, good, I thought I was gonna offend you for a second." Arnold shook his head. "My uncle would be so pissed if he knew I was here, you know? I don't care, but he has a right to be resentful, don't you think?"

Yassir stopped wiping the countertops, annoyed. It wasn't like the family here had asked his cousin to go to Afghanistan and get blown up. He couldn't imagine what they'd had to endure to get here.

"My uncle is always ranting on Facebook about shit, saying Islam is like a disease—"

Yassir couldn't take it anymore.

"Mike!" Greg called him from the hallway. Oh, thank *God*. "Since you're taller, can you use the step stool and reach for a tin on the top shelf of the parents' closet? I called an interpreter, and the family left . . . uh precious stuff up there."

Passports. IDs. Paperwork. Savings.

Yassir's parents had a similar tin they locked away, too. Gratefully escaping Arnold, he strode toward the bedroom, where he found a little boy, one he hadn't seen earlier. This boy was taller than the others, his face was slightly more hollowed out, like the babyishness of his cheeks was beginning to mature.

He was attempting to grab the tin.

Yassir tapped his shoulder. "Hey, it's okay. I got it."

He reached the tin in one quick swoop before handing it to the father, who smiled at him in gratitude. They finished up, loading everything into a giant van and the bed of the truck. With just the cleaning supplies left, Arnold made one last round, mopping the kitchen floors.

"Hey, where is our handheld vacuum?" Greg asked.

"Oh, shit, I left it way up there." Arnold pointed to the shelves above the kitchen cabinets.

"Mike?" Greg asked.

Yassir was already on his way, grabbing the stool. The family was taking a last glimpse of their apartment as the kids ran around, laughing. Just like his last time here. Chasing Ayah and Khaled around the living room. Tears threatened Yassir's eyes.

This isn't your family. This isn't your apartment. You left long ago. Everyone is gone now.

Everyone leaves.

Yassir reached his arm to the vacuum's handle as a gasp echoed. He turned and found the little kids staring down at a big puddle of cleaner.

"Shit, Mike, didn't you close this?" Greg asked, lifting the spilled bottle.

"I swear I closed it," Yassir murmured so quietly no one could hear him.

"Oh my *God*, it instantly fried a hole in the carpet!"

The family crowded around the new hole in their carpet as the little boy's head hung low.

"There goes the deposit," Greg sighed, rolling his eyes.

"Damn," Arnold said. "All this hard work, too! I changed my mind. *This* is worse than that old lady last week. Greg, what kind of cheap cleaning shit burns a hole in the carpet?"

"Watch your language," Greg said, although he had just sworn less than a minute ago. "C'mon, Mike, just grab the vacuum and we'll go. No deposit is ever guaranteed anyway."

"Maybe we can talk to the apartment manager?" Yassir suggested. His eyes were stuck to the little boy, whose face was now stained with tears.

"Mike let's go, *please*," Greg said.

"Got it," Yassir said, finally grabbing the vacuum's handle. The father reached his hand out to his son, but instead of striking the boy, he pulled him close and rubbed his hair and hugged him.

Then he kissed his cheeks.

He forgave him.

The little boy wiped his face as the mom convinced all the kids to step out the door.

How could it be so fast? So easy? When was the last time Baba had forgiven him?

"C'mon, Mike!" Arnold said, smacking Yassir's back, making him lose his balance and crash to the floor.

20

KHALED

FIFTEEN DAYS BEFORE

Fifty kilometers awaited as the Arbaeen walk commenced.

Each step farther away from Ayah.

Yet each step closer to the shrine of Imam Hussein.

Once Khaled clutched the bars of the shrine window and asked for forgiveness and guidance, he would be brave enough to face her.

He could not see where the congested dirt roads started and where they ended. Between the city of Najaf and Karbala, each street was lined with endless stands of food; lamb shawarma, kabobs, falafel, bread, rice, marags, tea, and cups of fresh-squeezed green, yellow, and orange juices. Everything free.

Many Iraqis saved up money for months just to serve the pilgrims of Arbaeen who had come from all over the world. To feed them a meal big enough for a small army and offer them a bed to sleep on, a place to shower and rest. For the next few days, this was what his life would look like, sleeping in the houses of complete strangers.

"Please, my son, take this blessed food and may Allah grant you a righteous ziyarah," an old man told him, shoving a cup of hot boiled leblebi into his hands.

Each stand they passed was the same.

Please my love, eat.

Oh, pilgrim, may Allah bless you!

Eat, eat, you must all be so exhausted!

Khaled nibbled on a roll stuffed with barbecue lamb kabob, fried eggplant, potatoes, and Iraqi salad made of raw cucumber and tomato chunks, feeling love in each bite. He knew he came from a culture drenched in hospitality, but he couldn't quite find words for people who didn't have much but gave everything they had to each other anyway, all to honor a man who had stood up for justice.

Imam Hussein didn't just symbolize the survival of Islam itself—he inspired millions of others to stand up against their oppressors. Imam Hussein and his seventy-two companions, including women and children, had stood against an army of one thousand, refusing to submit to a tyrannical government, even if they faced death or imprisonment.

In the end, Imam Hussein was brutally executed. Beheaded. He had not even won the battle, but there was dignity in rejecting oppression. In being a martyr. In standing up to something higher than yourself, for the sake of your people, for the sake of good, and for the sake of God.

It was impossible not to see his own family's pain reflected in that history.

Khaled always tried to embody the actions of Imam Hussein, to speak out despite the risk, to honor his faith even when others doubted it, and to sacrifice for the sake of the truth. But he was not sure if fighting (and losing) against faculty at Chapman High counted.

He hadn't protected Ayah when he should've, or known her well enough to see the truth behind her pain. He had never questioned Kawther when she abandoned their family and had never done anything to stop Yassir from self-destructing. As much as he valued truth, he was still afraid of facing his own realities. When things got tough, he drank.

He was just like his parents, his sisters. He couldn't help but run away from his own shame. Yet here he was, walking among people who were embracing a painful past, and his family could still not bear theirs. He kept moving.

"Khaled!" Hassan panted as he caught up with him, Khalee Jafaar just a few steps behind. "You'll grow tired if you walk this fast. Why are you in a rush?"

The bottoms of Khaled's heels already burned. Did it look like he was running away from his sister as much as it felt like he was? The rest of the family caught up to them. Kawther offered him a soft smile, pushing up the top of her abaya as it kept falling from her head.

"Hold hands!" Khalee Jafaar shouted a few steps behind as the crowd multiplied. "Hassan, come hold on to Maha's."

Hassan dutifully pulled away to hold his younger sister's hand while Kawther trudged forward, offering her hand. It wasn't like Khaled hadn't held it as a kid, clasping his sister's hand at the playground or grocery store, looking to her for guidance, for all the answers. The answers to his homework, the answers to Baba's occasional sour moods or Mama's distance. The answer to why they were so different—why she wore hijab, and why they prayed on turbahs when other Muslims didn't—and why some people hated them for that. For the first part of his life, he had relied on her, trusted her, depended on her to be his guiding light.

No matter how badly he wanted to reach out to her, the fact that she had been the one to let him and Ayah go all those years ago—that was why he couldn't just take her hand now.

They continued forward, Kawther's arm brushing his, until the crowd began to thin as they headed toward the farmlands. Khalee Jafaar caught up to them, clasping a hand to each of their shoulders.

"So, now that we've spent a day walking, would you have thought this is the same Iraq your parents talk about?"

"I remember when Mama left the first time." Kawther spoke up as they trudged along. She sounded healthier today, her voice clearer. "Khaled and Ayah were too young to remember, but I kept crying at the airport, holding on to her jubbah, thinking the bombs they kept showing on TV would hurt her. Obviously, I know there isn't an active war anymore, but when I thought of Iraq I only thought about death." She quieted, glancing at Khalee Jafaar nervously.

Mama had left to visit their sick grandmother before it was too late to say goodbye. She'd arrived two days before their grandmother died. Before that, Mama had acted more like her extended family. She had been full of life, inviting friends over for izzemas, rewatching Disney movies with them despite not understanding more than a few English words, testing out new recipes for everyone—including the Al-Azzawis—but when she came back, she began to stare at the walls and hardly left her bed.

With the truth about Faizal revealed, Khaled understood now why his parents always went to Iraq separately, and without the children. When Baba went alone, he always complained to uncles at home that the Iraq he knew had changed too much. Even the parts he loved—picking golden dates from palm trees, swimming in the Euphrates River with the water buffalo, praying fajr in Imam Ali's shrine—the parts not full of pain and bad memories—had changed. Khaled always wondered how it would feel to return home and no longer recognize it.

Now he knew.

Khaled glanced over at Kawther, studying her tight expression. "But I see how much it is more than that," she added. "I felt like the Iraq I was given was only in tragedy, but I know it's just a component of who we are. We are also this."

She gestured to the crowds in front of them. During Saddam Hussein's reign, Shias were forbidden from gathering for religious observances. They were targeted and killed in masses for decades, just like Faizal and the other revolutionaries were. Khaled wished Faizal could see that his efforts to fight against a tyrant had been worth it. That now the walk for Arbaeen had become the largest pilgrimage in the world. He wished Faizal could be walking among them, too.

"Agreed." Khalee Jafaar smiled at Kawther warmly, lovingly pushing a hand through Khaled's hair, a gesture Khaled had gotten used to since he arrived. "What about you, habibi?"

"It's different." Khaled mustered up a reply. "Different than I thought it would be."

"Different good or different bad?"

Khaled turned to look at the next set of stalls that wrapped around the road. In America, his people were always painted as villains. But this was who they were. Golden milks and soft smiles and people who embraced pain and love. Crumbling concrete and shelled buildings left over from the military occupation. Zealous celebrators who cheered for the national soccer team for months after their win, making homemade soccer jerseys, like he'd done with Ali and Yassir. Grievers who had survived centuries of destruction, yet their laughter and joy still echoed.

"Good," Khaled finally said. "I wish people could see what I'm seeing right now. Kids at school would never believe this is Iraq. They only know it through violence—through Saddam, and the US military, and ISIS . . ." He paused, remembering the snark comments from his presentation. He didn't mean to, but he was implicitly agreeing with Kawther. "We're more than what people think we are back home. Baba always taught me that."

His head buzzed, this time with pride rather than alcohol.

"And how do you feel?" his uncle asked after a moment, his words discreet. From the arch of Kawther's brow, Khaled wondered if she understood what he meant. "Different good or different bad?"

"Different good," Khaled said, hoping whatever sobering effect Iraq had would stay with him, as his parents intended. "Inshallah."

“It’s okay if you don’t change so easily, Khaled,” Kawther said to him, switching to English. “You can’t expect this trip to magically change you. I’m sorry Mama and Baba are so harsh on you.”

What did she know about change? About pleasing their parents? No one’s actions toward him were harsher than her own. “You’re sorry?” Khaled scoffed, unable to hide the sudden anger in his voice. He saw Khalee Jafaar frown at his tone, although he did not understand the words. Khaled kept his voice low. “To who? To Ayah? To me? To them? Do you ever think about the fact that maybe none of us would be so miserable if it wasn’t for you? For all the secrets you still keep. You’re never there when I need you, only when it’s too late to matter.”

Kawther flinched at his words, as if he had struck her.

“I’m only here because of you.”

But as soon as he said it, he knew it wasn’t completely true.

It wasn’t like she was around when he took his first sip of alcohol. She hadn’t been there at all. Maybe if she had been there to stop him, they would not be walking this path, and their family would not have fallen apart.

Silence stuck between them as they trudged forward under the heavy sun. She did not say anything more.

He stayed a few steps behind his uncle and Hassan. The crowd squeezed around them. After a while, he saw Kawther fall back with Khala Samira and the girls. Though she was walking behind everyone else, every so often he would see her look over shoulder, like she was searching for someone who did not exist.

21

YASSIR

THIRTEEN DAYS BEFORE

"You currently have a D-minus," Mr. Porter said, locking his door. "I don't know if you'd be able to get that up to passing without the presentation you were supposed to complete with Khaled—"

"He left the country," Yassir said quickly.

"So, what are you asking for?" Mr. Porter asked. "Another extension?"

Yassir nodded, no longer nervous after approaching all his teachers about making up assignments due as far back as August.

"And Khaled?" Mr. Porter continued. "Is he going to present his slides virtually?"

Yassir shook his head. "Well, Khaled and I . . ."

He didn't know how to summarize the events of the last three weeks to his teacher. Yassir simply pointed at his face, at the left eye that was finally healing. The one Mr. Porter had stared at for the past few weeks each time Yassir walked in. If only Khaled had punched him after finishing the presentation, he'd have one less thing to worry about.

"We're not really on speaking terms," he finally said.

Mr. Porter blinked. Apparently, he wasn't subscribed to the gossip of Chapman High. "Was he the one that hit you before?" Even though he was referring to Baba's bruise, Yassir nodded, his rib cage burning with shame. Both injuries were Khaled's fault anyway.

"We fight all the time," Yassir said, which wasn't exactly a lie. "I don't think I can work with him anymore. Also, he got suspended and I don't even know when—"

Mr. Porter blew out an exasperated breath. "Don't worry, I won't have a student deal with another who abuses him. I didn't know Khaled was capable of such violence . . ." He broke off, making Yassir's insides scream with guilt.

Even when Khaled was gone, Yassir still hurt him.

"If you can present your half of the slides over lunch tomorrow, I'll give you a grade for the assignment."

"Thank you!" Yassir said, attempting a smile as he limped away.

When he got home from community service, Mama and Baba had just stared at him, puzzled. Another bruise on his face. A hurt ankle. Zero explanations. Arnold and Greg had diagnosed him with a sprained ankle, but Yassir hoped he could shake it off. At home, he attempted to ice it, but Yasmin kept trying to steal the bag and crawl away with it.

It would feel better soon. Eventually. Probably.

Now all he had to do was read a third of his physics textbook to know what the hell to present about tomorrow at lunch. He should probably check out the textbook from the library, since he had no idea where his own copy was.

"Mikey!" a familiar voice shouted behind him.

Yassir paused. He hadn't tried to avoid Alex, but he didn't want to explain what had happened between him and Khaled, which Alex had asked about every three seconds.

Alex stared at his ankle, wrapped haphazardly with Ace bandages. "You're falling apart, Mikey."

Yassir shrugged. "Trying not to."

"I'm honestly falling apart, too," Alex sighed. "My best friend punches my other best friend in the face, he won't tell me why. Is it something I did?"

That was a new record. Two seconds.

He slung an arm over Yassir's shoulder. Yassir shook his head. "Alex, absolutely no one would fight because of you."

"Tell that to my parents." Alex frowned, his eyes suddenly glassy. Shit. The divorce. Yassir had completely forgotten. "They keep telling me it's not my fault, but they literally only argue about me. Why do the people I love most keep splitting on me?"

Yassir bit his lip. "I'm sorry, Alex. This is just life. People . . . don't stay."

Yassir knew it was naïve to ever believe they would.

"Gosh, you're bleak," Alex sighed, pulling away. "Where you headed?"

"The library?"

"For what?"

"A passing physics grade."

Alex stared at his left foot. "I'll come with you. In case you topple over."

They squeezed through a small crowd gathering near the cafeteria entrance, students walking away from a table with a green camouflage shirt with CLASS OF 2019 embroidered on the sleeve.

"Well, I guess it's a good thing Khaled isn't here," Alex whispered in his ear. "First he gets kicked out, then he punches you. If he saw this table, he'd flip it."

Yassir stared at the men in uniforms. Every winter at Chapman High, the US Army sent recruiters to speak to students. While most of the students would prefer Harvard over the Army Reserve, some of the Chapman scholarship kids seriously considered it for the free college education. The kids who couldn't quite keep up with the Chapman academic standards who were not yet expelled—kids like him—were often singled out by recruiters. Yassir was sure if he checked the mailbox at home, he'd find a personalized invitation waiting for him.

"Oh, shit, is Miles actually signing up?" Alex gasped, lingering in the hallway. "Doesn't his family think one dead son is enough?"

A pen was in Miles's hands. Brooks was scratching his name on the sign-up sheet, smiling like the cat who got the cream.

"You boys interested in serving your country?" A tall man in uniform with a shiny pink bald head approached them. "The army offers a variety of career paths and excellent education opportunities for kids interested in all sorts of specialties. How does free college sound to you?"

"My dad's paying for my school," Alex said. "Or my mom. They keep fighting about it."

"Well, lucky duck," the bald man said, his blue eyes fixed on Yassir. "How about you, young man? I know this school is filled with talent. Even has the best ASVAB scores in the state."

Alex put an arm over Yassir's shoulder. "Oh, this guy got the highest score in the tenth grade. He got a giant gift basket. Best roasted peanuts in my life."

The bald man raised an eyebrow at Yassir. "That so? Well, that's extremely impressive. What are your post–high school plans?"

Get a job. Take care of Yasmin. Maybe get a degree one day. Move out. Survive.

Once upon a time, Principal Delpy had said he was a shoo-in for Harvard. With his current GPA, he probably couldn't even get into the local community college.

The bald man continued his spiel, undeterred by Yassir's uncomfortable silence. "You could get help with housing. Good health care. The army offers you security. The best years of your life."

Yassir needed all those things. But he also remembered the plumes of smoke from the Arabic satellite TV. The screaming women. Bloodied bodies. Khaled's Blackwater presentation. The brain that slid out of that little Iraqi boy's head after military contractors shot him. "N-no thanks."

"Just take the flyer and think about it. Call us anytime."

Unable to refuse, he took the flyer and turned around, nearly crashing into Brooks.

"Oh, *you're* joining the army?" Brooks laughed. "I don't get it. If you need to go hunt down terrorists, doesn't that mean you would just have to kill yourself?"

"Where's your cousin, anyway? Family drama?" Miles chimed in. "Did he run off to join ISIS like his sister last year?"

Yassir's fists clenched, crumpling the flyer. Khaled hadn't told anyone the truth about Ayah's leaving. *No one at Chapman deserves to know. They wouldn't understand*, he'd told Yassir last year at the start of the school year. *She hates that place.*

Ayah hated it, and Yassir had never done anything to make it better.

He was ashamed. Ashamed for every word he didn't say. Ashamed that he hadn't stood up for either of the Al-Hakims, nor himself. Ashamed that he hadn't corrected Arnold about the Afghan family. Ashamed that he still didn't know what to say when people spoke like this. Even if he didn't feel connected to his religion, he was sick of everyone acting like the God they worshipped was violent and wrong, and that *they* were violent and wrong, too. The language they spoke. The way they dressed. The way they worshipped.

If you don't stop being such a fucking coward, everyone in your life will leave you behind.

He was tired of feeling ashamed. Tired of being left behind.

"Fuck off," Alex said, grabbing Yassir's sleeve and protectively wrapping an arm over his shoulder as he guided him to the other side of the hallway.

"Yeah, fuck off," Yassir finally said, his voice only loud enough for his own ears to hear it.

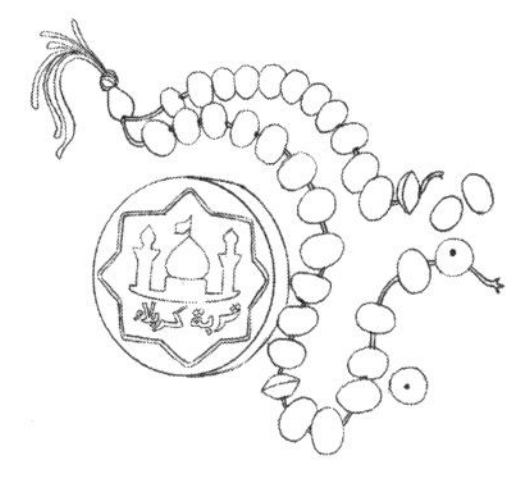

22

KHALED

NINE DAYS BEFORE

No longer a distant glittering star, Khaled could put his hand up to the sky and measure his palm against Imam Hussein's shrine. Enormous palm trees gleamed crimson under the molten sky, embracing the lustrous golden dome and its accompanying minarets. The heart of Karbala glowed before him. And something inside Khaled's stomach ached.

Right now, halfway across the world, his debate team had just finished the championship in first place, and Sabrina Parker, the team's vice president, had earned the scholarship.

He wished he still didn't care—that he wouldn't keep checking his phone for updates—that he could pay attention only to the wonder in front of him. Once he prayed in the shrine, he would promise himself to stop looking at the competition results. It would be a marker of the journey he'd made, and the mistakes he would not return to.

In Islam, anything—birth, marriage, death—could be moved on from after forty days. It only made sense to be here for Imam Hussein's

Arbaeen. Forty days since his death anniversary. Forty days since Khaled's last drink.

They finally reached the shrine after a five-day walk from Najaf to Karbala. They had spent their nights staying at the houses of different strangers, who would offer a hot shower or a wash, endless meals, and thin twin-sized cushions on the floor to sleep on.

But even inside, Khaled could not escape the faces of the dead. Last night, he had stared too long at a photo of a man hanging on a wall, and the little boy who lived there had explained that his father had been shot several times in the face by US soldiers while trying to retrieve medicine for the boy's youngest brother. Khaled shivered, thinking of how casually the boy had delivered the story.

"This way," Khalee Jafaar said, pushing toward the opposite direction from the shrine, where dimly lit tents surrounded the chaos of pilgrims still walking in the night. Maha was on his shoulders, Hiba in her mother's arms, and Hassan was soaked in sweat.

The city was illuminated in ruby and gold, the lights reflecting off the shrine's gilded dome. Latmiyats and drums echoed into the neighborhoods as pilgrims from Iran, Pakistan, Nigeria, India, and Bangladesh filled the roads, holding their own countries' flags with pride. It was amazing to see so many Shias from all over the world—many who could not openly commemorate this day in their own countries found solace here, too.

But the more they walked, the farther they pulled away from the stuffy crowd. Was there a shortcut around the back? The shrine shrank behind them as they walked.

"Why are we walking away?" Khaled finally asked. The shrine was so close, it felt like he was only a few steps away from touching the sacred floors that led to the entrance.

"It's impossible to get in." Khalee Jafaar shook his head. "There's millions of people here. We'd suffocate."

Khaled knew his uncle's words weren't an exaggeration, but he didn't want to accept them.

"When will it clear up?" he asked.

Hassan nearly snorted. "Probably not for another two weeks."

He and Kawther did not have another two weeks.

Had Baba known he wouldn't get a chance to see the shrine and sent him here anyway? Khaled felt his phone burning a hole in his pocket. Every vibration reminded him of what he had done, what he had lost by coming here. How could he possibly change when he wasn't even given a chance?

"Sorry, habibi," Khalee Jafaar added, as if it would soften the blow.

"But all of this . . . was for nothing?" Hiba asked her mother tiredly, taking the words right out of Khaled's mouth. Khaled couldn't believe he shared his frustrations with a six-year-old. "Why did we come, Mama?"

"For the journey, 'umri." Khala Samira smiled at her six-year-old, kissing her cheeks. "Every step you take is for Imam Hussein. For his family, too. Not a single inch you walked is wasted."

"Next time, inshallah." Kawther spoke, looking at Khaled with a soft, placating smile. "We'll come back."

Khaled stared at her. There was no we.

Hell, he didn't know when they would return. Threats still loomed. From what he'd heard from his family, the country was stabilizing, but ISIS still lingered. Just two years ago they had targeted a group of Shia pilgrims during the Arbaeen walk. Growing up, he'd known that some years were more dangerous than others. A year from now, where would they be?

He knew better by this time than to think anything was ever guaranteed.

Khaled sulked as they walked farther from the heart of Karbala.

He sat on a stoop outside a convenience store as more strangers handed him free food and drinks, his lap filling by the second. Everything before him was full, yet he still felt empty. He pulled out his phone, unable to keep himself from staring again at the Instagram announcement of debate results, itchy heat behind his eyes.

If Yassir had just spoken up, Khaled never would've written that letter to Mr. Marks and been sentenced to academic probation. If Yassir hadn't lied to him all this time, Khaled never would've punched him and been removed from the team. If Yassir hadn't driven Ayah away, Khaled never would've found himself tempted to drink in the first place. He would have visited Iraq with only love in his heart—and not with his parents' punishment. Their disappointment.

Khalee Jafaar found him and quietly took a seat beside him.

"I know you're upset," he said, watching the streets. "You have no idea how long I've waited to meet you, Khaled. But I can tell something inside you is broken. Kawther, too. She's told me about how much she regrets not being there for you."

Khaled frowned. He didn't care to hear about her regrets right now.

"What is the point of losing a family member when they're still with you?" Khalee Jafaar continued. "I used to beg your mother to come back home permanently, but I know she has a new life in America. I know she will never live here again as long as you are all still there, getting better opportunities. But she worries for you." His uncle stood up. "How many days since you last drank?"

Khaled swallowed. "Forty."

His uncle's eyes did not waver in judgment, even if Khaled's answer meant that he had consumed alcohol on one of the most sacred days of the year.

"I'm supposed to pray at the shrine now," Khaled continued, trying keep his voice level. "Shouldn't I at least try? I'm thin as a stick, Khalee. I can squeeze in."

Khalee Jafaar chuckled, ruffling his hair.

"I get each step is for Imam Hussein. But why—" Irritation caught in Khaled's throat. "I don't get why we came all this way. If we don't get a chance to do what we're meant to, what's the point?"

It was the question he'd asked himself for over a year. How could he still not have an answer?

His uncle kept a hand over his head, softly brushing his disheveled hair the way Baba did sometimes. Guilt pulsed in Khaled's stomach. "Was it Allah's will that brought you here, or did your parents force you? Who do you think wants you to change?"

Khaled swallowed. He did not know the true answer.

"You cannot hide from your past here. Iraq is all open wounds. During Arbaeen we embrace pain because it is a human emotion. We spend forty days remembering what happened after Imam Hussein's death, and we end the observance with more closure in our hearts, but it does not mean our grief is over. Remembrance is an honor, not a shame. Whether it is grown men wailing about the tragedy of Karbala, or losing their sons as martyrs, we must walk with dignity, guided by Allah's will. We might not be perfect in doing so. In fact, we are broken shards most of the time, too. But we must try. Doing so can lead us to our true purpose. Do you think you can try?"

Khaled shook his head. His purpose in life felt less clear than ever. He murmured, "Maybe I'm not as strong as the rest of you."

Maybe part of my faith is irreparably broken.

Khalee Jafaar shook his head. "It is not about strength, Khaled. It is about acceptance. I'm sorry you cannot see the shrine today. It is truly magnificent. But remember, Allah is open for you at any time. Not just today. Of course, it makes us feel closer when there is a special day or prayer. Not just in the shrine. You do not have to wait to ask for mercy. If you are ready to change, keep that intention in your heart. When we come back home to Najaf, I will take you to see Ayah. We'll visit Imam Ali's shrine right after you visit her, okay? Praying there will give you the peace you need to move forward, just like it would've here. Inshallah."

"What if—" Khaled was breathless, feeling a tremor in his arm. The weight of the past several days—hell, the past year—was crushing him.

"What if I'm not ready? So much has happened . . . Why does it feel like I'm the only one who can't face her?"

"These are things no one can be ready for, Khaled," Khalee Jafaar said softly. "But it's something we slowly get used to as time moves on. Allah does not burden a soul more than it can bear."

Khaled huffed, the familiar words ringing in his ears.

Khalee Jafaar continued with a smile. "It may take a long time to bear it. But I won't let you go alone, I promise. Okay? Will you see her if I'm there?"

Khaled felt like a little kid for the second time that night. He longed for his father, who would remind Khaled of his purpose, to be brave when facing Allah's will. Instead, his uncle, who had a million reasons to hate Baba, and maybe even Khaled himself, offered up his hand. Khaled clasped it and was pulled from the stoop, squeezing Khalee Jafaar's hand in answer.

23

YASSIR

SEVEN DAYS BEFORE

Abbas and Yousef's video games blared from the back seat, making Yassir's ears ring. While he loved seeing his nephews, they only reminded him that he'd had to abandon Yasmin for this appointment.

His sister had accompanied him back to the court to make his first payment for the fine. He was short twenty dollars after he'd quietly paid off the deposit fee for the refugee family with his first paycheck. But he hadn't told Fatima that. She just stared at him, puzzled, and helped him make up the missing amount.

"Yassir," Fatima said as she drove to the counseling office just a few blocks away. "To be clear, that was the last time I will ever come with you to court. Next time, you're on your own. Unless you finally decide to change Yasmin's legal name, that's the only time I'll come with you. Okay?"

"Okay," he agreed sheepishly. Changing Yasmin's legal name was on his ever-growing to-do list. He felt like he needed to earn it, though. He just didn't feel like he was allowed to take away her connection to her original guardian just yet.

"Call me when you're done," Fatima said as she parked in front of an aging black building. "Don't try to walk home. Understand?"

Yassir nodded, waving goodbye to his nephews before the silver minivan flashed away to a nearby Kids' Zone.

Alone, Yassir stepped into the cold brick building, winding through several hallways until the security officer showed him the correct office.

"Name and birth date?" the secretary asked, along with a dozen other questions. Yassir was momentarily transported back to the DNA testing center eight months ago. Except Khaled wasn't there to speak for him.

"Mich—" Yassir began, realizing his mistake. "I mean, Yassir. My name is Yassir Al-Azzawi."

The lady raised an eyebrow and stared at him. "Spell for me, please."

When he was done signing paperwork, ignoring the parent and guardian portion, he was directed to a hallway. The therapist was waiting for him behind the last door. He entered the room. Unlike the fancy sofas he always saw on TV, this office only had a small green couch and a leather La-Z-Boy.

"Get comfortable . . . Yass—"

"You can just call me Michael."

"Oh? Nice to meet you, Michael," the blond woman said, shaking his hand. "I'm Dr. Evers. I'll be your therapist during these five sessions. Okay?"

He nodded.

"Now, I know you're here because you've been ordered by the court, but I wanted to let you know that in conjunction with talking about your relationship with alcohol, we can discuss whatever else you need to in these forty-minute sessions, okay?"

Yassir shrugged.

"So, tell me a bit about yourself and how you came to be in my office today."

Yassir cleared his throat. "Um. I'm seventeen years old. I'm, uh, a senior at Chapman High—"

"Oh, the private school?" Dr. Evers interjected.

He nodded.

"You must be very smart."

"I used to be."

"What do you mean, 'used to be'?"

Yassir shifted uncomfortably in his chair. "I'm failing a lot. During freshman year, they were saying I was going to be valedictorian."

"Then what happened?"

He shrugged again. "Lots of things."

She stared at him with a soft smile. It was strange to hear how naturally these statements came out of his mouth. She seemed to like it. He tried to think of an answer she'd like to hear

"My girlfriend broke up with me."

It wasn't quite the truth. Ayah was not his girlfriend, but she also wasn't just a friend. It seemed like whenever high school kids in movies got broken up with, their actions were easily forgiven.

"So, is that why you started drinking?"

He didn't answer. "I'm not supposed to drink," he said instead. That was the truth.

"Of course, no one at your age—"

"I mean religiously. We're not even allowed to touch it, let alone drink it."

"How does it make you feel to break legal and religious rules?"

"Bad, I guess."

"Because you're not supposed to, or because you got caught?"

Because I'm forced to attend fajr prayers. Because drinking made me a dad. Because my own dad hates me. Because alcohol fucked up Khaled. Because I'm here.

"Because I got caught."

"Does anyone in your family drink?"

Yassir shook his head. He was the first and only sinner.

She scratched something into her notepad. "Sometimes we drink because it's fun. Because it's a social activity. Other times, we drink to self-medicate. I have a questionnaire to help identify the root of your drinking. You can just respond yes or no, okay?"

He nodded. This would be easier than talking.

"I drink because it makes me feel good around my friends," she began.

Alex's eyes lit up whenever Yassir said yes to his Jeep invitations. Yassir himself was indifferent.

"No."

"I drink because it makes me feel connected to my social group."

Since Yasmin, he'd stopped sneaking out to parties and socials and dances. Unless Cheese Puff Jeep therapy sessions with Alex and Khaled counted.

"No."

"I drink because it helps me numb my feelings."

He felt numb before he drank, he felt numb after he drank. What was the difference?

"No."

"Okay." Her blue eyes met his. "I have a few more questions."

"Okay."

"I drink because I had a relationship change."

Yassir tried not to roll his eyes. She already knew that.

"Yes."

"I drink because of domestic violence in my home."

He could still feel Baba's harsh slap on his cheek. Khaled's knuckles smashing against his face. The pain that still pulsed in his jaw whenever he smiled at Yasmin. Drinking was what had led him here, not the other way around.

"No."

"I drink because of the death of someone close to me."

Yassir went still. Silence filled the room.

". . . Michael?"

"Yes."

"Whose death?"

His lungs burned.

"Mother?"

"No."

"Father?"

His head was heavy again. It was always heavy. Why did Baba wake him up to pray for what he didn't believe in? So Allah could forgive him for his sins? Every morning he gave his body to God, and nothing changed. No matter what he did, Baba would never forgive him. Khaled would never forgive him. *Ayah* would never forgive him. And frankly, he'd never forgive himself.

"Is it your father, Michael?" Dr. Evers said.

"No," he replied, his voice hoarse.

The biggest lie he'd told himself was that he didn't care about her. He still wanted to have fun. He wanted to grow up on his own and not rush into anything like she had. There was so much responsibility in getting married—hadn't their own siblings tried it and failed?

Still, even now, as hard as he tried, he couldn't stop himself from calling her every night. From hoping she would come back to him one day. But if she were here, he knew she wouldn't recognize him. He had pushed her away, and in her absence, he had become a dad. A failing, flunking, fucked-up teen dad.

He always tried not to think about who Ayah had become, what had happened to her after she left him. But he wanted to be better. He wanted to stop being a *fucking coward*. He wanted to tell the truth, even if it tasted like poison in his mouth.

After a long silence, he whispered, "My girlfriend."

"I'm very sorry to hear that, Michael."

Yassir stared at the floor.

"How long ago was it?"

"Over a year ago," he murmured.

"Is that when the habit started?"

He nodded.

Dr. Evers moved closer, and he knew he'd made a mistake. "Tell me more."

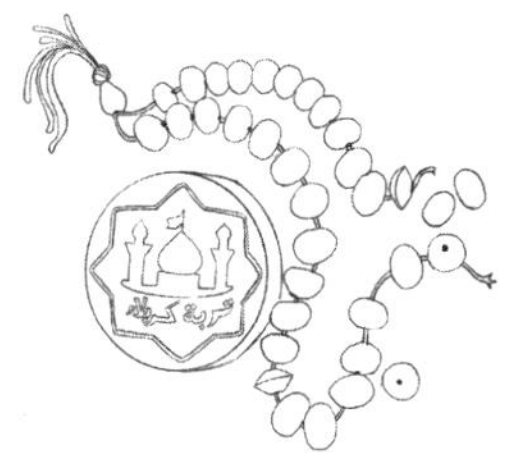

24

KHALED

SIX DAYS BEFORE

The billowy column of smog bit into the clotted clouds like a welt. It only felt natural that the purple sky over Wadi al-Salaam resembled a bruise.

Birds flocked around them, their squawks a song, as if they were practicing a ritual. Bibi Amal was right. From a short distance, the dome of Imam Ali's shrine gleaned bright under the rising sun. Although Khaled didn't have to walk across cities to reach this shrine, it had always felt so far away. So did Ayah.

Khaled felt his insides crumble.

His sister was just in Ohio. Still married. Ignoring him after he told her getting married at seventeen was a mistake. She was in Ohio being a new wife, doing whatever else she thought would make her happy. She was still in Ohio baking cinnamon rolls on Sundays. She was in Ohio, being loved.

Had she not been loved?

It had been one thing to watch his parents wail in the masjid, to feel the uncles kiss his cheeks softly and give their condolences. It was another to visit her grave.

I'm sorry, Khaled whispered with each dragging step as they entered the cemetery. Each step was a step on the dead. *I'm sorry*. Trash and empty pink bottles that were once filled with holy water to douse the gravestones lined the entrance pathway.

"Remember, there are unwanted things here," Khalee Jafaar whispered to him and Kawther as they continued forward. "Say bismillah and keep Allah in your heart."

Wadi al-Salaam was the biggest graveyard in the world. In the tenth grade, Khaled wrote a paper about it in his geography class. Ancient Mesopotamian kings were buried here, along with six million other bodies. Everyone in his family was buried here. When they were young, Baba used to proudly tell Khaled to send his body here when he died.

Why can't you stay near me, Baba? Khaled would ask, and Ayah would nod curiously.

Because on the Day of Judgment, the souls buried by Imam Ali's shrine will rise with him.

It took twenty minutes to make it to their family's plot. Pictures of men lined one side of the path, photos of the martyrs killed by ISIS lined the other, their gravestones in pristine, single-file lines. Quran echoed all around them, like smoke hanging in the air. Nearby, Khaled spotted other families paying their respects. There were flowers lining the path and bakhoor burning near the gravestones. The sound of wailing. From a short distance, he could spot several women grieving, their bodies on the ground. When Mama had come with Ayah's husband to bury her, he knew she had cried the same way.

Last year, Khaled could not bring himself to see his mother that way. Baba had stayed with him in America as she went on her own. He still hadn't forgiven himself for that.

"Read al-Fatiha, children," Khalee Jafaar instructed as Khaled stared at the gravestones in front of him. Mama's family.

Faizal, his grandmother, his grandfather, and a few other uncles' names he did not recognize. The gravestones were pearly white, each of their names looped and engraved in Arabic calligraphy.

Ayah.

He'd learned how to write her name in Arabic before he learned his own. It was easier. Alif. Ya. Ta Marbuta. He could recognize the letters. When his fingers traced over the Arabic, it was ice cold.

Why are you getting engaged? Without talking to me first?

Her expression had cut him. *I don't need your permission, Khaled. I'm not asking you to like Haydar, I'm just asking you to accept him. Don't be so shocked, nearly every Iraqi girl in our community is engaged to someone.*

What about Chapman? You're just going to drop out? What about your friends?

Ayah laughed coldly. *You think anyone cares about me there? Why do you think I want to leave?*

Was this what leaving had earned her? A grave in a land she never got to see while alive? She only lived as a bride for five months before her heart stopped. Just because it could. Aunties still called her 'arusa—the bride—at the memorial. She never got to grow up and live her full dreams. The kind that left smudges of paint around her fingertips, the unfinished designs still stuffed into her computer files. The college degree she'd started. She would always be known as a version of herself that Khaled didn't recognize or understand.

Sudden cardiac arrest. That was what the coroner in Ohio had told them. Hypertrophic cardiomyopathy could not be ruled out—a genetic disease. His parents still wondered if it was the same condition that had killed Abdalla all those years ago. Perhaps it wasn't the poor conditions of the camp, perhaps it was something inherited instead. Since Ayah, they'd all had testing done, and no one else shared the diagnosis.

He still wondered what could've triggered it. Was she stressed? Was this new transition to adulthood too much? Did her husband do this to her? How could he not have caught any symptoms if he slept beside her? Khaled would've noticed if his sister was sick. He would've noticed the signs.

But he hadn't known that his sister had longed for and loved Yassir. Why didn't they tell him? Why did they assume the worst of his reaction? Perhaps Khaled would've allowed it. If they really loved each other, he would've helped bring their families together to make it work, to mend Kawther's mistakes. Instead, his sister had left, and Yassir had let her go. Khaled had let her go.

Now she was here.

Khaled stood up and walked in the opposite direction. "Khaled," Khalee Jafaar said, attempting to catch his sleeve.

"Sorry, sorry," Khaled whispered to the dead as he stepped over their plots. "I'm so fucking sorry."

He could hear Kawther whisper the same thing. Half of her face was buried in the dirt, just like the grieving women.

You were the one who acted dead all this time to us, he had overheard Mama tell Kawther when she came home for the memorial. It was the cruelest thing he'd ever heard her say. *It should've been you.*

The next morning, Mama was locked away in her room and Kawther was gone again. For the first time since she'd left eight years ago, Khaled was beginning to understand why. It was not so easy to face your regrets after all.

"Khaled," Khalee Jafaar whispered. "Do you want to say goodbye one last time before we leave?"

He turned around. Kawther was still sobbing, telling Ayah she was sorry for not seeing her sooner, for not seeing her at all. Khaled swallowed his grief whole. He walked back to the gravestones.

He turned and faced Faizal.

He recited al-Fatiha out loud for his uncle.

Then he turned to Ayah's stone and braved a whispered Fatiha for her, too.

Slowly, Kawther wiped her face and stood, joining him in the recitation. Their voices shook, the words repeated when he couldn't finish them because of the tears clotting his throat. When they were done, Khalee Jafaar put an arm over each of their shoulders, holding them close. Khaled took one last glimpse of the cemetery city.

"This will make you feel better," Khalee Jafaar said as they walked to Imam Ali's shrine, wiping their tears. They passed the stalls and markets. They passed the people whose grief probably outweighed Khaled's by a long shot, who had lost more than he could even imagine. He took in their smiles and tried to remind himself that he would try to bear it. Just like they all did.

"Keep Allah in your heart. Keep Ayah in your heart with every step, too," Khalee Jafaar explained to them. "Kawther, are you sure you're all right walking in alone? I should've brought your aunt today to be here with you."

Kawther wiped her face, her voice hoarse. "I'll be okay on my own. Promise."

She was probably used to it by now. Being alone. Khaled's heart panged as she offered a weak smile and walked away.

Khalee Jafaar lightly wrapped an arm around Khaled's as they stepped toward the shrine.

Khaled padded barefoot onto the shiny white marble tile to drink in the view, his mouth gaping at the sight. Glass chandeliers glistened above him, dripping light in every direction. Diamonds lined the walls from the floor to the ceiling domes, gold filling the crevices. With bombs and dust and movies depicting Iraq as an endless barren war zone, it was hard to look at this and think it was the same country. Despite Baba's stories explaining the shrines and the golden sunsets kissing the Euphrates and Tigris Rivers, Khaled hadn't been able to imagine it until now, until he stood inside the shrine and felt the verve of its veins pulse beneath his feet.

Was this what heaven was? Clean and golden and shiny?

He hoped this was what Ayah's afterlife looked like. She deserved nothing less.

Khalee Jafaar handed him a green cloth to bless the silver-latticed window that separated them from Imam Ali's tomb. Khaled reached up through the crowd and wrapped his cloth, making wishes for each knot.

Ya Allah, please let Ayah forgive me.

Knot one.

Ya Allah, grant her the highest heavens.

Knot two.

Ya Allah, forgive my parents for giving her away so young. Forgive us all for failing her.

Knot three.

Ya, Allah, please keep me honest.

"Khaled." Khalee Jafaar pulled at his sleeve. "We have to go now. People are waiting their turn. Sorry, habibi."

Khaled was not the only mourner. He looked around him like he had at the cemetery and tried to remember what all these people had in common. How they, too, still showed up to pray for the family members they had left behind.

Khaled nodded, tying the fourth knot, the last unspoken prayer still in his mouth.

Grant me your mercy.

Then he turned to where his relatives were waiting for him, to return to a country, and a family, that he was sure did not love him back.

25

YASSIR

ELEVEN HOURS BEFORE

"I was hoping you wouldn't look so . . . surprised," Delpy said as she tapped her red fingernails against her chin. "All students and their parents were made aware that the deadline for scholarship renewal is at the end of each quarter. We've had several meetings about your academic standing this year, and there have hardly been any real improvements."

Yassir stared at the letter outlining the termination of his scholarship and the printed-out bill beside it.

One that easily cost more than what Baba made in a year.

He'd thought, when she cornered him, it was to give a statement about Khaled. It was a conversation he had successfully avoided despite her attempts to call him down to her office these past few weeks.

"Now, this isn't for *this* semester. That's already paid for. While the school board has a process in place to make students pay back the tuition when they lose their scholarship, I know that would be hard for your family."

"I still have like . . . two more days until the end of the quarter," he said as tears threatened the back of his throat. There were more assignments he could submit. Maybe it would raise his grades to passing. Maybe it would be enough to save him.

"No." Delpy shook her head. "There's no school Friday for grading. Last day is tomorrow."

He tried to keep his voice steady. "If I don't pass by tomorrow—do I have to pay next semester?"

"Unfortunately, yes," she sighed. "Listen, you have some time to appeal this decision if you feel that you're being treated unfairly. The appeal would go to a committee who would decide on whether or not to release your scholarship funds for the spring semester. I really tried to warn you, Michael."

Mr. Porter had finally input Yassir's grade for the presentation he'd missed, which moved his D- to a D. All the assignments he had turned in had barely made a dent in his grades. Despite everything he'd done, it still wasn't enough.

Each time I saw you with someone else, I thought I wasn't enough for you, but you weren't enough for me, Ayah had told him. *I can't keep waiting for you to change.*

"I informed your father," Delpy said. Yassir's stomach turned. "He said he won't be able to afford the tuition, so he will have to transfer you to a different school by the end of the semester. I'm sure that's not what you want, but he said he'd talk to you about your options. He said he'd wait for you in the pickup lane."

If Baba wasn't inside, it meant that a deep, full-throated scold awaited him. Delpy blew out a breath, staring at her computer where his current grades were displayed. "Again, I'm just trying to figure out what's happened with you. You never used to have this issue before. You were our top student."

She handed him the paperwork, including the scholarship appeal form.

List the extenuating circumstances that have caused hardships this semester. Please attach any related documentation.

His extenuating circumstances for fucking up?

Father of an eight-month-old baby who he still didn't know how to take care of.

Double DUI.

Failing Ayah.

Ayah being dead.

Ayah being dead.

Ayah being dead.

Except Delpy didn't know any of that, and it was best if she didn't. The scholarship termination would go into immediate effect if she found out about his criminal record.

"I'm still getting my grades up," Yassir said. "I swear. I have almost everything turned in. I'll ask about extra credit. I'll talk to all my teachers again. I just . . . I can't get kicked out."

I need this diploma from Chapman. I can't keep messing up for Yasmin. She's the one person I'm not willing to let down.

"If you insist you can turn this around within the next day—"

"I can." He stood up, and the burning pain in his ankle shot up his leg. He handed the scholarship termination paper over. "You won't need this, I swear."

She waved goodbye with a soft, pitying smile before he stepped out of the office.

"Mikey!" Alex called to him from across the hall. "Been looking for you all day. Where the hell have you been?"

"Can't talk, need to find Mrs. Britton and beg for extra credit again." Her English class was the easiest way to boost his GPA. Earlier that week she hadn't noticed when he turned in a recycled essay Khaled had written back in tenth grade. Yassir reasoned that if Khaled had still been his friend, he wouldn't have let him fail. He'd have been sitting in the library with Yassir, smacking the back of his head while begrudgingly pushing up his sleeves and revamping old assignments to ensure that Yassir passed. Just like he'd done the last two quarters. And Khaled wasn't there to object.

"I thought you worked after school on Wednesdays. Want me to give you a ride?"

Yassir blinked. Work. Right. *Yes.*

He was one paycheck away from paying off his court fine. Working at Hajji Majid's shop had turned out to be a blessing. Business was stagnant most days, and he was able to do his assignments there with minimal interruptions. It was a lot easier to write an essay without a baby drooling on the keyboard. Yassir crossed to the end of the hallway.

"Yeah." He nodded, his heart hammering at the thought of everything that still needed to be done. He didn't want to fail anymore. He wasn't supposed to fail anymore. He was supposed to do better. He'd had one more chance and he had still fucked it up. "I'll take you up on that. I'll meet you in the Jeep."

Yassir successfully got another extra-credit assignment from Mrs. Britton, due at midnight, then spoke to three other teachers before heading toward the student parking lot. In the distance, he spotted Baba's bright yellow cab waiting by the curb. He felt his phone buzzing, but he knew what awaited him in the cab. Yassir turned off his phone. His ribs ached as he got into Alex's car and ducked his head before they drove away.

NINE HOURS BEFORE

"Yassuri, you done?" Hajji Majid called from outside as Yassir finished restocking potato chips. Yassir eyed his homework pile. He'd be back for it. "Come help me with something, habibi."

Outside, Hajji Majid's rusty red truck was parked adjacent to the shop. Stacked inside the bed of the truck were bags of charcoal.

"Delivery truck accidentally dropped this off on my side. Can you unload these in the Hajji's shop? Laith is out sick. The Hajji has a bad back, you know, and so do I!"

Yassir knew that some uncles had been tortured back at the refugee camps after protesting the poor conditions. Hajji Abu Abdalla was one, so was Hajji Majid. As a toddler, Yassir used to jump on his father's back during prayer. He'd learned at an early age that he couldn't do the same with Khaled's dad.

Hajji Majid tossed Yassir the keys. "Here, drive the car to the end of the lot. Okay? Don't carry it all from here."

Legally, I'm not allowed to drive, Yassir wanted to say, but he didn't want to remind Hajji Majid of his indiscretions. He took the keys and nervously switched the ignition on, slowly driving over the rocky gravel between the lots closer to the Al-Hakims' shop. Luckily Hajji Majid was inside, although he probably heard the truck wailing in anguish.

Yassir walked to the bed of the truck and pulled out each shipment box, then stacked them neatly toward the back of the building. He imagined Khaled scolding him if the bags weren't perfectly aligned.

Yassir made his last round, and when he looked up, he found Hajji Abu Abdalla staring at him. His eyes were dim, not ignited like they were on Laylat Ashura or on the day Ayah left forever.

Stay away from my daughter. Do not touch her. Then the accusation. *Are you the reason she's trying to leave?*

"There's one more bag."

Yassir blinked and stared back at the Hajji, who pointed to the bed of the truck. Yassir turned around and grabbed the last bag of charcoal and slammed it down with the rest of them.

Yassir took a small step closer to Hajji Abu Abdalla.

Why did you take Ayah away from me?

Why did you have to take Khaled, too?

When their families had first stopped talking when Yassir was ten years old, he had asked the Hajji these exact questions. Baba had pulled him away and scolded him. *Do not speak to that man or Khaled unless I tell you to, understand? Give them your salaams and respect and nothing more.*

Even during Ayah's memorial at the masjid, Baba had instructed him not to say anything to the Al-Hakims. Although they knew they were not welcome, his family sat in the corner and paid their respects. Khaled's head was in his mother's lap. The Hajji had given Yassir one glimpse, his face broken with rage.

A car screeched into the parking lot, and Yassir saw the yellow cab at the corner of his eye.

He jumped into Hajji Majid's truck, and when he peeked at the rear-view mirror, Hajji Abu Abdalla was already gone. Yassir pulled into the shop parking lot, where the yellow cab was waiting for him.

Baba didn't have to speak.

Yassir could see the anger in his eyes.

Baba shook his head, blowing out a breath. "I've looked everywhere for you. Fatima was looking for you."

"I went to work—" Yassir said, stating the obvious.

"Ya Sayed! You're here!" Hajji Majid called from a distance. "Come! I'll make chai!"

Baba put a hand over his heart, squinting at the man with a smile, shaking his head before he turned back to Yassir. "Get your things. We're leaving."

"Work isn't over."

Baba sighed and Yassir held his ground.

"I'll get home by myself. Just go, Baba," Yassir muttered as he fished Hajji Majid's keys out of his pocket and walked back to the shop.

"Do you think I like following you around?" Baba called after him.

Yassir kept walking.

"Would it kill you to answer your phone?"

Yassir kept walking.

"You're failing school. They're kicking you out—"

"I'm fixing it!" Yassir shouted in a rush of frustration. No, he *roared*. "I'm fixing it! Don't worry about it."

Luckily, Hajji Majid was inside, already brewing the tea Yassir's father did not want. Yassir was just a few steps away from drowning his father out. It was too much. He couldn't take two fathers staring at him in disgust.

"Fixing it?" Baba's voice reverberated across the lot. "What have you fixed? You even missed Yasmin's appointment!"

Yassir stopped walking.

Yasmin?

Shit. Shit. Shit.

"The doctor's office could not get ahold of you, so Fatima took her. You want to be a student? Fine. Be a student, do your homework. You want to make money? Fine, go to work. But don't say you've fixed anything. You've fixed nothing in your life. If you keep doing this—" Baba breathed down his neck. "Then don't bother coming home."

Hajji Majid walked out, steam wafting from the foam cup, but Yassir's father was already gone.

26

YASSIR

TWO HOURS BEFORE

Yasmin was sleeping in the center of Mama and Baba's bed. According to Fatima's text, she had cried herself to sleep. She'd been given a flu shot. She had taken Tylenol. The doctor said she was fine. Yet she whimpered as she slept. She winced in pain, a rosy flush stroking her cheeks like a kindled fire. His rib cage burned with guilt.

"Yassir," Mama called from the hallway. "Habibi, shut off the light, let her sleep."

Yassir planted a soft kiss on his daughter's cheek before tearing himself away, finding Baba standing in the hallway. Baba hadn't spoken to him since the shop.

Baba was right, too. Yassir couldn't fix anything. Hadn't he told Ayah the same thing months ago, when she pulled away from him forever? Hadn't he told Khaled this back at the coffee shop before he left for Iraq?

Yassir couldn't even drive himself home, so Hajji Majid had given him a ride after his shift was over. The alarm clock in his bedroom blinked past midnight. He still had three essays left, a physics assignment, an economics paper, and four calculus quizzes. He'd promised all his teachers he'd have them done by the morning.

"Go to sleep," Baba whispered from the crack of his bedroom door. "I'm waking you up for salat."

Yassir didn't say anything. He stared at his homework and knew he wouldn't be sleeping. He picked up his phone and looked up Ayah's number.

This was her fault.

If he had never loved her . . . if she had never loved him back, he wouldn't be here. He wouldn't be Yasmin's dad. He would still be Yassir, the kid with the good grades and the parents who smiled brightly at his report card and the kid who drove his beat-up snow-white Toyota Camry down the street, pride and freedom mixing in his stomach.

He rested his hand on his chin and realized there were tears on the backs of his fingers.

It was so dumb to cry.

It was so dumb to be mad at a dead girl. It wasn't really her fault. But he wished she had never waved at him in the hallway during freshman year. He wished his heart had never twisted at the sight of her smile. No one else had made him feel that way. When he was with her, he felt like he was home. Whatever the hell home was.

He wiped his face, then glared at his homework.

Over the next several hours, Yassir wrote the rest of his essays. After he'd emailed them to his teachers, he opened his physics textbook. His eyes burned. His chest was tight. His ribs ached. For a few minutes, he just needed to breathe.

Light spilled into the dark hallway as he slowly opened his bedroom door. He grabbed his hoodie, phone, and wallet, and when he was sure he could still hear Baba's snores, he gently opened the garage door and walked into the frigid night air.

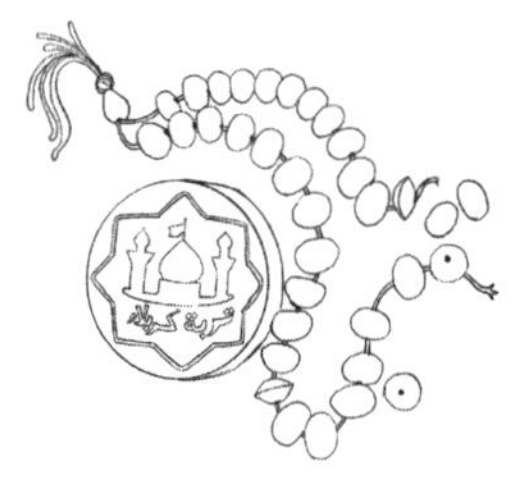

27

KHALED

ONE HOUR AND THIRTY MINUTES BEFORE

At the airport, they were not hugged by Mama, nor by Baba. After putting the suitcases in the trunk quietly, Kawther slid the van door open, and Khaled followed her in. As kids, he and Ayah had sometimes giggled so hard they'd set off Mama's migraines. Kawther would sit between them and ensure that they behaved. Khaled now sat all the way to the window, resting his head. The space beside him was empty.

"How are you, Mama?" Kawther asked after a few minutes of silence. She had purchased for their parents special sajadahs made of silk and chadars made of satin, bottles of mai Zamzam, and wrapped green cloth she had tied at Imam Ali's shrine. Even when she explained this, a tinge of excitement in her voice, their parents said nothing in reply.

Khaled watched his sister's face fall like it had when he yelled at her during the Arbaeen walk. But she did not cry now, like she did not cry then. There was a familiar defeat in her eyes. She stared at her phone, shifting in her seat.

His family did not speak about Ayah.

His family did not speak about Faizal or the family or Iraq, either. They drove in silence, into the thick of night, until they arrived home. Mama retired to her bedroom, telling them there were rice and marag still warm in the kitchen, and Kawther disappeared into her room, exhaustion rimming her eyes, disappointment still clear on her face.

"Khaled," Baba said before Khaled could escape. "Come outside."

A gust of cold wind rushed through the air. Winter growled closer and closer. But Khaled was still haunted by last summer. He watched the small billow of smoke enter the air before he turned to face his father's shadow in the backyard. Baba wasn't supposed to smoke. He'd tried to quit so many times, always threatening Khaled if he ever picked up the habit himself.

"Khaled." Baba whispered his name. "The trip . . . did you change? You won't act the way you did before, right?"

Despite the numb feeling he'd had since his tearful goodbye with his family in Iraq, a small festering anger reignited in his stomach.

Khaled had done what his parents had told him. Khaled completed the Arbaeen walk. He'd seen the beauty of Iraq, its scars too. He'd told Ayah he was sorry. Yet . . . his stomach was still in knots. The emptiness, the anger, the sadness, they felt like they would never go away. The true trial wasn't in Iraq. It was here. And he was scared to fail again.

"I don't know, Baba." Khaled spoke honestly.

"You don't know?" Baba asked, smoke leaking into the air. This was not the answer he wanted. "Are you choosing to not know? Or do you truly not want to change?"

Kawther was right. His parents expected him to magically shed his past and become a new person. How could he when even they were still haunted by their own pasts?

"I made a mistake, Baba," Khaled whispered. "I'm not going to drink again. I already told you that before I even boarded the plane, but you sent me anyway. To punish me? To make me feel miserable? I don't get it."

"Punishment? I did not send you to be punished. I sent you back to remember who you are." Baba grew breathless as he stared at the night sky. "No matter how many years we live here, it will never be our true home. So many people still don't want us here. Why should my son grow up in a world where he is rejected for who he is? And when he falls into the temptations of this land, he loses himself? I sent you there to save you from a worse path, habibi. I have seen it before."

"Then why do I still feel like I'm being punished?" Khaled said, feeling defeated, eyes to the faint scattered stars.

Baba's breath was heavy in the cold air. "If all you felt was punishment, Khaled, then I am afraid you have not learned anything at all."

No. I also learned that our family hates you. I learned that no matter what I do, I can't run from death. I learned that sometimes no matter how hard I try to cover them up, all my mistakes catch up to me anyway.

Does your mistake still haunt you? Is that why you think mine will haunt me forever, too?

When Khaled could not offer any more words without insulting his father further, Baba shook his head, blowing smoke for a few more minutes before crushing the cigarette beneath his slider. He retreated to the house, telling Khaled to eat before bed and lock the doors. But Khaled stayed watching the moonless sky, his breath clouding in the air, until the cold made his face burn.

THIRTY MINUTES BEFORE

Back in his bedroom, Khaled's life from only three weeks ago seemed unrecognizable. He still had a red ticket from that college party he and Yassir had attended with Alex last year—the one that earned Yassir his first DUI. Khaled's regional debate medal sat next to it in the drawer. He grabbed them in a fistful and threw them away.

He was due at school as soon as this weekend ended.

Maybe he shouldn't go back to Chapman, either. How could he face Yassir? Delpy and his teachers? The debate team? He'd only proved to everyone how violent he was by punching Yassir in the face.

At least he still had Alex. Kind of.

Alex had sent him endless messages while he was gone. Mostly updating him about Yassir.

Michael tried to get recruited by the army.

Michael twisted his ankle.

Michael might actually pass the semester!

I think you should apologize to Mikey, I know I shouldn't take sides but I don't think you should've clocked him.

Khaled placed his heavy head on the pillow. He hadn't slept much, worried that the man who sat next to Kawther on the plane would keep trying to "accidentally" touch her. He wanted to suggest switching seats, but he hadn't. Instead, he'd watched as sister sat uncomfortably and endured it.

Why did he want her to endure it? Hadn't they both been through enough?

Did you change?

The clock blinked at him. It was nearly two in the morning now.

He closed his eyes, annoyed by his conversation with Baba. Perhaps he was becoming just like Yassir. Regretful. Bitter. Lost. Insomniac.

Khaled wondered if Yassir had changed.

If he had done his homework, like he said he would. If he had complied with the court orders that Khaled had recklessly caused for him. He wondered how Yasmin was.

Although he promised himself not to look again, he found his fingers gliding over the phone, opening the location app, searching for the little blue dot.

When they were kids, Khaled was the one who would wander aimlessly. Not Yassir—not yet. Khaled was so curious, so ready to eat the world up, that one day, during the second night of Muharram, he walked away from Yassir and the small group of boys playing with globs of Play-Doh and Hot Wheels along the carpet while their mothers observed a latmiyat.

There was a small brown cat with a striped tail that purred at him on the bright sidewalk. Mama and Baba didn't let him have a cat, and Yassir was afraid of them, so he followed the cat down the small patch of raspberry bushes near the old masjid, along the sidewalk, where the soft grass still lined the streets. Then he stepped into the shadows. He followed and followed the cat, but when he looked back, the cat was gone, and so was the view of the masjid. Strangers who had stepped out of the house were staring at him, phones to their ears. Cars zoomed past the street. And he couldn't remember where he was going anymore.

When an older kid from the masjid spotted him down the street, he screamed his name, but by then the police had arrived. Khaled had stared at the Play-Doh carved in his fist while a police officer barked at Mama about child neglect.

You can't speak to my mother like that, Kawther, only twelve years old at the time, told the tall man.

She'd always loved to question authority, just like him. It earned them both distrust and exile, but at least she had a shiny degree to complement it.

When the officer left, Yassir sat in the parking lot and cried. So did Mama and Kawther. Then Khaled watched Khala Zainab publicly scold Fatima, who was supposed to be watching him and Yassir that afternoon.

"Don't blame her," Mama said, wiping her tears. "It's not Fatima's fault. It's Kawther's fault. She should be watching her brother."

"Khaled is my son, too," Khala Zainab said, livid, as Fatima hung her head in shame. "She needs to watch him like he's her own brother. Not just Yassir."

Fatima grabbed each of their hands and took them to the nearby gas station for Popsicles.

"Don't you two ever leave again," Fatima had told him, squeezing their hands so hard it finally got Yassir to stop crying. "You can't just leave without saying anything! Understand? Now choose your flavor."

That day, Khaled and Yassir licked their respective rocket pops as they each swore to God that neither of them would wander away again. But Yassir kept whimpering, even hours later. Ayah took tissues to his cheeks and attempted to wipe the invisible tears away.

Now Khaled sat up, sweat lining his neck, restless. The clock struck two.

Did you change?

Though he'd never wandered off again, sticking to the playground or the sidewalk in plain sight, he was still the curious little boy afraid to disappoint his parents.

But he had also broken the rules. He'd drunk. He'd been friends with Yassir. He'd lied to his parents. He'd hidden the complaints about his behavior at school from them. He had done many things that he knew would disappoint them. He'd always thought he'd remained the same while everyone he knew changed in ways that made them unrecognizable.

What would it truly take to change?

Khaled stared at the dark window, moonlight now peeking beneath the clouds. He looked down at the tiny blue dot moving on his phone. Then he slipped on the fake fuzzy Nike jacket Ashraf had gifted him from a mall in Najaf, tiptoed out of the house, and sank into the shadows once more, as he had all those years ago.

SKY

Outside the hospital, I still hear the whimper.

I watch as the other humans flood in and out of the mouth of the warm building. Some linger at the building's teeth, smoke escaping their noses as they suck on tiny little sticks, wiping tears they don't want others to see. Most who come through have no relation to the whimper. Panic overfills their eyes, but it is a different kind of pain.

When I see the whimper's parents enter the building, they move quickly, the type of panic I anticipated flooding their eyes. Just like I remember, it is the same way they once looked at me.

Years ago, leaflets dropped from my belly and a revolution ignited in their first land. The war had not yet fizzled, blood still stained the streets, and within days, bodies piled up.

Bodies and bodies and bodies.

I saw children running. I saw them captured. I saw them beaten. I saw the way the wisps on their faces had not fully bloomed, and they became corpses, instead of men. I saw the women crying over their dead young.

I saw the boy with guns in his holster get kidnapped. I saw the way they grabbed his head and smashed it against the concrete. I saw them do it again before they replaced their kicks with gunshots.

I still remember his whisper.

Many families ran that day.

Bullets showered over the fleeing. Men huddled close to their wives and children. The whimper's parents made it to the borders, a baby boy clasped at their side. They, like others, looked up at me and prayed, their hands cupped.

The prayer was not for me.

They, like others, were sent over to a land of tents and dust and torture chambers. Their tent neighbors—a husband and a wife and a baby still inside her. I had seen her waddle, her belly protruding with an orb. One evening, the pregnant woman was about to give birth. The husband of the pregnant woman twirled the whimper's brother around excitedly. Finally, the husband would become a father, too.

The soldiers are taking too long, the pregnant woman complained as her stomach quivered. Hours later, they were escorted to a small hospital. After two days passed, I saw her walk out, a baby wrapped tightly in her arms. But I could not see its face. I never did hear it whisper.

Later that morning, a small grave was dug for the baby. The whimper's mother held on to the woman as she wept, her face nearly buried in the dirt.

She sobbed and sobbed, and I swear I heard a rattle leave her body.

We'll go home someday, her husband kept whispering, attempting to lift her. *We'll go back. We'll leave this hell behind. We'll have a whole family. We'll try again and again until it's true.*

I know the sound humans make when they lie. Even when they try not to, a small broken chord vibrates in the air, echoing their deception.

When the woman let go of her husband's hand, she knew he was lying, too.

Eventually, a doctor and a nurse came over, checking the woman's pulse. Together, they carried her back to the hospital.

Later, years later, she'd emerge with a baby girl and she would lovingly stare at the baby's face and point toward me and the few stray clouds cast over that day.

This new life—this new hope—made the possibility of living real again. She symbolized a future and not just a haunted past. She would lead them out of here. She would crawl on real rugs and not just tent tarpaulins. She would play with real toys, instead of donated canned beans. She would read and write in two languages, not just Arabic. She would dance in her wedding dress without bombs ricocheting outside. She would get what they did not have—freedom. She would speak her mind. She would speak her heart. She would love and be loved.

She just had to live.

The whimper's parents joined the new mother, the families opening their palms and looking straight at me. Threat and desperation clung to their tears.

Keep this baby safe, they prayed. *Keep this one alive.*

28

KAWTHER

TWENTY MINUTES AFTER

For the fourth time in Kawther's life, she packed her things in the middle of the night, never to return home.

The very first time, their apartment was burning down. Baba screamed for her and Mama to get out, but Mama kept trying to grab things, a hijab, government documents, the photo album of her childhood in Iraq, and Kawther had tried to push as many stuffed bunnies into her arms—the kind Baba was good at winning from claw machines at the grocery store—before she followed her parents down the stairwell. Fire licked the windows as smoke from their upstairs neighbors unraveled and billowed into the air, lighting up the night sky in scarlet streaks.

When daylight came, they dragged a small bag of clothes that had not been incinerated, and moved in with the Al-Azzawis, who lived in a smaller, cramped apartment. A month later, they moved next door and stayed for several years.

The second time she'd left, blood leaked from the bandage on her face as she grabbed Mama's suitcase, the one her mother had reserved for her trips to Iraq, and poured in every item she thought she'd need for a week. Before she could close the suitcase, Khaled had caught her.

Where are you going? His voice small and scared. *Is the wedding back on? Are you moving in with Ali?*

He had asked a few more questions until she grabbed his arm and made him swear not to tell anyone, that she'd be back after her school trip.

He agreed after she stuffed five dollars into his jeans.

Then she left again, just last year, the day after Ayah's fatha. After Mama flung the words that Kawther still couldn't erase from her memory when she looked at her mother.

It should've been you.

The past year, after failing over and over again at her first job, she'd felt that her mother's words were still true. Sixty-three days since returning and Mama still did not acknowledge her, and Baba only used her to get Khaled to behave, just like when she was younger.

Most of all, though they had spent over two weeks together without their parents, Khaled had not forgiven her. But how was he supposed to when she did not even forgive herself?

Now, for the fourth time, she packed up her things, and this time, she didn't want Khaled to find her. But she heard a door creak open, heavy steps padding through the hallway, and she froze.

Had he finally finished talking to Baba?

When she'd first arrived two months ago, they'd seemed so close, chatting and praying together all night long on weekends, almost like they were companions and not father and son. It was hard to tell when she came back the first time—when her parents sat in the dinge of the quiet living room, unmoving for hours, Quran filling the quiet between them, Ayah's wedding photos splayed on the coffee table, Khaled reminding

Baba to pray and Mama to eat—what their relationships had truly been without her.

Just fine, and yet completely falling apart.

The house quieted, the footsteps retreated, and she closed her eyes for a moment, imagining herself being pulled out of bed all those years ago, feeling the fire lick the flames of the walls, wondering what it was like to leave home and never return.

Had she been scared then?

She had only thought of the bunnies—all the ones she'd lost over the year between laundry washes and subsequent moves—and nothing else. Yet she remembered her chin on Baba's shoulder, and Mama's hands lifting her up and away from the earth.

She opened her eyes, darkness beating over her vision.

She was wrong. She'd left home *five* times in her life.

The first time must have been at the Rafha camp. She couldn't quite grasp those memories anymore. She remembered the shape of the tents and the heat of the air and the sand in her eyes and Ali's small round face.

Ali's face.

Crying. Quivering.

He was always crying in the beginning, and when they first arrived in America, too.

She could still feel him. His hands caressing either side of her face. Her letting him.

She could feel him lean closer and closer until she opened her eyes again, seeing the pale light painting the ceiling.

She sat up, sweat stuck to her neck, her head pounding as she lifted it, finding the suitcase and her clothes splayed on the floor. Sunlight bled from the window. When had she fallen asleep? She checked her phone, realizing that several hours had passed. She returned to the message she had received days ago from Mona, her old coworker and former classmate in LA. The message she could not stop looking at.

Mona was the first Iraqi girl she had met outside the community she grew up in.

Mona's mom never made her daughter choose between her dreams and her duty as her child. She was proud that Mona became a lawyer—even if it meant living away from home. While Kawther had forgiven her own mother's limited dreams for her, she wondered when Mama would forgive her for choosing a life on her own terms. For abandoning her siblings, even when Mama needed the help. For breaking apart the only family Mama had in America, the family that didn't hold a grudge against her for leaving Iraq. For leaving her to wash Kawther's little sister's dead body alone. To bury her alone, too.

During the first few years of college, Mona's mother had tried desperately to reconcile Kawther and Mama—but each phone call ended with Mama agreeing to have Kawther back only if she returned permanently. Now that Kawther had finally mustered up the courage to do what she'd asked, it was too late.

She would not be forgiven.

Layla said she'd give you a second chance. Blink once if you want it. You can stay with me and Samir, we have an extra room. Or you can stay at Mama's until you get back on your feet. She loves you like her own.

At least Kawther still had a place where she was loved. Even if it had all fallen apart since childhood, this still remained.

Blinking, Kawther finally texted back before she stood up and resumed her packing.

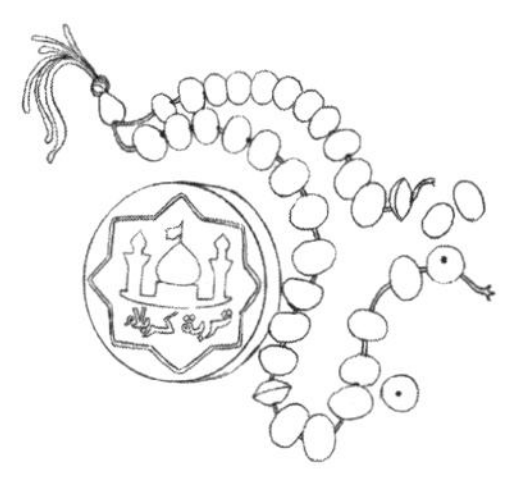

29

KHALED

THIRTEEN HOURS AFTER

By the time Khaled awoke, he felt that several days had passed, rather than just eleven hours. Last night, he had only made it to the end of the street before he'd retreated to his bedroom. He had watched the blue dot move without him, wondering, if he'd met Yassir, would they have talked? What would he have said? He had fallen asleep watching the map.

Now his phone was dead, as was his will to get up. He stared at the trash can—the things he threw away last night—and buried his face in his pillow again. He missed Iraq. He missed the scent of sweet chai first thing in the morning and the chickens that clucked next door. Even the annoying gas truck that woke up the neighborhood every morning, selling propane. He plugged his phone in and watched it come to life.

He hadn't told anyone his return date. Yet his phone dinged with a series of notifications. He had local news, global news, and an independent news line about Iraq, too, that fed him headlines every morning.

400 Americans to sue Jameson Company for Iraq Bribery. Local Man Found Beaten at 21st and Main Street, Police Searching for Suspect. The Best Pumpkin Cheesecake Recipe This Thanksgiving.

On Thanksgiving, the Al-Azzawis used to come over, and Kawther and Fatima would make three pots full of mashed potatoes while Mama and Khala Zainab stuffed chickens like the Americans did to the turkeys. He and Yassir and Ayah would go to the grocery stores with their fathers to pick out premade pumpkin pie and whipped cream, and Ali would stay sleeping in his room until dinnertime. But when salat al-maghrib would commence, he'd lead the prayers and serve everyone's plates while their sisters cleaned the kitchen and their mothers brewed chai. He and Yassir would take turns squirting the whipped cream can into their mouths until Ayah told their fathers on them.

Khaled sighed, wincing as he opened Instagram. He hadn't posted any Iraq photos yet, even though he was proud, even though Hassan had stolen his phone and taken four dozen black-and-white selfies. He wanted to show the glitter of crystals from Imam Ali's shrine and the sunbaked dirt and thick green palm trees that lined the sky.

The only person who would comment on his posts at this point was Alex. Kids at school followed his account. He didn't even know why he allowed them to, like there was a sliver of hope that they accepted and liked him, even though he knew it was far from his reality. Last year he'd posted himself in his dishdasha and black-and-white agal during Muharram and two kids from his chemistry group had called him Osama bin Laden's long-lost twin.

Why do you take everything so seriously? they scoffed when he confronted them. *No one can ever joke with you.*

He scrolled mindlessly through all the Halloween photos he'd missed. Offensive. Viking. Slutty Bunny. Offensive. Freddy Krueger. Offensive. And then he saw it.

#ToKillAMuslimDay

Breaking News: Three Muslims reported injured in the tristate area.

This wasn't an old, stupid Halloween post.

Khaled clicked on the linked article.

Three Muslims from three separate communities found beaten. Weapons and motive being questioned. A document titled Kill a Muslim Day *was found by each of their bodies. More details to come.*

Something sank to the bottom of his stomach. He clicked on the hashtag, where more stories generated.

Breaking News: Five Muslims found beaten on the same night. Kill a Muslim Day point system found.

Breaking News: Eight Muslims . . .

Breaking News: Eleven Muslims . . .

Khaled put his phone down. Then he closed his eyes.

This was a bad dream.

Another dream about being hunted.

Khaled was unsure how much time had passed. When he opened his eyes, he got another notification. *US News.*

Multiple People Attacked. Police Suspect Muslims May Have Been Targeted.

A chill entered his body. The second headline, before the Thanksgiving recipes, had been about a local man getting beaten on Main Street. The masjid was tucked into a corner a few blocks away.

Shaking, Khaled opened the local news article.

Veteran Saves Local Man's Life:

Ashton Milton was looking for a homeless shelter when he found the body of an unconscious man at 21st and Main Street around 2:39 a.m. on November 8th. No details about the victim have been released, but police confirm he is in critical condition. This is a developing story. More details to come.

Every image of the uncles at the masjid entered Khaled's mind. Baba was home, right?

Despite their argument last night, he braced his nerves and called. But when his father didn't answer after a few rings, Khaled jumped out of his bed and ran into the hallway. Mama was in the living room, a fresh cup of chai steaming nearby, her cell phone pasted to her ear. She looked so . . . normal. Which meant she was speaking on the phone with his family in Iraq.

"Mama . . . where's Baba?"

Her eyes brightened. Her lips turned up happily when Khalee Jafaar's voice echoed through the speaker.

"Oh, you're finally awake. Your aunt and uncle wanted to make sure you came home safely. They wanted to say hi to you on the phone." Mama blinked at him expectantly just like she always had whenever she had randomly shoved the phone at his ear over the years. "Here he is!"

Khalee Jafaar's cheery voice welcomed him. "Khaled, habibi, we missed you at breakfast today. Maha started crying for you." Heaviness panged in his chest. They missed him already?

Khaled didn't even know he could be missed like that.

"I miss you, too," he said, realizing he had only said the word twice in his life. Once, about Yasmin, and once to Kawther when he got her on the phone in the sixth grade, asking if she'd come back home.

Everyone at home is so mad, but I miss you.

He tried to keep the conversation with his uncle short, and luckily the connection cut out. Mama frowned at the phone, but before she could call them back to pretend she was okay, he questioned her again.

"Mama, where's Baba?" he repeated. "Did he leave last night?"

Mama shook her head. "He's at work now. Why?"

Khaled looked at his phone, his voice suddenly shaking. "I think someone from our masjid could've gotten attacked last night . . . the news—"

"Attacked?" she echoed, confused.

"The news . . . I saw it on the news, Muslims got attacked, all over the United States—" He began to fumble, unable to keep translating his thoughts into Arabic. "And I think one was attacked here."

"Attacked here?" Mama sat still, shocked for a moment before she began to click through her phone. "I'll call Khala Nasreen, she'll know if something happened."

Khaled began pacing. He would get confirmation in no time. Nothing ever got past Iraqi aunties. If the victim was even an Iraqi. Or even Muslim. What if it was a coincidence that someone was attacked here on the same day?

Khaled dialed the auto shop to see if he could reach Baba directly, but there was no answer. What was the point of keeping a Bluetooth earpiece in your ear at all times if you didn't answer the phone? He dialed again and watched as Mama mumbled something on the phone and stared at him.

"Baba's still not answering," he said breathlessly. He refreshed the news page. It had been hours since it was last updated. "What did Khala Nasreen say? Did she know anything?"

"She knows," Mama muttered, blood draining from her face. Khaled felt his bones unravel.

It was someone they knew.

"Are they okay?" He didn't even know who *they* was. *Ya Allah*, he prayed silently to himself. *Please let them be okay.*

"They're still alive," she said. "That's all I know."

"Who?" he said, refreshing the local news page. "Who is still alive?"

Local Teen Found Beaten at 21st and Main Street.

The word *man* was now replaced with *teen.*

No. No. No.

Last night was Thursday, the men's congregation always gathered for prayer. It could've been Abbas or Kareem or Bassim or any of the other boys at the masjid. It could've been Hakim or Karrar or Mohammed . . .

But then he thought back to the blue dot on his phone, moving toward Main Street at two a.m. He stared at Mama; she was sitting now, frozen. Then she looked at him, a gloss in her eyes, and whispered, "It was Yassir."

Khaled began moving before his brain could register what he was doing.

"Khaled, where are you going?" Mama tried to grab his arm, but he was already down the hallway.

He pushed the door open and found Kawther, messy bun swirled at the top of her head, the innards of her suitcase spilling out. She wasn't unpacking; instead, she was piling her clothes inside. Eight years ago, in the middle of the night, he'd found her doing the same thing. She'd stolen Mama's suitcase and stuffed her things into it.

Don't tell anyone. I'll be back. I'll be back, I swear.

She stared at him, startled. "Khaled . . . what's wrong?"

"I need you to take me to the hospital."

"Are you sick?"

He shook his head. "I need you to take me to the fucking hospital and do something for me for once in your life," he said as he took the black hijab draped over the chair of her vanity set and tossed it at her. She caught it. "We need to go right now! Understand?"

"What happened? Did someone get hurt?" she asked, eyes wide. But she was already out the door, wrapping her hijab, obeying his orders. For the first time in his life, she was listening to him.

There was no time to dwell on that miracle.

His ears began ringing.

It was Yassir.

It was Yassir.

It was Yassir.

"Khaled, tell me what's going on?" Kawther exclaimed. "Where are we going? Are you sick?"

Khaled walked back to Mama, who was staring at him bewildered.

"Mama, why isn't your hijab on?" he asked her seriously. Was his mother just going to sit here after Yassir had been attacked?

She stared at him blankly.

Yassir had been attacked and she didn't even care?

"Grab the keys, Kawther, let's go," he said, giving up on his mother before sliding on his sneakers, which were parked at the doorway. No socks.

"Khaled, it's dangerous!" Mama yelled as he stepped outside the house. *"Khaled!"*

He didn't care.

The aging Honda Accord beeped open, and Khaled slipped into the passenger seat, staring at his mother, who continued to yell at him from the doorway to come back as Kawther brought the car to life and drove them away.

30

KAWTHER

THIRTEEN HOURS AND THIRTY MINUTES AFTER

"Are you cold, Khaled?" Kawther asked her brother.

He was shaking.

Her own bones rattled as the car's engine squeaked out of the driveway. Mama called them several times and Khaled shook his head when Kawther attempted to pick up.

"Just drive," he mumbled, not looking at her. Even after two and a half weeks together, he could still hardly look at her. "Go to the Riverside hospital. It's closest to Main Street."

"You're scaring me," she whispered. "Did something happen to Baba?"

He shook his head and at the red light, he showed her two headlines that made her stomach fall to her feet. The first, *Kill a Muslim Day, 13 victims identified*. The second, *Local Teen Boy Found Beaten on Main Street*.

"Do you know who . . ." Her words lingered in the air. She had followed him out of the house, not knowing what she was getting herself into.

"Yassir," he whispered, his voice cracking, a surge of pain echoing in it. She thought a sob might escape him.

Her throat tightened as she was hit with disbelief.

Yassir?

The last time she'd seen him in the courtroom, he'd looked so scared. So skinny. So tired.

Tears automatically crept up her throat.

"I need you to promise me something," Khaled said as she took the wrong left turn. She did a U-turn before he could correct her. She still didn't know this place, still couldn't remember the blueprints of her childhood. She had wanted to leave before she could be forced to remember it all, and her brother had caught her running away yet again. "Say wallah you'll do it."

Kawther hesitated, waiting for him to explain, but only silence filled the air. "What is it?"

"Swear first," he repeated, pointing her in the right direction. She shook her head, following his lead, and turned at the light. "Say wallah you'll do it."

"Khaled, I don't even know what I'm—"

His body shook again even though the heater licked warmth onto their faces. He needed something from her. For the first time in eight years, he needed something from her again and this time she could not deny him.

"Wallah," she whispered.

"Promise me that you'll be his lawyer. He's going to need one. Once these details start to come out, he'll need someone on his side. You know they don't have money and he's going to need someone to defend him. You saw him in court. He's defenseless." Khaled continued to shake, but his voice stayed firm. "The police are going to get involved. They're probably already involved . . . he has a criminal record, and I don't want anyone to blame this on him. He has no one else. You have to do it, Kawther."

"His family wouldn't want—" She stopped herself again when Khaled's eyebrows furrowed at her. She had already promised God. *This* was what she'd promised? "What . . . what if . . ."

What if Ali was there?

She reminded herself that he had a wife, maybe even children now, he could not just appear out of thin air. Something she'd had to keep reminding herself in Iraq each time she thought he could be around, staring over her shoulder.

"What if they don't want me?" she said instead.

"They won't care," Khaled muttered. "It's our family that rejected them, not the other way around."

His words were so bitter, so raw. Yet not true at all.

"You don't know everything, Khaled," Kawther said.

"Then tell me," he said as she pulled into the hospital driveway. "Tell me how it wasn't your fault." A news crew sat by the front entrance; a sea of minivans filled the parking lot. There was a group of Iraqis, old faces she recognized, making their way into the hospital.

Her mouth dried. She didn't know where to start. So much had been taken away from him the past year. She did not have it in her to take Yassir away from him. Especially not now.

"Just keep your promise, like I kept yours all those years ago," Khaled sighed after a long silence, unbuckling his seat belt. She caught a glimpse of herself in the rearview mirror. She was still wearing pajamas. Her hijab was disheveled, dark curls poking out from the fabric. Khaled seemed to be noticing himself, too. He took the half-drunk bottle of water in the van's cup holder and washed his face, then wiped off droplets of water with the back of his jacket sleeve. He tried to put a hand through his hair to smooth his bedhead but gave up.

"Let's go," he said, stepping out.

"Bismilllah." She blew a heavy sigh before she stepped out of the Honda and followed her brother to face the people she'd run from eight years ago.

31

KAWTHER

EIGHT YEARS, SIX MONTHS, AND FORTY-TWO DAYS BEFORE

Kawther crumpled the MASH paper and stared at her best friend. She ignored what Fatima had written on the blue lines of the notebook paper under the "Husband" column. *Who*, she'd written on there. She had meant it as a joke, but she could read the truth in Kawther's eyes. She always had. Each fib and fear, Fatima always knew before she could even speak a word.

And somehow, she knew this, too.

The only secret Kawther had ever kept from her.

Fatima began giggling. "I can't believe you like Ali! For how long, Kawther? We were all in diapers together!"

Kawther wondered if it was obvious in her eyes each time he came by and made a joke or smiled back at her during her sleepovers with Fatima, back when Fatima was still living at her parents' house. All these years she had silenced her feelings. She'd been sure not to stare at him too long, as if every curve in his face was not already delicately engraved into her mind. She did not know if she had permission to love him that way.

Embarrassed, Kawther pulled out her laptop and opened the essay for the Future Law Scholars program her college advisor, Mrs. Mackenzie, had begged her to apply for. She didn't have the heart to finish it now that Fatima was here and knew her secret.

They were too old to keep playing MASH. Her best friend was already married, she already had a home to attend to, her eighteenth birthday was coming up and she was already trying to get pregnant. Fatima thought Kawther was falling behind, just like Mama did, comparing her to the other girls in their Iraqi community who were already getting married, too. Sometimes Kawther didn't know why she tried applying to programs like this. It wasn't like her parents would let her move out unmarried anyway.

It didn't feel fair for her parents to cling to a traditional version of being Iraqi when plenty of boys and girls in Iraq, no matter their religion or what city they came from, spent years studying on their own in universities. Hell, Iraqis were descendants of the most educated people in history. But for Mama and Baba, who grew up without a chance to go to school, who were forced apart from their own families, the idea of their daughter going to college far away was too difficult to wrap their minds around.

Fatima pulled the computer away from her. "You're turning red! I didn't even think that was possible! For how long, Kawther? Just imagine, we could become actual sisters!"

"Not that long," Kawther murmured to herself.

"So, what? When we went to elementary school?" Fatima pressed. "Before? In the camps?"

Kawther rolled her eyes. All she remembered about Ali at the camps was a boy who cried more than she ever had. For so long, he was just that to her, a sensitive boy whose tears she tried to silence. Then, on the first day of Ramadan in fourth grade, everything changed.

That morning, Mama finally wrapped a lilac-colored hijab around Kawther's face, the one she had begged Mama to wear for months, and pinched the fabric around her chin. "It's time," she had said. "You've grown."

Kawther wore the fabric like a crown.

At lunch recess, while Fatima's class had a different rotation, Ali, two grades ahead of the girls, would swing on the monkey bars and race with Kawther even though the older kids ignored them. But that afternoon they hung limply from the bars, torturing themselves with a conversation about strawberry ice cream and the taste of Khala Zainab's creamy red lentil shorba and chocolate and German chocolate cake and what they would do when they finally broke their fasts.

"Hey, you." A kid from Ali's class walked up to them as blisters erupted between the lines of her palms. "I didn't know you had two terrorists in your family."

It was not the first time Kawther had heard those words.

On her parents' television, rubbled buildings and plumes of black smoke filled the screen. Her parents would eat breakfast, clicking their tongues as they watched dead Iraqis being pulled from the dust. Yet on the television she shared with her siblings, the American evening news would come on after their cartoons, and a blond news reporter would talk about how many US soldiers were being killed by terrorists in Iraq and Afghanistan. *The Connection Between Immigration and Islamic Terrorism.* Story later, at nine.

"What did you say?" Ali asked the boy, both of their bodies still suspended in the air. "What did you call her?"

"A terrorist," the boy spat. "Just like your sister. Are you bald under there, too?" he asked Kawther. "Or are you hiding a bomb?"

Ali clenched the yellow handles of the monkey bars, swinging his legs forward and kicking the boy straight in the mouth. Blood dripped on the ground as a whistle blew in the distance.

"Don't call our parents, please," Kawther begged the principal. The pin around her hijab felt so tight that she could hardly breathe. "Ali was just defending me."

Ali held on to her sleeve protectively, something he did when they walked in the dark, playing boogeyman in the apartment neighborhood near sundown. The principal sighed, not knowing what to do with one student in a hijab, let alone two, now that Kawther and Fatima both wore them. Despite Kawther's protests, she called their fathers anyway. The two men sat, merely nodding at the principal. Although her father tried to fight back against Ali's two-day suspension, his limited English only left blank stares on the principal's face.

Kawther and Ali were excused from class for the rest of the day, and on the trudge to the parking lot, the Sayed kept a protective arm around Kawther, softly tugging at her hijab.

"Choosing to wear this is the bravest thing you can do," the Sayed said. "Braver than Ali. Braver than any of us. Okay?"

Kawther nodded, tears stuck in her throat as she and Ali sat at opposite ends of the passenger seat of Sayed Rahman's cab.

"Fuck that principal," Baba whispered. Her father rarely swore in English, but when he did, the words ricocheted like bullets in his mouth. Baba twisted around in the passenger seat of Sayed Rahman's cab and stared at Ali with pride in his eyes. "Thank you for protecting my Kawther. She's my habiba, you know?"

"I know," Ali said, a nervous smile appearing on his face as Kawther looked away in embarrassment.

"Don't praise him," Sayed Rahman said, shaking his head in disappointment as he began to drive. "Ali, this is not the way. Don't let anyone tell you what Islam is. Islam is love. Islam is forgiveness. It is protecting, not kicking, or hurting."

"I thought we were supposed to defend when people attack us, just like Imam Hussein defended everyone," Ali said. "Why can't I defend Kawther?"

"Exactly!" Baba added, agreeing with him. "Rahman, stop being so stubborn. Ali, I'm buying you a gift for protecting our daughters."

Sayed Rahman shook his head again. "No need for that. Save your money."

But Baba winked at Ali, who smiled in relief. Kawther could tell he didn't regret what he had done—in fact, his fists were still curled. That night for iftar, Baba bought Ali German chocolate cake, and Ali cut a slice for Kawther first. When he accidentally got coconut frosting on her hand, he rubbed it away, his topaz eyes ignited at her. For the first time in Kawther's life, she felt her chest burn in longing.

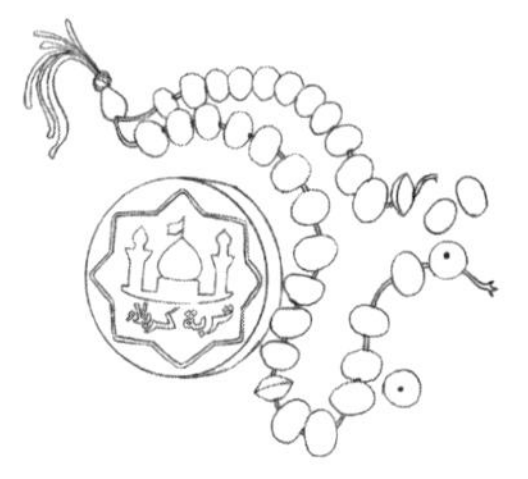

32

KHALED

FOURTEEN HOURS AFTER

"I'm sorry, only immediate family members are allowed in the ICU." The waiting room was filled with Iraqis and the attending nurse was trying to kick them all out.

"Khaled, is that you? When did you come back, habibi?"

Hajji Majid stood before him, his eyes red and wet. Khaled let the man hug him and kiss his cheeks like he always did, but something in Khaled's body shook at the contact.

"It's okay, it's going to be okay," the Hajji whispered to him, as if he were consoling him because he was crying. But Khaled wasn't. He was not the one who had been attacked. "Pray for him, understand? Everyone here needs to make duas!"

Khaled pulled away. Yassir had been attacked, but how badly had he been beaten? Was he awake? Maybe he could be discharged later today, maybe—

"He's in surgery." Kawther came to Khaled's side. When had she left him? As she looked down at her feet and said her salaams to Hajji Majid, Khaled noticed everyone staring at them. They were in pajamas and disheveled, here to visit a family that loathed them. No one used to blink twice when the Al-Azzawis and Al-Hakims were together. They were one and the same. But now they were out of place.

"Khaled," Kawther said, taking his arm as she sat him down in the waiting room chair. "They're kicking everyone out, so I told that lady I'm his lawyer and you're his cousin. But if his family comes out and kicks us out, there's nothing I can do."

Khaled nodded and watched as the Iraqis put up a fight, chanting a salutation for the Prophet before reciting Surat al-Fatiha for Yassir's recovery.

"We just want to pray over him!" a Hajji shouted as he and his wife stepped out, the nurse holding the door open. In minutes, the waiting room was empty save for the families of other patients, who seemed relieved that the noise was gone.

"It's been a circus since this morning," the nurse sighed to the assistant. "The family was so panicked last night. Cherrie told me everything."

Kawther put a hand on Khaled's. He let her.

"This is a bad dream," he whispered. "Right?"

"I'm still waiting to wake up," she murmured.

He wasn't sure how long they waited. They sat still.

He felt his phone vibrating in his pocket but didn't look. If he answered Baba's calls, Baba would tell him to come home immediately. He would remind Khaled of what Yassir had done. That Khaled had no business trying to see him.

Despite how much his parents despised the Al-Azzawis, they had allowed them to pay their respects when Ayah died. Would they not pay their own respects to the boy they'd helped raise, even if they hated him? Even if Khaled still hated him, too?

He wanted them to swallow their pride, like he had, despite the years of pain that stretched between them. He waited for his parents to set aside their hate and walk through the door, take a seat next to him and Kawther, and pray for Yassir's healing.

But they never came.

33

KAWTHER

NINETEEN HOURS AFTER

"It's the middle of the night," Mama said, waiting by the door. She had probably heard the squeak of the tires from the driveway and readied her scolding, just like old times. Kawther hadn't seen Mama out of her bed this many times since she'd returned. "Where is Khaled?"

"At the hospital," Kawther said, watching Baba's eyes fall to his feet. "He's not going to come home, so don't ask me to bring him back."

Kawther sidestepped her parents and walked to her room. Quickly, she changed out of her pajamas and into a black blazer and matching pants. She put on a green hijab and lightly dabbed on blush. She added mascara, gloss on her lips. Then she grabbed her suitcase and closed it tightly before setting it to the side. She stepped into Khaled's room and bathroom and gathered his things: a change of clothes, his toothbrush, and deodorant.

She had left Khaled asleep, head dropping to his chest, as they waited for news. She hoped that by the time she returned, the surgery—whatever it was—would have been successful, that Yassir would recover, that they could drive home and she could finish packing and disappear. If Yassir ever went to court for whatever had happened to him, she could come back to help. Perhaps this was how she was meant to reunite with her family. In spurts, not permanence.

She realized she'd forgotten her phone charging at her nightstand, and walked back into her bedroom.

"Where are you going now?" Mama asked at her door. The last time Kawther remembered Mama visiting her bedroom was when she gave her *the talk* days before her khatib al-khatab with Ali.

"Back to the hospital," Kawther said, heading to the front door, Mama following her, Baba still waiting in the same spot. "Do you want to come? Or have you still sworn to God never to speak to them?"

Mama and Baba didn't say anything. Kawther knew she wasn't entitled to be this harsh to them anymore, but she didn't know how else to say it.

"I'm going to be Yassir's lawyer. I don't know when I'll be back," she said, her commitment feeling real now. She did not owe the Al-Azzawis much, but perhaps after she helped them they could all stop hating each other. Her parents stared at her wordlessly as she closed the door between them once more.

She called Mona as she drove.

"Holy hell, did you read the articles I sent you this morning? The firm is taking on two clients. One in Santa Monica the other in Oakland. Honestly, we could really use your help. I already talked to Layla this morning and she said she'll take you back immediately; you'd still be on probation, though."

Take you back.

She really had a second chance.

But she had promised Khaled. And she had promised God, too.

"Actually, forget my text from earlier today. Monie, remember the law firm that does pro bono work here? The one I sent a few applications to?"

Mona sighed heavily, understanding what she meant. "Kawther, did someone get attacked near where you live, too?"

Kawther didn't think her voice would start to shake. That tears would slip out of her eyes when she said, "Yes."

"Oh, God. I didn't see your city named in the reports . . . what happened?"

"I don't know much. It happened late last night, and I don't even know if it's connected. Can you get me that contact with them? You're friendly with one of the partners there, right?"

"Yeah, Rebecca. She's fearless, I swear. I'll contact her and have her reach out to you for this. I'm sure the firm will back you up."

Kawther wiped her face. She knew her way to the hospital now. "Okay, thanks."

"Stay safe, all right? Don't walk out alone, don't drive alone. You still have that pepper spray I gave you? And the pocketknife?"

Kawther nodded. "I have the pepper spray. TSA wouldn't let me keep the pocketknife, remember? Almost got detained for that."

"Right," Mona sighed. "Who is the client? Someone you know? Hopefully no one you were trying to avoid."

"Yeah," Kawther murmured as she stepped out of her car, the tall hospital building welcoming her back. "I know them well."

TWENTY-ONE HOURS AND THIRTY MINUTES AFTER

Khaled was awake and disoriented. He looked up from his phone and stared at his sister in panic.

"Here, get changed," she whispered, shoving the small grocery bag with his things in front of him. "Packed your toothbrush. Any updates?"

"They won't tell me," he said, standing up. "Why didn't you wake me? At least text me. I woke up and you were gone."

"Sorry," she whispered. "I'm back now. Didn't think a lawyer should show up in pajamas."

He nodded, hugging the small bag of clothes to his chest. His hair was sticking out in several directions, and she wanted to run a hand through it, like she used to every Eid, as she slathered gel into his loose waves.

She kept her hands to herself and took a seat next to him.

"Someone died."

Her head spun so she could look at him. "What?"

"Someone died from the attack. In Philadelphia."

"Ya Allah," she whispered as she began to scroll social media. "Inna lillahi wa inna ilayhi raji'un."

To God we belong and to God we return.

If she was going to become Yassir's lawyer, she would need to know what was going on. One death. Eighteen victims according to the Washington Press, and she wasn't sure if Yassir counted. She would probably have to notify the Muslim Media League herself. Or maybe the law firm would?

She didn't know how to do any of this.

We won't be extending a full-time offer, Layla, her old supervisor at Mirza & Associates, had told her as she slid over a business card for a therapist's office. *I'm telling you this as your mentor, Kawther. I think you need professional help.*

She'd spent two years interning there. Her coworkers had become her friends, another new family after her classmates had departed for other journeys after graduation. It felt like the last place she could hold on to, and they didn't want her around anymore, either. Her superiors seemed to agree that despite her stellar grades and dedication in her classes, she had yet to become the professional she was supposed to be. Something was holding her back.

When she first moved to LA, her family was all she could think about. Every day without them made her physically ill. She spent her weekends too sick to move, barely able to muster the energy for her classes, wondering if she had made the wrong decision. The vitriolic voicemails her mother left her every couple of weeks didn't help. But her professors admired and encouraged her in a way she had never experienced before, her classmates seemed to genuinely like her, and she was doing well in class. She began to think there was no way she could ever regret her decision. Even if she spent the holidays and breaks alone, with Mona's mom dragging her to Eid prayers and Muharram majlis on occasion. It was a freedom she would not be able to get back if she ever returned home.

But when Ayah died, she could no longer lie to herself. For the first time since leaving home, she regretted not marrying Ali. She regretted not flying back home to convince Ayah not to marry Haydar. She regretted the long, vague messages she'd sent instead of being there for her little sister in person. She regretted not telling Ayah the truth of what had happened between her and Ali. If she had, perhaps Ayah would never have tried to repeat Kawther's mistake. Perhaps she would have stayed.

She would still be dead.

After Ayah's funeral, the life she had stubbornly built for herself in LA had slipped from her fingers. She could barely keep up at work, lying on her side, staring at the walls for hours, just like Mama did, so Layla had let her go. Kawther had tried seeing the therapist.

Perhaps it's time to try reconciling with your family, the therapist had said. *It might not be easy, but enough time has passed. They might forgive you and you might find yourself forgiving them, too.*

With no job, she packed her bags and left LA. She had taken the universal bar exam for this reason—she always made room to come back. But now that she was here, all she wanted to do was disappear.

Her promise to Khaled was all that was truly keeping her now.

"He's going to be okay," she finally said, unsure if she was trying to make Khaled or herself feel better. "Inshallah."

Khaled rubbed his hands over his face, as if making wudu. "I'm gonna go pray."

She watched him disappear into a small private room. Her phone vibrated.

Jones, Jacobs & Associates is on board. They'll contact you soon. It's better if they back you up. Don't do this alone.

Thanks, Monie, she texted back.

Damn Islamophobes. I was so close to getting you back home :(

Kawther put her phone down, and when she looked up, she found Fatima staring at her. Just like in the courtroom, anger rekindled in Kawther's stomach the moment their eyes locked. Fatima was a stranger now. Not because Kawther had left her behind eight years ago, but because she had become a different person before Kawther could even leave.

Fatima looked away from her and moved to the nurses' desk.

"Congratulations, I heard the surgery was successful," the nurse said.

"Thanks." Fatima's voice was hoarse, like she had been crying for hours. "I was told there was a lawyer waiting for my family."

The woman pointed at Kawther. "She's right there."

Fatima turned around and stared at her. She blinked, as if she remembered why Kawther had been gone for so long. As if they hadn't seen each other in court weeks ago. "Sorry for the misunderstanding. Also, please make sure no reporters are let in. Some community members want to pay their respects. Can they do it once he's moved to the recovery floor?"

The nurse nodded. "We can do five at a time. We just can't have them flood the ICU. It's a safety precaution."

"I understand."

"So that woman is not your family's lawyer?" the nurse asked as Fatima turned back toward the hallway.

"No," Fatima said, enunciating clearly. "She's not."

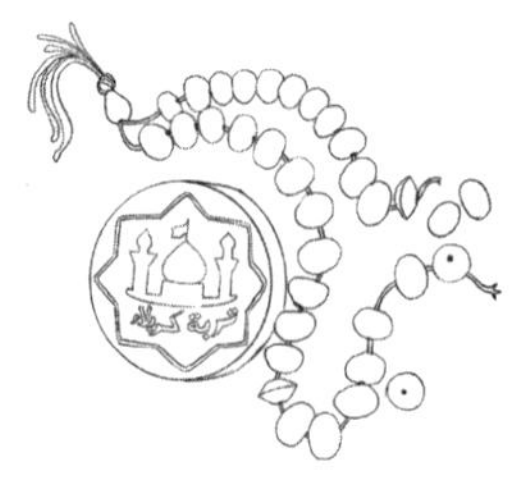

34

KHALED

TWENTY-TWO HOURS AFTER

Khaled watched as his sister stood up and grabbed her things to leave. Was she always this weak?

Fatima stepped into the hallway and paused at the sight of him. "You should go."

"Wait," Khaled said, stepping in front of her. "Tell me first, is he okay?"

She sighed. "He got through his surgery successfully."

Alhamdulillah.

"What kind of surgery? It must be bad, right? They don't just do emergency surgery for bruises."

She began walking. "Go home, Khaled. I told you he's okay."

"No." It felt stupid, like the past few weeks of hating Yassir hadn't mattered, but Khaled could not just leave without knowing if he was okay. He didn't even care if Yassir would ever do the same for him. Yassir was still the oldest friend he had, and he cared about him, even though he wished he didn't.

"Khaled," Kawther called him from the hallway. "We need to respect their choices. Let's go."

Of course she didn't care about protecting Yassir or the Al-Azzawis. If he hadn't made her swear, she would probably be boarding a flight back to California.

Khaled shook his head. "No."

"Let me guess, he was with you last night. Is that it?" Fatima accused him, and he instantly shook his head. "Whenever you two are together lately, things get worse. When the police come back—"

"I wasn't with him!" Khaled cut her off. "You can yell at me all you want, I don't care. But he's going to need a lawyer. This is going to get legal. This whole Kill a Muslim Day shit—"

"We don't know if that's what it is yet," Kawther and Fatima both said, startling Fatima, motivating her to walk even faster.

"Even if it's not, someone beat him up! You're gonna want to press charges!"

Fatima shook her head. "I don't have time for this. Okay? I need to go back to my parents—"

Khaled pushed himself closer to Fatima and she paused, staring at him. Maybe she remembered the time she got in trouble for not watching him. When she squeezed the bones in his right hand and made him promise he'd never wander away. How she held him close and hugged him. How she said he was her brother, too.

"Fatima, please. Forget our families for a second. Just think about him. You can yell at me all you want. Hell, you can hit me if you want. Just . . . just let us help. Let Kawther help him. He's going to need someone to talk to the police on his behalf, to notify the authorities, to talk to reporters. Kawther will help for free. She graduated top of her class, she's the best option you have. If you get someone else, they're not going to understand him. They're not going to understand . . . us."

When Kawther had gone back to the house, he had looked her up on LinkedIn and had seen her accolades and the internship she'd completed. He'd never done that before, always wanting to avoid any knowledge of her life without him. While he still didn't know much, it was clear that Kawther had what it took to be a decent lawyer. At least, on paper. Moreover, she was his excuse to be at the hospital. After the incident at the gas station and the punch he'd thrown, he knew he shouldn't be here at all. It was clear on Fatima's face, too.

"I can get him a new lawyer." Fatima sighed again.

"You have a good one right here!" Khaled said, but Fatima looked unconvinced. If Kawther weren't so weak, it wouldn't be so hard to persuade Fatima that this was true. "I'll leave him alone after this. I swear to God if you want me to never see him again, I won't. But he needs someone to protect him."

Pain flashed across Fatima's face. Tears suddenly poured out of her eyes, and Khaled felt bad for yelling at her. He couldn't imagine what she was going through. Probably interpreting every question between the doctor and her parents. Probably making sure her own kids weren't frightened. She had to be the strong one, like she and Kawther had to be when they were kids.

She wiped her face. "Okay."

"I'm sorry for yelling," Khaled whispered.

"Just follow me," Fatima said, defeated.

"I'll leave for now," Kawther said, retreating to the waiting room. "I need to meet with the firm that's going to help me handle his case. I'll be back. Okay? If the police come, let me talk to them. That's really important. Understand?"

He and Fatima nodded at her before Fatima led him to an elevator, then up to the seventh floor. Machines whispered and linoleum shone so brightly he could see his own exhausted, deranged reflection.

In a small room without a bed, Sayed Rahman had a Quran in his hand, praying, and Khala Zainab had her hands over her face.

"Salaam 'alaykum," he whispered, and they both looked up at him, bewildered.

He was expecting them to yell at him. Ask if he was with Yassir last night, too. Instead, Khala Zainab's face brightened. "I'm so happy you're here, habibi."

Then she stood up and hugged him and kissed his cheeks, and he held her as she began to sob. Khaled felt a tightness in his throat. It had been so long since he had hugged her, the woman he'd considered a second mother.

"It's all right, they said he'll be all right," Sayed Rahman said, but tears poured out of his eyes, too. Near the Sayed's feet sat a car seat, where Yasmin was fast asleep. Two little boys, Yousef and Abbas, Fatima's sons, were also asleep in their own chairs. "We can't keep crying. He got through his surgery successfully. They'll be back soon to move him to a new room. He's going to be all right. Okay?"

Khala Zainab pulled away from Khaled, nodding; then she grabbed his hand and invited him to sit next to her. As they waited, Khala Zainab pushed her fingers through his hair, as if it comforted her more than him. As they waited, the shaking that had taken over his body since he'd first heard the news finally stopped.

35

KAWTHER

FOUR DAYS AFTER

"I'm so sorry, Monie," Kawther whispered into her phone from the hallway of the law firm. "How is the family dealing?"

Two more victims had died.

One in Buffalo and one of Mona's clients in Oakland.

"They've been crying in our offices all day, trying to make a public statement," Mona said, her voice shaky. "It was an older sister. She was driving back from a friend's wedding late. She had a hijab on, got attacked in the parking lot of a gas station." A small sniffle echoed through the receiver. "Screw all of this. We were supposed to get an update yesterday from the FBI official and we've heard nothing. There must be fingerprints on these damn Kill a Muslim Day documents—they still won't even send us the full document. My mom is trying to convince me to get a police escort to the firm each day. As if that would help."

Fear was officially taking over. People weren't leaving their homes. Women were making videos about not wearing hijab to stay safe. Some men, like her father, still went to work, unafraid.

I've been through worse, she'd overheard Baba say when Mama was arguing with him about keeping the shop open this morning. It wasn't so far from where Yassir had been found.

When she stopped by the house to change clothes and attempt to get a few hours of sleep, Kawther would overhear her parents arguing, or Mama would stare at her wordlessly, angry that she hadn't brought Khaled back with her. He practically lived at the hospital now. Although Yassir's surgery had been successful, he had sustained traumatic brain injury and still had not woken up.

"You need to go into the hospital room," Mona said. "I know it sucks, but there's no way the cops haven't come by. I mean, you could just call your brother again—but you should be with them. At least send some paralegal to babysit the family."

The police hadn't come back since the initial reporting. At least, if they had, no one had told her.

"I don't think I have the right to ask that from the firm, they're already doing me a massive favor," Kawther said. "In fact, Rebecca said that if I do well, she might hire me on, anyway."

"Or . . . you could just come back here after it's over. It's been two months. What you're doing now has already convinced Layla you're ready to get back to work," Mona said. "Besides, everyone misses you. And I know it's been shitty for everyone these past few days, but I can hear the brokenness in your voice. It's okay if it didn't work out with your parents. You tried, you're even helping the family that you—"

"I have to go, Mona," Kawther said, because she could not bear listening to someone repeat the same thoughts she'd been having since she'd made her brother the promise four days ago.

Kawther stared at room 705.

Her fingers clasped the cold metal of the door handle for the third time in the past five minutes; then she let go and stepped away. She walked down the opposite hallway, stopping when she found Fatima crying on a chair as her two sons played games on a shared cell phone in the clustered seating near the family room. The little boys looked so much like her. The dark golden curls, their sandy warm skin and light brown eyes.

She could keep walking and Fatima might not even notice. But then one of the little boys looked up and Kawther couldn't turn away, caught in her cowardice.

"Mama, someone is here," the little boy said, nudging their mother.

Fatima looked up and immediately began wiping her wet face.

"Is Uncle Yassir going to die?" the younger boy with the wavy bronze hair asked, as if reading her own fear.

"No, Abbas." Fatima sniffled, putting a crumpled tissue she fished out of her pocket to her nose. "Stop asking that."

"Mama said to say inshallah he gets better," the older boy said, tugging at his brother's light gray sweater.

"Inshallah," Kawther whispered to the boy. "Are you okay?" she asked Fatima.

Fatima stared at her, tears filling her eyes again, and when Kawther nervously took a step forward, her old friend took it as an invitation to embrace her.

Startled, Kawther felt the girl who had wrapped her arms around her dozens of times over the years squeeze her shoulders. She felt Fatima's spine beneath the black button-down abaya. Fatima wept and Kawther stood frozen.

How badly she had wanted to be held this way after Ayah passed. When Kawther had come back last year and had gone to the masjid, her mother had grieved with Khaled's head on her lap, and Kawther had sat in the corner and shivered alone. Some aunties tried to kiss her cheeks, shocked to recognize the face of the girl they hadn't seen in years. She couldn't remember if Fatima came by that night. She mustn't have, caught in her own shame. Kawther wasn't sure if she should know better than to comfort a girl she'd trusted more than anyone, who had broken her heart just as much as Ali had.

In the face of tragedy, perhaps the past didn't matter all that much, even if it still hurt.

Fatima sobbed. "I shouldn't have been so harsh on him. What if he left that night because of me?"

"What do you mean?" Kawther asked, her hands brushing the black abaya Fatima wore. "Did you two have an argument?"

Fatima let go, taking a few steps back. She shook her head. "No."

"Then why do you think it's your fault?" Kawther asked.

"I don't know. I shouldn't have shamed him . . ." Her voice broke off.

"Did you talk to him that night?"

Fatima shook her head. "I sent him a text message telling him to do better. I took Yasmin—his daughter—to the doctor's office. I was so mad at him . . ." Her words faltered. Kawther knew of Yasmin. She had overheard Baba talk to Mama about how reckless Yassir was now and that they couldn't let Khaled end up with the same fate. It was why they'd both insisted on sending him to Iraq in the first place, hoping that the separation would prevent him from making the same mistakes.

"Do you know what happened that night?" Kawther asked, pulling her notepad out of her briefcase.

Fatima shook her head. "The police are talking to my dad and brother right now. You can ask them. They're in the family room."

She pointed to the small room at the end of the hallway.

Kawther's stomach dropped. *The police are here?*

"They're not supposed to talk to the police without me. *Remember?*"

"Oh." Fatima frowned. "I think they're just giving them an update. I just got here a few minutes ago. I thought Khaled might have told you the police were here."

Khaled had made her promise to stay and represent Yassir, but he'd barely bothered to talk to her unless it was to ask for updates she didn't have.

Then the words hit her.

"Your brother?" she echoed. "Wait, is Yassir awake?"

"No." Fatima's voice was small. "Ali is here. His flight landed this morning."

Kawther's face heated up, sweat trickling down the back of her neck in an instant.

"He heard what happened and came straight here. Just . . . you can avoid him if you want to," Fatima murmured.

But she was Yassir's lawyer. And the police were talking. And Sayed Ali Al-Azzawi was back. She shouldn't have come. This was a mistake. *This was a mistake—*

Suddenly the door across the hall opened and two police officers walked out. Then they were heading down the hallway. She should stop them.

Right?

Right.

"Excuse me," she called, making her voice loud enough to echo in the hallway. A nurse down the hall stared at her curiously. "I'm the family's lawyer. You can't question my clients—"

The officer turned around and stared at her quizzically. "Sorry, who? What's your name?"

"Kawther Al-Hakim."

"Got a business card?"

Embarrassed, she shook her head. She didn't even have the temporary contract with Jones, Jacobs & Associates fully processed yet, although they had given her the green light to get started on building the case. The officer with the blond hair spoke. "Well, they didn't say they had a lawyer. We just asked a few questions."

Kawther sighed.

The second officer shrugged, like her presence bothered him.

"Can I get a record of it?"

The officers began walking away. "Call our office. Get a copy from the secretary."

"But you must have notes—" She held her tongue as they walked away.

Assholes.

Fatima and the boys stared at her, and she felt her skin flush. She was pathetic. So pathetic.

Coming in was definitely a mistake. It was different being a lawyer when your clients actually *wanted* help. This would be impossible if the Al-Azzawis kept her out of the loop. She was about to step away, for good, but then she heard a cry.

When they lived together after her parents' apartment caught fire, the Sayed's father had passed away in Iraq. Baba had held the Sayed as he cried, after they thought everyone had fallen asleep, but she and Ali were awake, eavesdropping.

She recognized the sound now.

Slowly, she entered the room and found Sayed Rahman crying into his hands as a man held a tissue box up to him.

Age had made his body bold. The thin wisps that once danced over his chin now connected into a golden-brown stubble, the same color as the thick waves that overlapped messily at the top of his head. Somehow, he had gotten more handsome with age, and she hated him for that. The last they saw each other, they were kids trying to play the roles of adults. Now they were grown and all she could remember was how she missed their lives as children.

Her gaze met Ali's, his eyes the color of the topaz stones they used to toss at the lake shore each summer. Two thick dimples dug into the curves of his cheeks like chasms. The kind of smile that could break the earth.

As a child, she would poke her finger into his dimples whenever he laughed, when she was still allowed to touch him, and then again at their khatib al-khatab, when he'd smiled once, only once, as Fatima flashed a camera and they agreed on their Islamic marriage contract, and she had done it as a reflex. Her hand burned at the memory of it.

Ali tried to speak. Her name became a mumbled breath. "Kaw . . ."

Sayed Rahman looked up and stared at her.

And even though they knew her name, even though they had known her since the day she was born, they were strangers.

"Amu, it's me, Kawther. I'm Yassir's lawyer," she whispered, stepping closer.

I'm here to protect you, she wanted to say. But instead she asked, "Did the police question you?"

The Sayed's eyes blinked, red. Voice thick. "Yes." He sniffled.

"What did they say?" she pressed. She took a seat on an orange armchair and scooted closer to them. She kept her eyes on the Sayed as she pulled out her notepad and pen. "Did they tell you any new information?"

"Nothing." The Sayed stretched his spine, his head now kissing his knees. "I should've watched him more. I heard him leave that night. I knew he left all the time, but he always came back and I did . . . nothing to stop him. What kind of father falls asleep when their son is outside in the cold?"

A small sob escaped the Sayed's body and she and Ali became still, like they were still holding their breaths, eavesdropping on their fathers from the hallway eighteen years ago. Ali's hands were limp now, the box of tissues hanging uselessly.

Tears rose in her throat. The black ink of her pen bled onto the notepad. It slipped from her hand and dropped to the floor, rolling toward Ali. She scooped it up quickly, her eyes still focused on the floor, instinctively. Her mother had taught her long ago that unmarried people should lower their gaze.

"Did you tell the police this? That you heard Yassir leave that night?"

The Sayed nodded. "I told them what I knew so they could help catch who did this."

Well . . . shit.

Kawther could only sigh. "Don't talk to them if they ever come around. Okay? Not unless I'm here, because they'll try to twist your words." This was her fault. She hadn't been there to remind him to remain silent because she was still too much of a coward, hiding herself when she shouldn't. "Can you tell me what happened that night?"

Ali shifted. "I'll talk. My dad is tired."

"You weren't there," she said. "You're not a witness."

The Sayed sat up, wiping his face clean, reminding her of Fatima earlier. "I'll talk after I pray. I know you're trying to help." A soft smile appeared on his lips. "It's good to see you, habiba."

Habiba.

He still spoke to her like she was his daughter. When she'd lost him, and her biological father, she'd never expected him to treat her this way again. And the boy who took it away from her was only a few feet away, and every nerve in her body was on the cusp of exploding.

"Baba, go rest," Ali told his father, who did not look at him. Another sob escaped from the Sayed's lips and Ali stood. "Baba," he pleaded. "Please."

The Sayed finally nodded and walked away. Then it was just her and Ali.

She hoped to see regret in his eyes. She wondered if this was how her parents felt, staring at her like she was a ghost that had returned to haunt them. Hoping she regretted leaving them.

Just come back, he'd told her one day after school. *Let's just get married. I'll put this behind me if you do.*

Spite gnawed at her. She hoped he was as miserable as her.

He swallowed.

Who would break down first and say how they felt?

Kawther swallowed the lump in her throat and walked away before she could find out.

36

KAWTHER

EIGHT YEARS, TWO MONTHS, AND SIXTEEN DAYS BEFORE

"Change into something nicer," Mama said as she plated purple turshi. Ali's favorite.

Kawther was wearing what she had worn to school that day.

"Why? It's just Fatima's family," Kawther said as she prepared the kettle for chai in anticipation of their parents asking for it once dinner finished. She had nailed this routine. She knew exactly what Mama needed when guests came around.

Normally, guests meant Kawther had to smile stiffly and dress in her finest clothes, and she and her siblings had to stay quiet when their parents were talking. But the Al-Azzawis were an extension of their family. She wore old jeans and wrinkled shirts, she spoke loudly and incessantly, and she didn't need to worry about faking smiles when they were around. Not once, in her seventeen years of knowing them, had she needed to change to be more presentable. Until today.

"Change," Mama simply repeated. While Kawther was puzzled, wondering if some other Iraqi family was going to randomly tag along to their weekly izzemas, she changed into the salmon-pink hijab she'd bought for Eid al-Fitr that year and a plum-colored dress with a black cardigan.

Mama nodded in approval as the doorbell rang. When she heard Ali's voice greet her family from the hallway, it immediately beckoned her eyes. She focused instead on Yassir, who ran up to her and hugged her torso, something he always did before Khaled shoved him.

"Hi," Yassir said, a missing baby tooth at the center of his smile.

But Ayah got to him before Kawther could even tousle his thick curls, looping her arm over his before pulling him away.

"You look nice today." Fatima smiled as she stepped inside. Despite having gotten married months ago, she still reserved every Thursday evening for these dinners while her husband worked night shifts. "Doesn't she look nice, Ali?"

Kawther scowled at her best friend. Fatima hadn't told Ali her secret, had she? She hadn't even seen Fatima since their last MASH game.

"Kawther always looks nice," Ali said, but his voice did not dance with the warmth it usually did. Kawther did not look back at him. If they'd embarrassed him at this moment, there would be a soft flush near his cheekbones, only an inch away from where his dimples were buried in his face. Instead, he just looked . . . sullen.

Another family did not come, so Kawther was puzzled why she was dressed so nicely. Perhaps it was the birth anniversary of one of the Imams and she had forgotten, but she was too embarrassed to ask Fatima if she looked *too* nice in case Ali heard. Dinner was served. The kids played games instead of eating as their fathers spoke of politics as they always did, and their mothers spoke about the rising prices at the grocery store in between correcting their husbands about political issues, as they always did. Fatima spoke to Kawther about what color drapes she should buy for her new apartment, affectionally joking that her husband was color-blind. But Ali stayed quiet, focused on the plate in front of him, and when Mama offered him more chicken, he took it gratefully, but he did not touch it.

After dinner and prayer, tea was served, and her mother put the tray in her clumsy hands. "Give one to Ali, too."

"Ali doesn't like chai," Kawther said.

"It doesn't matter." Mama waved her away.

When she entered the living room, the men were not speaking. They stared at her silently, and when she placed the chai in front of Ali, he did not look at her or say he didn't want one.

Kawther stepped away to head back into the kitchen to finish scrubbing the dishes, but Fatima put a hand on her arm, dragging her back to the living room. Mama and Khala Zainab clasped their hands around each other's, which they did often, but there was a look in their eyes she did not recognize.

Sayed Rahman's hand lightly pulled at Ali's baby-blue sweater before he stood up and stared at his feet, too. Had something bad happened? Was that why Ali looked so sad? Had he failed his college courses? He'd only just started community college. Had he lost money? Was he sick?

Ya Allah, she silently prayed to herself. *Please let Ali be okay.*

Sayed Rahman stood up and spoke, his eyes glued to the floor. "Our families have shared three countries. We each have three children. Neighbors in exile. Neighbors in America. Subhanallah, it is rare in life when you find people who you can truly consider your own." Sayed Rahman was the only one looking at Kawther. "And today I am respectfully asking Akhooya Mustafa and Akhti Abeer if they would give their blessing for a union."

A union? Was Ali getting married?

No. No. No.

Kawther's heart thumped so hard—just as it had when she was nine on the playground—that she put a hand on her chest to calm herself.

"I'm asking you, Kawther Bint Mustafa, to consider Sayed Ali to be your husband. I am asking if you would consider joining our family. If you could become Fatima and Yassir's real sister. Of course, I know this is a big decision, so I want to give you time to think about it. As much time as you need. Ali has already agreed and said yes."

The room was blanketed by silence, and Kawther could no longer feel her heart bursting in her chest. She had imagined this moment many times. She'd always known that if she was lucky enough, Ali would tell her father that he wanted her, and that she would learn it from them. A proper union.

She'd thought it would happen on the spur of the moment, like with Fatima, who was washing the breakfast dishes on a normal Saturday morning when her mother approached her with a proposal from the man who had become her husband a few months ago. Kawther had thought she might be wearing pajamas and acne cream when the question came, or maybe Khala Zainab would approach her first, putting her hand in hers, as she did often, as she asked, *Do you want to be my daughter?*

Though this did not follow the Islamic tradition, it was even better than she had imagined, because her entire family was there to witness it. The Sayed was right. Perhaps they were made for each other.

Allah had created human beings from clay. Had she, the eldest daughter of Hajji Abu Abdalla, and he, the eldest son of Sayed Rahman, been placed on this earth for each other? Their fathers had escaped Iraq on the same night, escaping the same bullets, witnessing the same dead bodies lining the roads, as Kawther and Ali held their mothers' hands and stepped into a new beginning together.

Her spine tingled in excitement.

But why did Ali, her Ali, look so sad? She had only admitted her crush to Fatima a few weeks ago, and now he was asking for her hand in marriage. He must think of her the same way. He must. When she tried to make eye contact with her best friend, Fatima looked down at the floor.

Why couldn't anyone look her in the eye? Only the boy she loved, who she had always loved, finally stared at her as the rest of the room looked down respectfully at their feet. For the first time in her life, when she stared into his stormy eyes, they lay empty.

In her panic, in her elation, in the dream she had imagined over and over again since the fourth grade, she whispered a yes.

"Are you sure?" Baba asked her quietly. "Do you want to take more time to think, habiba?"

Her eyes found Mama's, who nodded at her in agreement. "Take all the time you need. No rush, Kawther."

But Kawther shook her head. She had dreamt of this moment for nearly a decade. "I am sure."

After a few quiet breaths, the room exploded in cheer; her mother was kissing her cheeks and his mother was kissing her cheeks. And when Ali looked away, his cheekbones flushing above his dimples, she foolishly convinced herself that this was the first sign of love.

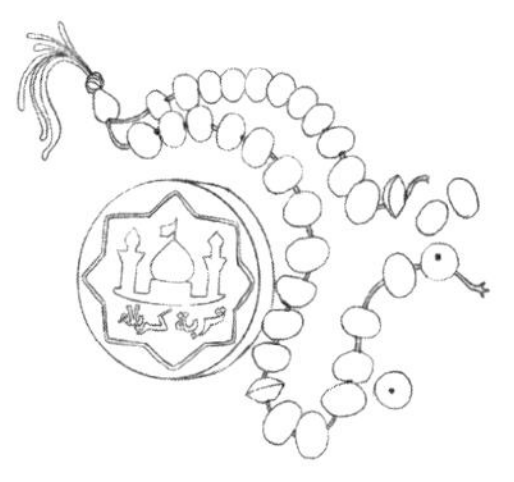

37

KHALED

SIX DAYS AFTER

Since the age of four, Khaled had dreamt of Saddam Hussein hunting his family.

The dream was always the same.

He sat in a single room, a bed neatly tucked into the corner, two white wooden doors serving as a closet. However, the room was not empty. At the center, his mother, sisters, and father lay fast asleep on the floor. When he pushed open the closet doors, it looked awfully like the closet he and Ayah shared as children: a few coats on a hanger, half-folded clothes stuffed into the tiny chest where he would store his soccer ball.

The dream always moved so quickly.

One moment his family was asleep and the next moment, the sky bled crimson with bright explosions illuminating the room. A large green tank thundered through the street. Lights flashed, followed by a series of bangs. Bombs shattered outside the window and bullets rained across the room. The room was being invaded.

Yet his family stayed asleep. As much as he tried to shake them awake, they did not move. Right before the door of the bedroom was smashed down violently, Khaled somehow pushed his entire sleeping family into the closet. Through the cracks in the doors, Khaled watched a man in a dark green uniform and a straight-cut mustache pace around the room with the largest AK-47 he could imagine.

In this dream, Saddam was as tall as the ceiling, his eyes bloodshot, his hair the same unruly gray as when the soldiers found him lying in that ditch in 2003. After throwing Khaled to the side, Saddam uncovered a knife from his pocket and stabbed Khaled's sleeping father. Then both of his sisters. He slit their throats, blood pooling so thick Khaled could swim in it. Then Saddam pulled out a knife and fork to feed on their flesh.

Khaled always woke just as blood splashed on his face.

Just as he did now, sweat dripping down his back.

The digital clock plastered on the wall blinked. Five a.m.

As a child, he would wake up in a sweat, screaming. His parents would whisper surahs into his ears and Baba would rock him to sleep each night until the dream disappeared. He would not tell them what the dream was about because, even at six years old, he did not want to remind them of being hunted. He knew that in New York City, Saddam kept a torture chamber where his men would torture Iraqis who had escaped to America. Saddam was known to execute at least two citizens before his breakfast, and despite the distance, that fear never left Khaled.

He still remembered the day Saddam finally died. His parents and the Al-Azzawis cheered in their living room the day of his hanging. The man responsible for so many innocent deaths was dead. He and Ayah snuck into the apartment complex's computer lab and watched the video with Yassir, as their parents forbade them from watching the man bellow his last words to God. The rope silenced him and his twenty-four-year dictatorship. Khaled could still remember watching his body swing back and forth eerily. It was that day that Khaled realized that not all deaths were a bad thing.

He'd always wondered if that was what men in power thought, too. Whether each time Saddam targeted Shia Muslims or Kurdish people or anyone else who dissented, he thought he was saving people from evil. Or if the Kill a Muslim Day people—whoever they were—thought they were doing the world a favor by trying to eradicate Muslims.

Faizal had been hunted. Khaled's and Yassir's parents had been hunted. And now Yassir was perhaps being hunted, too.

Different people. Different times.

Khaled shifted in the lime-green hospital chair, reaching for the laptop he'd left half open. He must have fallen asleep, trying to find more details about Ashton Milton, the veteran who had found Yassir. He didn't have a criminal record. But he had served two tours in Iraq, right after the invasion.

Khaled rubbed his eyes, the dream still fresh in his head. He wanted to shake it away—but some nightmares stayed true long after he was awake. He closed the laptop but noticed a movement in the dim light. Sayed Rahman was standing above Yassir, pressing a small cloth gently onto his face. He whispered Ayat al-Kursi into his son's ears, like he was a newborn. He prayed on behalf of Umm al-Banin and never stopped playing the recording of the Quran. Because sheikhs only came to town during big observances, a sheikh from California had recited a prayer through the phone last night.

Khala Zainab had not stopped praying, either. She kept a Quran under Yassir's head unless the hospital staff asked her to remove it while they checked his wounds. As a toddler, Yassir used to jump on Sayed Rahman's back while he prayed and rest his head on Baba's leg as he made istikharahs.

Now he'd been the victim of an attack for a faith he no longer believed in.

Eight people were dead now. Five-minute segments on major news channels and Muslim activists posting updates on social media kept Khaled in the loop.

Last night, a father of four—an immigrant from Ethiopia—had died of his injuries. He had been stabbed. Others had been shot. Yassir had been beaten. Despite that difference, whoever had attacked Yassir had wanted him dead. They hadn't stolen a thing. His wallet—including his ID—was still in his yellow Chapman hoodie pocket when the paramedics got to him.

Yassir was the youngest victim, too.

Khaled stared at the cutesy animal stickers lining the top of the wall. Yassir was still technically a child. Sometimes Khaled forgot he was just a kid figuring it out. When he'd punched Yassir in the face weeks ago, he'd blamed him like he was another man who'd taken his sister away.

Adhan quietly beckoned from the Sayed's phone. Khaled watched the man grab the sajadah and point it toward Mecca. Then he kissed the turbah so hard, with so much mercy, Khaled wondered if the clay would crumble.

Khaled made wudu in the hospital room sink, unfurled his own sajadah, kissed his turbah, and stood near the Sayed, who gave him a soft smile.

Since Khaled had reunited with them, he didn't know how to leave them. He helped with Yasmin. He helped translate when Fatima wasn't around, busy with her own kids. He made sure they ate their meals, just like he'd done for Mama and Baba after Ayah passed.

"Come pray right here, habibi," Sayed Rahman said, his eyes red and wet again.

When Khaled was around them, the pain felt more bearable. The anger subsided. His purpose felt clear, like Khalee Jafaar had told him it would. People wanted to kill them because of the way they worshipped. And for the first time since before he'd started drinking, before his belief in Allah's plan had begun to waver, before his soul had become soaked in anger and sadness, Khaled felt like his prayer was grounded in truth. The past few days had proved to him that no matter what happened, no one would take this away from him. It was his choice, and he would keep with it.

Khaled took his place next to Yassir's father. They prayed side by side, without a word to each other, speaking only to God.

"Khaled, you're not supposed to look at this," Kawther said, grabbing the file from his hands. "Stop going through my briefcase."

Khaled had already half memorized the results of Yassir's injuries from the police report he'd found when looking for a report about Ashton Milton. Moderate contusion. Two fractured ribs. Punctured liver. Dislocated right shoulder. Sprained ankle. Although according to the Al-Azzawis, Yassir had hurt his ankle a few weeks before the attack.

Even with a hurt ankle, Yassir couldn't resist leaving at night.

"How much did you read?" his sister asked, putting down the greasy tray of hospital fries in front of him. She would barely tell him a thing. So he looked for his own answers. Had the police even bothered questioning Ashton Milton?

"Barely saw a thing," he said.

Kawther shoved the file closer to her chest and pushed the fries toward him.

"They're out of veggie burgers and there's nothing else halal here. Eat."

He shook his head, scoffing.

"You're shaking again."

His sister placed a cold hand on his trembling arm and he shrugged her away, stuffing fries in his mouth so she wouldn't keep nagging, hoping the shaking eventually would stop.

It had begun after Ayah passed. He trembled when he thought of her. When his guilt over letting her down got to him. He trembled when he was angry for her, too. He used to have it under control. But lately, he couldn't stop. Maybe it was the hospital. Maybe it was the thought of Yassir lying on the ground, defenseless. The thought of Khaled's fist hitting his face weeks ago.

Kawther zipped up her briefcase, sipping on a hot coffee and pressing a hand over her temple, like Mama sometimes did with her migraines. "The documents in this bag are confidential. I could get in serious trouble if anyone sees you with them."

"Screw confidentiality," he said, grease on his fingers. "That doesn't count with family."

Kawther shifted, shaking her head. "If you're bored, go home. Your grades are slipping, your principal keeps calling, reminding us that you're about to hit the ten-day unexcused absence limit for the year. In fact, Baba keeps calling me, too, because you're avoiding him and your responsibilities at the shop."

He couldn't believe that after eight years of ignoring his pleas to talk to their parents, she was lecturing *him* now about Baba.

"Tell him to come here," Khaled said stubbornly. Kawther was here, Ayah was dead, what more could his parents be running from at this point?

"You know he won't," Kawther said, opening her laptop, where her press conference notes stared back at her. She swallowed. It was scheduled for tomorrow morning. "Why are you always asking questions you know the answers to?"

"Do I know the answers?" Khaled murmured. "I don't know why you're always hiding in the cafeteria, for starters."

"The nurse kicked us all out an hour ago, remember?" she said. "Besides, it's hard to concentrate—" Her eyes fell to the table and she stopped speaking as Ali and Fatima stepped into the cafeteria. Fatima had her arms folded and Ali pushed his hair frustratedly out of his face.

They spotted Kawther and Khaled, Ali rushing over in an instant.

Kawther nearly shot up out of her seat, as if she was in trouble. As if she wanted to disappear. Perhaps it was awkward, seeing her ex-fiancé this way. Technically, before she ran away, they were married Islamically, but they hadn't yet had their wedding party or moved in together. They had still touched long ago in a way Khaled didn't like to think too hard about, but a way that would make a Muslim boy and girl not look each other in the eye again, he was sure.

"Is it true?" Ali asked, pacing nervously around the table. Khaled had only remembered him calm, but in the past few days since he'd arrived, the panic over Yassir's condition had made Ali antsy, too. "Are they still not counting Yassir as a victim of this Kill Day shit? Muslim League of Lawyers posted a list of victims' names today and Yassir's name wasn't on it."

Kawther sighed, her eyes on her hands. "They're only publishing names with categorized hate crimes, and the police haven't categorized his assault as a hate crime."

"Why not?" Ali asked. "Do you need help doing this, Kawther? Maybe this is too much for you."

"Ali, shut up." Fatima unfolded her arms. "It's better if his name isn't all over the news. Mama and Baba want it this way. In fact, I came over to tell you to cancel the press conference tomorrow."

"Cancel . . . ? We shouldn't. His name and school were already released," Kawther said, side-eyeing Khaled because she knew he had told Alex, who had then told everyone at school. "He's a minor, he's supposed to be protected. This press conference is meant just to clarify our stance in pursuing this case as a hate crime and to put pressure on the district attorney to press charges when a suspect is found. But . . . if you don't want to do it, we don't have to."

"Do it," Ali said at the same time as Fatima gave a definitive *no*.

They always used to bicker like that as kids, too. They glared at each other.

"Maybe we can do one after he wakes up," Fatima said. "But you see Mama and Baba, Ali. You see how they're torn apart. Don't make them feel more scared and embarrassed."

Embarrassed over what? Khaled wondered. *Embarrassed that their son, who never listened to them, was beaten to a near pulp? Or embarrassed over details of Yassir's personal life getting out there?*

"Fine, cancel the stupid press conference," Ali muttered. "Do you at least have a lead yet? Please tell me the police are doing something."

Kawther looked between the siblings and stared at her computer again. "I called for updates every day and there were none. Because he's the only minor potentially connected to these attacks, they're still skeptical—"

"Potentially?" Ali echoed. "What do you mean by potentially? It's a fact—"

Kawther gathered her things, putting away the records. "It doesn't matter what we think. There needs to be proof of a hate crime. Inshallah Yassir wakes up soon so we can get this figured out. We have no eyewitnesses. No cameras. Zero leads—"

"Besides that veteran," Ali said, and Khaled nodded. So he wasn't the only one thinking of Ashton Milton. "How could anyone think it's not strange that a man who *volunteered* to hurt Iraq didn't target my Iraqi little brother?"

"Exactly," Khaled huffed.

"He was homeless," Fatima interjected. "Lots of veterans are. It's not that odd he'd find him. It's just a coincidence."

"Coincidence? Do you hear yourself?" Ali shot back at his sister. "You know there are soldiers who regret what they did, but there are those who are proud of it. Go watch some of the confessions online. How some of them laugh at their war crimes. Half the time they're only regretful because of how it fucked up their own lives, not because they're remorseful about what they did to our people."

Khaled merely nodded. He had seen the videos. Listened to the podcasts. Hell, even the Hollywood films that always memorialized the crimes, rather than the victims.

"They killed a million Iraqis. What's another one to them?" Ali spat.

Fatima huffed. "I know that, Ali."

"I don't know if he's innocent, but Milton had an alibi," Kawther interjected, pulling her briefcase toward herself. "They're not going to keep questioning the man who found him, the media has touted him as a hero for now. I'll . . . I'll email my boss about pushing the press conference until after Yassir wakes up. Khaled, please go home."

"Why? We need him here," Ali said, putting an arm over Khaled's shoulder. A warm feeling of nostalgia hit Khaled. "I think the nurse should be done doing whatever she's doing by now. Let's go, Khaled."

They left the two women staring at each other. Ali didn't move his arm away from Khaled.

"You know I missed you the most?" Ali said. "Well, outside of Yassir, of course. I missed your smart-ass remarks."

Khaled tried to smile but it felt weird in this moment, so he just nodded and let the man steer him upstairs.

"I'm glad you haven't abandoned him," Ali said. "We all abandoned him except for you."

Guilt crawled up Khaled's throat.

"I'm sure your parents are mad that you're here, I can tell by Kawther's voice, but don't go, please. Not until he wakes up, at least. You're a part of us. You've always been so brave. Remember when you got attacked by that snotty white kid? And you went to this exact hospital and even though you had to get stitches on your chin, you didn't even cry. Everyone cried besides you."

Khaled could still remember Mama crying, holding his head close, something Khala Zainab usually did.

We need to leave, Mama had pleaded with Baba. *I never wanted to live here. Look what they're doing to us!*

And where should we live? Baba had said. *Beneath the bombs?*

Nearly ten years later and they were back. Same hospital. Different boy. Different injuries. Same violence.

"We need to do something," Ali said. "The police seem to think my dad might have something to do with this."

Khaled blinked at him, shocked. "Your dad? But Kawther didn't say anything . . ."

Why was she so full of secrets?

They found themselves back in the hallway waiting room; the nurse still had the room closed off. "Tell me everything about the cops and your dad."

As Ali explained, Khaled felt anger burning deep in his gut.

Even though he had forced Kawther to defend them, they were still defenseless. She was failing them, just like Khaled had failed Yassir so many times.

"What are you thinking, Khaled?" Ali asked as Khaled reached for his laptop in his backpack, immediately opening a blank document.

If they had to prove that Yassir could've been attacked for being Muslim, then he would prove it. For the first time since the attack happened, Khaled knew what he needed to do.

38

KAWTHER

SEVEN DAYS AFTER

Kawther sat at the shiny oak desk at Jones, Jacobs & Associates and listened to her new boss finish her call between sips of black coffee. Rebecca had been quick to hire her and introduce her to a set of attorneys and paralegals, who'd offered her some stiff smiles.

What Jones, Jacobs & Associates didn't realize was that she had applied for two vacant attorney positions at the firm. She'd been rejected for both before being considered for an interview.

Outside of a tall Asian attorney, she was the only person of color on the team. She admitted, it had shocked her a bit to see them jump on Yassir's case with her, but the attack was already becoming highly publicized. If they pulled it off, it could put the small injury law firm on the map.

"Thanks again, Gerald, we'll get Reese in court for that tomorrow." Rebecca hung up the phone, her frizzy brown hair bouncing at the ends, as she pressed a faint smile onto her lips. "That's a beautiful color," she said, pointing at Kawther's powder-blue hijab.

"Oh." Kawther tugged on the bottom of her scarf absentmindedly. "Thank you."

Rebecca's eyes descended to the file in front of Kawther. "This score sheet is extremely interesting, don't you think?"

She pointed to the page left open in Kawther's file, the one that had made Kawther cry this morning when she found the Kill a Muslim Day score sheet on the desk she was assigned to.

While news reporters had discussed vague details about the list, it had yet to be released publicly. A copy of the page-long diatribe about Islam and its followers' corrupting America had been found along with nearly every victim. Except Yassir.

KILL A MUSLIM DAY

They killed our people. Now we kill them. Kill the most to save our democracy and save the American people from those who threaten our freedom. The law may punish you, but God will reward you greatly. Whoever earns the most points will be blessed in the afterlife.

Punch a Muslim — 10 points
Liberate a Muslim "Woman" from hijab — 20 points
Defile a Muslim "Woman" — 22 points
Stab a Muslim — 30 points
Shoot a Muslim — 50 points
Eliminate a Muslim Family — 100 points
Burn Down a Mosque — 500 points
Eradicate a Congregation — 1000 points

"It feels like a joke, doesn't it?" Rebecca said, sighing. "A rep from the FBI called this morning; they say it may actually have started as a joke and gone too far. They have yet to find the source, but it was leaked online this morning. If it hadn't, they probably would keep withholding it."

Kawther's eyes quickly glanced over the words again. The pin holding up her hijab felt tight. Her skin prickled. "It's only a two-point difference."

Rebecca raised her eyebrows, staring at her.

"Liberating or raping me. It's a two-point difference."

Rebecca nodded. "I'm sorry. It must be heavy to do this work when you're so close to the subject."

You have no idea.

"If you ever feel like this is out of your scope, just let me know. The press conference, for example . . ." Kawther's fingers shook. She knew this was why Rebecca had called her in. "I know you and the family share the same cultural background, which is why Mona recommended you and why we're pulling some strings to have you join the team. You've done a wonderful job so far collecting the police reports and media details. But we still need a statement from the family. A teen boy getting attacked in the evening screams gang violence, not hate crime. If we can humanize the victim, show them he's a good kid, we can get public support. It would only help our case and put pressure on the police."

It angered Kawther that they had to humanize Yassir at all. He'd been attacked in the middle of the night. Defenseless. And still, people would blame him for his own blood spilled on the concrete.

Kawther cleared her throat. "They said they'd be open to it once he wakes up."

"*If* he wakes up." Rebecca blew out a breath and Kawther's spine vibrated. The woman was helping. Kawther had to remember that Rebecca was paying her, though they'd taken the case pro bono. That Rebecca's firm was carrying the weight of what had become a politically charged criminal case. "Sorry, I know we should be hopeful, but we should always plan for the worst . . ." Rebecca shook her head. "I'm praying for his recovery, of course. But you need to get them to reconsider *now*."

Kawther nodded, scribbling notes that Rebecca couldn't see.

Convince the family that betrayed me to listen to me.

"If you feel that's too much . . . I don't mind taking over. I went and visited this morning, hoping to see you, but I couldn't find you."

Shit.

"Sorry, I was probably in the cafeteria. It's easier to concentrate there," she said, embarrassed at the pathetic excuse.

Rebecca nodded, frowning. "The father shouldn't speak at the conference, not with the police questioning him. The mother didn't look like she understood any English, and the sister wasn't friendly. But there was a teen boy who had a lot to say. He kept talking about how Yassir was bullied at school for being Muslim. He looked his age, but they didn't look alike. Is that his brother?"

She must be talking about Khaled. Not Ali, who she luckily hadn't seen.

If Kawther told Rebecca that Khaled was her brother, would Rebecca immediately throw her off the case?

If she told Rebecca that the family she had promised to protect was the one who had ruined her, would Rebecca let her go? Would she be freed from her obligation to Khaled?

For the first time since she was in high school—since she sat in Mrs. Mackenzie's office—she wanted to spill her secrets.

Rebecca continued while Kawther kept silent. "If he's not a minor, he should make a statement as well. Or if he is, with parent permission. Think you can ask him? I didn't get his name before the nurse came in and he ended up interpreting for the family."

Kawther pressed her lips. "I'll ask."

Like hell he'd speak publicly about this.

She'd drag him straight to Baba herself. If he shared any of his thoughts about the situation with the world, this whole case would be over before it could even start.

"One more thing before I let you go back to the hospital," Rebecca said. "An article was published today in the victim's school newspaper. It's retaliatory toward Ashton Milton, the veteran who reported the crime. Normally this wouldn't be on our radar, but it's getting a lot of traction online and we've received a few calls about it already today. The article was written by a student named Khaled Al-Hakim. I'm sure you have a common last name, but I wanted to make sure. Is this someone you know?"

39

KHALED

EIGHT DAYS AFTER

Khaled's phone had been blowing up all afternoon.

Around six a.m., he saw his piece published and a smile spread over his face. The new quarter had started, so technically, he was allowed to submit again and had been accepted within minutes. It helped that Jia, the cute half-Nepali senior who occasionally flirted with him, was in charge. As soon as Jia confirmed the publication, he forwarded it to Alex, who forwarded it to the kids he knew . . . which was most of the senior class.

I can't believe you wrote this, **Alex texted him.** Everyone is going to fight you.

But that was precisely what Khaled wanted. He wanted people to get riled up enough so that maybe the truth would spill out. Someone had attacked Yassir, and while he still thought it could be the veteran, he wasn't ruling out anyone from Chapman, either.

Khaled sauntered into school for the first time in a month to see if anyone would crack with information. He didn't even make it halfway to the library before he was stopped by Miles's voice calling him. Khaled kept walking until his arm was pulled back, forcing him to look Miles in the eye.

"How do we know it wasn't you?" Miles said gruffly. "You're the one who punched Michael in the face before you went to get recruited by ISIS, right?"

"Don't bother," Brooks said, his gaze cutting into Khaled. "The truth about them will come out. It always does."

"*Them*?" Khaled echoed, pushing away from the two boys. "Can you elaborate, Brooks? What is it about us that comes out?"

"You always cry fucking crocodile tears," Brooks spat. "It has nothing to do with your cousin. We don't give a shit about your religion or your country, we just don't like you, Khaled. Is that so hard to understand?"

They shrank back as he came closer. He was not going to physically fight with them, it was the last thing he needed. But they were afraid of him. Threatened by every word he said and had yet to say, long before he'd ever stepped into the school.

"From the bottom of my heart," Khaled said, raising his hand, which caused Brooks to flinch, even as he put it over his own chest, "fuck you."

Then he twisted around, hearing them swear all kinds of things under their breaths. Only a few steps later, he felt another pull on his arm. He turned, ready to elbow whoever it was.

"What are you doing?" Alex asked, eyes wide, ducking. Khaled straightened. He hadn't seen his friend in weeks. Alex huddled Khaled under his arm, pushing him through the crowd, away from the eyes watching him. "You finally show up to school for this? Do you want to get beat up?"

Khaled shrugged. "Maybe I can find the perpetrator if I do."

Alex sighed. "I thought maybe you'd come back chilled out."

"How can I be chilled out when people are getting hunted, Alex? Are you even paying attention?"

"I'm trying, I'm just overwhelmed by it all," Alex admitted, shaking his head. "You don't even answer my texts. The news stopped saying Michael's attack was connected—"

"Fuck the news, Alex." Khaled cut him off. "When have they ever been on our side?"

The media that often painted Muslims as villains was not a media that would paint them as victims. The intercom roared with static before Khaled even reached the library doors for first period.

"Khaled Al-Hakim to the principal's office. Khaled Al-Hakim—"

"Well, that was faster than I thought," Khaled muttered.

"Man, what if you get expelled this time?" Alex asked, worry in his eyes.

Khaled spotted Miles and Brooks still standing in the middle of the hallway. He quickly walked past them, avoiding their dirty looks, as he headed toward the office where his favorite principal was waiting for him.

☽

Principal Delpy was seething. She wasn't the type to seethe.

"Welcome back," she muttered. "You missed more days than you were excused for, including your suspension."

Khaled shrugged. "There's sort of a community crisis going on, not sure if you heard . . . or cared."

Her ears turned red. "You don't think we care about Michael?"

"It's Yassir," Khaled corrected under his breath. "If you cared so much, why did you take away his scholarship? Alex told me."

"That is confidential information—" She stopped and sniffed before shaking her head. "I didn't realize you and Michael were on good terms again, since you *did* assault him before you left on your trip."

Khaled stared his principal down. He hadn't resolved shit between Yassir and him yet. Even if Yassir woke up, he didn't know if they could go back to normal. But Khaled sat by his bed and prayed he'd live another day so he could tell him he was sorry.

Delpy sighed. "Khaled, I didn't call you in about your attendance, although I did talk to your father, and he said he would get you back in class regularly. I called you down because my phone hasn't stopped ringing all morning. What you wrote today in the school paper . . . it's gone beyond the Chapman community. Did you know you made the twelve o'clock news because Fight for Freedom, the veteran-run support group who volunteers at our annual fundraisers, issued a response? Did you also know that they're threatening to retract their donations? I understand it was an opinion piece, and we do promote diverse thinking in this school, but it doesn't mean what you wrote was acceptable."

Silence filled the air, and Delpy began typing something on her computer.

"Do you think something bad is going to happen to me?" Khaled finally asked. "People seem really angry about what I wrote, right?"

"No, I don't think anything bad will happen to you. I think you should think about who you've hurt in this moment instead." She pushed a printed copy of the article in front of him. "There were many complaints specifically about the last paragraph of your piece. Can I read it over to you?"

She didn't wait for his response before she recited the words he'd viciously written less than twenty-four hours ago.

"Perhaps our society is not yet ready to condemn the crimes of those who served overseas for the sake of our so-called freedom. Ashton Milton could be innocent, but without a thorough investigation, we're letting a potential criminal—one with a history of killing innocent Iraqis—go free. If we refuse to consider Milton a viable suspect and seek someone else to blame, look no further than the classmates who have spewed Islamophobic vitriol for years. Maybe even a teacher. Chapman High is a miracle of a school, consistently producing stunning sporting championships, Ivy League hopefuls, and racists alike."

Delpy stopped reading. She stared at him.

"*This* I do not take lightly, Khaled. You could potentially be sued for what you wrote."

Khaled swallowed. Sue?

"My sister is a lawyer," he said automatically, surprising himself by thinking of Kawther first.

"You won't have to worry about any legal action unless this goes further. I'm giving you a chance to issue a retraction and publicly apologize to all the students, teachers, donors, and parents. I plan on speaking with the rest of the newspaper staff this afternoon. We can send a mass email together."

"But—"

She shook her head. "I do not have time for this. We are all thinking about Michael and his recovery. As soon as we heard the news, we sent flowers to the hospital. We've extended all of his assignments and exams and I talked to the board about his scholarship. We'll figure it out once he wakes up. What happened to him was unfortunate. But there is absolutely no evidence that his attack is even remotely related to this school."

She blew out a frustrated breath, a stern look in her eyes that seemed reserved only for him. She must have been relaxed these past few weeks without him.

"I've also consulted Mr. Marks, and we've concluded that due to your consistently unacceptable behavior, you will be removed from your American government course for the rest of the year and will do the assignments independently with Mrs. Marsh. We have decided that if you commit any more offenses at this school, we'll be forced to expel you. Understand? I expect a draft of your apology by the end of the day."

He returned to class in a daze. Alex nudged him for an update, but Khaled shook his head, planting his face against the cold desk while trying to get his body to stop shaking.

40

KAWTHER

"Rebecca called me. She's furious." Mona's voice echoed from the phone. "Why didn't you tell her this was a conflict of interest? Kawther, this family is the reason you left and—"

"I'm handling it, Mona," Kawther said as she circled the school again in her shaky Honda. Where the hell was he? If it hadn't been his first day finally back to school, she would've pulled him out of class. But she needed time away from him to calm herself down.

"It's okay to quit. It's okay if you never see them again."

"Listen, I'm picking up my brother from school. I apologized profusely to Rebecca. The article was already taken down."

"The reposted screenshots are still going on both sides. Muslim Twitter is very keen on blaming Ashton Milton now, too . . ." Mona blew out a loud breath. "I'm sorry. The last thing you need is someone to yell at you, I know that. I've been just so tired and frustrated. It's been hard to keep dealing . . ."

She stopped talking. The Santa Monica patient wasn't looking well, and neither was Yassir. He still hadn't woken up. Kawther was afraid at this point he would be added to the increasing death toll. She didn't want to think of him succumbing to his injuries.

"I have to go," Kawther said, feeling the tears rising in her throat again. "I'm sorry. I'll call you later."

"Okay. Stay safe."

Kawther hung up and stepped out of the car. She spotted Khaled walking out, eyes to the ground like he didn't know where he was going.

"Here!" Kawther shouted, waving at him. He looked up and around, then slowly made his way to the car. He got inside, shaking. She took the bagel she'd bought him this morning and shoved it into his hands. "Eat. Or I'm taking you to the hospital to be admitted as a patient."

Kawther, you're shaking, have you eaten today? Mrs. Mackenzie once asked her, leaning close enough that she could feel the woman's warm manicured nails momentarily touch her left arm. *Shaking means you're hungry, you're sick, or there's something that's really bothering you.*

"Let's get the fuck out of here," he murmured, grabbing the bag. She did not like her baby brother swearing, but he took a large bite of the bagel, and she forgave him. She always forgave too easily.

When he finished eating, she decided to scold him.

"The article you published," she said as she drove. "Why didn't you tell me?"

"Why?" he asked. "You never would've let me publish something like that."

"Because this hurts the case!" she shouted. "The firm is getting hit with negative press. If people find out the author of that article is my brother, they'll think the Al-Azzawis agree with your accusations, and we'll lose public support. I'll be fired. The firm won't represent him anymore." She bristled with rage. "Baba called me, furious, because your principal called again—" She stopped, glancing over to see that he was still shaking, eyes glossed over.

"Are you in trouble?" His voice cracked. "Did this get you in trouble?"

She parked in front of the hospital. She couldn't keep the next words from coming out of her mouth. "What if I break my promise?"

The gloss in his eyes turned into fire. "You can't, Kawther, I won't speak to you again—"

She sighed, pulling the keys out of the ignition. "Let's just go inside."

He pushed himself out of the car. "You should be doing better. If you were actually doing your job, I wouldn't have had to make sure everyone is talking about Milton's involvement. If you quit, you can't even pretend that you're my sister. Or that you care about me at all."

You should be doing better.

She wondered what more she could possibly do to convince him that she was on his side.

"I am your sister, and I do care about you," she said, defeated.

I'm doing this for you, she wanted to say. *For Ayah. For all the moments I could no longer protect you.*

"You're a fucking coward," Khaled said, slamming his door and walking into the hospital without her.

She blew out a hot breath, slamming her own door with annoyance before she followed him. On the ICU unit floor, the Al-Azzawis were standing in the hallway. They were probably waiting to fire her before she could quit. Maybe they thought she was a failure, too, just like everyone else. But when her gaze locked with Fatima's, she noticed the familiar fear in her old friend's eyes. Then she saw the uniforms. The two tall officers were back, their eyes trained on Khala Zainab.

41

KAWTHER

EIGHT YEARS, ONE MONTH, AND ELEVEN DAYS BEFORE

As soon as Ali's rusty Toyota drove off, Kawther purchased a single movie ticket. Even though she hated him at this moment, even though she'd lied to her mother when she asked what romantic things Ali had done for her on their dates, she still loved him.

She had not told her parents about this. Or Fatima.

Just a week ago, in the comfort of Mama and Baba's living room, among a crowd of community members, they'd agreed on their Islamic marriage contract. Both of their mothers had cried, kissed each of their cheeks, elated that their families had officially become one.

Although they were Islamically married, Iraqis in their community didn't consider them officially married until their wedding party. For now, she was culturally engaged. This was the way they could date halal. Touch each other, if they chose to.

Ali had yet to do so.

At first, she thought Ali was just too shy to see her without her hijab. His cheeks flushed when their skin brushed as he put the thin wedding gold he could afford around her neck, and when Fatima forced him to put his hand in hers, he laughed and said he'd forgotten he could.

But tonight he looked at her in a way he never had before.

"I need more time," he said on what was supposed to be their first date, dropping her off to go who knew where and do who knew what, maybe kissing who knew who instead of her. She'd worn red lipstick, his favorite color, tonight. "Before I can do these things with you."

She didn't know what "these things" meant.

Holding her hand or kissing her cheeks or maybe even her lips. Now she sat in the empty theater and thought about all the ways he could touch her, how it would make her feel, and whether it mattered if he had touched someone else like that first.

On the screen, the man kisses the wrong woman. The other woman leaves.

It did bother her.

Kawther shoved another handful of popcorn in her mouth, tucking her engagement ring in her pocket because it felt too heavy at this moment. Before the credits rolled, her phone vibrated. Hope in her heart thudded. Maybe he'd changed his mind.

But the number was unfamiliar.

Mrs. Mackenzie had said the Future Law Scholars committee selected candidates from all over the world. She'd said they might call Kawther at an odd hour if she'd earned a spot. Kawther knew she should've retracted her application, but everything had happened so fast with Ali, she had forgotten to update her advisor. But if they offered, she'd simply tell them no. She was technically a wife. Her husband just needed to fall in love with her first.

Kawther stepped out and answered the call. A familiar voice repeated her name.

"Kawther," Ali breathed. "Kawther. Kawther. Can you come get me?"

This didn't make any sense. They had driven his car tonight, not hers.

"What do you mean?"

More static. A brief pause.

"I—my car is parked. I don't want it towed. We'll get it after. I need you to come get me. Do you have the credit card with you?"

"Ali, where—"

"Do you have it?"

She had it but hadn't touched it yet. He'd given it to her with the promise to take her furniture shopping, but he hadn't found the time.

"Okay. Then just come. Riverside Police Department."

"Why are you at the police station?"

Static. The call disconnected.

She thought about calling Mama. She thought about calling Baba. But she was an adult now. She shook off the panic in her stomach and called a cab, praying that one of her dad's friends would not be driving it.

A thin, quiet white woman drove her to the police station. She called Ali's cell phone, but he did not answer.

"Can I help you, ma'am?" a stout woman asked at reception.

"Um. I think my fiancé is here."

They had yet to do the legal paperwork at the courthouse.

"Name."

"Ali Al-Azzawi."

"He's been in the holding cell for about forty minutes. You work fast."

"Holding cell?" Kawther echoed. "For what? Is he in trouble?"

"He got called for a disturbance at a residence. Lucky for him that he just turned twenty-one or this could've been ugly."

She didn't understand what the woman was saying. "What do you mean?"

"Your fiancé was found drinking and trespassing on private property."

"Drinking?" Kawther echoed.

"Bail is set at five hundred. How would you like to pay?"

Kawther slid the credit card over, and the woman used money meant for their future expenses—furniture, henna, and the wedding party to celebrate and finalize their union, the first month's rent for their first shared apartment. A small ticket spat from the machine.

"You can take a seat. He'll be released soon."

When he came out, his eyes were as empty as when his father had proposed on his behalf in the living room a month ago. There was a rancid stench on his clothes that she had never smelled before. Ali grabbed her hand and squeezed her fingers immediately, as if he knew how each molecule of his touch stirred her. It was the first time they'd held hands since their khatib al-khatab. If it were not for Fatima putting his stiff fingers into hers, she never would've known what it felt like to touch this Ali's hands. Not childhood Ali. This Ali, who was a man. Soon, she would regret the familiarity of this new touch.

"Why did you lie?" she whispered when they found his car in a manicured suburb.

"I never lied," he said, his eyes red and tired. She had seen him look this way before, here and there, when she thought he'd just woken up after a long nap. Perhaps this was what he looked like after the drinking stopped affecting his body. When he became sober.

Sober.

She never thought she would have to think that about Ali. The boy who had taught their brothers how to pray. The boy who always prayed before breaking his fast in Ramadan. The boy who had just sworn to God that he would be her husband and take care of her in the way she was supposed to be taken care of.

"So, you go around drunk, trying to break into strangers' houses?"

He laughed. "That wasn't a stranger. I wasn't breaking in, I got caught sneaking in and got the cops called on me."

"Who is it?" Her voice trembled.

"My girlfriend . . ." he whispered, staring at his hands. "Kawther, don't look at me that way, please. You don't think my parents didn't look at me that way, in disgust, when they first found out about her, too?"

She opened her mouth and closed it. And when the tears descended her cheeks, she did not know what they even meant.

"Shit . . . I—I'm sorry. Please don't tell my dad, don't tell anyone. I'm done with that shit, I swear. I'm never going back there. She just watched as they took me away . . . she just watched." His voice broke.

"So, each time you're supposed to be on a date with me," Kawther said, "you're really with her?"

Ali put a hand on her hand. "I never wanted to marry you, Kawther," he said, and the words seemed to ricochet, stinging her chest. "But maybe this is my wake-up call. Maybe I needed to go through this shit to see that Lexi isn't worth it anymore. Maybe I just needed—"

She pulled her hand away from him and he grabbed it again, this time more forcefully. She stared at him, trembling, and he let go.

"Kawther, I see the truth now. I'm meant to leave that shit behind and be with you. You came immediately. You've been there for me. I don't remember where you begin and where you end. You're always a part of me, and I've neglected you."

She stared at the dim white moonlight. It was nearly midnight, and Mama had not yet called her to check up on her because Mama trusted Ali. They all trusted Ali.

His fingers found hers again, gentle this time.

"Drinking, Ali? How could you—" Her voice cracked as he rubbed circles into her hands. Her pulse accelerated under his touch.

"You don't know what kind of hell I've been through," Ali said. "I'm sorry, Kawther. I'm sorry, I'm sorry—"

And then he began sobbing and she couldn't stop herself. She wiped his cheeks and told him it was going to be okay, just like she had when they'd first arrived in America, when he would burst into tears as if he suddenly remembered something that scared him. Although she knew he had been with someone else just hours earlier, even though he smelled like something sour and vanilla and roses, she let him scoot closer to her. His hand spread over her cheek, and she did not pull away.

When he murmured that he would try harder as his breath tangled with hers, she believed him. If he had not had a semblance of love for her, would he still have tilted her chin and delicately laid his fingers on either side of her glistening cheeks, kissing her for the first and last time?

Soft and sweet like German chocolate cake. That was what he tasted like.

He pulled away, his bottom lip still lingering over hers, murmuring *Let's start over* and *Don't tell anyone what happened tonight*. If she had known what was to come, she would not so easily have obliged.

42

KAWTHER

EIGHT DAYS AFTER

Two officers, one in a coffee-colored two-piece suit, the other in uniform, extended their hands. Khala Zainab kept her hands to herself, and Kawther politely rejected their handshakes, quickly explaining that Muslims didn't shake hands with the opposite sex.

"Are you the interpreter?" Coffee Suit asked, looking around the enclosed prayer room she and Khala Zainab had been shuffled into moments ago. They each sat in orange upholstered chairs, a small shiny coffee table between them.

There was no way he'd already forgotten who she was. "I'm an attorney with Jones, Jacobs and Associates. I'll be representing the victim and his family in the case," she said, her voice more confident than she imagined.

"I'm Sergeant Montgomery." Coffee Suit pointed to his chest. He gestured to the blond man in uniform sitting next to him. "This is Officer Matthews, who was at the scene after your son's attack."

Khala Zainab blinked at the men. She knew as much English as Kawther's mother. More than she'd let on, secretly understanding her children's words but rarely acknowledging it or replying, unless they were misbehaving.

Kawther interpreted for the woman. Her Arabic pronunciation wasn't amazing, but it had been good enough to help her parents decipher bills and notices and apply for Medicaid and food stamps since elementary school. Baba used to check her out of class so she could attend doctor appointments with Mama.

"I'm surprised you'd come all the way here." Kawther cleared her throat nervously. Their timing annoyed her. *"Again."*

"We wanted to ask you a few questions, Zainab. This investigation has gained a lot of media attention, and we just want to make sure we're doing our job and will catch whoever did this to your son. Do you understand?" Montgomery said.

Kawther translated, and Khala Zainab's eyes flitted between her and the men. She nodded.

"Yes," Yassir's mother whispered quietly in English.

Officer Matthews shifted in his seat.

"Zainab, can you tell me where you were between the times of eleven p.m. and three a.m. on November seventh and eighth?"

Kawther felt her hands become clammy.

Ya Allah. Ya Muhammad. Ya Ali. Please don't let this go wrong.

Kawther translated and looked back at the men after receiving Khala Zainab's answer. "She was asleep, and her husband was asleep, too. Yassir was working on homework, so she slept near the baby whenever Yassir had to study."

"The baby?" Sergeant Montgomery said. "Is that your son's baby? Hayley?"

It was easy to forget that Yasmin hadn't fallen out of the sky and into Yassir's arms. Kawther had forgotten that she was technically a half-white baby belonging to an American teenage girl who'd abandoned her. At least, that was what Khaled had told her a few days ago.

Kawther nodded. "Yes."

The men stared at Zainab.

"Yes," she confirmed in English.

Officer Matthews wrote something down. "Was your son home at eleven p.m.?"

"Yes." Khala Zainab understood that.

"Tell me about your relationship with your son?"

Kawther received her response and spoke with urgency. "She says her relationship with Yassir is loving. She takes care of his daughter while he's at school and teaches him how to properly take care of her. Every night, she cooks for him, and she watches him go to school in the morning."

"What's your husband's relationship like with your son?"

Kawther looked at Khala Zainab and received a quieter answer. An embarrassed answer. But Kawther knew they were being recorded, so her translations had to be accurate. She felt sweat lining her armpits.

"They have a more strained relationship. They still love each other, but they don't always see eye to eye."

Kawther bit her lip. She knew there was more, but Khala Zainab kept her words to a minimum.

"Has your husband ever physically hurt your son?"

Kawther attempted to relax her face. She knew the Sayed had slapped Yassir on the eve of Ashura, and there had been witnesses. It was unlike Sayed Rahman to ever hit his children, yet it had happened. She hoped Khala Zainab would lie.

"No," Khala Zainab said after Kawther explained the question.

"Okay." Officer Matthews clicked his tongue, writing something down like he didn't believe her. "Has your husband ever punched, slapped, kicked, or hurt you in any manner?"

Kawther felt bile rise in her throat. The officers weren't here to ask if Khala Zainab knew anything pertinent or saw something happen on Kill a Muslim Day. They were still trying to pin the crime on Sayed Rahman.

Khala Zainab's stare was drenched in confusion.

Right. Kawther needed to translate. She hesitated, but she knew the truth, even if she did not know this family anymore.

"No." Khala Zainab stared at the men, a scowl on her face.

Officer Matthews kept his eyes on Khala Zainab. "I understand that you and your son might not have the same religious beliefs. I have a daughter, and trust me, she doesn't want to go to church sometimes." He chuckled to himself. "But in America, this is a free country. I want you to listen to me really carefully." He sat up straight in his chair, leaning his hairy arm closer to the table. Kawther felt her blood pressure rise. "In America, we see cases like this. With Muslim victims especially. I know people want to claim racism and Islamophobia and all that. I'm not saying that it doesn't happen, but I'm saying that many times, with thorough investigations, it turns out to be family members instead. When it's a child, like your son, sometimes parents do these things because the kid isn't following the rules. And I know your son has run into issues with the law. Do you understand me?"

Kawther caught herself rising from her chair. Khala Zainab's warm hand forced her to stay put.

"Don't give them an excuse to blame us," the woman whispered in Arabic.

Kawther did not care to be nice. These were her clients. They had been her family, and she would not let anyone try to vilify them this way.

"Officer Matthews." Kawther kept her voice steady. "You do not have any evidence pointing toward Mr. Al-Azzawi. He has an alibi from his wife. She gave her statement moments ago, and you have a recorder to rewind if you'd like. Since the tenth of November, I've requested that this investigation be forwarded to the FBI, and your department has denied my request. I want you and Sergeant Montgomery to understand that if Muslim communities hear that Yassir's attack is being circled back to his father rather than to the string of attacks that took place on the exact date of Kill a Muslim Day, well, you're going to have a problem. I'm just stating that as a fact."

"You don't need to threaten the department, Ms. . . ." Sergeant Montgomery stumbled on her name, leaving himself breathless. "Your law firm has done that enough. We're backed up with calls already. Crime is rising, especially near the holidays."

Officer Matthews pressed his pen into the notebook. "Honor killings aren't just for girls, you know? Boys get killed, too."

"Honor killings aren't inherently a Muslim problem or an Arab problem," Kawther said. "Surely if you don't understand that, then you shouldn't be accusing one of my clients of hurting his own son when there was a string of similar crimes on the same night as Yassir's attack. When my client awakes, I'd be more than happy to sit you both down with him so you can hear a child's voice crack when you try to accuse his father of such heinous things."

"What's happening, Kawther?" Khala Zainab whispered softly.

Kawther told her gently. "They're trying to blame Amu Rahman."

Khala Zainab shook her head and began to swear in Arabic beneath her breath. *Sons of dogs.*

Sergeant Montgomery pulled closer in his chair. "You're going to have to translate that, too."

Kawther did, and the men stared at her in shock that she didn't sugarcoat it. It was the same expression she'd earned from classmates and professors in her law classes. They easily stereotyped her in their heads. When she walked into a courtroom, even judges stared at her in surprise. A hijab-wearing lawyer seemed too far-fetched in their imaginations of what a Muslim woman could be.

"Next time bring a separate interpreter," Sergeant Montgomery grumbled.

Officer Matthew continued his questions. "Did you hear your son leave that night? Were you disturbed in your sleep?"

Khala Zainab shook her head. "No."

"Your husband was."

"She says she was asleep," Kawther said.

Silence.

"Any other questions?" Kawther spoke with arrogance. She did not want to tell Khala Zainab to remain silent unless she felt she must. In this moment, she needed to make the family look confident.

She watched the men leave. Khala Zainab took both of Kawther's hands in her hands like she used to.

"Shukran, habibti," Khala Zainab whispered, squeezing and letting go. The faint wrinkles under her eyes were wet. Kawther wanted to hug the woman she had hugged at least a million times throughout her life, but she refrained, held back by the pain of the past. Fatima stepped into the room, and Kawther relayed the information about her father.

And at the end of the conversation, she did not tell them *I quit*, although the words lingered in her mouth, alongside the million other words she wished to tell them.

She stepped out, turned at the end of the hallway, and found Ali waiting for her. His eyes locked with hers as he slowly approached.

"What happened?" he whispered as he got closer.

Her eyes searched for Khaled, but he was probably back in 705, watching over Yassir. "I handled it."

Ali stepped close enough she could smell the overpowering cologne on his clothes, just like all those years ago. "Thank you."

Kawther stared at the dimples deeply implanted in his cheeks. She said nothing, only felt her own cheeks warm, perhaps from embarrassment, from proximity to him, she did not know. She needed to go back to the firm and talk to Rebecca, who was waiting to scold her. Just as she stepped away, she noticed his hand lingering on her sleeve.

"I've missed you so much, you have no idea. I know you don't answer my messages," he whispered. "But I'm really glad you're here."

She thought back to the messages he'd sent her over the years. Facebook messages. Email. Texts.

Let's be together again.

I regret what I did.

Once you're done with school, let's put it all behind us. I miss our families. I miss us.

The latest one was last year. It was the same year he posted a photo in Najaf with his wife, standing in front of the shrine of Imam Ali.

Kawther shook her head, freed herself from his grasp, pushed back the heart that was loosening from her chest, and walked away.

43

KHALED

TEN DAYS AFTER

"If you fall asleep, I'll have to mark you absent," Mrs. Marsh called from her desk, the clack of her fingers echoing against the keyboard.

Khaled had yawned at least six times in the past two minutes, and Mrs. Marsh, the librarian, kept giving him a dirty stare. She did not like babysitting him, even if all he did was quietly sit behind the biographies and doze off over the war documentaries Mr. Wells had assigned.

He picked his head up and tapped a finger to his temple. He'd had about three hours of sleep last night. He didn't want to admit it to the Al-Azzawis, but spending the night on the padded windowsill at the hospital was wrecking his sleep, as was the nurse, who kept checking on Yassir's oxygen levels as they went up and down. Each time Khaled closed his eyes he wondered if he'd wake up to a code blue and watch his oldest friend die before his eyes. The nightmares weren't helping, either.

Khaled was starting to wonder if he, like his parents, was destined to lose everyone he loved.

The library's phone rang, and Mrs. Marsh stared at him as she answered it, her eyeglasses slipping to the bridge of her nose. Khaled checked his phone, seeing another message from Baba appear. Come home after school. This time, written in English. Khaled clicked his phone off, putting his head down again, his forehead kissing the cool table.

"Khaled." Mrs. Marsh's voice echoed in the hot blow of the space heater she had on at all times.

"I'm not asleep," he pleaded, pushing his forehead one inch up from the shiny oak. "I'm awake and reading about the unhinged rhetoric of Dwight D. Eisenhower that Mr. Wells assigned for me. Did you know that Camp David is named after his great-grandson? Eisenhower. Not Wells. I mean . . . duh? Mr. Wells is a hot forty-six. Did you know George W. Bush went to Camp—"

"Khaled," Mrs. Marsh sighed, silencing him. "Principal Delpy needs you to come down to her office. She said there are police officers here for you."

Surat al-Fatiha. Falaq. Ikhlas.

Khaled repeated the prayers in his head for protection as the police station appeared before him. He had never been in a police car before. It smelled like the inside of an armpit, worse than the boys' locker room after track and field practice. He remembered the blue and red lights that had stopped him and Yassir what felt like lifetimes ago.

Before he'd left school, Delpy had told him she'd call his father to notify him of what was happening. Because Khaled was eighteen, he could go on his own. If Delpy was suing him, she could've at least told him before he got into the cop car.

At least they didn't handcuff him. But that didn't stop several pairs of eyes from watching him as they left the school building. Alex already knew about it, texting were you freaking arrested with a million question marks. The car parked, the brakes squeaking.

"This way," the tall blond officer named Matthews said as Khaled pushed his way out of the car. They stepped into the building, which felt like a furnace in comparison to the biting wind outside.

"Can . . . I call my sis—lawyer?" he asked. "We all get one call, right?"

"Just use your cell," Officer Matthews said. "You're not arrested. We just want to question you. Is it okay if we check your cell after?"

He had nothing to hide, so he made the call and left a message for Kawther when she didn't pick up. Then he handed his phone over, afraid of what they would do if he didn't comply.

He tried to keep his thoughts calm, repeating the surahs in his head over and over again as they led him to a bright white room, where they left him alone for a long time. He tried not to fidget much, knowing they could see him through a tiny dark window somewhere. Luckily, he was wide awake now.

When the officers came back, they sat across from him. Each had a file in hand, and he could see his phone peeking in the brunet officer's hand. He briefly introduced himself as Sergeant Montgomery.

"Bet you're happy you got to skip some school?" Officer Matthews asked.

Khaled kept his mouth shut, wishing he had done the same weeks ago, when the officer had stopped him and Yassir outside the masjid.

After several minutes passed, the door squeaked open and Kawther stepped into the room, breathless. The men straightened up and cleared their throats, as if they were nervous.

"I'm here," Kawther said as the blond officer scooted a metal chair for her. Kawther put down her black briefcase, her hair slightly poking from her hijab, which told him she had truly run to get herself here. His heart clenched.

What had he done?

He wasn't sure.

"Do you represent everyone connected to this case?" Matthews asked, annoyed.

"I think it would be easier if you questioned everyone at once. Might save us some time," Kawther said, folding her arms on the table. "Let's get this over with."

Khaled's mouth nearly dropped. Did . . . his sister just talk to two police officers that way? His stumbly, muttering sister?

"Trust me, we'd prefer that, too," Matthews retorted. "But we got some new information this morning from a few students at Chapman High School, so we had a few questions for the administration. First of all, it's Ka-led, right? We saying your name correctly?"

"No," Khaled said, although the man was close. Closer than most of his teachers. Maybe he'd arrested a lot of Khaleds around town.

"Can you tell us where you were between eleven p.m. and two a.m. on November seventh and eighth?"

This . . . wasn't about the article? "You . . . you think I did this to Yassir?"

Kawther nudged him again. "He has an alibi. He was picked up at the airport around half past midnight and spent the night at home with his parents. His father is already on his way to give a statement."

Baba's coming?

This scared him more than the fact that he was sitting in a police investigation room. He had been very careful to return home at random intervals—in the middle of the night, or when Baba was at work and Mama was lying in bed—for a quick shower and change. He had avoided both of them until now.

Officer Matthews continued. "We have a school record that you assaulted the victim right before you left the country, and you came back the night he was attacked. That doesn't sound odd to you at all?"

That was what Miles had implied earlier, too. Did people really think he could've done this to Yassir? That he was this violent?

"He was attacked on the night of the Kill a Muslim Day," Khaled began, although he felt Kawther's foot press over his toes. *Shut up*, she was signaling him. "Why would I attack a fellow Muslim?"

"Tell us about your relationship with the victim," Sergeant Montgomery inserted, ignoring his words.

"He's my best friend," Khaled said automatically, although it wasn't true anymore.

"So why did you punch your best friend at school?"

Khaled swallowed, remembering the rage he'd felt that day, and the regret that had sat in his gut ever since, even when he tried to convince himself that Yassir had deserved the punch. Although Khaled tried to control his body, it shook until Kawther put a hand over his. She couldn't answer for him because she did not know him well enough.

"I was . . . angry at him. But it had nothing to do with what happened to him now."

"And what do you think happened to him now?"

"I think he got assaulted by that veteran who found him," Khaled said, and pain shot through his toes as Kawther's heel dug into the front of his sneaker.

"Right," Sergeant Montgomery said. "You wrote an entire article . . . seems like you're trying to deflect the attention to someone else. Is that why you wrote it?"

"He wrote the article because he's angry and scared," Kawther interjected quickly before he could speak again. "Not because he's deflecting attention. Like I said, he has an alibi."

"Who are your other friends?" Officer Matthews asked. "Did you ask them to beat up Yassir?"

"Didn't you just check my phone? Did you see anything where I'm asking people to beat up my friend?"

Kawther's eyes widened at him. "You took my client's phone?"

Officer Matthews nodded, his eyes still on Khaled. "You were tracking the victim's location. Did you follow him on the night of the attack?"

"Don't"—Kawther spoke in Arabic softly to him, her foot pressed over his again—"speak a word." She sat up straight, eyes on both officers. "They're close friends. They have each other's location, and my other client, lest you forget again, frequently walked the neighborhood at night."

"So why were you checking his location on the night of the attack?"

Khaled stayed silent.

"You sure you didn't want to finish the job, Ka-led? Maybe you had a little fight. Maybe a big fight. Was it drugs? A girl? Is that why you followed him that night and nearly killed him?"

Khaled's knuckles pulsed. Only twice in his life had he felt the urge to punch someone in the face. The first was Yassir. The second was this officer.

"He has an alibi," Kawther reiterated. "That statement is coming in. If you want access to the cameras outside Khaled's residence, you'll need to provide a search warrant."

The cops exchanged a look before they both stood up, Montgomery sliding the phone back to Khaled. "Fine, no other questions for now. We'll get the statement and assess. Thanks for your time, Ka-led," Officer Matthews said, pronouncing his name wrong again.

Kawther didn't say another word as they left the room, although her eyes said she was going to grill Khaled with a dozen questions soon. He followed her out of the building and found a familiar pair of eyes staring down at him in the parking lot.

Khaled tried to avoid eye contact, but Baba was already stepping toward him and putting a heavy hand on his bicep, just as he had on the night of Laylat Ashura. Khaled hadn't seen his father for nine days. He felt and looked like a stranger.

"As soon as I'm done, you come home with me, understand?" His voice was soft, but the rage was alive beneath his words.

Khaled shook his head. "Not until he wakes up."

"Where is your shame, Khaled?" Baba's hand tightened around his arm. "You hit him just a few weeks ago. Do his parents know? Do they know why? Do you even remember why?"

Kawther stared at them, puzzled.

Days ago, he'd told her he'd fought with Yassir, but he had not told her why. He wondered if, when she knew the truth, she would stop representing him.

"I remember," Khaled finally said. "I'm not abandoning him."

"Do you want to be attacked, too?"

Khaled shook his head, knowing his father would hate the next words that came out of his mouth. "I don't care."

"You don't care about your own life?" Baba scoffed, his voice rising, and Kawther reminded them that they were in public. But Baba, triggered, continued. "What have I told you since you were young? You are not American. You are Iraqi. You are Muslim. You will never be enough for them. They will kill you. See how they're already killing us!" His father's voice cracked. "Do you want to be in the hospital bed, too? Is that where you will follow Yassir?"

Khaled shook his head. He would follow Yassir to the ends of the earth. It was what Faizal had done. That was what friends did. That was what he always should've done. Even if he still hated Yassir. God, he still hated Yassir Al-Azzawi. But he loved him too much, too.

"Baba." Kawther came between them. Khaled hadn't realized how tight Baba's hand was around his arm. Khaled felt numb. "They need your statement. I'll help you, c'mon. Khaled, stay in the car."

She pulled Baba away, tossing Khaled the keys. Khaled watched as they both disappeared back into the police station.

"They're just gonna take turns blaming the attack on us," Ali whispered to Fatima. "Get your statements and facts straight about the night Yassir got attacked."

"What did they say exactly, Khaled? Just because you have his location, they think you did this now, too?" Fatima asked, taking a seat next to him in the hospital room. He needed to explain what had happened because they deserved to know.

The truth. The entirety. He didn't want them at risk, too, in case the cops came poking around. His eyes were trained on Yasmin and the drool pooling onto his jeans as he explained what had happened between Yassir and Ayah.

When Ayah passed, Ali had sent Khaled a long condolence message on Facebook. On the first day of her memorial, Fatima gave her condolences at the masjid door, her face wet, walking away before Baba could spot her and cause a scene. Khaled was scared to bring Ayah up, but he knew it wasn't their fault they were disconnected from her when she was still alive.

"You guys know how close all three of us were. I felt so deceived. He knew how hard a time I had with her leaving after Kaw—" Khaled's voice cracked, and he knew he should stop talking. He didn't want to hurt Ali by reminding him what his sister had done. "But I shouldn't have punched him. I regret it. I regret it so much."

Khaled had spent his last months with Ayah making her angry, and he'd spent his last moments with Yassir Al-Azzawi punching him in the face.

Before his body could begin to shake, he stood up, taking Yasmin with him.

"I'm gonna put her to sleep."

He had done so nearly every night. When he'd walked around the hospital hallway a few times, she'd slowly tuck her head close to the crook of his neck and doze off. The nurses smiled at him. They thought it was precious that a teenage boy put a baby to sleep.

He'd hold her for a while, apologizing for everything.

"Sorry I punched your dad," Khaled whispered, patting her back. "I should've checked on him that night . . . I shouldn't have made his life worse."

Shame spilled out of him. After Ayah had died and Yasmin had come into his life, Yassir had been so stressed, so upset, that he couldn't sleep anymore, walking around aimlessly to pass the sleepless hours. Khaled had thought he knew what Yassir felt like the night he arrived back in America, when he'd slunk into the dark, lost and unsettled. But now, in the dinge of the hospital, holding Yassir's daughter, he felt the weight of loneliness Yassir must have borne this whole time. The weight of shame, knowing he'd let someone down. The weight of fear, of not knowing what was to come next. The weight of duty, of feeling helpless to protect the ones he loved.

Yasmin whimpered and Khaled breathed heavily, starting to sing the ridiculous lullaby Yassir would whisper to her. *Hush, Yasmin, don't you cry, or Daddy's going to have a full-on mental breakdown.*

Yasmin must have heard it enough times from her dad, because when he sang, as he had every night, her eyes began to flutter closed.

"I'm sorry he left home that night," he whispered as she tucked her head into his shoulder. "I'm sorry people are sorry you were born. Despite it all, and the shitty circumstances that brought you to me, I'm glad you're here."

After a few minutes, she was fast asleep. Khaled stared toward room 705, wondering if he would ever get the chance to tell Yassir the same.

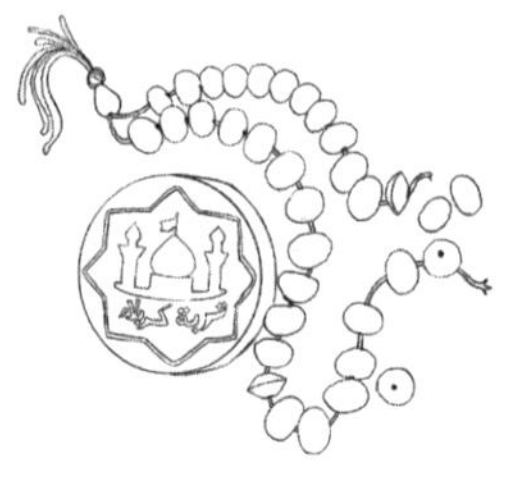

44

KHALED

SEVEN MONTHS AND THREE WEEKS BEFORE

"Can I talk to you?" Yassir's eyes were wide as he handed Khaled his cell phone, the sounds of the cafeteria bustling around them. Alex was out with the flu, so Khaled sat alone, as he did often when Yassir was caught up with other friends, other girls, other plans. But he was here now.

"What is it?" Khaled asked, giving up on the soggy cheese pizza on his plate, Chapman High's only halal option. "Whose heart did you break now?"

Whenever Yassir preferred his company lately, it was usually because he was hiding from a girl. Yassir Al-Azzawi had never liked confrontation.

"Just press play." Yassir was breathless.

Khaled did as he was told, playing the voice message, an older woman's voice nearly static through the speaker. *I've been trying to call you. I think you know my goddaughter, Emily? I think it's important you come see me. Emily had a baby a few weeks ago, and, well, she told me you were the father. If you can come by, my address is eighteen ninety-nine East Elm Street South—*

Khaled stared at his friend. "This is clearly a prank call. What are you freaking out about?"

Yassir's eyes were now pink. Khaled felt his blood turn cold.

"Do—do you remember the girl I was talking to at that party we went to together last year? Her—her name was Emily," Yassir stammered. Khaled did not remember the names of all the girls Yassir had spoken to. "Coul—could you drive me? I don't have a car anymore. I just want to know if it's true. I can't tell my dad. *Please.*"

Before tears could spill down Yassir's cheeks, Khaled grabbed his sleeve and stood up. "I have my Buick. When do you want to go?"

"Today?"

Khaled was due at his dad's shop that afternoon, but Yassir looked so desperate that Khaled called his father and blamed debate practice for his work absence. They spoke little on the ride to the large three-story redbrick house that was nearly three hours away. Yassir panted for a few minutes, head between his legs, as Khaled parked the car.

"Fuck," Khaled whispered. If Yassir was the father, Khaled was sure he'd immediately pass out. "Look, I'll do the talking, okay? Just relax. We don't even know if this is true. What if we're walking into a murderer's house? If I get murdered, wallah, I will haunt your ass if you survive."

Yassir had nodded seriously, and Khaled had looped an arm over his shoulder and led him up the stairs. After a few knocks on the door, an older woman with dark brown hair flecked with gray streaks answered. She was wearing jeans and a fitted white T-shirt that said LOVE IS FOR EVERYONE.

The woman's eyes widened before she started talking a mile a minute. "Hi, I'm Stephanie, come in! Come in! I'm so happy you're here. You have no idea how scared I was that you wouldn't show up. Are you Yaseer?" she asked, staring directly at Khaled. "My goddaughter wanted to give this babe up for adoption and, well, I thought—what if the father wants to be involved? So she gave your name, Michael, but I couldn't find a Michael with your last name in your school's directory, but I found a Yaseer, and I'm sorry, I sort of went down an internet rabbit hole but found your Facebook page and found your number on yellow pages which matched the one Emily had given me and now you're here!"

She stared at Khaled expectantly, but he shook his head. "Um, sorry, you're mistaken. I'm just a friend. Here for support." He tightened his grip on his frozen friend. "This is Yassir."

All the color had drained from Yassir's face. He was going to throw up in this stranger's house. Khaled was sure of it.

"Take a seat. I'll get the baby."

Yassir stared at Khaled in horror.

They were meeting the baby? Shouldn't they talk first? They didn't even know if it was Yassir's.

"Uh, Stephanie, right? Can we speak first?" Khaled called out as she came back into the room with a sleeping one-month-old baby in her arms.

"I can't leave her alone—the baby monitor stopped working."

Stephanie sat down on a leather recliner, holding the baby close. Yassir swallowed.

"Look, I'm not here to judge. It's why I didn't ask you to bring your parents yet. I don't need to get into details about my goddaughter. I love her like my own. Her parents kicked her out some time ago. They think she's too rebellious, and she *is*. If I'm honest, this isn't her first pregnancy scare. I have children of my own and yes, I'm religious, too, if you're wondering, but I don't believe in leaving anyone behind. Including this little bundle . . ." She sighed, staring at the infant. She let out an exhausted breath. "But I'm moving back to Nevada because my mother is sick. She just got diagnosed with dementia and needs someone to watch her."

"Sorry," Khaled said.

Stephanie smiled down at the baby. "Her name is Hayley. I named her since Emily already waived all her rights. Sorry, but I didn't know what culture you were from until I found you online. I'm sure you could change her name later . . . if she's yours. I have a number where you can take a paternity test. Already got baby Hayley's DNA sample. I've already been granted rights for her guardianship, but I'll waive it once we identify the father. If that's you, and you want to keep her, let me know. You can bring your parents. We can sit with my husband. Talk this through. All right? If not, don't worry. We can forget this happened and she'll go up for adoption. Okeydokey?"

No wonder Emily had found comfort with this woman. She was responsible and caring and it showed, even within five minutes of meeting her. She gave them the number of the paternity test center, and in minutes they found themselves back in the car.

"We should call—" Yassir shoved the sticky note with the number of the test center into Khaled's face. "Here. Call, *please*. If they're closed, we'll come back tomorrow."

First thing the next morning, Khaled had called from the school hallway and scheduled the appointment at the testing center for Yassir. They would need to miss lunch and fourth period. Khaled filled out the paperwork as Yassir shook in his seat, tears threatening to spill from his eyes. He even forged Sayed Rahman's signature—he'd had it memorized since they were kids forging field trip permission slips. It would take five to ten business days to get the results.

A few days passed. Yassir didn't sleep and Khaled stumbled on all his practice speeches in debate, something he hadn't done since the weeks following Ayah's passing. On the sixth business day, Yassir received a call during first period from an unknown number. He refused to pick it up or check the voicemail. He handed the phone to Khaled at lunch after dragging him off to the courtyard outside, both shooing a curious Alex away with iced macchiato orders for the local coffee shop down the road.

Khaled had watched Yassir's lips tremble. "I—I can't listen. Just tell me."

Yassir had stared at his hands, almost like he was making a dua. Maybe he was. Because his parents were going to kill him.

"Um . . ." Khaled had spoken carefully, aware that each word he uttered would alter Yassir's life. "It's positive. I'm really sorry, Yassir."

For a moment, Yassir had stood still, and Khaled had wondered if the news had broken his friend. Or had given him a heart attack.

"Yassir?" Khaled had put a hand on his shoulder, shaking him.

Yassir's eyes welled with tears again. "Okay. We should go, huh? Go get her?"

Yassir was talking about the baby.

It was a Thursday, Laylat al-Jumu'ah. Khaled's father expected him to be at the masjid in a few hours, but he nodded. They arrived at Stephanie's house even faster than the first time. When Khaled had called her earlier, she'd said she'd have Hayley's stuff ready when they arrived. Yassir was lucky. This could've been messier. Pregnant Emily could've shown up at his doorstep and his parents could've killed him long ago. They could be having a custody battle. Emily's family could have come and started issues with his family.

"What the hell?" Khaled whispered to himself in disbelief.

"What?" Yassir asked as they turned into Stephanie's neighborhood.

"So we're just gonna take the baby and you're going to go home with it?"

Yassir nodded. His eyes were steady.

"And your parents don't know?"

"They'll find out. Stephanie said if she's mine, she'll help me with the whole transition. That includes talking to my parents."

"What if they kick you out?"

"I don't think they will," Yassir said confidently. "But I don't think this will be easy. I would ask you to come home with me, but I know how things are between our parents. I just—I don't know what other choice I have. I've thought about this every single moment of every day since I got that phone call almost two weeks ago. If that baby is mine, I have to keep her. She's my responsibility. I don't fucking know why, but I feel like I couldn't live with myself otherwise."

"Okay." Khaled parked outside the red house. "Okay. We don't have to get out yet. Whenever you're ready."

But Yassir opened his car door and practically ran to the front door of the house. Khaled watched as Yassir awkwardly held her after Stephanie showed him how. Richard, her husband, said they'd come with Yassir to break the news to his parents. Richard had become a father as a teen, too, but he didn't know until seven years later. That was why Stephanie had been so adamant about calling Yassir. She didn't want Yassir to lose time with his daughter the way her husband had with his son.

"Is it okay if . . . the baby rides with us?" Yassir asked when it was time to depart. They had spent the past few hours getting to know each other. Stephanie and Richard had asked about their families' immigration story, about Chapman, and about Yassir's dreams—which nearly caused him to cry in panic. Richard assured him that dreaming takes time, especially when he started to have children too. By the end of the conversation, Yassir's shoulders had relaxed, though his eyes were still filled with uncertainty. Khaled kept an arm over his friend's shoulder.

"Of course, we'll drive behind," Stephanie said with a smile.

"You sure? It's far," Yassir said. "I don't want you to waste—"

"Making sure the right baby goes to the right parent is worth it. Don't worry, we'll come along, give you the birth certificate, all the supplies, and help explain what happened to your parents now that we have the DNA test. This baby is yours," Richard said to Yassir, putting a hand on his shoulder. "You treat her like she's the most precious thing in your universe, because now she is all you have. Your family might hate you for this. Your friends might get scared. But she's yours. Forever."

Khaled wasn't sure if Richard was trying to be encouraging, because his words made bile immediately rise in his throat. At this point, he wanted to burst into tears himself, but he needed to be strong for Yassir.

"I'll drive really slow. I promise," Khaled said, realizing he had never driven with a baby in his back seat. He had never been an uncle before. All his life, *he'd* been the baby of the family. Now he felt intimidated. What if she started crying? What if she needed a diaper change?

He slowly backed out of the driveway and turned on a recording of Quran for the ride home. Yassir sat by the new baby, who was half white and had a white girl's name.

"Um. What are you going to call her?" Khaled mumbled as he merged onto the freeway, as soft snow began to fall from the sky. He made a dua the weather would not escalate. And as they continued driving, Richard and Stephanie's Nissan still in the rearview, the snow let up, as if the sky itself had listened to his prayer.

"I think . . . Yasmin," Yassir said after a while.

"Yasmin? Isn't that close to your own name?" Khaled scoffed. "Self-centered. Just call her Yassir junior, why don't you?"

"You have a better name?" Yassir had rolled his eyes. "I didn't want anything too religious."

"Surprised you chose something in Arabic, *Michael*."

"She can call herself Jasmine when she's older," Yassir said. "So no one at school makes fun of her for it. But my parents might *actually* kill me if I name my child anything other than something in Arabic."

Khaled's words dissipated as reality set in. "Right, when she's in school . . ."

In school? Yassir would have a daughter in school in a few years?

"Holy shit," Yassir muttered, his voice finally cracking. "This is really happening. What the hell did I do?" Khaled caught a glimpse of his best friend's face in the rearview mirror.

Huge tears poured down Yassir's cheeks. Just like when he was five and hurt his foot badly on the sprinklers outside and Khaled carried him home on his back before he got stitches on the left side of his heel.

Or when Khaled talked back to their Sunday school teacher after she scolded Yassir for not getting any of his Arabic homework right. Or when Yassir received the first DUI fine, and Khaled handed him a small wad of cash to pay it off.

Protecting Yassir Al-Azzawi had always come naturally for Khaled. In that moment, he realized his protection would be extended forever to Yasmin, too.

Yassir cried and cried, and Khaled said nothing, just listening to him weep. He turned the volume of the Quran recording up and prayed that Allah would protect them on the road back.

SKY

I listen outside the hospital for a long, long time.

I listen to the other noises that filled the earth. I cup their chins. We whisper our goodbyes.

"He still hasn't woken up," a man in a uniform said over the phone, sucking on the stick that leaked smoke into me. "Tell me about it, the lawyer is a pain in the ass. Some straight-out-of-law-school amateur. If he passes, this will become a homicide case . . . That's what I'm saying. I don't have time for this bullshit, either—"

I know the faces of humans when they give up.

The whimper's father steps outside in the dim of sunrise, his hands cupped toward me in golden light, tears staining his cheeks as he begged to give his son a second chance. This is not the first son he's prayed for. I've heard his prayers and pleas.

I remember when he was as young as the whimper is now, forced to hold a gun and run away from men in uniforms. I've heard the sum of his prayers out loud.

I've heard him thank God for the first dollars he earned in this land. I've heard him beg God to save his family in the last land, and the one before it, too. Despite all the trials and vicissitudes he's endured, I have never seen him so desperately wanting his prayer to come true as now.

But in the glass of his eyes, I see that he no longer believed the words on his tongue. He has given up, and I wonder if it is time for me to give up, too.

On the eleventh day, I no longer heard the whimper.

45

YASSIR

TWELVE DAYS AFTER

First, it was nausea.

Then sharp lights that hovered over his face.

For a silly, small second, Yassir wondered if he was remembering what being born felt like. But then his parents' faces obstructed the lights, peering into his eyes, tears drowning their cheeks, prayers shouted from their mouths.

"Allahumma salli 'ala Muhammad wa Aali Muhammad!"

He felt his mother's fingers on his face. He had felt them before; he was sure.

"Let him breathe!" he heard someone shout, but he didn't recognize their voice.

"Ya Allah. Ya Muhammad. Ya Ali."

He tried to sit up, but suddenly an older white woman stood before him.

A nurse?

She smelled like flowers. He felt sick.

"Ya Allah. Ya Muhammad. Ya Ali."

The nurse touched him everywhere. Checked his eyes, his arms, and started asking questions.

"Do you know where you are?"

He had to force himself to speak, but his throat felt full of salt. He could hear the beeps, recognized the smell of antiseptic in the room. "Hospital?"

"Do you know your name?"

"Yassir?"

"Can you try your full name, sweetheart?"

"Yassir Rahman Al-Azzawi."

"Very good. Do you remember your age?"

"Seventeen."

"Wow. Very good! Can you name everyone in your immediate family?"

"My parents. My brother, Ali, and sister, Fatima. Oh, and my daughter, Yasmin."

My daughter. Where is my daughter if I'm in a hospital?

"Very good."

His throat was on fire.

"Do you know why you're here?"

He didn't know. Or maybe he did but couldn't remember. Not right now. *Where is Yasmin?*

"Can I see my daughter?"

"Yes, just a sec. The doctor wants to come in and check on you really quickly. We are so happy to see you awake! I'll bring you some water, okay?"

He nodded, but oh, God. His neck. His *head*.

The nurse and his family disappeared. Several minutes, maybe even hours, of silence passed before a doctor came and repeated the nurse's questions. She was nice, tall and thin. White, but had a European accent of some sort.

“On a scale of one to ten in pain, how do you feel?”

He shook his head. “Six? But I think I might throw up.”

“That’s normal.”

“My throat hurts.”

“That’s because of the tube.”

“Oh.”

He’d had a tube down his throat?

“Can I see my daughter now?”

“Yes. I’ll let your family in.”

He didn’t want to see his family. He wanted to see Yasmin. As soon as they returned, they smothered him with kisses. Everyone’s face was wet and red—even his father’s.

Baba’s thumb ran over Yassir’s cheeks.

Weeks ago, under the amber streetlights, when Baba smelled of mouthwash and spicy cologne, Yassir had thought that was the closest his father had ever been to him. Now, it was this moment. His father didn’t let go. He put his forehead against Yassir’s and started reciting the Quran, and when the tears fell down his weathered face, he did not wipe them.

“Habibi,” Baba whispered into his cheeks, his body shaking. “Are you hurting?”

Yassir *was* hurting. He was always hurting. But he could not cry with them. He didn’t know why he should or why anyone else should. He just knew that his throat hurt. That he was going to throw up soon, maybe all over his father’s face if he didn’t move away soon.

What was even stranger was that he thought he saw someone who resembled his brother, but the man looked older and defeated, and sad, which couldn’t be Ali, who was hopeful and happy and pious.

Yassir didn’t know what was going on, but he knew he needed to see his daughter, not whatever apparitions his brain was making up.

“Yasmin?” he croaked.

“Asleep,” Mama answered. “When she wakes up, we’ll let her see you.”

He just wanted Yasmin. He wasn't sure if he had been asleep for so long that he had dreamt her up. But if his mother knew who she was, then his being a father was not a dream. And Baba holding him now . . . maybe Baba finally forgave him.

Baba pulled away, and when his red eyes locked with Yassir's, Yassir stared at him in disbelief.

Maybe *Yassir* was the apparition. Or perhaps this was an alternate reality where his father was no longer angry at him and his mother answered him without disappointment in her tone.

An apparition indeed.

46

KHALED

TWELVE DAYS AND SIX HOURS AFTER

As soon as Khaled stepped onto the hospital linoleum, he felt a lump in his throat. Of course, he hadn't been there when Yassir finally woke up, like he'd promised—he was too busy keeping his head down at school. His eyes stung. What should he even say? What if Yassir couldn't talk yet? What if he had amnesia? That didn't just happen in the movies . . . did it?

Maybe he shouldn't be here. Maybe he had only been tolerated until now. Just as he was about to run away, Fatima stepped out of the room, phone in the crook of her shoulder, and excitedly waved him over.

"Oh, Khaled!" An enormous smile spread across her face. Khaled hadn't seen that smile in years. "He's been asking about you!"

He stared at her. She was inviting him in. Inviting him to stay. He took a deep breath and whispered *bismillah* as he stepped into the room. The windowsills in room 705 were lined with fresh bouquets of flowers, oversized Mylar balloons, and faces he didn't recognize.

Khaled smiled nervously, blending into the background until the room mostly cleared, save for the Al-Azzawis. He looked around and found Yasmin in Kawther's arms. The baby looked moments away from bursting into tears. Just as Khaled attempted to reach for Yasmin, a faint, familiar voice said, "Finally, you're here."

Khaled turned around. The frown that always soured his friend's face turned up slightly, as if his mouth could not physically take more than a smirk. Red and brown bruises painted the eyes that had been closed for eleven days. Now they were open and eager. The lump in Khaled's throat felt bigger than ever. He opened his mouth to say something, but he couldn't.

For the first time in a very long while, a sob escaped him.

Khaled lost it.

All the feelings that had been simmering inside his body from the moment he had heard the news—the sleepless nights, squeezing Yassir's hands, praying at his bedside and combing his tangled hair as he slept—every emotion flooded out of him as he stared into his best friend's eyes.

Khaled held his hand against his mouth to keep the animal noises from escaping as he stepped closer to the bed and wrapped his arms around his best friend. The last time he had cried this way was the day after Ayah's memorial. They'd stood shoulder to shoulder in the lot of his dad's empty shop and Khaled had cried quietly to himself while Yassir patted his back for a long time. Now he felt Yassir's bones shake beneath him, his facial hair scratched at his neck.

They held each other for a long time and did not let go.

The word *sorry* repeated in Khaled's head, but he did not know if he could say it. Not yet. Not when he'd just gotten Yassir back.

"Fuck," Khaled whispered. "I'm glad you remember me."

Yassir laughed, his face twisting with pain. His voice was raspier than when he got bronchitis in the tenth grade.

"Me too."

"I'm never hugging you again," Khaled said, finally releasing him.

"Thank God. You suck at it," Yassir whispered as Khaled gently ruffled his unruly hair, careful of the bandages and gauze stuck to the top of his forehead.

Sayed Rahman cleared his throat. "More families are waiting to come in."

Khaled wiped his tears on the back of his jacket sleeve as aunties and uncles filed in. Their eyes flitted to baby Yasmin. Her presence was ultimate proof that she wasn't merely a rumor lingering in the community.

Khaled stood awkwardly in the corner by his sister and took Yasmin into his arms. She whimpered, frustrated with no room to crawl around. He tried to shush her without bringing too much attention to himself, offering her a silly face. She smiled at him.

"How has it been?" Khaled whispered to Kawther.

"Lots of visitors," she said with a deep sigh. "I haven't asked a thing. Doctors say he might have post-traumatic amnesia. He can remember us, but it will be less likely he can remember the attack."

So Yassir *did* have amnesia.

"Inshallah, he'll remember who did this to him," Khaled said to her before more Iraqis walked in to extend their well wishes to Yassir. He knew Yassir would be hating this attention. Khaled felt restless, defensive. "There are so many of them. They need to leave so he can rest."

"Shhh," Kawther whispered. "They'll hear you."

Khaled looked around. Ali was nowhere to be seen. "The ex?" Khaled whispered.

Kawther's face twitched. "Hiding somewhere. He disappeared before everyone came in."

Before he'd left for Iraq, Ali had never had to hide his face or be afraid of rumors. Khaled's good mood soured.

When the room finally cleared, the Al-Azzawis stepped out to talk to the doctors with Kawther. Yassir laid his head back, eyes pasted to the animal stickers near the ceiling.

Khaled's knuckles burned as he thought of the last time they'd seen each other. He swallowed his regret and spoke.

"Do you remember anything?" he asked as Yasmin squealed at the Mylar balloons dancing under the heater.

"I remember you hitting me. I remember you leaving," Yassir replied quietly. "I remember falling on my ankle. I remember trying to get my assignments in. I remember you hitting me," he repeated. "Are you still mad at me? For what I did?"

Khaled shook his head, thinking of his sister. Ayah and her soft, clipped laugh, which he used to find annoying. Ayah and her sadness. Ayah and her grave. "No."

But he was not sure if it was true.

"Did . . . you see her?" Yassir asked. "What was it like?"

He'd just been attacked and all he could think about was . . . Ayah?

Khaled felt something painful prick at his chest. "Yassir, just focus on resting. You have bigger things to worry about than feeling guilty."

A beat of silence crept between them.

"Did you do this to me?" Yassir whispered. "When you came back. Did you do this? Were you that pissed?"

Khaled eyes widened in horror that Yassir could think he could be capable of such violence. Just like the cops suspected. Just like the kids at school, too. "No. This was the Kill a Muslim Day shit! Did anyone tell you—"

"Khaled," Kawther said from the doorway, interrupting them. "The police are back."

47

YASSIR

FOURTEEN DAYS AFTER

Did your father attack you, Yassir? You can be honest with us. You won't get in trouble, the police had said to him. *Did he try to kill you that night?*

Yassir knew the answer more certainly than anything else in the universe, because no matter how much he'd disappointed his parents, they would never do this to him. Perhaps they would kick his soul and stab him with guilt, and that pain was different. Baba had only hit him once in his entire life and although he had not apologized for it, there was a sorry look in his eyes every time he glanced down at Yassir. Didn't they know Baba loved him?

Yassir knew that, too, didn't he?

When he'd answered the police, Yassir had protected his father. Something he had never done before. It felt good.

"Did you hear me?"

Yassir's eyes jolted open. "Huh?"

Ali clicked his tongue, worried. "I asked if you were hungry, twice."

Yassir was still not entirely sure he had not conjured up Ali with his imagination. He was so different now—he was not the young, smiling man Yassir remembered. But nothing was the same as Yassir remembered.

"I'm going to come back and bring you something you like." Ali fished out the keys to Mama's van as he turned to the doorway. "Oh, good. Khaled's back to watch you."

Yassir rolled his eyes. He didn't need to be watched. He needed to get out of here. It didn't matter if his head still felt like it was split in half and his gut was hot and flashing with pain and his surgery scar made him so sore that sitting up made his entire body ache. Bruises lined his face from his chin to his mouth, and even though his mother begged him to eat, it hurt to swallow.

Khaled stepped in, his eyes showing an awkwardness that had become familiar since Yassir had woken up. Yasmin was clasped to his chest. Thick yellow splotches painted her bib. It looked too thick for baby vomit.

"What's on her clothes?" Yassir asked immediately, unable to keep the annoyance out of his voice.

"Oh," Khaled said, tickling Yasmin's chin as he turned her to face her father. Yassir missed when she smiled like this, even if she hadn't smiled at him in days, scared of his bruises and bandages. Scared of him. "I got her ice cream. She loved it."

A pain deeper than all his injuries combined pulsed in Yassir's rib cage.

"Why are you feeding her ice cream?" he asked.

Khaled wiped drool hanging off Yasmin's chin with her bib. "You refused all my birthday treats, so I thought someone would appreciate it. She likes pineapple, just like you. I should've taken a video." He shifted under Yassir's stony gaze. "It's not like it's her first time eating ice cream . . . right?"

It wasn't like she would remember this, but Yassir would. Each time someone else was there for her instead of him, he would remember.

Khaled's face fell at Yassir's silence. "Shit. I didn't know. Are you mad?"

There were a lot of things he was mad about. He was mad that the police and reporters wouldn't leave him alone since he woke up. That strangers online knew his name—which meant they were closer to knowing Yasmin's, too. He was mad that the Iraqis in his community had seen her, without permission, that they'd seen him, too, without his permission. He was mad that his phone kept buzzing with new messages from people who were angry at him, thinking he blamed the veteran for the attack.

Khaled's words.

He was mad that Khaled was still here, knowing how much more trouble this was getting Yassir into with his parents, knowing there was still so much left unsaid between them. He was mad at Khaled for thinking he was Yassir's savior, for being here even when he'd said he was gone for good. He was sick of hurting Khaled, and he was sick of Khaled hurting him back.

Yet he was still, more than anything, mad at himself.

Did you have a fight with Khaled Al-Hakim? the police had asked.

How many times has he assaulted you?

Did you know he has your location?

Has he ever threatened to kill you?

Yassir had told the cops the truth, even though Kawther was standing there beside him. She deserved to know, too, that he and Khaled had fought over his lies about Ayah before Khaled had left for Iraq.

He says he's your best friend. Do you agree with that statement? they had asked.

Yassir had hesitated. *He's my best friend. He wouldn't hurt me like this*, he said, and he hoped it was true.

A hand brushed his forehead. Yassir couldn't help but flinch. Nausea filled his throat.

"Sorry," Khaled murmured, stepping away. "I didn't mean to touch you, it's just . . . You look sick and you're burning up. Maybe I should call the nurse."

"No!" Yassir shouted, and Yasmin startled at the sound. His phone buzzed in his lap. He took a deep breath as Khaled put a blanket down on the floor for her to crawl on. "I need to pass that checkup tomorrow. I'm never going to leave this place if everyone freaks out each time I cough or get a fever."

Yassir's phone buzzed again. He swallowed.

Khaled looked down at the notifications of more texts, emails, and comments. "Turn off those alerts. I told you I'll monitor Yasmin's name online, so you don't have to. I'll protect her, I promise. I only wrote that article to protect your dad, you know. We're family. We protect each other."

Yassir simply shook his head. It had been easier when Khaled was in Iraq. When they both no longer had to pretend that they had ever really protected each other. Even though everyone in his life had helped Yassir take care of Yasmin, he was her father. It was his responsibility to protect her, and he had failed, just as he had failed Ayah. His phone buzzed again, and he opened it so he wouldn't have to stare into Khaled's eyes.

He braced himself, but it was just his daily I'm so happy you're alive ☺ text from Alex. Beneath it was a reminder from Fatima that she was on her way to wish him happy birthday with her sons. He was glad he wouldn't be alone with Khaled much longer, and that Yasmin could play with people closer to her age.

He scrolled through his Instagram notifications. He hadn't used the account since sophomore year, but somehow the media had found it. If he looked at his message requests, he'd see a lot of vitriol, but also sweet messages, too. He didn't like the feeling of being loved and hated so intensely.

"If I ask for your phone, will you give it to me?" Khaled asked, his voice soft. He had been nicer to Yassir these past few days than he had his entire life. Yassir wished he weren't so suspicious of Khaled's kindness.

He shook his head and Khaled sighed, leaning down to Yasmin, handing her a teething toy, which she rejected to gnaw on the edge of a plastic block instead. She looked like an angry kraken. As Khaled played with Yasmin on the floor, Yassir sifted through messages from journalists requesting an interview. Kawther had told him to forward them to her, but as he was doing so, he realized that the last interview request was for an article that wasn't about him.

Hi Yassir, I'm wishing you a speedy recovery. Do you have any time to comment on your attorney's recent trip to Iraq?--Sam Sage, Daily US News

Yassir clicked on the thumbnail.

Islamophobic Vitriol Is Being Used Against an Attorney in the Kill a Muslim Day Investigation

Yassir scanned the article before putting the phone down. The words he read roiled his stomach. Yasmin babbled as she crawled toward the machine that still helped Yassir breathe at night. Khaled pulled her back, scolding her with the click of his tongue. She laughed. Yassir's heart hurt. If he was going to protect her and make things right, he needed this to end.

"Khaled," he said. "Is Kawther downstairs?"

"Why?" Khaled asked, scooping Yasmin into his arms as he stood. "Did you remember something?"

Before Yassir could react, Khaled took the phone from his hand, reading what he had on the screen.

"Khaled—" Yassir reached for the phone, but Khaled jerked it away.

Khaled read wordlessly, his lips tightening to a thin line.

"I'm dropping the case," Yassir said. "What if someone hurts her?"

"Dropping the case?" Khaled echoed, shaking his head. "Do you know how many people are working to ensure you get justice right now?"

Yassir swallowed. He hadn't asked for that. Or to be the face of a religion he barely identified with. Why did he have to be the one to endure it? Why did any of them?

"I thought you cared about protecting family," Yassir finally said. "Protecting everyone is more important than blaming someone they can't even find, Khaled."

"Oh, so you'll just let them go free? How does that keep anyone safe?"

"How is *this* keeping *us* safe?" Yassir echoed, unable to hide the rising anger in his voice. "Don't you want to protect your sister?"

"Don't lecture me about protection," Khaled said. "As if you ever protected Ayah."

There it was. The truth. Yassir was sick of hiding from it.

"We'll get this taken down, don't worry," Khaled continued.

Taking it down wasn't enough. The damage was already done. "Is she even here because she wants to be, or because you're making her? Be honest, Khaled. Unless you two miraculously became friendly in Iraq, I don't think you'd even let her be in your life right now if it wasn't for me being hurt. I see the way you still barely even look at her."

Khaled didn't speak, only pushed Yasmin's curls out of her face.

"Give me my phone and give me my daughter," Yassir said with finality.

Khaled hesitated, then put the phone in Yassir's hand and placed Yasmin on his lap. She began to cry, but Yassir hushed her between his words to Khaled: "Go home. The more you stick around me the more the cops are going to poke around, trying to figure out your motive."

Hurt flooded Khaled's face. "I didn't do this to you Yassir, if it wasn't fucking clear," he said, his eyes ignited. He planted himself in a chair by the window. "I'm not leaving you."

Yassir shook his head as he texted Kawther.

Can you come? It's urgent.

She responded immediately. On my way.

48

KAWTHER

Kawther had not walked four steps across the hospital parking lot before a warm hand gripped the back of her arm.

Her spine jolted and when she twisted around, she held the briefcase in a tight, angled position in case she needed to defend herself. She had stupidly left her pepper spray at the bottom of the briefcase.

"Sorry I scared you." Ali took a step back, and she closed her eyes for a moment. When she opened them, he was still standing in front of her. "Of course you're probably freaked out."

You freak me out. She kept her mouth closed. Now that they were no longer bound by an Islamic marriage contract, he was not supposed to touch her—but the rules had not stopped him from doing the things he wasn't supposed to before.

"Are you following me?" she asked instead.

Dimples sank into his cheeks like quicksand. She wanted to jab them again and again and say *You don't deserve to smile at me.* But she kept her mouth shut. She needed to stay focused. Though that was getting difficult when the man who could barely offer her a glance when they were engaged was now trailing behind her. When he looked at her in the way he did now, like he could swallow her entire heart.

"I'm watching out for you," he said. "You don't have security. You've acted brave, but I know you're scared."

She used her courtroom voice then: "So you *are* following me? You do remember what stalking is, right?"

Ali shook his head, his lips pressed in a nervous line. "No, I swear I'm not following you. I just got back here myself."

She noticed a plastic grocery bag in his hand.

"I got chocolate ice cream cake. Thought it would cheer Yassir up."

Ice cream cake. Despite the early-winter chill, they would eat it each year around Yassir's birthday, one big circle on the living room floor as their parents watched them in disgust at the sweet concoction, drinking their tea and spitting seeds. Their parents had never grown accustomed to American sweets.

Today was November twenty-second.

"It's his birthday," she remembered.

Her heart twisted. What a horrible way to turn eighteen.

"How are you going to get that past the nurse? They said the food visitors were bringing was getting out of hand."

He pointed to her briefcase.

"I was hoping you could hide it." His dimples burrowed deeper into his cheeks, and she could not say no. Yassir, who had been miserable since waking up, deserved some joy.

She took the bag, and they walked side by side just like they did in elementary school, crossing the street, walking to recess, walking under the sunset until Mama reminded them that a jinn would get them if they weren't inside before salat al-maghrib.

"You look nice today," Ali said. Kawther gripped the plastic bag to her side. "You always look beautiful in pink."

She tugged on her hijab. When he turned to look at her, she smelled something sour on his breath. She glanced over, watching him sway slightly where he stood. When the elevator dinged onto the floor, she swiftly walked out, leaving him a few steps behind.

Kawther nearly stepped on the little kids playing on the floor. Fatima's sons were building blocks with Yasmin as Fatima sat in the corner watching Yassir and Khaled. Fatima's eyes met Kawther's in a familiar panic.

Just give him another chance, Fatima had begged her eight years ago. *Ali doesn't know what's right and wrong . . . not anymore. We have to help him. You're his wife now. You can't just abandon him.*

Kawther had thought that if she removed herself from the equation, he would no longer have a reason to drink, that his family would get him the help he needed. But even after all these years, with the smell of alcohol on his breath and a glassy look to his eyes, it seemed Fatima had never figured out how to help her brother.

Ali trailed behind her like a shadow. To create more distance, she moved toward the bed, where Yassir and Khaled seemed to be arguing.

"Don't say anything," Khaled seethed, pulling the phone from Yassir, who could not even reach over and pull it back because of his injuries. Her brother was being cruel.

"I'm serious." Yassir shook his head, folding his arms in defeat. "What part of 'I don't want you here anymore' do you not understand?"

Khaled's mouth twitched, but he did not reply.

"You're just running away from all your problems and using me as an excuse. You hate me, still. I know you do. I can't even trust that you didn't really do this to me. Don't you see how much of a mess this is?"

"Yassir—" her brother began.

But Yassir cut in. "You're clearly still angry about Ayah. I know you hate me, so why are you pretending you don't?"

Ayah.

Yassir had mentioned her in the police report two days ago. He'd kept it vague, but from what Kawther understood, Yassir had had a relationship with Ayah without Khaled's knowledge. Once Khaled had figured it out, he'd punched Yassir. Ayah and Yassir had always been sweet together when they were younger, but she could understand Khaled's dismay.

Yassir continued. "Everyone at school is right about you. You're an asshole and attention-seeker. You only care about yourself and looking like a hero, even when everyone around you is getting hurt. No wonder Mr. Wells called you a thin-skinned poster child for social justice."

Khaled froze. Kawther looked between them, watching Yassir go pale.

"So you were there when Wells yelled at me." Khaled's voice was nearly a whisper. "And you didn't say anything to Delpy?"

Yassir became quiet.

Khaled scoffed. "She mentioned it to me, you know? That she saw you in the hallway footage. That you were a witness, just like Alex thought. But I let it go. You know how much I let go for you? Typical *Michael.* Always trying to avoid the problem even when it runs right up to you and punches you in the face—" He stopped, as if he'd just realized what he'd said.

Kawther watched her brother's eyes glistening as he tossed Yassir's phone onto the bed and crossed the room to grab his laptop and schoolwork. They'd tried to do homework together last night, until Khaled had found a crumpled flyer for the marines in Yassir's bag, and they'd nearly had a screaming match until Yassir had put the blanket over his head.

Maybe they weren't such great friends after all. Maybe, just like their families, they were irreparably broken.

"What's going on?" Kawther asked. "Why are you two fighting?"

Ali came to her side. "Yassir, stop this. Without Khaled, you'd be failing school even more than you are now. Mama and Baba would've been lost without him while you were asleep."

But Khaled did not listen. Her brother, stubborn—like her, like Ayah, like Baba and Mama—did not stop packing his things.

"Are you okay?" Kawther stepped closer to Yassir. "Did you remember something? You said it was urgent."

Yassir shook his head. "I'm sorry I'm wasting your time, Kawther. I want you to quit."

"Quit?" Ali echoed.

Was he firing her? Her heart sank. "Is this about the press conference?" she asked, shaking her head. "If you still don't feel well enough, I can get it pushed back. But you really should do it. The firm feels strongly that—"

"Fuck this press conference and fuck this case." Yassir raised his voice at her now, too. "Just drop it."

It wasn't that he hadn't hinted at this sentiment in the past few days, it was that she had never seen him so angry in her life. She tried to stare into his eyes, but he looked away. "Yassir, why are you fighting over a phone? Did someone post something online about you?"

She bit her lip. Last night, her paralegal had notified her about the recent discourse revolving around Yassir's faith. Khaled, Ali, and others had revealed his Shia identity early in their social media posts. After finding out he was Shia, some Muslims had threatened to retract their hospital bill donations and left crude comments. He was a kafir, they claimed. A sinner who committed shirk because he came from a sect that prayed on blessed clay and endearingly commemorated Imam Hussein each year.

She hadn't told his family yet. She was so focused on Islamophobes hurting Yassir that she didn't have the mental energy to focus on Shiaphobic Muslims doing it, too.

Why add extra stress? Why remind the parents who had escaped Shia genocide in Iraq that they didn't belong among other Muslims, either? She didn't know where they belonged anymore. Even in this room, she couldn't figure it out.

"Did someone threaten you?" she asked Yassir seriously.

Yassir shook his head but said nothing. "What's it going to take for you to quit?"

"Yassir," Khaled warned, putting his backpack over his shoulder. *"Shut up."*

"Khaled." She uttered his name as a warning. It was something she did not do often, as it was normally reserved for Baba or Mama, but her brother had interfered enough. Though they'd been difficult, the detectives had eventually interrogated the people she'd suggested based on Khaled's paranoid ramblings. The veteran. A kid from Chapman named Miles Guthrie. Some of Miles's friends. Even a grocery owner near Main Street who Khaled had interacted with passively. No evidence had been found.

People felt targeted, and now counter-articles were being written. Her brother needed to get out of her way.

"Hey," Ali said, grabbing the plastic bag from her. "Let's relax a little. Is Baba still praying?"

"What do you think?" Fatima suddenly spoke, an eyebrow raised. "I found him talking to Iraq again."

As kids, they always referred to their parents' calls to the homeland as *talking to Iraq*. As if their parents could speak to the whole country. But the way Fatima said it . . . Kawther glanced at Ali and saw the smile on his lips disappear. Had something happened back in Iraq?

"I got something to cheer everyone up!" Ali put on a smile. As if a piece of chocolate ice cream cake could solve everything. Like it could make the last several days, no, the last several years, bearable. Ali opened the bag and Yassir leaned back and stared at the ceiling. Kawther stepped closer to him.

"I have internet on my phone, too," she whispered. "I could just look up whatever you're worried about."

"Cake," Ali interrupted, pushing a plastic spoon into Yassir's face. He had a lighter and candles in his hand. "Let's sing 'Happy Birthday'!"

The kids excitedly jumped around as they all sang off-pitch, and Yasmin laughed as Yousef and Abbas blew the candles out. Yassir simply stared at the flame, anger still hot in his eyes.

"Eat something. You've lost so much weight being here." Ali gently put a hand on Yassir's unkempt hair, and his brother leaned away.

"Your cologne is making me nauseous," he said, putting a finger to his nose.

Ali's face dropped. He turned to Fatima and handed her a spoon, keeping his distance. He knew that if she smelled him like this too, it would confirm what Kawther suspected.

Ali had not changed. He was trying to re-create their entire childhood with a single dessert. He always stood defiant at the chaos in front of him, even if he was the one who'd created it.

I cannot be your friend, Baba had told Ali the day Kawther had admitted the truth. *And I cannot be your family.*

Kawther turned to Yassir, who sat with Yasmin on his lap.

He put a hand through her soft golden curls, the ones that resembled his own darker ones. Kawther's heart always seized when she saw the little boy she'd helped raise caring for a little girl of his own. Yasmin was all he cared about. He loved her, so much that whatever plans the Al-Azzawis had to "fix" Yassir, to get him closer to God, to make him feel regretful for his love for her, were futile.

Yassir Al-Azzawi did not need to be fixed. He needed to be loved, because it was the only thing that the boy with the small gap between his teeth knew how to do. But it was clear to her that Yassir was afraid of accepting love unless it leaned against him and nuzzled close to his neck as Yasmin did now. He loved fiercely, even if quietly.

"Here," Ali said, waving a spoon in front of Kawther's eyes. "I know this is your favorite, too."

Her heart squeezed. He was right—it was still her favorite. But by the look on Yassir's face when he put a spoonful in his mouth, it was no longer his. The boys crawled up to the bed and Fatima sighed, retiring her own spoon and focusing on not letting her boys get frosting on the hospital sheets.

Khaled tapped Kawther's arm. "C'mon, let's go. I need a ride."

"You too, Khaled." Ali pushed a spoon into his face. "And don't leave. If Yassir kicks you out, I'm leaving, too."

Yassir scoffed, feeding a small spoonful of ice cream to Yasmin. "Sounds like a plan. I didn't ask for any of you to come."

Khaled rolled his eyes. "You act like you're so much better off on your own and then you get hurt."

"And you think you're exempt from hurting me?" Yassir shouted.

"And you think you're exempt from hurting *me*?" Khaled shouted back, which startled the kids.

"Khaled, I'm not leaving until I get an answer," Kawther said, opening her phone. "Do you all forget why we're even here? This isn't time to hash out old arguments, Khaled. Yassir was attacked."

She searched Yassir's name, but there were no updates from this morning. She searched Sayed Rahman's name. Nothing new. She looked over at Khaled, who stared at her impatiently, annoyed, biting his lip. When she searched his name, it was all the same results as this morning. She huffed and looked around. Who was left? Had Yasmin been exposed? Search results . . . Nothing.

Kawther shook her head, and Fatima's eyes met her own again. She looked away. Fatima's eyes always gave her away.

I've always known, Fatima admitted eight years ago, her eyes filled with tears. *I just thought you would still love Ali anyway.*

Kawther deleted Yasmin's name from the search bar. Suddenly, it occurred to her that not once since becoming Yassir's lawyer had she searched her own name.

Her heart plummeted to the floor.

Terrorist Ties? How a Muslim Lawyer Tried to Cover Up her Client's Connection to the Islamic State in Iraq.

Kawther stared at an unattractive photo of herself on the article thumbnail. The article was brief, written by a conservative media group called the Righteous. It was only three paragraphs, but Kawther's temples ached as she skimmed through the words.

Ms. Al-Hakim, a rookie attorney, has connections to her home country, Iraq. It was reported that Al-Hakim came back from Iraq the night of the attack. She has accused only white men and has tried to pin the crime on innocent bystanders, classmates, and other community members who are now scared of being called racists or Islamophobes. A close source reported that Ms. Al-Hakim tried to cover up stories of her client's ties to gangs and potential recruitment by extremist Islamic groups . . .

Kawther scrolled down to the comments and when she noticed her hands shaking, she put her phone down.

49

KAWTHER

EIGHT YEARS AND THIRTY-TWO DAYS BEFORE

"What is this nonsense?" Mama said on the drive home. "Khala Zainab and I were preparing kleicha for your henna party and you're trying to leave the state for school? Does Ali know about this?"

Kawther breathed deeply. She couldn't believe Mrs. Mackenzie had called her parents and told them she had been chosen for the Future Law Scholars program. She'd described how capable Kawther was academically, how talented and hardworking she was. Even in their anger, for a moment, Baba looked proud.

It seemed like Mrs. McKenzie was trying to help in her own way. Kawther had told her the truth. That she was getting married, though she was not quite seventeen. It was legal. But when Mrs. McKenzie asked her if this was her choice, Kawther had become too emotional to speak.

It *was* her choice. It was just that her choice didn't want her back.

"Just ignore it, Abeer," Baba told Mama. "If Ali thinks it's good for her, he'll take her to California. Do you really want to go and abandon us, habiba?"

What did Ali know about what was good for her? He did not know her at all anymore.

"This is something to talk about between you and your husband," Mama said. "Not us. Really, Kawther, I thought you understood now . . . you're not a little girl anymore."

Kawther wondered when, considering all the times when her mother could not take care of them, she had ever had a chance to be a little girl in the first place. But she kept quiet as her parents talked about her future without her. Inserting the husband she did not even really have.

☽

"Pick up the first time I call you. I don't want to have to come inside and find you."

Ali stared straight ahead, annoyance on his face. Lexi had probably broken up with him again. He was going to try to get her back. Again. It was probably why his breath smelled sour.

Kawther got out of the car without a word, and when he drove away, she did not even go inside. She sat at the curb in front of the theater and watched couples walk past her. Holding hands. Whispering in each other's ears. A secret between them.

She had secrets, too. Almost all of them were Ali's.

She had one secret.

She emailed Mrs. Mackenzie to accept her spot for the Future Law Scholars program on her behalf. She forged her parents' signatures on the extensive form before scanning it back to her.

Your talk worked. Thank you, she lied. *My husband will be moving with me to California to make it work.*

Maybe on the day of their wedding, she'd tell him the news. He would have to obey her needs—everyone would expect him to take care of her now that she would no longer live with her parents. The apartment he'd secured had a month-to-month lease, so they could move to California when the program started, and he'd finally be away from Lexi so he could concentrate on Kawther. She planned to tell him the news today and was slowly working up the courage. She spent her time outside the theater practicing her speech, convincing him in her mind how great it would be. When she was twelve and he was fourteen, they had gone to California to accompany their parents for the first Iraqi elections after Saddam Hussein's regime had fallen. With so many Iraqis displaced across the world, they were allowed to vote at the closest embassy. It was a two-day road trip, staying in cheap motels, begging their fathers to stop at the beach, just so they could sink their toes in the sand for a few minutes and breathe the ocean air. They had exchanged jokes and smiles and stories about school. Ali still enjoyed her company then.

A few hours later, the Toyota pulled up to the curb in front of the movie theater. She stood up dutifully and walked to the passenger seat, only to find someone else sitting there. Kawther had not known how to imagine her. She looked like any cheerleader plucked from a TV show. She had big, beautiful eyes and straight brunette hair.

"That's my sister," Ali said. "Hurry. Becca got kicked out so I'm just gonna drop her off at her friend's before we get home. Your dad already called me, wondering where we are."

Kawther's spine tingled. *Becca?*

"Your sister is pretty." The girl smiled at her. "Nice to meet you. Fatima, right? I think we had science class together a few years ago."

Their wedding party was supposed to be in two weeks and three days from now.

Tears pricked at Kawther's eyes as Ali drove, but she did not cry. She watched as they dropped Becca off. She watched as Ali kissed Becca right in front of her. She stayed in the back seat as she watched the large four-story house neither Ali nor his father nor her father would ever be able to afford grow smaller and smaller in the distance.

It was clear to her now. No matter where they moved, in two weeks, in two months, or even in two years, she could be sitting in the back seat, watching her husband kiss someone else. She wanted more than that. She deserved more than that.

Ali did not say anything, even as he walked her up to her front porch. Not even an attempt at an apology. He was not ashamed. Baba opened the door to hug him as he always did while Ali lied about the places they'd gone and the things they'd done together, but this time, Kawther stopped him. She began to cry, and before her father could ask what was wrong, she spilled every secret she was not supposed to say.

50

KAWTHER

FOURTEEN DAYS AFTER

"Kawther," Ali said from the foot of the bed. "You look sick."

"Shit," Khaled whispered under his breath. "You found it, didn't you?"

He glared at Yassir, and Yassir ran his hand through Yasmin's hair once more.

Terrorist ties?

Mona would tell her to rationalize her emotions.

Focus on just one, she had told Kawther in preparation for the interviews at Mirza & Associates. *It will help you process your reactions in real time.*

Fear. Her stomach ached and her hands trembled.

Spite. She had put herself in this position. That pitiable guilt that festered and grew and swallowed her. She should never have said yes to this. She never should've been foolish enough to believe that people gave and received love because they were obligated to.

Anger. She was the villain, always the villain, and she was tired of being wrong.

"Kawther, your hands are shaking." Suddenly, Ali's hands gently laced with hers. Warm and rough, his hands rubbed a circle over her left hand.

She could not bring herself to look at him, so her eyes locked with Fatima's instead. At Fatima's shocked expression, she came to her senses and pulled her hands back to herself.

"What did you read?" Ali asked. When she did not answer, he grabbed her phone and read the article out loud. Kawther stood up, gripping her briefcase.

"Give me my phone back," she snapped.

Ali shook his head and began reading the comments from the phone. *"She is probably just an ISIS bride. Easier to jail her now. Better yet, deport her. They'll do the beheading."* Ali grabbed her hands once again and put the phone back in her left palm. "Kawther, I'm not letting you leave, what if someone hurts you?"

The center of her face ached. Strangers could hurt her and call her names. But no one had hurt her more than he had.

"This is why I wanted to drop the case," Yassir said, shaking his head. "Other victims who survived and their attorneys are getting death threats, Kawther. I'm sorry I did this to you."

Kawther shook her head, her voice breaking. "Yassir, this isn't your fault. Don't you dare think that."

Yassir stared at his hands. "I never should've left that day. If I hadn't, I wouldn't have forced you all to be here. You hate being here. You know how I can tell? Because the way you look on the outside is exactly how I feel on the inside." He pulled Yasmin closer. Kawther recognized the look in his eyes: guilt. "I'm so sorry, Kawther."

Khaled slammed his backpack to the floor with a jarring thud. "Yassir, this isn't your fault! It's a damn Islamophobe's fault, okay? This is why you can't keep telling her to quit or to drop the investigation. You have to make sure these guys are put away!"

"I'm the one who was attacked, not you," Yassir shot back. "I can do what I want. Unlike you, Khaled, I don't throw myself in front of danger."

Khaled shook his head. "You're being stupid."

Ali huffed. "There are people threatening our family and you two are *still* fighting? Khaled, sit and stay. Yassir, be quiet and eat your cake."

Kawther closed her eyes briefly. Her skull pounded. Ali's warm hand took hers again, and she recoiled once more. "Don't touch me," she hissed, as she should have done outside. *You are not allowed to touch me anymore*, she wanted to say.

"Kawther." Ali stepped close enough that she could have traced her hand over his stubble. "You've been protecting us. Let me protect you."

She ignored him. She stared at the boys. "Why were you trying to keep this from me?"

Khaled spoke softly. "I thought if you saw this that you'd run away from the case."

Was that all she was to him? A runaway girl?

She bit her lip. "After everything I've done for you these past few weeks, you still think I'm a coward?"

Khaled did not answer. Ali did not answer. Fatima did not look at her anymore.

Maybe she was a coward. Maybe she was born to run from every situation. Her parents had to flee. Maybe it was a genetic thing.

"Let's go, Khaled. You need to go home anyway." She looked at her client. "I'm not quitting. Yassir, tell me if something actually urgent comes up, okay?"

Ali stepped in front of her. "You're not going out there alone. Let me take you home, at least."

Khaled scoffed. "I think one Al-Azzawi in the hospital is enough."

Ali shook his head, his dimples exposed. He was laughing? "Your dad would never hurt me. That's ridiculous, we're family."

Everyone stared at him, dumbfounded. They were not family. They were never family, and Baba had made that perfectly clear to him eight years ago.

"Amu Mustafa loves me." Ali shook his head. "Look, I'm not saying our relationship is perfect. I haven't seen your dad in years, but you didn't think I'd come all the way back to America and not plan to see him? That's ridiculous. Our family has gone so long without talking. It's insane. This family is *insane*. Kawther, we did this. We can fix this, you know?"

Looking at him, it was clearer than ever: She did not do this. She might have run away from it, but it was not her fault.

"This isn't my fault," Kawther said aloud, watching Fatima's pained expression.

"If you had just stayed a little longer," Ali said, his words nearly slurring now. "I would've caught up to you, I swear. But you were so stubborn. Which is fine, you were young. I was young. But we're both here now. We're older. We know better now."

"What are you saying?" Khaled spoke the words that were ready in her mouth.

"I'm saying that fate brought us back together, don't you think, Kawther?" He took a step closer, until the bridge of his nose touched her own. She took a step back, feeling Khaled at her heels, holding on to her sleeve.

"Why do you keep touching her?" Khaled shouted at him now, but Ali's eyes were unwavering.

Tears filled Ali's eyes as she stared at him.

Buzzed Ali. Sad Ali. Heartbroken Ali. Twelve-Year-Old Ali Who Kicked Racist Kids in the Teeth for Her. Her Ali. No longer hers, but one who was too late. Always too late.

"Ali," Fatima hissed. "You have a wife back home, remember?"

Ali shook his head. "This is what you wanted, Fatima! You begged me to look at Kawther like a wife. Like a person I could love, and I couldn't back then. But when she steps into the room, I see it now. Do you believe me, Kawther? Because I will divorce my wife and start over with you. I will kiss the ground for your parents' forgiveness. I will do anything. I have been telling you this for years and you've ignored me. But now that you're in front of me again, do you I think I can just easily let you go?"

"Years?" Fatima asked, eyes wide. "What do you mean? Are you two still talking?"

"Talking is an exchange," Kawther said, her voice low and tight with anger. "I haven't responded to any of his messages. What is it that you want from me, Ali?"

"I want you," he said, clearly this time, his voice rising with each word. "I'm sorry for what I did. I'm sorry I hurt you that day. Not a day goes by when I don't think about it. I regret it. Wallah, I regret it. You should be my wife. You're not the coward. I am. I am! I swear!"

Kawther's heart beat and beat and beat. She was sure that if she looked down, her chest would be bruised. It had been bruised for years, as if from a welt earned after a passionate latmiyat. Ali's face trembled and she forced her heart not to collapse to the floor. She knew that when he sobered up, he would remember his role, and he'd go back to fulfilling his duties as eldest son, protector, husband.

"You know how I know you're lying?" Kawther whispered. "Because every time you let your guilt win, you suddenly remember who I am. Do you feel guilty? That you ruined everything?"

"Kawther." Ali's forehead brushed hers. The smell of his cologne mingled with the alcohol on his breath. She felt sick. "I love you. I'll always love you. I've never known where you begin, and I don't want to know where you end. Not anymore."

It took all her strength, but she stepped back once again. She turned around. Khaled's mouth was ajar, his hand tight on her sleeve, tugging, but she hadn't moved. Fatima stared at her, appalled, and Yassir's brows furrowed in confusion. The three children were quiet for once, as if they knew the weight of this moment. The cake melted in its plastic case, as the boy she had loved eight years ago finally told her that he loved her back.

There is someone who still owns your heart, Bibi Amal had reminded her weeks ago. *But it's time you take it back.*

There were many people who owned her heart, she realized, looking around the room, but Ali took up more space in it than he'd ever deserved. She still did not know where she belonged, but it was clear that it wasn't here.

"It should've been you." Ali knotted his hands, continuing to spill his foolish heart onto the floor. "If we'd stayed together, maybe none of this would've happened."

At once she understood that Ali blamed himself for what had happened to their families, but his only solution was to try to turn back time. His regret still haunted him and everyone in this room. She could not let it continue. This time, it truly had to end.

"Let's talk," she whispered. "Alone."

This time, she grabbed his wrist and pulled him behind her. They stepped into the hallway, and she dragged him one floor upstairs to a small roof courtyard. She would not do this in front of an audience. She would not do this in front of everyone. She would do this alone. Something she should've done long ago. She had been on her own for a long time now, perhaps for as long as she could remember. As much as she wanted her family or his family to save her from this heartbreak—she would be the one to save herself.

Of course, he took this as an invitation, and his fingers wrapped around hers. So strong. Firm. The sun twinkled in Ali's eyes like a slow riptide. He inched closer and closer, and they breathed deeply as they had that one time when he had kissed her under the moonlight in the car, wiping the tears that he had caused.

"Ali." The curve of his lips was close to hers as she spoke. "I have always loved you. I don't remember where you begin and where you end, either. I can't even think about my life before now without thinking about you."

Her fingers caressed the dimples digging into his cheeks.

She breathed deeply.

This moment she should've admitted to long, long ago.

"But you disgust me."

Lightning flashed across his eyes. "Kawther."

She said it because she meant it. She said it even as her heart snapped out of its strings. But she was not the same girl who would accept any little sliver of his love. She would not wait eight more seconds for him, let alone eight more years.

She could not love the boy who had never truly existed and expect him to love her back. It was not her job to keep them all together—she'd known that long ago—and even if everyone still blamed her for breaking their families apart, she knew in her heart that they were wrong. She decided that from this moment on, she would not regret her decision to let him go.

"I might have run away, but you abandoned me first. You all did. You abandoned me. It was never the other way around. Your parents, your sister . . . they set me up for a failed marriage. My mother wanted me to suck it up because she was afraid to lose you all if I broke us apart. But I couldn't just keep choosing your failures at the expense of myself. I was willing to give up all my dreams for you, but I'm glad I didn't. I want to fulfill them, and while I do regret leaving my family the way I did, I don't regret leaving you." Her voice trembled, but she kept a steady hand on his face. "If you had truly wanted me, you would've chosen me in the first place. But you never wanted me for me. You wanted me to save you. It was not my job then, and it is not my job now."

She put her hand down and stepped away, leaving him in the sun's embrace.

I love you but I cannot offer myself to you, and for once, that is enough.

She took the elevator back up, and when she returned to room 705, the little kids were on the floor, playing again, the ice cream melting on the corner of a countertop. Sayed Rahman was back in the room, and everyone stared at her.

Kawther grabbed her briefcase and beckoned to Khaled. "Are you coming with me?" she asked.

Khaled held on to his backpack and nodded. Fatima said nothing. She did not ask Kawther to love her brother like she had all those years ago, and when Kawther stepped back into the hallway, she noticed that Ali had not followed her.

She looked at the Sayed and smiled. "Ma'a s-salaama, Amu."

"Allah wayach." He stared, confused, but his eyes were soft and his smile warm. *God be with you.*

"What happened?" Khaled asked as they took the elevator and walked back to the Honda waiting for them in the parking lot. "Why are you crying? You're scaring me."

She put a hand to her face. "Oh."

A familiar feeling tugged at her chest.

Letting them go the second time was just as hard as the first, but both times had been necessary. Perhaps this was why it was so hard for Mama and Baba to let the Al-Azzawis go. Not just because of their parents' bond from the refugee camp to America, but because losing them was like losing half of their family at once, like losing themselves. Mama and Baba had already lost so much. Mama's brother Faizal. Baba's best friend. Their country.

But in her parents' attempt to create a new life, they had lost the dream they'd created, because their children could not love each other the way they wanted. Because she could not force someone to love her, just like they could not force a country to love them back.

But how dear it was to believe so. To believe that you could hold on to someone, to something, and have them love you like you wanted.

Kawther unlocked the car door, and they slid inside wordlessly. Snow welcomed the gravel. The engine sputtered a cry, and for a moment she was afraid it would cough into its demise. But this car would need to keep moving. She would need to keep moving.

"Kawther?" Khaled whispered as she drove. "Are you okay?"

He sounded just as he did the night before she left the first time.

Kawther slowed at the yellow light. "I lied, Khaled."

She closed her eyes briefly and opened them.

A tear reached the bottom of her chin, and she didn't bother to wipe it away. She could not lie anymore. She could not be something she was not, even for her brother. "I can't keep doing this."

"Doing what?" he whispered.

"I can't keep going back there. I can't be Yassir's lawyer anymore."

He stared at her. "Okay."

She sniffled as they drew closer and closer to home. She spoke the words that scared her. But she needed to know. "Do you hate me?"

"No." Khaled shook his head. "But I think it's time you tell me what's going on. Why did Ali say all of that to you? Is he the real reason you left us?"

Kawther trembled. "What if I tell you and you only hate me more? You still love the Al-Azzawis. I never wanted to take that away from you."

He shook his head. "Don't you think I deserve to know the truth? I'm so sick of everyone lying to me."

They parked in their parents' driveway. She could see the small ashtray perched on the railing. She could smell the spices wafting through the house. She cut the engine.

Kawther let out a shaky breath and told her brother everything.

51

KAWTHER

EIGHT YEARS AND TEN DAYS BEFORE

Ali was waiting for her after school again. In the three months they'd been together, he had never waited for her after school once. Now he was desperate to see her any moment he could.

"Give me another chance. Please, please. Do you know what it's like for your parents to look at you the way mine do? Give me another chance."

"Go away," she whispered, looking for Mama's van.

Part of her regretted it. Regretted that in her decision to break away from Ali, she had broken their entire families apart, too.

Mama had not looked at her in days. Khaled and Ayah lay around the house bored, complaining how they hadn't seen Yassir in years, although it had been less than a week since she'd broken down in tears and told her father the truth. Now her father banned them all from seeing the Al-Azzawis again. Ali had squeezed her hand, begging her to shut up, that night, but Baba had pushed him away from her and asked, "What have you done?"

The Al-Azzawis kept trying to come over. Ali begged on his hands and knees for forgiveness.

We were hoping you could help him, Sayed Rahman had confessed, his eyes glued to his feet whenever he spoke to them. *Kawther, don't you think you could help him? He might not be perfect now, but in a year, you don't know what he could become.*

"Kawther," Ali whispered as he stood up straight. Drunk Ali was functional. So functional that she had no idea how many times she had seen him this way without knowing.

"My mom will be here any minute," she whispered to him as classmates leaving for the weekend stared at them. Tomorrow would've been their wedding party.

"Good. She wants us back together, you know? This is all your dad's talk. I made a mistake, okay? I won't do it again—I won't." He grabbed her arm and she pulled free.

"Stop."

She began to walk away, and he pulled at her arm again.

"Please, Kawther, please. Please." He was starting to blubber. She had never seen him this way. Never this bad.

"Ali," she seethed, "let go of me."

He tried to pull her into a hug, and she pushed him away, so hard that he lost his balance and fell.

Drunk Ali was not so functional after all.

She dropped her phone, hands shaking. She needed to call Mama now. Or Baba. Or Sayed Rahman. A crowd was starting to gather around her.

She crouched down to grab the phone and he grabbed her legs. When she squirmed away, he kicked her. Hot white flashed over her vision. Blood poured out of her nose and her mouth. Her head rang.

"Oh, God, Kawther, I'm sorry. I'm sorry. I'm so sorry—"

He was blubbering again.

"Oh my God, are you okay?" a girl asked.

Kawther watched her blood drip to the ground.

Later, the officer asked, "Would you like to charge him with assault?" She shook her head. She knew assault was a minimum of three years. It was an accident. She knew that, too, even though it hurt. Her nose was not broken, according to the paramedics. "You said he was following you, right? He comes to your school nearly every day. You could get a restraining order. Is he a classmate of yours?"

She shook her head. "My . . . husband. Well, fiancé. Legally we're not married yet."

The paramedic seemed puzzled. "If he's not your legal husband yet, may I suggest you break it off before it gets uglier? Trust me, you don't want to get legally bound this way, and you don't want kids involved. Women like you deserve to be free."

She didn't know if the paramedic had said this because she wore a hijab or if she would say this to any woman who had been hurt by the boy she loved.

For a moment, Kawther realized that it had become past tense in her mind. Loved.

She had loved Ali.

But with her face pulsing in pain, she did not know anymore.

"What would that look like?" she asked, and the officer's eyes peered at her. "The restraining order, I mean."

"You would file paperwork, then go to court."

She stared at Sayed Rahman talking to Baba in the back of the police station, his eyes sad.

"If you don't legally restrain him, he can keep doing this to you, you know?" the officer said. "I see cases like this all the time. Sometimes it helps to have a piece of paper to threaten them with."

Once more he'd get on his hands and knees and apologize. Once more, they would ask her to help him. Six more times. Eight more times. Ali did not want her. He just wanted the disappointment and shame to stop.

Ali stepped back into the hallway with their fathers. Baba's eyes filled with tears, and she saw him reach to ruffle Ali's hair, then pull his hand away when Ali bowed his head, apologizing profusely like he used to when he made a trivial mistake as a kid.

She could see the heartbreak in Baba's eyes. She knew it would be hard for her father to stop treating him like a son.

But she couldn't do it anymore.

This had to end.

"What do I have to do?"

☽

The courtroom was cold. Fatima's stare on her back, colder.

"Assault charges have been dropped."

Ali nodded gratefully at the judge.

"But the defendant would like to obtain a restraining order."

Ali's eyes were upon her, and she knew that when she looked into them, they would be empty.

"Don't tell anyone about Ali," Baba had said on the night she told him about Ali's cheating and drinking. "Not even Ayah. Not even Khaled. I don't care if you do not marry him, but you cannot shame him this way. Only let Allah judge him."

The Future Law Scholars program was giving her her own dorm room, free tuition. All she had to do was go and leave this all behind.

"This is our family, they are not strangers," Mama had pleaded earlier that morning. "Ali is your husband, not a criminal. Anything can be forgiven, Kawther. I did not teach you to live your life this way. Ali simply made a mistake."

A mistake that would keep him forty feet away from her at all times. She drove herself to the court because they would not accompany her, claiming that she was shaming the boy she had loved for so long. It was the first time in her life that Kawther realized she was truly alone. It was the first time regret began to knot in her gut.

You don't need to marry him, but how could you do this? Baba asked later that night. *My daughter is not vengeful. She is forgiving.*

That evening, she sat on her bed and sobbed. She didn't know what daughter she was anymore, and when she asked Baba if she could go to California, he told her never to bring it up again. *If you are not a wife, you are our child and you will live your life as before.*

Except nothing was like before.

She did not even have Fatima to call anymore. The only family they had truly known was no longer theirs. And everyone blamed her for it.

When Khaled opened the bedroom door and caught her packing her bag, she ordered him to go back to sleep. When he asked her what had happened to her nose a week ago, she told him her boyfriend had done this to her. She had no husband. Just a boy who used to be a friend who hurt her.

She promised she would be back. She had to see something else, something new. She had to see if there was something greater waiting for her elsewhere, if it could hold her delicately, and for once, love her as much as she loved it back.

SKY

When I came to see if the whimper was still alive, I found his brother staring at me on the rooftop of the hospital. Unlike his father, he did not speak much when he looked at me. When he lived in the land of the tents, he'd do this, too. He'd stare after seeing something that made him shake. The baby that was buried. A young man who was dragged by the officers before he was returned bloodied and bruised. The explosions that rained over my belly. Even though his father tried to shield his eyes, he saw the dead bodies on the way to the border. Every time, I tried to warm him. To comfort him. To show him something beautiful and good.

Perhaps this is why he clasped a small bottle tightly in his fist so many times when he looked at me. Why he held it toward me before taking a sip. As if he was toasting in victory to all that haunted him still.

52

KHALED

TWENTY DAYS AFTER

"You do your lawyer voodoo magic or whatever. Scare the hell out of Delpy," Khaled whispered as they walked through Chapman High. It was late Wednesday afternoon, so the halls had mostly emptied.

"My purpose today is that we discuss the lawsuit," Kawther said.

"Fine, but at least frighten her a little," he said.

"Am I scary?" she asked as they approached the glass doors.

"Terrifying," Khaled said. "When we were kids, Ayah and I used to call you . . ."

He stopped talking, embarrassed to admit he missed talking to his sister like this.

"The Dictator?" Kawther responded. "Quite an insensitive name, considering Mama and Baba actually endured and escaped a real one."

Well, shit. Maybe they weren't that secretive about the nickname.

"You wouldn't let us watch the TV past nine. You limited the number of cookies we could eat. You were cruel."

Kawther shook her head, smiling as they stepped into the principal's office. Today was D-Day. Again. But this time, he had an arsenal.

"You don't deserve to be treated like this, Khaled," Kawther said. "Even though you're kind of a pain in the ass."

"Kind of?" he echoed as they knocked on the office door. Within seconds Delpy opened it, her signature fake smile plastered to her face.

"Wow, you look just like your sister. How is Ayah, anyway?"

"I need to be at a work meeting soon," Kawther said, ignoring her question. "Thanks for letting me come in. I heard you threatened Khaled with a lawsuit." Delpy's face visibly contorted at the word *lawsuit*. "The article was taken down the same day it was posted, and while I know you want a public apology issued, he will only consider it if you and Mr. Wells also issue him a public apology."

Delpy's smile thinned until it disappeared. "Why would we do that?"

"Well, you allowed a student, who, according to your policy, was participating in diversity of thought, to be verbally assaulted by his teacher over an assignment. Then he was forced out of the classroom despite following the rubric for said assignment. When he filed a complaint, you ignored it, and did not notify your vice principal despite standard procedure. So Khaled took matters into his own hands."

Khaled couldn't help but smile as Kawther continued, her voice unwavering.

"I looked deeper into the district's policy; the last time a student had to be permanently removed from a classroom, it was under review and guidance of the board of trustees. Khaled knew this, which is why he notified the board himself. However, instead of discussing the incident with the entire board or completing a thorough investigation into the incident, you delayed the process without due cause. Then you threatened him, without an attorney present, with a lawsuit after he wrote an opinion piece for the school newspaper, which was within his right as a citizen with free speech and, as far as I can tell, did not at any point break Chapman's code of conduct."

"Debatable," Delpy simply said, wringing her hands.

"Agreed," Kawther said, leaning forward, her expression unamused. "Which is why you cannot punish him without following procedure. In fact, while we're discussing procedure, I'd like for us to review all of Khaled's complaints, and Ayah's former complaints, too. We'd like to take them to the board to seriously investigate the incidents of Islamophobia and racism at this school. There was a good reason that a few students at Chapman High were investigated by the police after Yassir's attack; there were many things students said that made Yassir feel unsafe. In fact, Yassir has recently agreed to give his eyewitness statement about what happened between Khaled and Mr. Wells."

Shock buzzed in Khaled's stomach. Was that true? Would Yassir defend him now?

"He's more than welcome to give a statement, but the decision has been made." Delpy frowned. "Superintendent Marks will have to decide if his statement is substantial enough to reopen the investigation."

"Fine." Kawther nodded. "If the investigation reopens, I'd love to get an updated statement about it, as I've already added myself to the guardian list on Khaled's school record. I'd also love for a letter to be sent to home to my parents, with updates, too."

Delpy smiled at her. "Okay."

But Khaled knew Kawther wasn't done.

His sister raised a brow at Delpy. Pompous, yet professional. "As for the culture at Chapman, it seems your school has a consistent Islamophobia problem. If I continue to hear of it—or of the school ignoring protocol and unfairly punishing their Muslim students— you will be hearing from Jones, Jacobs and Associates about a discrimination lawsuit."

"That won't be necessary," Delpy said immediately. "Khaled, apologies if you've felt targeted, but please know I've taken your and Ayah's complaints seriously. Trust me, if I didn't want you at this school, I wouldn't have advocated for the board to renew your scholarships.

You wouldn't have been nominated . . ." She became flustered when Kawther gave her that look.

The Dictator look.

Or maybe just a very serious lawyer look.

"Khaled, we already discussed your status to stay in independent study. However, you will still need to make up all your classwork, and if your grades stay where they are, well, there will be another conversation about your scholarship at the end of the quarter. Unrelated to our previous discussion, of course."

"Of course." Kawther smiled, satisfied. "Well, I have to get back to work. Any questions or anything else you wanted to discuss?"

Today she would finally facilitate the press conference—a last-ditch effort to build the hate crime case for Yassir.

Delpy shook her head. "Give Ayah my regards."

She's dead, Khaled wanted to blurt. But he and Kawther simply nodded and walked away. Ayah didn't deserve pitiful regrets or empty apologies. She'd deserved to have those before, when she was still alive.

"Thank you," Khaled said quietly. "For . . . defending me. For defending Yassir when I asked. For . . ." He stopped talking. His family was not one to express love or appreciation, and he felt his stomach grow fuzzy at the words. "Just, thanks."

"You're welcome." Kawther smiled at him. "You're brave, Khaled. You care so much about the truth, just don't forget to keep yourself safe, too."

"What if I can't . . ." he said quietly. "What if I care about the truth more? I want people to know the truth about what happened to us. I want them to care. But it seems that each time I try, they only hate me more. I'm the one always painted as violent. I don't regret what I did in Wells's class—now less than ever."

Kawther sighed softly. "The truth can only be experienced if the people open their hearts to believe it. You don't have to regret what you did in class. Everyone should be proud of you defending us. But you're not . . . violent, Khaled. I know you regret punching Yassir. That's not you. Hold yourself accountable."

He nodded.

"So . . . I think you're clear for now. But seriously, let me know if it ever happens again. I'll come back so fast—" She unlocked the Honda but paused for a moment, not speaking at all, before she quickly got inside the car. After Khaled climbed in, too, he craned his neck toward the back window and saw it. The old snow-white Toyota Camry Yassir used to drive, parked at the very edge of the lot, where the manicured concrete bled over to a rockier expanse. Ali ducked when he saw Khaled.

"Kawther," Khaled said as she began to back out of the spot. "I saw him."

"I know," she said.

"How long . . . will you endure it?"

She didn't say anything.

"Turn around, I'll kick his ass."

Kawther simply shook her head. "I'll figure it out, Khaled. You have enough to worry about."

Silence filled the drive.

"Kawther—" he said as they approach their neighborhood. "If you want to leave again, I won't hate you anymore. I swear. I won't."

She stayed silent for a long time. It wasn't until she was about to enter their street that her hands began to shake.

"What if I—"

"Just park for a moment, 'kay? Turn left and stop at the gas station."

She listened to him.

All along he had thought she had left him because she did not love him enough. It could not have been further from the truth. She had left to protect him from the truth, hoping their families would reconcile without her there to remind them of the pain. She'd protected him, and for once, he would protect her, too.

"What if I hate myself? I can't just leave our parents again."

Khaled shook his head. "Hate . . . it's a strong word, Kawther. I think Mama and Baba resented you. I think they were angry. I think they didn't understand, but I don't think they hated you. Me, on the other hand . . ." He gave her a pointed look and Kawther laughed, wiping her face. "I hated you. And I'm sorry. You didn't deserve it. I just didn't understand why you left us. Why you would keep the truth from me and Ayah. And . . . they might not understand if you leave again. But you deserve better than being haunted by a past like this. You're better than here."

"Is this your subtle way of kicking me out?"

He shrugged. "Damn, if I had just said it that way, would've been faster."

She ruffled his hair. "You're such a smart-ass."

"I know," he whispered softly. "Do you want to go back to LA? Do you miss it back there?"

She nodded. "I was going to leave the day Yassir got attacked. I missed it, but I was scared, still. I think I can go back, this time with a few less regrets, now that you know the truth about what happened." Silence lingered between them for a few moments. "Will you visit me?"

Her voice was hoarse as more tears fell.

He nodded. "Yeah, I'll visit you."

"Will you miss me?" she asked quietly.

He nodded again, feeling the tears fill his eyes, too. "Yeah, I'll miss you."

53

YASSIR

TWENTY-FIVE DAYS AFTER

"Thanks for coming," Kawther said, her eyes on her brown paper coffee cup. "I told you I could meet you at your house."

"I thought it might be awkward," Yassir said, eyeing Fatima, who was sitting at a different table with her kids as they drank hot chocolate and ate cake pops the shape of snowmen. He'd only been out of the house for eighteen minutes and he already missed Yasmin, who he had left sleeping. "Besides, I needed to breathe a little."

Kawther wanted to talk to him one last time. I'm going back to LA. Your case is being transitioned to another attorney, she'd texted him last night. Can we chat about next steps? I also want to see how you're doing.

"How are you feeling?" Kawther asked.

"I'm alive," he said because it was the truth, and she smiled.

Things could've gone much worse, Dr. Bozic had told him when he finally passed his cognitive test five days after his birthday. *You could've never woken up, Yassir.*

His brain was no longer swollen, but he was still concussed. Four days after his discharge, he wasn't as disoriented, but he had to wear sunglasses when he watched TV or went outside. The headaches were duller, but sometimes he'd have to hold himself upright to quell the wave of nausea overtaking him. Each time Baba looked him in the eye, pushing a turbah into his hand, reminding him to pray and thank Allah for saving him, or lightly putting a hand to his cheek, asking if he was all right, Yassir would swallow the urge to vomit.

He was not all right. The idea of walking outside alone made his vision darken. He couldn't imagine it. If he did, he'd wake up in a hospital again. His spine would shiver. His body would ache. And he would almost die again.

The only thing that had been stolen from him that night—besides his health—was the small sliver of peace he'd had left. Even as the headlines finally faded along with the bruises across his skin, Yassir wouldn't get it back. Everything in his life had changed once again, and he wasn't sure anymore how he could hold on to anything, or anyone.

"Sorry, it was a stupid question." Kawther passed over a file with his name on it. "This is everything I've collected about the case so far. I wanted to give you a copy. Unfortunately, if your memory doesn't come back, or a confession isn't made . . . this might become a cold case. I'm sorry I don't have better news for you. The veteran denied his involvement. There was no camera footage and the checklist wasn't found . . . you haven't remembered more since we last talked, do you?"

All he could remember was the sensation of looking back, turning, his vision going black. All he could remember was the scream from his own throat. All he could remember was the burning.

He didn't want to think about it anymore.

"How are you, Kawther?" he asked, shaking his head. The last time he'd seen her, she had walked his brother outside. Ali had later disappeared for the night. She had looked scared. Ali had grown more antsy since then, constantly asking questions of Yassir, aggravated when he didn't have an answer about the attack. Ali didn't seem like the brother Yassir knew, who used to be gentle and patient. Perhaps he never really knew Ali at all. "The article about you . . ."

She smiled at him. "You're sweet to be concerned, but I don't want you to worry. I'm working on getting it taken down with the attorney who will be taking over the case." She stared at him again, guessing what was on his mind. "I know you want to close this case, but what good does it do to constantly wonder who hurt you?"

He blinked at her. "What good does it do to hunt someone down? What would it solve?"

"Yassir." She clicked her tongue, just as she had weeks ago when he'd first asked her to drop the case. "It's worth knowing who hurt you."

"We have no leads. It's become a political argument. I don't . . . I don't want to be a part of this whole Kill a Muslim Day thing . . ."

"I know you're in denial about this, but—"

"But I'm not Muslim!" he shouted. Fatima stared back at him, her face worried. "I'm just saying . . ." He lowered his voice. "Those other people that got hurt, I'm sad and sorry for them. But I don't think that's why I got hurt."

"Why do you think you were hurt?"

He shook his head. "Even if that veteran hurt me . . . even if he tried . . . it's not going to bring true justice. It's not one person. It's never been one person. If he did do it, do, you think they'd even hold him accountable? It's not like they've done anything to all the others who hurt us. Khaled must know this, too. We have no evidence. I don't know if it was him. I just . . . I need to move on. No more press conferences, either. It's riled up people again. I'm sick of it."

"No more press conferences, I promise." She nodded. "But I still want you to keep the file and the case open. As long as that person is out there, they could hurt someone else. The new attorney will be there to help if you remember anything or if there's any more harassment online. Okay? If one day evidence comes to the surface, and you feel ready to pursue justice, you should. Maybe it won't lead to anything, but it's worth trying, isn't it?"

He could only nod. He hoped, one day, if the time came, he would be brave enough to face it.

"Oh," she said, pulling out her phone, "you have more donation funds set up for you. A few weeks ago, there was some uproar about you being Shia and some people retracting their donations, but after the press conference other people caught wind of your case and were upset about others being upset about your Shia background . . . Anyway, you have more money to use for your hospital bills. Some was even donated by classmates, classmates' parents. Not everyone hates you at Chapman High, no matter what Khaled says. But I recommend you pay off your court fine with anything left over."

She took a sip of her coffee, and he sipped his own. The last time he was here Khaled had begged Yassir to save him from going to Iraq. Yassir had secretly hoped Khaled would show up today, but he hadn't spoken to his best friend since he'd kicked him out of the hospital. Yassir's parents made comments here and there, how Khaled would put Yasmin to sleep, how helpful he'd been, and Yassir realized how awful it was that he'd thought for even a moment that Khaled might have been the one who'd attacked him. How he'd bought into the same stereotypes the police and kids at school labeled him with.

Khaled would never hurt him like this, even if they had both hurt each other in other ways. Yassir needed to apologize, but he didn't know how.

Kawther grabbed her things and stood. It occurred to him that this might be the last time he would see her. At least now he could say the goodbye he never got to say before. But how could he say goodbye to his big sister when he'd just gotten her back? When the look in her eyes was steely and steady, like it always used to be, but the minute she looked away, he could see the hurt in them.

"Wait . . ." Yassir said, tugging on her sleeve. Surprised, she sat back down, eagerness in her expression, as if she believed he'd already changed his mind about the case. "Before you go . . . before you go forever . . . would you tell me what happened between you and Ali at the hospital?"

She shook her head. "I think it's important that you hear his side."

"Kawther," he whispered. "I want to hear your side. When you left, everyone made it seem like it was your fault that the wedding was broken off. Khaled once said you had a secret boyfriend. He never told your parents, but he did tell me and Ayah. Listen, I know what it's like to have everyone look at you and to see the disappointment and hurt in their eyes. Why does everyone in my family look at you that way?"

Her mouth set in a straight line. Her hands trembled.

"I'm not mad at you for leaving. I think as a kid, I couldn't understand how you could leave your family. Leave Ali. But I do now. I understand what it's like to want to leave everything behind. When you feel too ashamed to face the truth. I just want to know why you actually did it."

Kawther swallowed and quickly nodded. "Okay."

While she spoke, Yassir did not look her in the eye; instead, he looked at Fatima, who was busy wiping the mouths of her children, changing the videos on their tablets, tickling them until they giggled and hugged her. Part of him wanted to stand up and yell at her. The other part wanted to understand why she had let Kawther get hurt. Why she had let Ali hurt her.

When Kawther stopped talking, she wiped her eyes, although they were dry. Maybe she was sick of crying, too.

"I'm sorry," Yassir whispered. "I'm sorry they hurt you. How could Ali . . . why would he?" He broke off and blew out a frustrated breath, his eyes still narrowed at Fatima. All this time he'd thought he had shamed Baba as the one and only sinner in the family. The one who drank. The one who made reckless mistakes. But all this time, Ali had not been the perfect son, either. It was almost a relief to know he was not the only one.

"I'm not asking you to hate him," Kawther said. "He loves you. He wouldn't come halfway across the world the minute you got admitted into the hospital if he didn't. Promise me something, though, okay? You won't tell your siblings what I just told you. The only thing I ever wanted . . . was for them to admit they were wrong. For *someone* to admit it."

She put her hand over his. He hadn't realized that he was trembling now, too. That tears were threatening his eyes. Kawther's voice had not cracked, not once in her story, and he would not crack in front of her now.

"I have to go now," Kawther said. "I'm not okay, Yassir. Sometimes I wonder if I ever will be. But there are things that make me feel better. Even if they hurt, too. It hurt seeing Khaled every day, knowing that he resented me, but I don't regret coming back for him. When I left LA, I had gotten fired for unsatisfactory performance . . . but I want to pick myself back up again. I want to be okay, and I want you to be okay, too."

Hadn't Ayah told him something in that vein?

It hurts if you don't love me the same way, Yassir, but I don't mind loving you anyway. Even if it's different for us now. You'll be okay. I'll be okay. Separately this time.

"I'm sorry about Ayah," he said. "I'm sorry I caused her to marry early, I'm sorry that I . . ."

Loved her.

The words he couldn't say to Ayah, although they were true. He'd loved her and he'd let her leave.

"Failed her," he finished. "I failed her. I bet Khaled told you."

"Yassir," she said seriously. "You can't apologize for something that's not your fault. Not everyone is brave enough to love." She grabbed his hands like she used to when he was small. He missed the life they'd had, the life they'd never get back. "In another life, it was you two who were meant to be together, not me and Ali. Things don't always work out the way we want. But . . . now you have Yasmin," she said. "Don't be afraid to love her. Don't ever be ashamed to love her, either. She loves you and she's beautiful and you can't let her go. She needs you, okay?"

She patted his hands one last time, leaving him with those words.

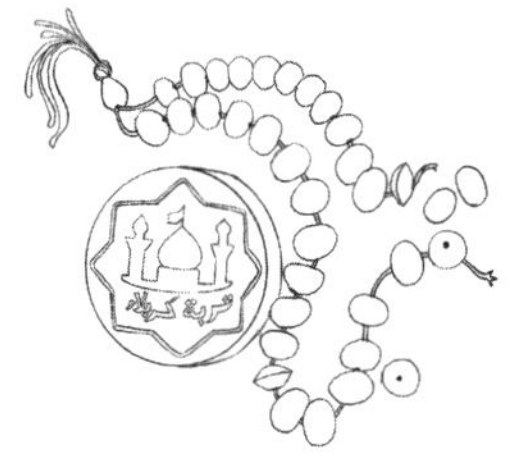

54

KHALED

TWENTY-SEVEN DAYS AFTER

Having watched his sister run away twice, this time, Khaled was helping her leave. Kawther had told everyone, including Yassir, but Mama and Baba still did not know.

"Do you want to come with me?" she asked. "You could come to LA for college—"

He shook his head, folding a hijab and sticking it in her suitcase. "I can't leave them."

Kawther sighed, a messy bun tied at the top of her head. "It's not your responsibility to stay. You're the baby of the family—" She paused. "I could wait longer. I don't have to do this now."

Khaled folded another hijab. "Don't worry, I'll be fine. That's why you put me in therapy, right?"

Last week he'd found himself in Alex's Jeep, his mind filled with uncertainty again, though Alex had agreed not to bring alcohol around him anymore. Khaled's prayers were consistent. So was his attendance at school. But the sadness that had made a home in his gut—the kind that made him shake—still lived inside him. He was not sure how much longer he could last, so when Kawther suggested counseling, he'd agreed to try.

"That's not the only reason, Khaled. You're not fine," Kawther said, putting her things down. "Neither is Yassir. You won't agree, especially after everything, but I do think you two need each other."

Khaled huffed. "I think we're bad for each other."

"If anyone in our family deserves each other most, it's you two," Kawther said.

Khaled wrinkled his nose. "What does that mean? Because we're both moody assholes we deserve to stay friends?"

Khaled looked up, and the expression on Kawther's face told him he was about to get a lecture. He was surprised to find he wasn't unhappy about it.

Kawther rolled her eyes. "I was going to say you're both filled with angst and seem a little lost in life, but you could go with your words instead." She sighed. "You both made mistakes. You can't keep punishing each other—or yourselves—for these secrets. I'm sorry he didn't tell you about Ayah, but Ayah kept the secret from you, too. There were a lot of reasons why she left. Yassir can't take all the blame. I deserve some of that responsibility. So do Mama and Baba. So does your school. It's not any one person's fault . . . I know you think you failed her, too."

A short tremor snaked up his arm. He wondered when he would stop feeling so guilty for letting her down. Even if he had tried his hardest to keep her.

After they finished zipping up the suitcase, they stared at her empty bedroom. When Kawther left the first time, Ayah had taken over this room because it was bigger and had a nicer closet. He'd silently stand at the foot of her bed, and she'd accuse him of doing it to annoy her, but sometimes he just wanted to imagine that Kawther was in this room again. She could've read her law school textbooks here. He would've behaved. They could have been happy.

When Ayah moved out, he didn't bother taking the bigger room for himself. Maybe he knew it would belong to Kawther again someday.

Kawther blew out a soft breath, putting a hijab to her shoulders. Her flight was in a few hours, and he couldn't even drive her there. He would say goodbye here.

They opened the bedroom door and the scent of dolma wafted through the kitchen. The kitchen smelled like childhood. Kawther's favorite meal. His, too.

"Do you think Mama knows you're leaving today?" Khaled asked his sister, an eyebrow raised. "It's true what they say. You can't get anything past an Iraqi mother. Their intuition is insane."

He and Kawther had spent hours quietly packing, eating donuts in her room. He imagined his mother gutting eggplants, zucchinis, and peppers before stuffing them with rice and meat and folding each grape leaf as she probably cursed him and Kawther under her breath for not helping. Not that she ever asked for help, anyway.

Kawther stood frozen. Khaled pulled at her sleeve.

"Bet she's in her room now," Khaled said. "Bet she's lonely again. Not that she'd ever admit it."

Kawther nodded, her face stony as they stared at the empty living room. Sometimes he could still imagine Ayah lounging on the couch, drawing, scoffing at his impressions of the uncles in the masjid while Mama tsked with her tongue as she picked basil and mint from their stems for dinner. "Where's Baba?"

Khaled felt a wave of anxiety. He was still not ready to talk to their father. They stepped into their parents' bedroom cautiously. Mama lay on her side, eyes closed, breaths shallow. She was not asleep.

"Mama," Kawther whispered. "Come have dinner with us."

Mama shook her head, eyes still closed.

They stepped closer until he could smell the cucumber-scented soap on his mother's skin. "You worked so hard on the food, don't you want to eat it, too?"

"C'mon, Mama." Khaled stepped closer, went to the other side of the bed, and leaned his head against her arm, his hair rubbing her skin. "Please. I'm hungry."

"Then go eat," Mama muttered without looking. She would not acknowledge them.

"*Mommy*, I'm hungry," Khaled said, this time in English. His eyes met Kawther's, and neither of them could keep from laughing.

"What, are you five?" Mama's eyes opened. "Stop being such a nuisance."

Khaled shrugged. "I don't know how to."

It was true; he didn't. Khaled nuzzled closer to his mother, and while he did not expect her to hold him, she did not move away, and for now, that was enough. He gestured to his sister to do the same. Kawther hesitated, but after a few breaths, she joined him and they all lay on the bed together wordlessly.

Whenever Mama felt this way when they were small, Baba would ask them all to pile into the bed together to keep her company. Yassir would join sometimes, too. Mama would pat his hands and get out of bed if he asked her to, as if she remembered he was a guest in their house.

Khaled waited for his sister to break the news, but perhaps now was not the time. Just him and his sister and Mama breathing. Would it ever be this way again?

"So, I'm the one working all day, and no one invited me to sleep?"

They all turned their heads at once, finding Baba at the doorway.

Baba took a seat at the edge of the bed, and Khaled held his breath.

Did you change? Baba had asked him weeks ago.

More than he'd ever thought he could. More than he'd ever wanted to.

He hadn't recognized himself for a long time, but now, he wanted to. He wanted to be honorable like Faizal, but perhaps he was more like Ali, stuck in the past and intent on a future that could not exist anywhere outside his mind.

"Mama, Baba," Kawther whispered. "I'm leaving again."

"When?" Baba asked.

"Tonight."

A quiet lull seeped through the room.

"I quit being Yassir's lawyer," she said.

Another quiet beat.

"You didn't do all that work just to stop being a lawyer." Baba shook his head, lying down on his side. Khaled nuzzled closer to his mother, who was staring at the ceiling now. "Don't tell me that family ruined this for you, too? Not after you worked so hard."

"I did work hard, Baba," Kawther said, smiling softly. "But no, they didn't ruin it for me. I'll still be a lawyer in LA. My friends are waiting for me there. I want you to meet them one day, if you want to."

Baba nodded. "Inshallah."

Mama blinked, nodding, too.

And they lay there, breathing, for a while.

Another lull fell between them.

Eventually, they all fell asleep. When they woke up, Kawther was gone.

55

YASSIR

TWENTY-NINE DAYS AFTER

"So . . . who exactly is the parent or guardian?" Dr. Evers blinked at the three pairs of eyes staring at her from the black leather couch.

Yassir slumped back in the single armchair adjacent to his family and his therapist. He already wanted to crawl back into the space between his bed and the cold wall.

Last week, he'd received a warning from the courts that if he did not resume his appointments, he would face a larger fine. So he'd been escorted to therapy by Baba, who Ali didn't trust to take Yassir alone. Ali had decided to tag along, which made Fatima, skeptical of both of them taking Yassir, also insist on coming. They left Yasmin with a sighing Mama, who knew this wouldn't end well.

The reminder messages for this appointment kept insisting that a parent or guardian must be present, and Yassir didn't understand why until Dr. Evers recommended medication.

"I'm eighteen now," he told her. "Do they . . . do they need to be here?"

Dr. Evers clicked her tongue, staring at her paperwork. "It says here that you're not eighteen until next week. The second."

His cheeks went warm. The past year, he had done that more often than he'd like to admit, getting his dates and words mixed up. He must have dropped a two somewhere, or written the date of his first appointment incorrectly. In any case—it made him look incompetent.

"He turned eighteen on the twenty-second." Ali snorted. "That must have been his dad sleep deprivation."

"Dad sleep deprivation?" Dr. Evers echoed, her eyes now on Yassir.

Shit.

"Yeah, because he's a dad?" Ali said incredulously. "He has a seven-month-old daughter."

"Eight months," Fatima automatically corrected.

Dr. Evers blinked in shock. "I hadn't realized . . ."

"Oh, don't tell me he lied about this, too." Fatima sighed to herself, exasperated. "Aren't you supposed to be truthful in therapy, Yassir?"

Yassir swallowed. Now that his bruises were healing, his steps steadier with his cane, it seemed everyone was getting comfortable with being disappointed in him again.

"Michael, would you like to clarify?" Dr. Evers asked him directly now. "Do you have a child?"

Yassir swallowed. These were his therapy sessions—his version of the truth—a truth that was focused on one fuckup at a time. He just hadn't quite gotten to Yasmin yet. He didn't know if he ever would.

"Yes, he has a kid." Ali spoke for him. "Also, why do you keep calling him Michael? Do you keep getting him mixed up with another patient? It seems that you know nothing about him."

"I call him that because he asked me to," Dr. Evers said, her eyes still pasted on Yassir's. "What would you like to be called?"

He avoided his family's inquisitive stares. "Just call me Michael. It's easier for you to pronounce it."

Ali groaned, just like Khaled would have if he'd been in the room with them.

"Is that why you asked to be called that?" Dr. Evers asked. "Because it's easier for people to say it?"

He nodded.

But it was more than that. It had always been more than that.

It was a barrier to help set him apart. From his family. His heritage. His religion. It was supposed to protect him. Why hadn't it protected him?

"What about what *you* want?" she asked.

Yassir's mouth dried. It had been a long time since anyone had asked him what he wanted. He simply shrugged, hoping to end the conversation. "Michael is fine."

"As you wish." Dr. Evers nodded. "I'd love for everyone else in the room to respect your choice, too, if that's what you want."

"Clearly, he doesn't." Ali scoffed. Yassir could smell his cologne. He wondered if his brother was sober. He seemed riled up in the way that reminded Yassir of Khaled when he was too buzzed. "He's just embarrassed about his whole life, if it isn't obvious."

Beyond the bruises and fractures, Yassir's skin burned.

"Ali." Fatima silenced him. "Stop being rude. If Yassir wants to be called that, then so be it."

"This is the issue." Ali shook his head. "You all just let him do whatever he wants and look where that's landed him! He almost died under your so-called watchful eyes. This is why I'm staying permanently. He needs real support now."

Baba quietly shook his head at that, not speaking. This seemed to be news to him, too.

"So, who is the parent or guardian?" Dr. Evers asked, bringing them back to the real issue. The medication. Fatima and Ali both pointed to Baba, who simply nodded awkwardly, his lips a thin line.

"So, are you his brother and sister?" Dr. Evers asked as she pushed the paperwork on the coffee table toward Baba. "You have a beautiful family," she told Baba. "And I can tell they care. I can see a lot of love in this room. I do. But I don't feel it."

"What do you mean?" Fatima asked, lips twisted. She looked skeptical of Dr. Evers now, too.

"When you look at your brother, I can see the love in your eyes. But when you speak to him, it seems you're more focused on his faults than what he's doing well. I think now, more than ever, he needs empathy for his situation."

Yassir blinked at the woman. Was she . . . defending him in front of his family?

"Michael exhibits comorbid insomnia. I believe his lack of sleep contributes to his anxiety, which causes him to drink. I'm suggesting he take these over-the-counter sleeping pills if he still has trouble sleeping. Even if you are eighteen, now, Michael, with your drinking history, I'd feel more comfortable knowing there's a parent who is aware of the medications you'll be on, in addition to the pain medications you were prescribed by Dr. Bozic. Dad, do you feel comfortable signing?"

Baba stared at the paperwork while Fatima and Ali immediately crowded around it, helping explain in Arabic what she meant. Dr. Evers looked on with a serious expression.

"Michael also exhibits signs of depression; however, I've asked the state for an extension of care so I can do further assessment before I prescribe anything. Because of your unfortunate attack, they approved this free of charge. Looks like you'll be seeing me a few more times." She flashed a sympathetic smile at Yassir. "Maybe I can get the full story when you're ready."

His attack had earned him four more therapy sessions. Great.

Dr. Evers started talking about *healthy family dynamics* and how to have *honest conversations* and even suggested family therapy, which his entire family quickly shook their heads about, until the timer went off, concluding the appointment.

Yassir grabbed the prescription. "We done here?"

As they walked out of the building, Baba spoke his first words. "What's this nonsense about you staying, Ali?"

Fatima shook her head in disgust. "Did you forget you have a wife waiting for you back home? What's your plan, to move here and bring her over?"

Ali didn't say anything.

"Get another divorce?" Fatima asked, exasperated. "Are women a hobby to you?"

Ali became quiet. No answer.

Yassir felt anger burn his stomach. Ali tried to put an arm around him, to steady him as he balanced on his cane, but Yassir shrugged him away and slid into the back row of their mother's minivan alone.

Yassir stepped inside the house first while the argument about him among Ali, Fatima, and Baba continued in the car. Inside, Mama was still cooking a meal too large for the kitchen itself. Wrapped trays of rice sat on the couch in the living room, hot and steaming, waiting to be taken to the masjid. She had done this before—honoring the wishes that had come true—usually by making elaborate meals or passing out newly slaughtered lamb to the poor. She had done this when his uncle got through his kidney surgery successfully in Iraq, and when Fatima gave birth to Youssef, and now, to keep Yassir alive.

"Yassir." Mama stepped outside the kitchen, a cheetah-print hijab tied tight over her head like a turban, a bowl full of herbs in her hand. This was her serious cooking look. "Ali's old dishdasha should fit you. I left it on your bed."

He shook his head. "I'm not going. I'm tired."

He was sure the Al-Hakims wouldn't even be around, knowing his parents were offering the dinner, but he was sick of the pitiful stares and prayers. After that disastrous therapy session, all he wanted to do was be alone with Yasmin. Maybe, if no one else was there to distract or comfort her, she might finally accept him again.

"How can you miss your own dinner?" Mama asked, puzzled.

"I didn't ask for the dinner," he said, stepping toward the playpen, where Yasmin was sound asleep, her curls slightly damp with sweat under a stretchy white flower headband. She was dressed, not in pajamas, but in black-and-pink overalls. Her outside clothes.

"You're taking Yasmin?" he asked.

Mama blew out a frustrated breath. "You think she's going to stay here alone with you?"

"Yes," he said, feeling heat in his words now. "She's not going. I'm not going."

"Everyone knows she exists, Yassir. Enough with the embarrassment," Mama said. "When you were in the hospital, everyone was happy to meet her. We have learned to live with it. When will you?"

He swallowed at her question. The front door swung opened, and Ali stepped in first, then Fatima.

"Mama, something is burning," Fatima said.

Mama rushed away. "Make sure he tries on the dishdasha!"

"Are you always this disrespectful to Mama and Baba?" Ali asked. "Didn't I teach you that in Islam disrespecting your parents is a sin?"

Yassir couldn't take it anymore. The hypocrisy. His brother spoke like he could teach him about Islam—but Yassir wondered when his brother would learn the lessons he preached. It was harder to keep Kawther's promise than he'd thought. He gently gathered his daughter in his arms despite Fatima's quiet protests.

Yassir quietly made his way back to his bedroom, careful not to disturb Yasmin. If she awoke now and cried, and he struggled with soothing her, he'd prove himself wrong to them. So he prayed—unsure to who anymore—that she stayed sound asleep. She did. He pushed the dishdasha to the end of the bed and lay down, feeling the heat of his bruises brushing against the mattress.

Before he could close his eyes, he heard Baba's gruff voice. The argument continued in the living room.

Mostly Baba's exasperated voice, Mama joining, Ali sighing but not talking back.

Iraq. It was still about Iraq. And the wife Ali was leaving behind. And maybe much more that Yassir didn't know. Although his family was angry about the secrets Yassir had held these past two years, he knew now that they hadn't been honest with him, either.

At one point, their voices woke Yasmin. It started as a whimper, as it often did in her dreams, until the cry amplified. He whispered *smallah* in her ear—something his mother did whenever Yasmin stirred in her sleep suddenly—but this time it wasn't enough.

He sat up, resting her chin in the crook of his shoulder before he began tapping her back. This was the only way he knew to quiet her. The past few weeks, he had tried to hold her like this but had found his bones burning each time. She still had to relearn this routine with him after everyone else had taken care of her at the hospital. She still had to get used to the bruises on his face, but he would try and try until she felt comfortable again.

"Hush, Yasmin, don't you cry . . ." The words were familiar on his tongue again. "Or Daddy's going to have a full-on mental breakdown."

After a few more minutes of repeating this, his hand tapping a consistent rhythm on her back, she began to quiet.

"Alhamdulillah." The word was foreign, yet soft under his breath. He hadn't said that in a long time. Never on purpose, although it felt like the only word that could carry his relief. When he'd been attacked, all he could remember was saying God's name before everything went black. He hadn't admitted that to anyone yet.

Yassir continued to pat Yasmin until she fell back to sleep and he slid her down into his arms. Although his muscles pulsed in pain, it was worth it. Yasmin was always worth it.

He gave her a soft kiss on her temple, and when he looked away from her cute sleeping face, he found his brother and sister staring at him from a crack in the doorway. He braced himself.

Fatima's face was wet. "One minute I was holding you just like this. And now you're holding your own daughter. It's hard for me to handle sometimes, Yassir, but I feel like I've never realized it until now."

"What? That I'm messed up?" Yassir asked bitterly.

"That you're a good dad," Fatima whispered. "Khaled kept saying that in the hospital. That you would never let her down. I'm sorry I didn't believe it until now."

Yassir stared at her in shock. Sometimes Khaled didn't make sense to him at all, but the thought of him understanding Yassir, even if he didn't tell him to his face, felt too raw to handle.

Ali approached him, now dressed in a white dishdasha. "You sure you don't want to come with?"

Yassir shook his head. "I'm sure."

"We'll come back early. But if you start to struggle with her at all, just call me and I'll come back immediately." Ali sighed. "Fatima, tell Mama and Baba he'll be fine. They'll listen to you now more than me."

Fatima wiped her face and stepped away. Ali put a gentle hand through Yassir's curls, like he'd done when Yassir was little. His eyes softened as he looked at Yassir.

"I meant what I said at the therapist's office. I'm going to protect you and Yasmin now."

Yassir shook his head. "You don't need to protect me, Ali."

"Why? Clearly no one else has," his brother huffed.

But someone had tried to protect Yassir, and he'd tried to protect that person in return. Sometimes trying to protect someone only hurt them more. Was that not what Baba had done to him all this time, too? Tried to protect him from sin—and only hurt Yassir in turn? Yassir knew that better than anyone.

Ali shook his head. "I'll move us out. I'll get you the best doctor to help you get your memory from that night back. I'll talk to the Al-Hakims—" He stopped talking as Baba called him from the living room to start packing up the van.

"Ali." In a sudden burst of bravery, Yassir grabbed his brother's sleeve before he could turn away. "What happened between you and Kawther at the hospital?"

His brother shook his head, a sad smile on his lips, and walked away.

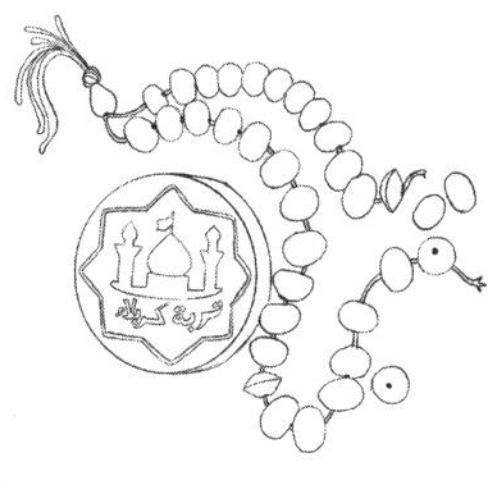

56

KHALED

THIRTY-TWO DAYS AFTER

Salat al-fajr commenced before the winter's dull sunrise could emerge. Khaled's eyes blinked down at the location tracker he had fallen asleep watching. Kawther had been invited to attend a fancy Berkeley social justice conference and had an early-morning flight.

Landed. Go to school, **she texted.** Don't give Delpy another reason to expel you.

She could use another death glare, **he texted back, and Kawther sent him an eye roll emoji.**

Nearly a week had passed since Kawther had left, and since then—save for silent shifts at Baba's mechanic shop—he had tucked himself away, lonely. He ate alone. He did homework alone. He began going to the gym—running off his pent-up energy, which used to be released in debate team—alone. He was practically the quiet boy he'd become in Iraq.

Alex tried, at least. He had lunch with Khaled every day even if it was both of them sitting in the Jeep, quietly watching the clouds crowd the sky. Khaled helped Alex pick out a tux for the winter dance. He'd had a life without Yassir, before, in middle school. But he'd had Ayah then. Now he had neither of them, and he wasn't sure how or when he'd get used to it.

He prayed he would.

He prayed alone, too.

Despite the urges here and there to upend all he was working toward, he still tried to keep himself as close to Allah as he could. The recording of adhan softly echoed from the living room. Sighing, Khaled put his phone down, pushed his body out of bed, and made wudu in his bathroom. He returned to the center of his room, unfurling his sajadah and grabbing his turbah, ready to set it down, but the coolness of the clay stone sent a shiver down his spine.

The empty space beside his shoulders felt unbearably cold now, too. He missed being sandwiched between his uncles in salat. He missed Sayed Rahman praying beside him at the hospital. But most of all, he missed Baba's gruff morning voice reciting each word with care.

"You can choose the way you return to them," Kawther had told him over the phone last week. He had been complaining about their parents' silent treatment again. "You don't have to fall back in the same place, Khaled. You've grown. Things are allowed to be different."

Bismillah.

He slowly curled his mat back up and rose, then stepped into the hallway, swallowing his nerves. He found Baba kneeling, reciting his last rak'ah.

He parked his prayer rug next to his father, who did not look up as Khaled commenced his own prayer. For the first time since the morning of Laylat Ashura, before his world had fallen apart for the second time, Khaled prayed with his father. Sober.

Some words were quiet whispers, others heavy with announcement. When he finished, he found Baba's eyes on him, dark bags glistening beneath them. Baba leaned forward, handing Khaled an envelope with Chapman High's emblem printed in the corner.

Khaled paused before reaching for it.

Dear Parents of Khaled Al-Hakim,

We're notifying you of your student's current status in regards to his American government course . . .

Yassir still hadn't gone to school, as far as Khaled knew. Even if he had, Khaled had wondered if he would finally tell Delpy the truth. So, Khaled's status was the same for now.

"I read it already," Baba said. "I know."

"Did you understand—" Khaled stopped. He knew his father had trouble reading English, understanding all the words, all the awards and debate titles; still, he'd always trusted that Khaled was doing what he was supposed to. "What did you understand?"

Baba rarely swore, but when he did Khaled knew how serious it was. "*Sons of dogs.* Get the diploma, that's all that matters. Take what you deserve."

He wondered if Baba still wished Ayah had gotten her diploma last year, a year ahead of schedule, instead of leaving. Rage rekindled in Khaled's gut.

You don't have to fall back in the same place, Khaled.

Khaled nodded. "Ayah deserved better, too."

Baba merely nodded, jaw tensing. "I know."

"I can't stop wishing I'd tried to make things better for her when she was still here. Maybe then she wouldn't have wanted to leave."

Baba nodded again.

"Do you know why I really started drinking?" Khaled asked his father.

Baba's eyes descended to the floor, to the round turbah placed over his dark blue sajadah. Baba had never asked him why he had done it; he'd just assumed it was Yassir's fault. Now Khaled understood why: Baba was scared they'd both become like Ali. Khaled had lied to himself and to his family for so long about who he was and what he felt. He'd run from his feelings, chasing a higher purpose in protecting Yassir, in being a pariah at school. He wasn't ready to face the truth then, but he wanted to now.

"I wasn't just angry that Ayah died. I was angry that you and Mama and Kawther let her get married. When she was suddenly engaged, that's when I first considered drinking. The night after she got married was when I held my first beer, but I didn't drink yet. I came to my senses. But after she died, Allah yarhamha, I felt like I lost all sense." Each word felt heavier as he spoke, like a ripped bag of sand piling on his tongue. "I was angry you let her go—that if she was meant to leave this earth, why did she have to go when I was so angry at her? I was angry at you and Mama, I was angry at God, too. How could I just accept all that happened? How could I not be angry or lost? But I couldn't show it to you. How could I show it to you when you'd already lost so much—"

"Shhh," Baba said softly as his warm hand rubbed Khaled's back. A sensation he did not recognize anymore. "Shhhh."

Khaled felt the tears running down his cheeks. He tried, as hard as he could, to make them stop, but just as it had when he'd hugged Yassir at the hospital, the sadness poured out of him. It felt never-ending. He was afraid it would be, although he prayed that one day, like Khalee Jafaar had told him, it would become more bearable.

Khaled looked up and found tears on Baba's cheeks, too, just like during every Muharram procession. Just like when he'd broken the news about Ayah to the family. The wound was just as fresh as it had been over a year ago.

Baba's voice was shaky, but his words were clear. "I just wanted her to be happy. She begged me to find her someone good, so I found the best person I knew. He was the son of a man who lived in the camps with us. I know you don't even speak to him, but he is a young man who cares for his deen. I knew he'd be a good match. I didn't know—"

"None of us knew," Khaled whispered. "I'm not blaming you for her death. I'm not blaming anyone anymore, not even Haydar. It's not in our hands, I understand that now, but I was angry and that's why I did what I did. And even though you won't believe me, it's not Yassir's fault, either."

He couldn't believe the words he was saying. He was still so angry at Yassir, for hiding from him, for trying and failing to protect him. But Khaled knew he was almost ready to forgive Yassir.

Baba blew out a breath, rubbing his face. There was regret in his expression, Khaled could see it so plainly now.

"You don't have to forgive him, but you can't force me not to," Khaled said, then hesitated. "Kawther said we need to stop punishing each other and ourselves for our secrets. Our mistakes. I know you blame yourself for Ayah . . . but you shouldn't. It's not your fault. You don't have to blame yourself for Faizal, either."

Baba looked up, jarred by his words. "How did you . . . ?"

"Bibi Amal told us in Iraq," Khaled admitted.

Baba stayed quiet for such a long time, Khaled wondered if he had ruined it all. The sun painted the living room with pale morning light. He would need to get ready for school. But then Baba shifted, blowing out a light breath.

"You're just like Faizal, you know? Running after a boy who didn't know how to look back," Baba whispered. "Who didn't realize what he was doing. If I could go back in time, I would never have shown him how to shoot a gun. I would never have let him go into danger. I was a kid, too, but I should've known better."

"It's not your fault," Khaled repeated, wondering when they would all figure out the difference between responsibility and regret. He thought back to Bibi Amal's fortune. "Nobody knew what was going to happen in Iraq. Nobody can tell the future. Maybe Mama's family will forgive you now."

Baba stared at his turbah, shaking his head. "Some things are too shameful to forgive, Khaled."

"I don't know about that," Khaled said, knees to his chest. "I thought Allah was all-forgiving if we change our ways? If we do better?"

"Allah is," Baba said quietly. "But we are not God. We are not close to perfect. Sometimes we don't forgive."

"Do you forgive me for what happened on Laylat Ashura?" Khaled asked.

"I'm trying."

A quiet lull sat between them again.

"Go see him," his father whispered. "I can't lose another child. If that's what will keep you here, go see Yassir." He looked up at Khaled, shaking his head. "It's not like you ever listen to me anymore, anyway. You are just like your uncle after all."

Khaled nodded, a soft smile on his face.

He owed Yassir an apology, but he still felt too ashamed to see him now that his friend was healing. He wasn't sure if they had a friendship left to mend, anyway.

Baba leaned back against his prayer mat and began to fold the corners. But Khaled didn't want this to end yet. This moment with his father that he had longed for.

"Wait. Can you tell me a story? About getting kicked out of school?"

Baba wiped his face. When Khaled met his father's eyes, they did not feel so daunting to look into anymore. "Didn't you get kicked out of school once?"

Baba shook his head. "You and Ayah always loved those stories. Maybe I shouldn't have told them. Look how these rebellious stories shaped you." He gestured to the letter on the floor. Yet a soft smile appeared on Baba's lips as he unfolded the rug, and the memory, once more.

57

YASSIR

THIRTY-FOUR DAYS AFTER

Yassir felt dozens of eyes on the back of his head as he limped through the halls of Chapman High.

"I've asked all your teachers to give you an extension," Delpy said, her heels clacking against the freshly buffed tile. "If you need to lie down in the sick room, let me know. We have a nurse on standby."

Although he'd assured Principal Delpy that he'd be fine, she insisted on escorting him to first period. Perhaps it was Khaled's accusations that someone from the school could've attacked him, but Delpy seemed to want to prove a point that she had his back, that she did not condone Islamophobia. While he wasn't sure he could face Khaled now, he had asked Kawther to warn Delpy of his knowledge about the Wells incident. He'd promised himself he'd tell the truth.

But now, with a crowd of students behind her staring at him, just didn't seem like a good time.

"Michael," Delpy said as she walked him to the door. "If anyone says anything to you about your incident, let me know immediately.

You can come straight to my office. All your teachers are aware of what happened. We watched the news, and although you weren't a part of this whole . . . *attack*, you were still hurt."

Yassir nodded, and she smiled at him as he stepped into Mr. Wells's classroom. Wells paused a documentary about the Vietnam War and stood up from his desk to welcome him. He even started clapping.

The whole class followed suit.

Yassir tried not to groan. He already missed Yasmin. He missed falling asleep beside her. He missed her giggles when he stuck his tongue out at her. He missed her warmth. He also missed having fewer eyes on him, although at home, Iraqi aunts and uncles still came around to check on him at least once a day.

"Welcome back, Mikey!" Alex shouted as Yassir took his seat.

In seconds, the class was back to normal, with the documentary resuming. The first image that played was a bomb exploding in a field.

Yassir's spine tingled. Alex tapped his arm.

"Mikey," Alex whispered, wiping his wet face. "You could've given me a little warning that you were coming back. Last time I saw you, you were still passed out."

"You visited me at the hospital?" Yassir asked.

Alex nodded. "I'm so happy you're back."

"Hey," Miles whispered to him from two seats over. "Is it true? You weren't even attacked during that Muslim Death Day? It was all a lie?"

"Shut up, Miles," Alex spat.

"No talking, take notes," Wells said, not looking up from his computer.

Miles's eyes locked with Yassir's. "I'm just saying if it was a lie, then maybe you should apologize for tricking everyone. You know the cops came and questioned some of us, right?"

"Leave him alone," Alex said, seething. "He's been through enough."

Although the room was dark, Yassir could see Miles shaking his head, annoyed. "Whatever."

The documentary continued. Bombs rained from the sky. Darkness filled the screen. The back of Yassir's head ached with a migraine. Nausea filled his throat. He hated this sickening feeling.

He was sick of letting everyone down, scared of what people would think of him, playing it safe—as if real safety existed. More than anything, he was sick of letting himself down.

"Fuck off," Yassir finally said. Not caring if anyone heard him, he stood up and walked out of class.

"Michael!" Wells called after him, but he ignored it.

You throwing up? You need help? Alex texted him immediately. I would walk out but I think I'll get a zero on the quiz :(

Yassir went to the only place he felt he belonged. He limped to the library and found Khaled resting his head on a stack of debate books. Although debate season had ended and he'd been kicked off the team, Khaled was probably preparing extra early for college. Wherever college was now. Yassir didn't know what that meant to either of them anymore.

Yassir plopped down beside him, ignoring Mrs. Marsh's confused stare. He realized Khaled was sound asleep. Red marks pressed around his neck and cheeks. Drool dangled from his lips.

"You're not supposed to be here," Mrs. Marsh called, marching toward them. "Mr. Al-Hakim, I have told you *several* times not to sleep during independent study."

"I'm not asleep," Khaled muttered, his eyes still closed.

Yassir scoffed. "You're fucking asleep."

"Watch your language, Michael."

Khaled jolted awake. He stared at Yassir, eyes wide.

"Care to explain, Michael?" Mrs. Marsh asked.

"Um, it's Yassir," Yassir responded, not looking at her. "That's my name."

Michael wouldn't protect him. It never had.

"What are you doing?" Khaled asked him, a scowl framing his face.

"I'm protesting," Yassir said.

"Protesting what exactly?" Mrs. Marsh asked, exasperated.

"Khaled's exile."

Mrs. Marsh shook her head and blew out a sigh. "It's too early to deal with nonsense. I'm calling Dr. Delpy."

She walked away. Khaled tapped his arm. "Why are you doing this?" he hissed.

"I just told you. I'm protesting."

"You? Protest?" Khaled shook his head. "Go back to class. One of us deserves to have a real education."

Yassir shrugged. "That class isn't so good for my PTSD. Wells shows too many war movies."

"Ah, yes, because you battled so hard in the war of 1776." Khaled shook his head. "Wait. Did you remember something?"

Yassir shook his head. "I don't like to watch people get killed in documentaries. I don't like hearing the bombs. I don't like the way I feel in there. I don't like the way they look at me, either."

It was the truth. The kind he never admitted—always pushing down his discomfort to fit in. Always trying to hide from who he was.

Khaled nodded.

A tense silence fell between them. It wasn't the first time the two of them had sat side by side, even after their friendship had ended. But how could anyone end a friendship that was woven in the womb?

Khaled shook his head and rummaged through his backpack, pulling something out. The purple jelly of Yasmin's teething toy squeezed in his palm. "Accidentally grabbed this a few weeks ago. Return this to the owner, yeah?"

"Khaled," Yassir scoffed. "You're being overdramatic."

Khaled placed the toy between them and went back to his textbooks. Only the sound of his pen scratched against his notebook, filling the quiet library.

"I'm sorry—" Yassir finally whispered, words he should've said long ago. "I'm sorry."

"For what?" Khaled murmured, not looking at him.

It was like a dam had burst. Yassir, who had kept so many things hidden for so long, couldn't help the words that poured out of him now. "For not standing up for you. For kicking you out at the hospital. For blaming you for my attack. For Ayah. I'm sorry I didn't love her . . . No, I did, I just . . . I didn't know how. I didn't know she'd leave. I got scared and let her go and—"

"Shut up, Yassir," Khaled said, his voice cracking. "I'm the one who's fucking sorry."

"For what?" Yassir asked, the teething toy between his fingers now.

"For punching you in the face, for abandoning you, for calling you a coward, for doing things without your permission."

Khaled sniffled. Yassir could see tears leaking from his best friend's eyes.

"Are you . . . crying?" Yassir said, knowing his own tears had already started to descend his cheeks the moment he'd taken Yasmin's teething toy in his hands.

"No."

Yassir wiped his face, and Khaled stared at him, eyes red.

"It's not your fault she died. It's not your fault that she left, either," Khaled whispered. "I've stopped blaming you, and I think it's time you stop blaming yourself, too. Just . . . don't keep any more secrets from me, okay?"

Yassir nodded. "Okay."

Yassir was surprised to find how easy it had been to forgive him. He hoped it was the same for Khaled.

"Michael!" Delpy rushed in with Mrs. Marsh following closely behind. "What is this about you protesting? Unless you have something to say to me directly, Khaled is staying in independent study. This was a mutual situation between Khaled and—are you both crying?"

They both looked up at her, tears streaming down their faces. She gawked at them.

"It wasn't," Yassir said, wiping his eyes. "It was never a mutual decision. Wells was the only one who got what they wanted in this situation. You should probably get Mr. Marks on the phone, so he can hear my side of the story, too." He met Khaled's eyes. "Unless we both can go back, I'll just stay here."

"Those war documentaries aren't so good for this guy." Khaled patted his back. "You should probably let Ryan know."

Something always fabulously stung about calling your high school teacher by their first name.

"What am I going to do with you two?" Delpy muttered to herself. "Should I schedule an appointment for you both to see the counselor? You both seem distressed."

"What we really need is an A, and as you know, we're both failing right now," Khaled said. "So, if you'll excuse us . . ." He pointed down at the open textbook in front of him. For show, Yassir reached into his backpack and pulled out one of his overdue assignments.

Delpy sighed before walking away in defeat.

Yassir and Khaled exchanged a smirk and began to work in silence.

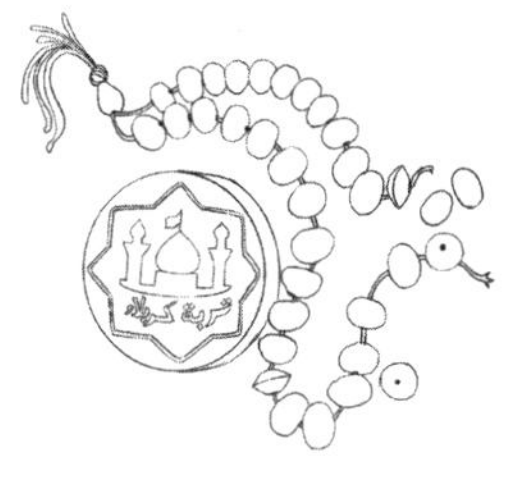

58

KHALED

THIRTY-EIGHT DAYS AFTER

Khaled glanced at Yassir wiping the sticky countertop for the fourth time as he took the trash out once more. Arnold was texting on his phone, laughing at something.

"You can do community service at the masjid, too. You could help me throw out trash once in a while," Khaled said, hauling another bag over his shoulder.

"These people need help," Yassir said. "I don't think the people at the masjid need help."

"On the contrary," Khaled said. "Those people need help desperately. Hajji Majid needs help putting flavor in the tashreeb. I love that man, but it's an insult to our culture, honestly."

Yassir cracked a smile. "Stop complaining, you volunteered here today."

"Yeah, you have a soft heart, Kaden," Arnold piped up.

"It's *Khaled*."

No matter how many times Khaled corrected Arnold, he still said his name wrong. Khaled rolled his eyes and stepped out of the apartment. It was the same apartment they had lived in long ago. When Khaled closed his eyes, he could still see Yassir and Ayah playing on the playground, skipping hand in hand. He could still imagine everything as it had been. Who they were before. Before Kawther left. Before Ali left. Before Ayah left, too.

Kawther had told him that Yassir knew about what had happened between her and Ali. *Your brother ruined my family*, he wanted to say. *Your family ruined my family, not the other way around.* But it wasn't Yassir's fault. And he had just gotten Yassir back. Yassir and his lingering guilt.

It was why Khaled was even here. Yassir's community service hours had finished, but he kept volunteering. Maybe his near-death experience had convinced him to help others. Whatever it was, Khaled preferred that Yassir stayed by his side, which was why he'd offered to accompany him today. Baba had driven him here himself. Though Baba still didn't talk to the Al-Azzawis, he'd kept his word and let Khaled continue their friendship.

Khaled walked back into the kitchen as Yassir attempted to step on the ladder.

"Oh, hell no, not like last time, Mike," Arnold said. "Plus, aren't you still injured?"

"Yeah, take a seat, dude," Khaled said, forcing Yassir to sit down. "You're still bruised and—"

"I like doing this," Yassir interrupted. "I mean, not cleaning. I like helping people. Greg said he might hire me on as a coordinator if I keep it up."

"And not breathe car exhaust and secondhand smoke at Hajji Majid's?" Khaled scoffed. "Traitor."

"I need to do *something* with my life," Yassir pointed out. "One of us has to."

"For your information," Khaled said, "I've just applied to *the* prestigious Riverside University. You know, the school with an eighty-nine percent acceptance rate. Five-thousand-dollar scholarship."

"Same." Yassir frowned. "They're stingy, yeah?"

"I mean, you failed two quarters and I got suspended, so . . ."

"So we'll show Delpy. Part-time night classes for me, you can go make their debate team piss their pants."

"And when we're rich, we'll really show her," Khaled laughed. "Especially you making millions as . . . a future social worker?"

Yassir shrugged. "Dunno. Was thinking of something that wouldn't make me an asshole. You?"

"Was thinking about something that would let me be an asshole."

"On-brand," Yassir muttered, dusting the top shelves.

"You might not realize it," Khaled added, "but you doing all this is pretty on-brand with Islam."

Yassir rolled his eyes. "What does this have to do with being Muslim?"

"Everything," Khaled said. "We're supposed to help each other. Feed each other. Be kind. When I walked the Arbaeen pilgrimage, everything was free."

"Man, I knew you were Muslim!" Arnold interjected. Khaled had forgotten the kid was still standing there. "Just something about you."

"How can you tell?" Yassir asked, annoyance in his voice. "It's a faith, not a race."

"Yeah, but you think shitheads like me know the difference?" Arnold said. "Mike probably isn't even your real name, huh?"

For half a second, Khaled liked Arnold. "It's not. It's Yassir."

Arnold slapped his hand down on the countertop dramatically. "Damn, that's much nicer! Why don't you go by that?"

"I do . . . kind of," Yassir said. "I'm trying."

"You got that Middle Eastern vibe. So, if you're not from Afghanistan like that one family you ruined the deposit for . . . where is he from, Kaden?"

"Iraq. Same as me."

"Iraq?" Arnold echoed. "That's wild."

"Why is that wild?" Khaled asked.

Arnold shrugged. "I dunno. I just see your people on TV, blowing shit up."

"Thanks, Arnold." Khaled laughed dryly and Yassir stopped cleaning. "But you know not all Iraqis are blowing shit up. Our people get *blown* up."

"I mean, I know that, but other shitheads don't," Arnold said. "Is that why you got beat up? I heard that a veteran did it."

Yassir shrugged as he moved to the kitchen sink and began washing the pile of crusty dishes. "I don't know."

"You still don't know who did that shit to you?"

Khaled sighed. "We don't know who did it. We don't know why. If it's related to this whole Kill a Muslim Day—"

Arnold shook his head. "Nah, man, I heard that shit is a hoax. I mean, think about it? Muslims getting attacked? Seems far-fetched when Muslims are—"

Yassir dropped a spoon loudly into the old porcelain sink. "Shut up, Arnold."

Khaled blinked, surprised at Yassir's reaction.

Arnold shrugged, throwing old cups in the garbage. "Just speaking my mind."

"Then you must have brain rot," Yassir muttered, and began washing the dishes again.

"Ever heard of a 'difference of opinion'? I mean, I'm sorry you got attacked, man. Seriously. I just doubt it had to do with that Kill an Islam Day stuff."

"Arnold?" Khaled asked. "You ever heard of Blackwater?"

Yassir sighed. "Shut up, Khaled."

"Okay."

"What's Blackwater?" Arnold asked.

Khaled listened to his friend for once. He kept his mouth shut. That was something else he was working on.

When neither boy responded to him, Arnold whipped out his phone for the answer. After a few minutes, he put a hand over his mouth. "Oh, shit. Those soldiers just shot people up?"

"It wasn't just them, either," Khaled said. "There's a lot more stories like that."

He thought about Mr. Marks and Delpy watching him make his presentation last Friday, after deciding to reopen the investigation thanks to Yassir's testimony. He thought about how their faces had dropped in shock at all the things he spoke about. They'd concluded he had followed the rubric after all. He received all the points Wells had taken away from him, and his transcript would be amended. The administration had agreed that Khaled was too disruptive to stay in class, but that Mr. Wells would be on probation himself for the rest of the school year, too. Khaled didn't always get justice for what he wanted, but he refused to regret trying.

Arnold shook his head. "Why did they kill them? Because they're Muslim or Iraqi?"

"Maybe both." Yassir shrugged. "I think both."

"Is that what you think happened to you, Mike?" Arnold asked.

"Let's stop talking about this," Yassir said again. "Please."

Arnold clicked off his phone, obviously annoyed, but kept his mouth shut. Silently, they continued to clean. After a few hours, Greg returned from whatever task he'd left to accomplish.

"Why does everything look exactly the same as when I left it?"

"No matter what we do," Arnold cried, frustrated, his hands full of dusty soda cans, "everything feels the same. You know how much work we put into this, Gregory?"

Greg rolled his eyes and began to stuff more bags with trash.

From the corner of his eye, Khaled noticed Yassir's shoulder shaking as he sighed at Greg's melodrama.

"You good?" Khaled walked to Yassir and put an arm over his shoulder. "You tired?"

"I'm good," Yassir said, pointing to another bag. "Take out the trash, ihmar."

"Okay, ihmar."

59

YASSIR

FORTY DAYS AFTER

"You don't have to come inside," Yassir told his brother, who had insisted on driving him today. Khaled had a scholarship interview for another local college this morning and had gone to work right after. The idea of taking the bus alone exhausted Yassir, so he'd allowed Ali, who sat restlessly at home and continued to beg to spend time with him, to take him to work. Yassir hoped on the ride over his brother would finally confess something.

But as Ali drove, it occurred to Yassir that he hadn't been able to detect lately that his brother was drunk.

When he had listened to Kawther's story, it had made sense. Ali's behavior at the hospital, touching her, practically begging for her to love him despite his having a wife back in Iraq—a woman Yassir had never met before. Ali seemed sober now, which was why Yassir had agreed to get in the car with him in the first place. Ali drove steadily and his words were clear as he began talking about attending community college classes. He truly was planning to stay—even if it meant unraveling everything he had left behind.

When they parked at Hajji Majid's shop, he unbuckled his seat belt, too, noticing Yassir's confused stare.

"What? I need to say my salaams. I can't be rude to Hajji Majid, he's gonna be pissed if he finds out I didn't say hi after dropping you off. I'll never hear the end of it." Ali stepped out of the car, slamming the door behind him.

Nervously, Yassir nodded. Ali was always respectful toward uncles. He was the one who would push Yassir to them when he was a kid. *Shake their hand*, he'd command. *Let them kiss your cheeks. When they ask how you are, just say Alhamdulillah. It will shut them up.*

Hajji Majid's shop looked the same. The same black stains painted the white brick walls. Oil gleamed on the concrete floor. Yassir was grateful for the distraction the job offered, because he was not sure he could keep listening to his parents argue with his brother. Something he'd never thought he'd have to hear.

"Yassuri! Ahlan was sahlan!" Hajji Majid's silver teeth flashed at him. Yassir let the man kiss both of his cheeks.

"Ah, Sayed Ali." Hajji Majid's smile became serious as he looked at Ali, who stared around the shop. "How are you, habibi? Do you want chai?"

Ali gave the man a hug and they walked outside as they caught up. Yassir limped to the back of the shop and exchanged his yellow Chapman hoodie for a Majid's Oil Change & Emissions shirt. He sat behind the register and organized the files that sat messily in the cabinet beneath the counter.

It was weird, but he had missed it here. He didn't know he could miss a place that smelled like cigarettes and oil and car exhaust. But somehow, he had. After an hour of reorganizing customer files and calling those late on their payments, Yassir heard a ruckus outside.

Yelling.

When he looked out the window, he noticed that Mama's minivan was still parked out front. Yassir's blood turned cold as he quickly limped to the back of the lot where the Al-Hakim property connected with Hajji Majid's. There stood Ali, Laith, and Khaled, who was fuming.

"Where is she? I have something to tell her, I have something to tell her!" Ali was on his knees, grabbing Khaled's legs.

Laith was trying to pull Ali away, but Ali wouldn't move.

"What's going on?" Yassir was breathless. His leg hurt without his cane steadying him.

"This is so pathetic, Ali," Laith said. "Leave the kid alone."

"Yassir, get your brother off me, or I will punch him in the face," Khaled warned.

"Let's go back to work," Hajji Majid said behind Yassir, his voice panicky. "Yalla. Yalla. Say Ya Allah, and we go back to work, okay?"

Yassir grabbed the back of his brother's shirt, signaling Laith to help, but Laith stood dumbfounded, shaking his head.

"Ali," Yassir whispered. "Get up. What are you doing? This is embarrassing."

Ali wouldn't let up, even as Yassir pulled on his jacket, his arm. He shrugged Yassir off, and when Yassir wobbled backward, Khaled pushed Ali so hard that he slammed onto the concrete.

"Khaled," Yassir began, but Khaled shook his head, shaking Ali, still clinging to his legs, off him.

Khaled blew out a breath, hands on his hips as he began pacing in a circle. "He's looking for Kawther."

"What th-theee hell?" Ali's words were slurred now. "Whose side are you on, Khaled? Yassir? Laith? Whose side is everyone on! Why are there sides to even begin with! We're supposed to be one family! One!"

Ali stood up, blood filling his mouth. He staggered forward, swinging a fist at Khaled. Yassir reached out and pushed his brother back to the concrete; the action made his entire body feel like fire. Ali moaned before pulling his knees to his chest.

"Astaghfirullah," Laith said. "Now, this is pathetic."

Yassir locked eyes with Khaled, whose expression filled with sadness. A sadness that told him *I know everything.* Yassir leaned down to his brother. "Kawther left. She's not even in the state. I'm sorry I pushed you." He pulled on Ali's arm to get him to stand up. "What's wrong with you? Get *up.*"

Ali lay on the concrete. Blood still leaked from his mouth. "I came to see Hajji Abu Abdalla. I want us to start over. I want to apologize. I need to apologize . . ."

Yassir knew that no matter how hard Ali tried or how he begged, he could not start over.

Kawther was right. Life wasn't about starting over. It was about learning to be okay, to keep moving forward, even when it hurt. But his brother didn't want to feel that hurt. He wanted to erase it. As if the past didn't matter at all. But it always mattered.

Staring at his brother now, Yassir realized why Baba was disgusted by Yassir's drinking. Why Khaled's father was enraged by his relationship with Ayah. Perhaps they did not want them to repeat history. He wouldn't. Not like this.

Yassir gave Hajji Majid, who was staring at Ali in shock, an apologetic look. "Asif."

"It's okay. Take him home. Come back tomorrow, habibi."

Laith looked down at Ali. "He said he needed to talk to me, so I came out. He was drinking out of a water bottle, and I thought nothing of it. I didn't realize he was still like this."

Still like this.

"Yassir, I can't let my dad see this. Luckily, he's at a car auction right now," Khaled said. "I—I don't want him to see Ali like this again, either."

Yassir suddenly felt very aware of his surroundings. Lots of Iraqis hung around here. For some reason, Yassir didn't want to give his parents another reason to be embarrassed. He could try to drive, but legally, he still wasn't allowed.

Yassir fished his phone out of his pocket as his brother began to quietly sob in his arms.

"Everyone hates me, everyone hates me," Ali kept whispering. "I ruined everything."

"You didn't," Yassir whispered as a customer pulled into Hajji Majid's lot. *Not yet*, he thought.

"C'mon, Laith." Khaled pulled on the employee's sleeve. "We have customers coming back any minute. Yassir, you got this?"

Yassir nodded, his brother bleeding and broken on the ground. He dialed quickly.

"Baba," Yassir breathed as his father picked up on the first ring. "Can you come get me?"

☽

"Khaled, Laith, help me get him up," Baba said, so that Yassir wouldn't try to carry Ali, who was 170 pounds of deadweight.

Nearby, the customers watched them, and Yassir felt bad for Baba.

After his brother slumped in the back seat, Baba drove them home in the cab. Khaled waved goodbye in the rearview, having promised to check on Yassir soon.

Quran murmured through the speakers as soon as the cab breathed to life. Perhaps Baba needed the words of God to remind him to calm down as he swore under his breath in frustration. When his father made a right turn instead of the left turn at the main intersection, Yassir knew they weren't going home.

They zipped past the west side of town and went east where the houses became nicer, bigger, cleaner.

"Where are you going?" Yassir asked. This was the way to the Al-Hakims' house, the one they'd moved into all those years ago. The first step of separation. Yassir could see it only now, how it had been the beginning of the end for their families.

"Is this what you want, Ali?" Baba asked. Ali was slumped in the back seat of the car, half-asleep. "This family has waited eight years for you to change. They promised to give you forgiveness if you changed, didn't they? Do you think you're worthy of that?" Baba spat, his eyes shifting from the road to Ali in the rearview mirror. "You are not worthy under God's eyes. You know that?"

"Baba," Yassir said. "Stop yelling at him! That's not for you to decide. How is telling him he's worthless going to help?"

Despite how many times Baba had tried to save Yassir from sin—from moral failures—he wondered when Baba would stop repeating his own faults.

Baba glanced at him. He said nothing as Yassir continued.

"When are you going to stop making us feel like everything bad is our fault? Even if we're wrong, why do you make us feel worse? Let's go home, *please*."

Baba kept driving.

"Baba," Yassir pleaded. "Please."

Silence.

"Don't you always say Allah is merciful?"

At the next stoplight, Baba turned left, but instead of taking the road, he made a U-turn.

Baba met his eyes. They were wet. "Yes. Allah is merciful."

"Can you try to be merciful? Just this once?"

Baba blew out a breath. A tear escaped his eye. "Asif."

Yassir didn't know if the apology was for him or his brother. Although Ali was passed out, Yassir hoped he heard it in his sleep.

"Baba," Yassir whispered as the cab drove down Main Street. Yassir was hyperaware of their proximity to where he'd been found unconscious a few weeks ago. His spine tingled. "Why is Ali this way?"

Another tear fell down Baba's cheek.

"Your brother said he saw something, back when he was a kid, in Rafha. I tried to protect him, but I don't know what he saw. What could he possibly remember? But he did . . . and I think . . ." Baba's eyes flitted to the rearview mirror. "Your brother's faith is broken, Yassir. I don't think I can fix him anymore. I . . . I tried to, so many times. He's a good liar, the best I've met. It wasn't until the police started calling that I knew what was going on. The girls he kept seeing, the drinks he kept having, he had never been this way. He loved God, so why was he doing the things that hurt him? He said he wanted to change, so when I heard Kawther was interested . . . I thought . . ."

She could fix him.

"He hit her, Baba," Yassir said. Baba's face contorted.

"How did you . . ."

"She told me," Yassir whispered. "Even after everything he did to her, she still helped me. She helped our whole family, Baba."

"He didn't mean it . . . he accidentally—" Baba started, then abruptly stopped. He must have known that it didn't matter.

"There's no excuse for what he did." Yassir looked back at his sleeping brother. Bile rose in his stomach. A different kind of tingle entered his body and made his entire rib cage burn. "She left again because of him. It's our fault the Al-Hakims are separated again. Baba, how are you not ashamed?"

Baba shook his head. "You don't think we're ashamed? You don't think *I* am ashamed? Why do you think I never let you talk to Khaled? Why do you think I keep my distance? I know this is shameful! Your brother is shameful!"

"No, Baba, we're all shameful."

Baba sniffed.

Yassir stared at his sleeping brother, dark hair splayed on the black leather seat, blood drying near his cracked lips. Ali had said he'd come back to protect Yassir, but he still hadn't figured out how to protect himself from his own destruction.

Nausea filled Yassir's throat. He rested his head against the window.

"You look tired, habibi," Baba said, reaching a hand out to gently stroke Yassir's cheek. "Are you hurting?"

I'm always hurting, Baba. We always hurt each other.

Yassir nodded and told his father the truth, for once. "I'm so tired, Baba."

"We'll be home soon," Baba promised. "Inshallah."

At home, Yassir, Yasmin, and his parents listened to Ali retch in the bathroom.

He'd overheard his parents and Fatima discussing rehab before Ali returned to his wife. Whether he divorced her or not, she deserved an honest conversation about her husband. A truth they'd all owed Kawther long ago. Ali had never gone to rehab before, but according to Fatima, it was something she had been pleading for him to try since the last time he'd visited years ago.

Yassir wondered what it would take to make his brother feel better. Forced prayers and exiles didn't work—Yassir knew that all too well. He dared to hope that rehab would help his brother change.

When Ali had finished retching, Baba made wudu, his sleeves slightly damp at the roll of the fabric. Ali stared at Baba.

Praying drunk was not permissible. Praying with any alcohol in your system would not reach God. Although it seemed like Baba wanted to say these words, to remind Ali, who knew the rules well, he let him make wudu and unfurl his sajadah and turbah several inches away from his own.

The adhan for salat al-maghrib beckoned from the phone, and Yassir made a choice. Although he had a pile of homework waiting for him. Although his skin prickled at the thought of prayer, at the thought of sitting side by side with his family, he made wudu and unfurled the sajadah between his brother and father.

It had been 1,235 days since Yassir had made the *Allah is the most merciful, most compassionate* type of prayer. He did not know what it would really mean to return, if it promised anything, but sandwiched between his father and brother, he would try again.

"Remember," Baba said before reciting adhan. "Allah will forgive you. But you must change. You must mean it. All of us must mean it."

If they could change—if they could mean it—this moment was worth it.

Ali wiped his face, eyes pasted to his turbah, but did not say anything. Yassir nodded. And Baba sighed, wiping his face, too.

They began to pray maghrib and isha. Baba enunciated every word like he used to when Yassir first learned how to pray in Sunday school. Slow and serene. Yassir could hear each word and keep it in his mouth for a second before the next one echoed in the air.

As they lifted their bodies from sujud, Yasmin crawled toward them, stealing their turbahs. She drooled as she put the clay in her mouth. They reached their hands out, still in concentration, and she smiled as she returned two of the turbahs. But in their last rak'ah, she smiled so widely at Yassir, her gums pink and wide and probably still aching, that he couldn't help but laugh.

He messed up.

Laughing technically wasn't permitted in salat. Any interruption of focus would require the worshipper to start from the beginning. But Yassir couldn't help it.

Ali let out a soft laugh, too. Even Baba, who never broke concentration, sighed and smiled, shaking his head. He reached over and ruffled his granddaughter's curls. Yasmin lay between their rugs and rolled on her tummy over the dark green fabric.

Yassir took the last turbah back from his daughter and exchanged it for Baba's lime-green sibhah. He kissed the crown of her head.

Then they stood up, hands cupping their ears, and started over.

SKY

Sometime after, after the after, I heard him again.

The whimper had a whimper. He pushed her on the swing set on a rainbow playground and when she giggled into me, she sounded just like him. The sun was descending, illuminating us all in lilac and gray. The whimper pulled his daughter out of the swing and held her close. The whimper's parents were there, too. Older, their faces reflected all that haunted them, but all that made them smile, too. I watched as they walked together into the walnut-colored building. I braced myself. But to my surprise, when they came back out, the smiles on their faces had not disappeared. Something had changed. But not their joy.

It seems that outside of the delicate whispers, there is something else I like to witness about the humans. Something just as important to my testimony as all the rest.

It is their journey toward bliss. Even when momentary. Even when fragile.

ACKNOWLEDGMENTS

When you give an author of color a chance, you allow their entire community to be on the shelf. Thank you, dear reader, for picking up a book that is both unapologetically Iraqi and Muslim, and for giving my community a chance. While working on *In the Country I Love*, I found a community that supported me through what felt like an impossible endeavor.

To my incredible agent, Jenissa Graham, who took a chance on me and this book. You asked the right questions at the right time and helped me unlock a layer in this story I never knew existed (Sky was possible because of you). Thank you for your guidance and patience with me as I've navigated debuting, and for always reminding me not *if*, but *when*.

To my brilliant editor, Zoie Janelle Konneker, I am eternally grateful that you saw the true heart of this story and these messy, complicated characters for exactly who they are and loved them anyway. Your thoughtful editorial vision and care allowed this story to shine in its most authentic form. Not only is this book better because of you, but I am a better author for it, too. Thank you for being this book's True Blue.

To my best friend, Ban Naes. My sister and confidant, I wouldn't be here at all without you. You witnessed my discovery of writing when I was fifteen and always believed I would make it. Thank you for dreaming with me.

To my critique partner and soul sister, Narjis Sheikh. Allah answered my prayers when I asked to receive a fellow Shia Muslim writer in my life. You were this book's very first reader and cheered me on despite all my years of doubt. I truly don't know what I—or this book—would be without you. Thank you for walking along this wild journey with me; I can't wait to do the same for you.

To my dear friend CJ Hamilton, thank you for instilling hope in me again. When I was ready to give up, you held me steadfast on this journey and reminded me that the right editor would come along. Special thanks to Bear for being your guardian angel, and by extension, mine, too.

To Kiana Krystle, your soul is more beautiful than the entire sky. The moment I met you, I knew we were destined to be best friends. The universe seems to agree, as our lives keep intertwining in the most wonderful ways, and I hope it never stops. Let's keep growing together.

To Heba Al-Wasity and Zeyneb Holdridge, I always dreamed of having Iraqi writer friends, and how lucky I am to have found you both through this book. Heba, thank you for reading an early version of *In the Country I Love* and loving it as sincerely as you did. Zeyneb, thank you for endlessly encouraging me and designing such beautiful art for the story.

To my friend and QuillersSWANA collaborator, Ahmad Addam, your hope and advocacy for this story—and all SWANA stories—have kept me inspired and energized. May we see more books by us and for us.

Thank you to all the wonderful early readers whose insights were so valuable: Nesima Aberra, Taher Adel, Aamna Qureshi, Inès Ibanay, Hasan Namir, Sarwat Ara, Jasmine Danzy, Mary Nduonofit, Meryam Al-Barkawi, Anousha Vakani, Yuva Harish, Raidah Shah Idil, Sara Beg, Gillian

Sisley, Regan McDonell, Hana Ali, and Mis Hashmi. Thank you to Nabeel Sheikh for your insights on Yassir's and Khaled's spiritual journeys.

A special thank-you to the friends who have given support or simply a shoulder to lean on when I needed it: Sarah Mughal Rana, Sidrah Mughal, Baneen Al-Shamery, Kiana Webster, Yusof Hassan, Hajer Al-Awsi, Myriam Korichi. And to Jenan Al-Aetiaj, for being my first friend and chosen family.

To my first writers' group, thank you for reading early drafts and giving me space to grow: Ale Massenburg, Kamilah Cole, Alisa Altınay, Marwa Sarraj, Ryan Ram, Nadirah Ashim, Audris Candra, and Amani Salahudeen.

To my wonderful street team, for championing this book and spreading the word. I am so grateful to you all and always amazed by your creativity and enthusiasm!

To Professor Ranjan Adiga, whose classes and feedback gave me the bravery to write this book. To Emily Forney, for introducing me to the world of publishing during the earliest stages of my writing career—I am forever grateful to you for it. To the Highlights Foundation, for giving a space for Muslim authors to grow and connect—I am so honored to be part of this wonderful community. Special thanks to We Need Diverse Books for supporting marginalized writers and giving me the chance to work with the amazing Sarah LaPolla.

Thank you to my fellow Peachtree Teen authors who offer guidance when things get hard. Thank you to Lily Steele for bringing the cover's vision to life and making it so beautiful, and to the extended team at Peachtree Teen who made this book real and gave it a home.

This book was inspired by Punish a Muslim Day, an event that nearly took place in 2018 in the UK and the US, which was meant to hurt Muslims and be rewarded for it. While, thankfully, no one was hurt that day, it doesn't erase the decades of real ongoing violence against Muslims. To the Muslim reader who struggles with their faith and identity: There will always be a place for you.

To my parents, who were forced to leave their home in a country they loved, and then built us a new one in a land unfamiliar to them—may Allah protect you both always. To my siblings, Ahmed, Zahra, Duaa, and Mohammed Ali, and my sister-in-law Noor, for keeping a smile on my face and my life forever interesting. To my dear nieces and nephew, the greatest lights of my life, your endless abundance of cuteness made writing Yasmin so much easier. To my extended family, including my family in Iraq—my grandmother, aunts and uncles, and dear cousins—I see Iraq in its beauty because of you.

To the people of Iraq who have had to endure the cruel realities of imperialism: Your stories deserve to be told. May justice be granted to you in this life and the next, inshallah.

Finally, all praise to the Most High, whose plan led me here. Alhamdulillah for everything.

ABOUT THE AUTHOR

ALAA AL-BARKAWI is a first-generation, Iraqi American Shia Muslim writer. She is the co-runner of QuillersSWANA, a literary organization dedicated to Southwest Asian and North African writers, and serves as a Literary Peace Ambassador for Threads of Peace. Alaa holds a master's degree from Johns Hopkins University and has worked with refugee and immigrant students for nearly a decade. *In the Country I Love* is her debut novel. Visit her website at AlaaWrites.com and follow her on Instagram @AlaaAlBarkawi.